OF
DEATH
AND
BEAUTY

OF
DEATH
AND
BEAUTY

A NOVEL

BARBARA GRENFELL FAIRHEAD

SUNSTONE
PRESS

SANTA FE

Sunstone books may be purchased for educational, business, or sales promotional use.
For information please write: Special Markets Department, Sunstone Press,
P.O. Box 2321, Santa Fe, New Mexico 87504-2321.

Cover design › Tamzon Woodley
Book design › Vicki Ahl
Body typeface › Goudy Old Style MT Standard
Printed on acid-free paper

Library of Congress Cataloging-in-Publication Data

Fairhead, Barbara Grenfell, 1939-
  Of death and beauty : a novel / by Barbara Grenfell Fairhead.
    pages cm
  ISBN 978-0-86534-937-7 (softcover : alk. paper)
  1. Mothers and sons--Fiction. 2. New Mexico--Fiction. I. Title.
PS3606.A3783O35 2013
813'.6--dc23
                        2013002008

WWW.SUNSTONEPRESS.COM
SUNSTONE PRESS / POST OFFICE BOX 2321 / SANTA FE, NM 87504-2321 /USA
(505) 988-4418 / ORDERS ONLY (800) 243-5644 / FAX (505) 988-1025

For Jacques

CONTENTS

PART IV
HERESY

PART V
SALVADOR

PART VI
THE ZEALOT

PART VII
THE BIGGEST SKY IN THE WORLD

EPILOGUE

The Dark Wind

Poets live for it:
Heretics have died for it:
Every bullfighter knows it:
Everyone who lives close to the edge.

Anyone who loves beauty more than life itself:
Anyone who has dared to challenge death—will know
This dark wind that whispers in the heart;
That blows through us its terrifying beauty.

In the end it is all about beauty—
And our whispered conversations with death.

—Sebastián Chávez

Acknowledgments

I would like to acknowledge and thank the many people who have played a part in this book's long gestation and ultimate completion.

First for 'the unknown hand' that dropped the story out of a cloud and into my unsuspecting skull as I lay on a beach in the Cayman Islands, December 2001; to New Mexico, its vibrant people, its landscape and all those whispers on the wind; to the Duende who has haunted every page.

To Peter Fairhead for all the many times we spent in Casita Milagro in Northern New Mexico; Jay and Lesli Schutte for finding my first laptop and showing me how to open it; Jimmy Baigrie for his encouragement and for information on Catholic matters; Rykie van Reenen and Judith Wurtzel for listening to the many readings over the years; Di Steward for her appreciative listening and suggestions; Dorothy Kowan who has been such an inspiration over the years; Ian McCallum for the many extraordinary discussions as I wrestled with this or that character; Mike Nicol and Jill Gallimore for the extremely valuable feed-back and suggestions for the first draft and advice later; Glynn Woods for help with computer programs and Sherry Woods for showing me how to use them; Brian Rodford and Tony Meyer for their wonderful enthusiasm; Eduard Burle for his encouraging feedback on reading the final draft; Caroline Coetzee for loving the story; Mandy Dix-Peek, Robyn Cowie and Rodney Dart for their support and financial advice; Maureen Thelland for unscrambling my computer knots; Carli Coetzee for giving me some useful editing tips; Tracey-Lee Shuttleworth for handling everything but the writing; my six daughters, Jo, Toni, Tamzin, Geordie, Leigh and Trilby for all their support and love always, and finally, to my partner, Jacques Coetzee, for the exhilarating editing process, for his sensitivity and all the many in-depth discussions about the characters and their motives and for his remarkable capacity to hold the entire story in his head and still note the incongruities in the dates and the details.

—Thank you.

PROLOGUE

The Keeper of Stories

In the end it is all about beauty.

And it is about the forgiveness that comes from seeing, if only fleetingly, beyond the comfort of our illusions, into the starkly naked presence of things. It is about the mystery behind all things, and its workings in our lives.

This is a land surrounded by silences: a land of emptiness and solitude. A land of alpine plateaus and arid canyons: a land of river and desert.

It is a corner of the world where the dark wind that haunts the very edges of beauty, blows through the cottonwoods and down the dry arroyos, lifting the pink dust as if playing with the memories of those forgotten dead who lie buried beneath its eroded hills. It is a land of enchantment, and indifference; a land in which the interwoven threads of history and legend have made their peace.

It is within the embrace of this ancient remembering that I have come home to myself at last.

As I move into this, the final quarter of my life, with the remainder of my time necessarily short, I find I have returned to the immediacy of things close to me. Every moment is precious now. For every moment fades, leaving a memory that is little more than a shadow, which is soon erased or over-drawn by what follows it. Like old photographs, that every year grow less distinct, less readable, so do memories fade, leaving us with nothing but traces of the past. I am not sure whether I find this painful or merciful.

It is with this in mind that, like a child, I have come back to simple things, things soon to be taken from me, things which most of my life I have taken for granted: the smell of rain on dry earth; that breathless moment when once again, miraculously, the slow dawn stains the darkness with its light; the sound of wind moving through a forest; the taste of mountain air.

Daily I am astonished by that extraordinary bond that has taken thousands of years to establish, that I may know the uncomplicated love of the dogs that live with me.

I will miss the morning and evening chanting of the nuns, the voices of the workers calling out to one another, and the sounds of children playing. Most of all I will miss the beauty and the indescribable being-ness of wild things, for they carry for me the memory of where I come from.

I give thanks for the comforting intimacy of one I love at my side; that I do not go to sleep or wake up alone.

I am so acutely aware of the ultimate loss that awaits me that it is as if my senses would devour all of these experiences, all these images; as if in this way I could hold them inside me, so that death may not find my treasure. But I know this is futile, and that ultimately I must leave all of it.

There is a wind blows through me now, and death, that terrible and merciful friend, whispers in my heart—not urgently, not yet—but telling me I should not be too surprised if he opens that forgotten door and beckons me into his chthonic world in some pregnant, not too distant night of his choosing.

Some measure of what I wanted to offer to the world has been given, and a number of the many judgments that I held so intensely as a young man, and that on examination I have found to be ridiculously naïve, have been forgiven. For some time now an unfamiliar upwelling of compassion has found me tearful in the face of human courage; moved by that indomitable spirit that rises up again and again against all odds: moved by the humanity of it.

I have found that to look into the face of beauty requires courage, for she is a fierce goddess, and behind that shining face there sleeps the grinning skull, and the twin shadows of indifference and death. And yet, as I move beyond the fear that previously the very thought of death evoked in me, I have discovered, surprisingly, death's merciful gift: for who else could have opened that forgotten eye that I might see, ultimately, the simplicity of my life?

And so it is, at this late hour, that I find that I am called to tell you this story. Perhaps it is in my desire for closure that I tell it, or it may be some hopeless but very human longing to bring immortality to the passionate souls who live in it. Perhaps I tell it simply because I must. Whichever it may be, I have held too many secrets in my heart for far too long. So I must tell it now, in all its fullness, before that fearsome old midwife comes to claim me.

My story does not follow the more conventionally accepted forms of narration, such as are found in books today, and I do not have the skill or the inclination to arrange it in any such manner. So I will tell it to you the way it came to me, and if from time to time I pause to comment, I pray you may pardon an old man his lack of restraint, and permit this indulgence.

Much of what I will relate to you lies close to my heart, but there are parts that were told to me by others, who witnessed certain events that I did not. Other chapters I have had to piece together from fragments of memories held by the people who lived around these parts.

From the many diverse accounts and interpretations of the stories I have been told, there has emerged a rich tapestry through which a single thread weaves its way beneath the surface of things, linking everything to everything else: beauty. There may be certain errors in some of the dates and details, for much of what I have to tell you happened a long time ago, and there may be places where, from time to time, the line between what happened and what I imagined blurs a little. It is of no importance. Truth is never final or absolute, and indeed seldom proves to be true at all. What I will swear to is that the essential story, all the blood and bone of it, and all of the beauty, happened just the way I tell it.

PART I

MAGDALENA

Las Madres

A bare arm dangled out of the driver's cab window of the 1941 Chevy pick-up as it moved slowly down the dusty main street, the fingers playing dreamily with the currents of warm spring air.

There was something arresting about the lazy patterns drawn by those fingers which caused heads to turn and follow its passage up the street. Even the town's dogs felt compelled to raise their noses from their habitual scavenging, drawn by the new messages that were wafting towards them on those intricate whorls of warm air. The mid-morning sun lit the limb's bare contours, revealing the sheen of health and a degree of muscle that suggested it was an arm accustomed to work. The arm, bare to the shoulder, and the long, shiny hair that streamed out of the cab window like a sleek, black wind, was the first glimpse the people of Las Madres had of Magdalena Chávez.

The old woman, Elena Trujillo, who worked at the rectory, and who happened to be in the main street when the truck drove past, announced that evening to Father Octavio that a new fate had entered the town. Elena was known for the way she could read a person's character from one glance at their hands. Not their personal fortune: that was something else. She made this quite clear. But Elena caught the energy that floated out of those strong fingers, and she smiled.

"Mark my words, father," she said as she shuffled around the room, closing the shutters for the night, "this is no casual new arrival. There is 'knowing' in that hand. You may be sure, father—she is 'other'. I think I will go and light a candle. I feel sure that Las Madres is about to be blessed."

Father Octavio raised an eyebrow, listening attentively. He had a great fondness for this woman, who devoted her every breath and heartbeat to his well-being. She had never married, saying that to do God's work properly was more than one soul could undertake to do truly well, without a husband making all manner of unnecessary demands on one's time.

He was no longer surprised by Elena's strange announcements. Her predictions were well-known for their accuracy, although it had been noted by not a few that her idea of a blessing and that of the townsfolk often differed. But if Elena said that someone was 'other', she was invariably correct. 'Other' was not something to be taken lightly. 'Other' always brought about change. Whether this was always considered beneficial by those affected by it depended on the nature of the change and on the willingness, or perhaps the ability, of the people to accept it. Resistance to 'other' however did nothing to prevent the change from occurring. It merely made life uncomfortable.

Well! May the good Lord send us strength, then, he thought as she left to make her offering.

Las Madres was named after a small group of courageous women. They had traveled with their husbands up the Camino Real from Mexico to the Española Valley in the late sixteen hundreds. There all the men and older women were killed by Indians, but, by hiding in a reed-bed in the river until nightfall, a group of ten women and their children escaped. Under cover of darkness they made their way upstream until they came to a small, protected valley, where they built a rough camp. They managed to survive alone for six months. They were discovered by a mountain man who, seeing their smoke, came to investigate. When he reported his find to the authorities, he referred to the women as Las Madres, and the name stuck.

Las Madres became a small village, a center for the farming community which developed around it. In time a church, a school and a small hospital were built. A mayor was elected. The leaders of the community formed the necessary bodies to represent the village in the many political and legal matters concerning land and water legislation and to see that the village was informed of the new and ever-changing aspects of the law.

By the time Magdalena arrived Las Madres, now a small town, was very comfortably set in its traditions. Those who rebelled did so in the accepted manner, and their rebellion was contained by the social and religious mores of the community. The priest was not sure that Elena's 'other' would be welcomed by many.

"He found a buyer? I don't believe it!"

"Yes. A woman came, took one look and said it was perfect."

"A woman?"

"She's from out of town. She has a son. No husband."

Meaningful glances were exchanged.

Thus it was learned that a woman had bought the old Martínez place on Guadalupe, the dusty main street that ran through the ramble of shops, warehouses, offices and houses that made up the center of the small town. There was much speculation about what she intended to do with the old building that had stood vacant now for over a year. It had been widely advertised, and many came to explore its commercial possibilities. But all who stepped inside felt they could not live with the interior décor, nor did they feel comfortable about making any changes to it, such was the nature of its adornment. The agent tried his best to interest artists and gallery owners, but with no success. Everyone felt that the interior atmosphere was too overwhelming to be commercially viable. He was beginning to despair of ever finding a buyer for it when Magdalena appeared out of nowhere, took one look and promptly bought it.

Xavier Martínez, the previous owner, was a santero. He was born in the house on Guadalupe and lived there with his parents until they died, within days of each other, of some undiagnosed lung ailment. This had struck both of them so swiftly that their son hardly had time to become aware of the severity of the illness before it was over. On their death he saw no reason to move elsewhere.

"Come, Xavier. Now you're free. You don't owe them anything now. You can find your own place. Live a little. Marry."

But Xavier chose to make the house a shrine to those two loved ones who had been taken from him, he thought, so prematurely. He converted the back rooms into studios for his work, and by knocking down a few walls in the front he created a spacious gallery that faced onto the street. His living requirements were simple, and apart from the few hours he slept each night and the quick meals he took in the kitchen, he spent all of his time working on his passion, Los Santos—his extraordinarily individualistic paintings of the saints—and bultos, painted carvings of the same.

He was a prolific artist. Apart from the many hundreds of works he sold during his lifetime, he filled the interior of his house with depictions of the saints. It was impossible to sit anywhere in the house without finding the contemplative and often suffering eyes of some favored saint gazing down at you. Even the ceilings were painted, the most masterly portrayal being that in the gallery. Here was depicted a scene of Jesus being adored by Martha and the two Marys.

The group was surrounded by radiantly back-lit clouds in which there floated a host of pink angels, trailing ribbons of light and glory. The painting was particularly noteworthy on account of the aura of sensuality that surrounded Mary Magdalene, and the just short of lustful gaze that Jesus cast over her. It was the blasphemous edge that the artist had given to this painting, more than any other of his works that chased away prospective buyers.

At the age of ninety-seven Xavier Martínez died as he had lived, with paint-brush in hand, just as he added the last brush-strokes to his final masterpiece, a brilliantly painted carving of La Sagrada Corazón, the Sacred Heart—a voluptuous organ, carved, painted crimson, deeply etched with thorns of gold and with the flames of love painted in bright shades of violet, carmine and magenta springing from its cleft. This he had mounted on a cross of cedar upon which he depicted with exquisite mastery, but using the same startling colors, the Fourteen Stations of the Cross. It was a work which reached from floor to ceiling in the center of the front room.

He was found by his apprentice, stretched out beneath the painter's scaffold, the paint on his brush still wet from the last touch and a beatific smile upon his face.

Now, as the truck, red as ripe chili and with its chrome trim glinting in the sunlight, rumbled over the potholed street, throwing up clouds of pink dust, word of its arrival spread up the side-lanes. Soon the main street was populated by groups of curious inhabitants, waiting to catch a glimpse of the woman who had bought the most noted and controversial property in their town: and if they did tend to linger as they passed the 'old Martínez Place', it was surely only to enjoy the crisp freshness of the spring morning.

The realty agent described the new owner, Magdalena Chávez, as "a beauty!"

"She's a widow. She has private means, and she has a grown-up son called Sebastián who has recently finished school."

The townsfolk were intrigued. For a single woman to show such independence was indeed uncommon in this part of the world, but for her to buy such a bizarre property excited as much curiosity as the day the circus with the bearded lady had appeared in the town.

The truck pulled to a dusty halt outside a low adobe building. The arm was reclaimed to gather up the long hair and sweep it over a shoulder and into a loose coil. The cab door opened, and a woman stepped down into the street. The bystanders were not disappointed. The bare arm belonged to a tall, strikingly beautiful woman—the kind of woman men dream about, but seldom find in the flesh. But it was the energy she released that so caught their attention. She exuded a kind of sleek animal fitness. She had large, dark, almost black eyes that flashed a glance at the group waiting on the sidewalk, igniting all manner of desires in the male onlookers.

The men sighed appreciatively.

"Of such a señora one must only dream," whispered old José to the man standing next to him.

"This señora is no dream, my friend. Look how she walks. Like an animal. And that smile! And those dark eyes! Made for love. Oh yes, she could light a fire with those eyes."

"Wake up, Sebastián. We've arrived."

There was a scuffling sound, and the other cab door opened. A young man of some eighteen or nineteen years slid off the seat and moved to join his mother. He was tall and slender, his bearing aristocratic. His face bore that brand of dark, sultry good looks that excites women of all ages, and before which even the most sensible woman becomes undone. He had a flawless olive complexion, the same dark eyes, although fiercer than those of his mother, and a wide, sensual mouth beneath a strong nose with distinctively flared nostrils. His black hair, which he wore in traditional Indian fashion, fell in a thick plait down his back. He too, like his mother, exuded the quality of an animal in peak condition. But there was something else, something that the onlookers sensed immediately. It was a raw energy, like that of a wild beast; as if some fierce wildness was but momentarily contained, and might leap out at the slightest provocation.

Someone whispered—"¡Olé!"

"You will need to call los picadores to tame that one!" murmured another. "Those eyes! I would not enter the ring with such a toro."

This, however, did not apply to the two young women who worked in the store opposite. His glance, that lingered only momentarily upon them, was experienced by these two ladies as an electric shock. They stood staring at him, the most delightful flush staining their cheeks.

Sebastián stretched and yawned, and seeing so many eyes fixed on him, lowered his head and kicked at the dust. No one spoke.

"¡Buenos días!" Magdalena said finally. She met the eyes of each person individually as she smiled her greeting. "My name is Magdalena Chávez, and this is my son Sebastián."

Sebastián lifted his head, glanced around the small group with his dark eyes and gave a nod. The two young women flashed smiles at him and giggled breathlessly.

"¡Buenos días, Señora! ¡Buenos días, Sebastián!" the people replied, and then fell silent once more.

It was the Mayor who, having been informed that the new arrivals were due that morning, had contrived to be in the area, and now, aware that they were staring at Magdalena and her son in the rudest possible manner, stepped forward.

"¡Señora Chávez! ¡Sebastián! We heard that you would be arriving today. A warm welcome to both of you."

He made a small bow to Sebastián, and took Magdalena's hand in his and gave it a kiss. Still keeping hold of her hand, he said that the whole town was delighted that they had arrived safely.

"I hope you will soon feel at home. I personally would like to show you around, make you feel comfortable."

There were sidelong glances in the crowd, for it was well known that the Mayor could not resist a pretty woman.

"She can be grateful," said one woman, "that it is still early. With a few drinks, it will not be just her hand he is holding."

Magdalena, amused at the Mayor's transparency, smiled at everyone and tactfully retrieved her hand.

"¡Muchas gracias! Thank you, everyone, for the warm welcome. We are so happy to be here, and we look forward to getting to know all of you." She smiled. "And please call me Magdalena."

With this she turned to lift the first of the cases down from the truck.

Two men stepped forward and wrested it from her.

"Just tell us where you want everything, Magdalena. We will bring it all in for you. Sebastián will surely help. You must be tired."

Observing this, the older women, who regarded men generally as lazy, good-for-nothing lay-a-bouts, drew in their mouths. Well! It certainly hadn't taken long! There would be trouble. They knew it already.

It is true to say that an air of mystery is compelling, and Magdalena, a single woman of such assured independence, was a mystery to the people of Las Madres. She appeared to have no history.

Although they were told that Sebastián was her son, many of the women, who experienced powerful and instantaneous feelings of antipathy toward her, thought it possible that he was her lover, for he looked to be far more than the nineteen years he claimed, and they detected a closer bond than was natural between a teenage son and his mother.

"And where is the father, pray?"

For surely she was young to be a widow! There was just something about her, and it was their business to get to the bottom of it.

"You don't just arrive at a place where no one knows you unless you are running away from something. Take my word for it. And look at her! A woman like that! She just eats men. Look at what happened to Gustavo and Luis. 'Oh, we'll help you, Magdalena! You must be so tired!' Two of the laziest young men Las Madres has ever known, and she has them eating out of her hand."

The gossips, meeting for their regular Monday coffee and cake in the small café off Guadalupe, were having a field day.

"And that young man. She says he is her son. Well! You could fool me. Nineteen, she says. More like twenty-five. More like a lover than a son. I saw that at once! There is something unnatural about the way she looks at him."

She pressed the napkin to her tightly pursed mouth and looked meaningfully around the small group.

Still others whispered furtively behind their hands, suggesting he might be—heaven forbid!—both; and they crossed themselves.

"I overheard Señor Gonzáles telling the Mayor that he had heard that Señor Pérez knew that she was wanted in another state." She raised her eyebrows almost to the hairline. "You know what that means."

"I spotted it immediately. The moment they stepped out of that flashy, red pick-up. And what kind of a woman drives around in one of those? And there is something about that young man! Such looks! Such dark power. It is almost frightening. And those eyes! You have to admit it. He is just so beautiful. And when he turns those eyes on you! Holy Mother! It's enough to make one feel faint."

The mothers could not help but notice what effect he would have on an impressionable young girl: that splendid physique, the dark, burning eyes. He had about him an air of arrogant rebelliousness that the women found challenging and irresistible, and they found themselves sighing as they contemplated his lean body; his hair—that mane of shining blackness that from time to time he wore loose, so that it whipped about his face in the wind.

Not one word of this was ever mentioned—not even in confession. Some things are best left to lie as they are.

Magdalena paid no attention to the gossip, but set about making arrangements for the renovations to the property that she had purchased. For weeks the windows were covered with brown paper. There was a constant coming and going of workmen, painters and general handymen, accompanied by the sound of banging and sawing. Drapes arrived, and carpets, and a van filled with small tables and low chairs. The observers were mystified. A truck delivered a crate, which was opened on the sidewalk to reveal an upright piano. The town was humming with gossip and speculation.

In front of the low porch, on either side of the entrance steps, Magdalena planted beds of lavender which grew at such a pace that people commented with raised eyebrows that such growth was not natural.

Then one day the windows were cleared of the paper and cleaned; a sign was hung over the porch with the legend "Casa Magdalena", and the door was thrown open.

The curious who gathered to witness the opening saw a salon with comfortable chairs and low tables, set at intervals around the gallery room, with La Sagrada Corazón a central feature. A raised section for the piano stood beneath the figure of St Sebastián, his eyes raised heavenwards, a look of ecstasy upon his face even as the arrows pierced his torso. At the far end of the room Doña Sebestiana, a grotesque skeleton with long, red hair, sat in her death cart, La Carretta de la Muerte, and grinned down over a well-stocked bar. From every wall and corner the astonished eyes of Los Santos stared down on the occupants.

The few women who ventured inside retreated swiftly, appalled at the blasphemy. They could not have been more shocked if she had called it 'Magdalena's Brothel': and how she dared to have liquor in the same room as Our Lord and the many holy ones, blessed be their names, was beyond belief.

"For shame!"

But the men of Las Madres were delighted at such wicked eccentricity. They flocked into Casa Magdalena, filling it to capacity every evening. They considered that a certain balance had been introduced into the lives of those ascetic souls, who were now obliged to witness, and perhaps enjoy, the humanity of the convivial atmosphere.

Father Octavio, who was asked to bless the enterprise, had difficulty controlling his face on first stepping through the doorway, but apart from commenting on the unusual juxtaposition of sacred and profane, said he could not see any harm done.

"Indeed," he said with a twinkle in his eye, "perhaps a little sharing of their respective spirits would be beneficial for both parties. Personally, I think St Sebastián would benefit enormously from a little wine, while some of you,"—he raised his glass to everyone in the room—"might like to spend a little more time on your knees."

"Father! They will hear you," Carlos said, shaking his head. "What if they tell the Bishop?"

After the laughter and applause had died down, the Mayor, who was a little too full of the bottled spirit, and maybe, indirectly, the other kind as well, managed to hiccup: "Amen."

Later, when all things ordained had come to pass, the wives of many of the men who enjoyed their time spent in Magdalena's Salon said that they had known, right then and there, that there would be trouble. But that was later.

Casa Magdalena was an outrageous success. There was something about the atmosphere that Magdalena created that invited intimacy. She brought the warm, earthy tones of wisdom, humor and compassion; and something else: something that had been hidden or missing from the men's lives since ever they could remember. She brought beauty. She was unlike any woman they had ever met before, although they kept this information strictly hidden from their wives.

They enjoyed her spontaneity and her infectious laughter. In her presence they became relaxed and expansive. If they had been asked to consider or name just what it was about her that was different from all other women they knew, they might have come up with the notion of equality. Not the equality that is demanded so vociferously by radical political activists, the very demand for which, of necessity, becomes an obstacle to the possibility of its ever being experienced, but a spontaneous sharing of friendship, embracing mutual recognition and respect.

The men, however, were not given to undue introspection. Nor was Magdalena aware of how singular the experience was that she offered them. It came from her as naturally as breathing. It was Sebastián, from his place of observation behind the bar, who watched the development of these unique bonds with interest.

The men were not alone in their appreciation. It soon became apparent that the town's children felt it too. They crowded around Magdalena as she walked down the street to purchase her groceries and into the market to buy beans, cornmeal and chili.

"¡Magdalena! ¡Magdalena! Please, tell me a story with my name in it."

Little Perdita held on to Magdalena's dress until the story was almost all told:

"...and the name of the wonderful child who was so blessed was..."

"¡Perdita! ¡Perdita!"—the children shouted.

She laughed, and told them stories from the pueblos.

"There is a Water Serpent called Kolowisi and he lives in the rivers. He has a great horn, and he is like a god to the Zuñi people, because he makes the plants grow in spring." She paused, and bent down to add in a conspiratorial whisper that had all the children crowding around with big eyes, "But you must be very, very wide-awake if you meet Coyote. He's a Trickster. You must hold your candy very tight in your hand, or he will steal it."

The children begged Magdalena to go on.

"More!—More!—More!"

The mothers did their best to control them, but they were drawn to Magdalena like ants to candy, and no amount of scolding could keep them away.

In addition she attracted a band of cohorts in the form of a pack of town mongrels, a curious collection of yellow-eyed creatures whose interbred copulations had occurred so faithfully for such a long period that they had almost created a breed of their own. They followed her on her rounds, hanging around shop doorways or lying panting in what shade they could find, waiting faithfully for her to re-appear. The people came to know that if you wanted to find Magdalena, you only had to look for the pack of dogs, and she would be in one or another of the stores nearby. The women thought it scandalous, but she just laughed and tossed a few tit-bits to the dogs before returning to work.

And then there was Perro Mestizo. He was a stray who wandered into town from heaven only knew where, his tongue swollen for thirst and every rib painfully visible. From the day of his arrival he was rejected by the town dogs, and had to survive by snatching what scraps he could find before he was set upon by the pack. He had a dull coat, was a mass of bites and sores and had lost most of one ear. He was saved from being entirely forgettable by an arresting pair of pale-blue eyes.

But Perro Mestizo was invincible. From the day Magdalena arrived in town, he became her self-appointed protector, acquiring new status in the eyes of the other dogs, for he was the only one allowed into the Casa Magdalena. Under Magdalena's care he grew to be, if not handsome, at least remarkably fetching, soon becoming a regular feature of the salon and a favorite with the regulars.

No woman was ever loved more devotedly or served more faithfully than Magdalena by Perro Mestizo. At night he slept in the doorway to her room. During the day he followed her everywhere she went, and when she was working in the salon he frequently moved his position so that he could keep her in his sight.

Father Octavio commented: "If anyone wants an example of what it means to find meaning in life, they have only to look at Magdalena's blue-eyed dog: for surely he has found a great love, and has committed himself to it. If only I could inspire such devotion to God in my congregation, I would have achieved a great thing."

Sebastián worked hard in the salon, and soon became an expert barman, but he was an enigma to the men. He had about him an air of authority surprising for his age, that commanded respect. He was attentive, but unlike his mother he did not invite friendship. He neither sought nor invited intimacy, and avoided all forms of conversation that touched on anything personal. The men sensed that he was different from others of his age: there was something dark that seemed to lie behind his eyes; something which, for the most part, he kept hidden, but which from time to time flashed out with the brilliance and the power of lightning. Only when one of the men drew him out was he ever seen to enter into debate. Those who took the trouble discovered an intelligent and informed young man who could argue a point with the best of them, and who delighted them with his subtle and rather irreverent sense of humor.

"Is it not strangely poetic," Sebastián commented to three men standing at the bar, "that two such seemingly contradictory forms of spirit should have met so harmoniously beneath one roof? Could it be mere chance? And yet, hasn't wine been used since time immemorial to honor the gods?"

He gave an amused shrug.

"And is Señor García's ecstatic song any less reverent than the Gloria sung by a church choir? Do you think God cares that he is not dressed in white robes, and that his fingernails are decidedly not clean?"

The remark followed a performance by the Mayor, in all his inebriated glory and accompanied on the piano by Señor Fuentes, the music teacher, singing a passionate version of Cucurrucucu to Nuestra Señora de Guadalupe, who graced the shadows in one corner of the room.

But for the most part Sebastián remained on the outside of things, listening to the discussions, but seldom entering into the light-hearted banter.

It was Magdalena and her stories that brought the men back again and again. Not only did she have a fund of these engaging tales, but there was something about the way she told them that held the men spellbound.

There was, however, one story which they requested over and over again on account of its unsatisfactory conclusion. They hoped that in so doing she would grow tired of teasing them and give it a more acceptable resolution.

"Come, Magdalena. Tell us the story of Carmelita and Esteban, and let's hear the whole truth! Give us a happy ending this time."

"But I have told you all that I know," she responded, laughing at their persistence. "Not all stories are meant to have happy endings. Only fairytales end 'happily ever after'. And happy endings? Perhaps, if we halt in a happy place, then we might say, 'this is a happy ending'. But then there is always the next day. Life happens, gentlemen. And not all of it is as happy as we think we want it to be."

"Come, Magdalena! It's a story! Indulge us with a happy ending. Just for once."

"Gentlemen. A story has its own life and its own soul. I must tell it the way it wants to be told. We will see how this story ends."

Finally, after much teasing, she would allow herself to be persuaded.

A chair was drawn up. Perro Mestizo settled himself at her feet. Sebastián saw to it that everyone's glass was full. The room grew quiet and the saints leaned forward out of the shadows to listen, as she began the story.

Sebastián, who had heard it many times, wondered at how she managed to invest it with such immediacy, so much aliveness; for it emerged afresh with every telling, holding the audience captive right to the end.

Una Historia de Amor

"Gentlemen, I give you—Don Alonso Esteban Rodríguez Bautista, a Spanish nobleman of honorable ancestry. Don Alonso is possessed of a prodigious appetite for all things physical and sensual. His family is of proud Spanish origin, and in this country it can be traced back to 1590, the time of the heroic founder of New Mexico, Juan de Oñate, and before that to an adjutant to the famous Hernán Cortés. Through all the centuries it has been noted that this is a family of extraordinary valor. This last descendant is a powerfully built and exceptionally handsome man. He has a wife, Doña Corazón Flores Rodríguez, a bevy of lovely daughters and one son, Esteban Juan Rodríguez Flores. His wife is not able to bear him any more children, and so this son is to be the one to carry the illustrious name into the future."

The men settled back in their chairs. It was not only the story: it was the telling of it. She was beautiful, this woman, and a born story-teller.

"Don Alonso and his family lived in a grand hacienda, on a rancho with many thousands of acres, some twenty miles outside Las Madres. He renovated the house, which he had purchased in 1920, bringing many fixtures from Mexico, sparing nothing in his desire to convert it into a replica of the grand haciendas of that country of his birth.

"Nobody who took the narrow by-road off Route 84, known by the locals as Camino de Las Palomas, could fail to notice the elaborate entrance."

Magdalena paused, allowing the men time to consider whether they knew the whereabouts of the by-road.

"It was designed by an architect from Mexico who worked with a local artist, skilled in wrought-iron, bronze, tin and copper-work, and together they created a landmark of elegance or ostentation, depending on how you looked at it. It had two imposing adobe pillars supporting a double rainbow-shaped arc of wrought iron. Suspended between these two arcs, with the sunlight glinting off their wings, was a flock of tin and copper doves. These, in harmony with the vagaries of the wind, flew north in the general direction of Taos or south towards Santa Fe."

Magdalena indicated with an elegant gesture the directions of the wind.

"On each side, on a curving, six-foot adobe wall there was a group of life-size, prancing bronze horses, their wild manes and tails streaming about them."

The men tried to recall ever seeing such an exotic landmark—and couldn't.

"The Hacienda was famous for its many lively celebrations, musical evenings and dances, for Don Alonso loved to show off all his wealth. And even if some of the Anglos had more money than he, none of them could match him when it came to giving a party.

"'They just don't have enough red blood in them to appreciate what it is like: the longing, the romance, the nostalgia of having a first-class mariachi band play for you on a hot evening, with the scent of lavender and lilac mingling in your nostrils, and all around you the vast desert whispering its secrets to the warm night wind, and the sky with its millions of stars, and the full New Mexican moon sliding up over the mesa like a fat, ripe plum. And the sultry wind whispering its secrets ...'"

Magdalena's hand drew the passage of the wind with an arm as graceful as a dancer's. The men sat enthralled. They could smell the sweet, perfumed night. They could see the stars.

"Don Alonso attributed the success of his parties to two things: Spanish blood—for where else would you find such fire?—and chili.

"'Those poor Anglos,' he would say, 'they do not know the sacred qualities of chili; how to blend the subtle flavors to awaken the senses; how just the right amount of heat can light the fire in a man and bring a blush to the cheeks of the most refined of women. This can only be learned from the grandmothers. But those poor Anglo women—born in corsets, no doubt—they look like the colorless candles you find in the trading stores: pale, rigid and unlit. They are so stiff, it is a wonder they don't break in half when they attempt to dance. And how else can you know life if not through the body's fire and the dark wind of the Duende lifting your skirts, the way the bull's horns toss the matador's cape? That is the key to life: that strange wind on the back of your neck, making your hair stand on end.

"'The Duende! Those Anglos spend their lives trying to deny his presence. Poor fools! Do they think they can escape him—that emissary of death? How little they know of that terrifying caress that makes a man shudder when it touches him.'

"Yes, gentlemen. Don Alonso was a man for whom the gratification of the sensual appetites brought an intense erotic pleasure and meaning into life."

Magdalena rose, and went to pour herself a glass of water. The faithful Perro Mestizo followed her to the bar and back, where he resumed his position at her feet. The men were waiting.

"Yes. Don Alonso was a man of many passions; but his greatest passion in life was the breeding of thoroughbred horses for racing. To this end he spared nothing in converting the rancho into a show-place. He established himself as a breeder of superior reputation, producing creatures of such excellence that he became famous far and wide. With pride he would take his friends around the estate, showing them the fine stables, the shady paddocks and, of course, the progeny of the current bearers of all those centuries of impeccable breeding; youngsters who, unconcerned by the weight of their ancestry, raced up and down the pole fences, disporting their famous genes, snorting and bucking and generally making a spectacle of themselves.

"'Will you look, gentlemen—and ladies?', he would say as a three-year-old colt, with fire in his eyes and a coat more brilliant than sunset on the Sangre de Cristo Mountains, galloped around the enclosure, his tail raised like a banner and the thunder of his hooves throwing up buckets of dust behind him. 'Have you ever seen such a fine stallion, such a magnificent animal? See that neck muscle, that deep chest. And look how well-endowed!'

"Indeed, seldom had such a fine pair of testicles been seen in New Mexico. The ladies blushed, but their eyes returned inevitably to the site of these magnificent organs, fascinated, in spite of themselves, by such full-blown and unambiguous maleness.

"But surely such well-developed gonads will prove an impediment to speed? Delicacy prevented them from inquiring.

"'What a fine sire he will make,' Don Alonso continued, unaware that the ladies were suddenly feeling hot. 'I bred him myself! The Conquistadors themselves had no finer. See that action! See how effortlessly he moves, how he floats. He does not touch the ground. Blood, gentlemen! It is all in the blood! First I will race him, so he may show his colors, and then I am going to put him to my finest mares. Then you'll see horseflesh, gentlemen. Then you will see what excellence lies in that illustrious blood!'

"Indeed, more than once he had been heard to say that these steeds were descended from blood-lines which could be traced back further than those of most people he knew.

"For their comfort he planted several cottonwoods to shade the courtyard overlooked by the stables, and arranged for water to be fed to a fountain—ostensibly as a gift to his wife, Doña Corazón, but in actuality to provide the soothing sound of water spilling over smooth river stones for his beloved horses. Nothing, but nothing was too good for these classy steeds, the objects of his passion. No lover ever whispered sweeter endearments into the ear of his beloved than did Don Alonso into the pricked ears of his twenty brood mares and his two stallions.

"'Ah, Conquista!' he would say, running his hands over the glossy belly of his favorite mare. 'So how is this big baby coming along?' The mare would lean her head into his chest and allow him to scratch her ears, listening to the sound of his deep voice telling her how magnificent she was.

"Yes, breeding was his passion. It was all that gave meaning to his life. It was like a love affair, so intense was his devotion to these magnificent, four-legged descendants of the most famous names in equestrian history. Breeding was, you might say, his religion; what he worshipped; which, of course, brings us to his son. That is another story entirely!"

Here Magdalena paused to draw Sebastián's attention to the empty glasses.

"Esteban was every bit as handsome as his father, having the same Castilian, aristocratic profile, but where his father was shorter, more powerfully built, Esteban was tall and slender. He did not share his father's earthy appetites, being of a more refined and sensitive cast. He was romantic by nature, and introspective to a degree that infuriated his father. Where the older man was practical and pragmatic, a man of action, Esteban was a dreamer.

"'If you don't wake up, son, life will pass you by. Life does not happen in that dreamy head of yours. Life is out there. Wake up, Esteban! You need to roll up your sleeves and get your hands into the stuff of it.'

"Don Alonso had already chosen his son's bride-to-be. She was still a girl, barely sixteen, but they could wait a few years. Her family's name was also honorable, and although it could not be traced back as far as his, it was nevertheless beyond reproach.

"Perfilia Sabinita Gonzáles Laguna,"—Magdalena allowed the name to roll off her tongue like honey—"had fine features, and would be a beauty when she was a few years older. It was, however, in spite of these qualities, an odd choice for Don Alonso to have made, for in spite of her beauty Perfilia was curiously unlit. She had none of the fire and passion that usually attracted him to a woman.

"Doña Corazón mused on what had prompted his choice, and came to the conclusion that perhaps her husband would have felt uncomfortable for his son to have a wife, a female, with more fire than his own mate. Could it be, she wondered, that he was competing even with his own son? Truly! What an animal he was!

"Esteban was informed of the marriage arrangements, and had even taken tea with the young lady and her parents—an excruciatingly polite affair—but he paid scant attention to matters so far in the future."

Magdalena smiled at the men.

"Now, Don Alonso had a groom—we shall call him Miguel Valdez— his foreman, stableman and confidant, who lived on the property with his wife, Josefa, and daughter, Carmelita.

"Miguel's family came from Mexico. He could trace his ancestors back to the time when the fierce gods ruled from their airy mountain peaks; before the Conquistadors came to South America, before Hernán Cortés led his party off to conquer the Aztecs of Mexico City. He was part Indian and part Spanish. From his Indian ancestors he inherited an extraordinary knowledge of all things subtle, powerful and mysterious. He could interpret the messages carried on the wind: when a storm was imminent, or messages from the indigenous plants and from the coats of the horses that an early winter could be expected. And he could hear the 'speak' of animals.

"'We must put the mares into the east paddock tonight,' he would say to Don Alonso. 'It will be better so.'

"Don Alonso had learned not to question these irrational comments. The lightning that struck the large cottonwood in the west paddock, that same night, reducing it to a black stump, was very convincing confirmation.

"But his passion for horses came with his Spanish blood. Don Alonso, when he spoke about him, described him as a mestizo, a half-breed. He gave no thought to the man's splendid ancestry. Mixed blood was mixed blood in his eyes.

"Don Alonso had never stopped to examine his bigotry, or to consider how insulting this was to the man who worked for him. He had not paused to reflect that the same man he trusted most in the world, who was perhaps his most intimate friend, he dismissed as a mestizo.

"But in spite of this, and although there was between the men a huge difference in matters of culture and social standing, on one thing they were as one, and that was horses. They would both rise early and meet to discuss the program for the day: which of the youngsters would be lunged first, what mare was coming into season, which stallion she would be bred to, which of the two-year-olds they would keep and which they would sell. They examined feet, looked at teeth and discussed when they would break the next string of youngsters. Their love of horses knew no bounds. So, all was very well. A picture of success and happiness, don't you think, gentlemen?"

"Indeed! Go on, Magdalena!" they would urge.

"Well, of course, nothing that is so perfect can stay that way forever. Happiness is like the swallows, las golondrinas: they stay for summer, but when winter comes, they fly away. It has always been so. Nobody, not even a man as socially powerful and as wealthy as Don Alonso, can manipulate that law. It is perhaps at such times especially that one should pay attention."

There were nods and indications of agreement from the men.

"And so, let us consider Miguel's daughter, the beautiful Carmelita."

The men sighed.

"Because she was a girl, and the daughter of a groom, no particular attention had been paid to her by Don Alonso. Only her parents knew how exceptional she was, and they kept this to themselves. But they could not disguise her beauty."

Magdalena looked at the appreciative faces, and nodded. They had guessed right. So far the story contained all the necessary and entirely appropriate ingredients for a fine tale. Of course the groom had a daughter. Of course she was beautiful.

"She and Don Alonso's son Esteban grew up together. They were inseparable friends and playmates. They played children's games together, and shared all the joys, the small sorrows and disappointments of a happy childhood. They saw each other almost daily, exchanging the usual secrets that children love to share, living day by blessed day in that timeless way such fortunate children inhabit their world.

"Esteban particularly loved to listen to Carmelita tell her stories. Where she got these from he never knew, but she could hold him spellbound with tales of such intrigue, suspense and passion that often he would not notice the passing of time, and would have to be called in to his supper in the big house and scolded for being late.

"In return he brought her gifts: a necklace of little, carved white doves which he bought from a Zuñi Indian; a silver bear-claw bracelet inset with turquoise and coral, her most treasured possession. Another time it was a crystal embedded with four garnets which he had found when he and his father took a trip high up in the Sangre de Cristo Mountains—a Lágrimas de Cristo, a Tears of Christ crystal, so called because of its cruciform shape and its red garnet tears.

"On her birthdays, which were simple affairs, he never failed to bring her some little gift, a piece of turquoise from the trading store or a set of shiny Mexican button covers.

"Esteban and Carmelita lived their days in a state of blissful innocence. The world had not yet laid its hand too heavily upon them, and, although dimly aware of certain social and cultural differences, they were not yet fully aware of the implications of such disparity and the inequalities that lay behind it.

"Apart from her friendship with Esteban, the only close contact Carmelita had with the Rodríguez family occurred through her skill in beadwork.

Doña Corazón, seeing some of the bodices she worked, sent Carmelita into town for sewing lessons, where after she was employed to make all the party dresses for Esteban's sisters. The girls loved these dresses that so complimented their dusky beauty. There must have been some power in the beads that Carmelita chose for decoration, for when they went out—chaperoned, of course—the young men's eyes were drawn irresistibly to those shadowed cleavages that rose out of the glittering splendor of her handiwork. During the dances they would press the girls close to their hearts, leaving them flushed and breathless, a condition which the young ladies enjoyed enormously, but which caused many a hawk-eyed matron to intervene.

"When he was nineteen, Esteban went away to a college on the east coast to further his education. He stayed with an uncle who had a paper business in New York, and worked for him in the holidays to gain experience. He was away for three years. Carmelita stayed at the hacienda and helped with the work.

"It was when Esteban returned that it happened."

Magdalena paused, and pretended to fix a loose tendril of hair.

The men leaned forward.

"Yes?"

She patted the wisp of hair into place.

"Now, where was I?" she teased, and then laughed into the eager faces in front of her.

"Oh, yes! Well, Esteban arrived back home one late afternoon, tired from his long trip. He was about to enter the house when he caught sight of the most beautiful young woman that he had ever seen. She was walking across the courtyard, carrying a basket filled with lavender. She was tall and slender, and walked with the ease and grace of a young deer. With a shock he realized who she was. Carmelita!"

There was an audible sigh from the men.

"Well—from the moment their eyes met, it was as if an electric current ran between them, setting them both on fire. The lavender basket fell, spilling its fragrant load on the dry dirt of the courtyard. Esteban moved to her side.

"'Carmelita!' he breathed. 'Let me help you.'

"The two of them knelt down to retrieve the long, purple-headed stems. As Carmelita leant forward to gather up the blooms, her long hair fell across Esteban's face, and he caught the scent traces of earth and lavender, the slight tang of her perspiration and some sweetness which he could not define, but which caused his heart to race. He saw the smooth, swelling curves of her breast, a creamy, golden shade against the crisp white of her bodice. With her face so close to him he could feel the warmth of her breath on his cheek. He could scarcely breathe for the proximity of such loveliness."

Magdalena broke off to look at the men.

"She was just so beautiful, you see."

There was a murmur of appreciation. Magdalena continued.

"'I have missed you, Esteban. I am so happy you are home.'

"Simple words—but words that he repeated to himself over and over that night as he lay awake in bed and stared at the moon moving across his bed-room window.

"This powerful current, connecting them even when they were not in each other's sight, created an energy field of such potency that it flooded the entire hacienda with exquisite vibrations of erotic, trembling aliveness. For weeks the pair tried to deny this passion that left them trembling when, accidentally, they came face to face. Esteban took to staying indoors so that he would not see Carmelita, but he lay around, sighing so heavily and looking so pale and languid that his mother thought he must have caught some illness out east, and she urged him to go outside, to get some sun and fresh air.

"'Perhaps Carmelita would accompany you on a walk.'

"She had no idea what ailed him, or that she was fanning the flames that were burning in his heart.

"Carmelita had become dreamy, and on several occasions her mother had to draw her attention to flames leaping from the pan where she was refrying the beans, her mind quite obviously far away.

"'I think you had better go and help your father. Perhaps that will wake you up a bit.'

"So Esteban and Carmelita found themselves thrown together, accompanying their respective fathers on the stable rounds as they inspected the horses. Such was the energy between them that, on one occasion when they came too close to Don Alonso's jet-black prize stallion, El Estampido, the animal became inflamed, snorting and prancing, galloping around his small enclosure until he worked himself up into such a heat of passion that he jumped clean out of his paddock and into that of the mares. Here he mounted them with such vigor and vitality that they in turn began to thunder around their corral, screaming and showing the whites of their eyes.

"Don Alonso and Miguel shouted and banged their hats in their attempt to distract the stallion, but it was Carmelita who entered the paddock, seized the stallion's halter and led him back to his stable."

The men looked at Magdalena in disbelief. "Isn't that just a little too far-fetched even for one of your stories, Magdalena?"

"Not at all. Ever since she was a little girl, Carmelita had talked to animals. She had a way with them: dogs, cats, even wild birds, cottontails and coyotes. Her mother came from the old country. She was one of the wise ones—a curandera, a healer and a keeper of stories. She recognized when Carmelita was barely four that her daughter had inherited what was called 'the powers'; the ability to think in pictures. She would place her hands on an injured creature, and through some mysterious agency a series of pictures would flash through her mind which would tell her what the ailment was and which herbs and treatments were needed. This would always be followed by an image of the animal healed. Josefa taught her daughter all she knew about indigenous herbs and the art of healing, but with animals Carmelita was a natural. Quite instinctively, even wild creatures trusted her. There was no explaining it."

"Is this a true story, Magdalena? You make her sound so real."

"A story is a story, gentlemen. Please do not be distracted."

Magdalena settled them with an elegant gesture and continued.

"After witnessing his stallion's superb leap over the corral fence, Don Alonso instructed Miguel to raise the paddock fence by three poles. He wasted no time deliberating, but sent off for every bit of information that was available on steeple-chasing. He discussed with his groom, and a trainer, the possibility of sponsoring a famous steeple-chase event, with his name on it, naturally, to be held annually in the country. El Estampido would of course walk away with the prize.

"Eventually Esteban and Carmelita could deny their love no longer, and they succumbed to the inevitable."

There was a deep intake of breath from the men.

"Their first kiss was of such duration, and was so all-consuming, that their passion ignited a fire in the feed room behind the stables, where they had fallen onto the bales of hay and alfalfa, unaware of anything but this fusion of desire. Before they could beat out the flames, the smoke brought both the fathers running. One look, and they recognized instantly what had occurred.

"Well, you can imagine Don Alonso's anger and Miguel's embarrassment. Both fathers spoke to their wives and to their children. Both forbade their children to continue this foolishness.

"But love is not something so easily commanded. It is not a light that you can turn it off—just like that!"

Magdalena snapped her fingers.

"The fire of love was lit in Esteban, so that he glowed like a branding-iron, and nothing could hide the dazzle of love in Carmelita's eyes; not even the broad-brimmed hat that she wore to shade them was sufficient to fool her mother.

"'You'd best take off that stupid hat, and come and help me in the drying-shed.'

"But the fragrance of the pungent herbs only intensified Carmelita's passion. In desperation her mother sent her to help Ramona in the kitchen. It was here that some of her ardent desire must have entered the food that she prepared, giving it aphrodisiacal qualities, for it was noticed that after supper Don Alonso became unusually demonstrative in his affections towards his wife, escorting that blushing matron off to their bed-room without having his usual glass of after-dinner port—or his evening cigar.

"Esteban was no better. He woke each morning flooded with waves of love, a pain which burned and throbbed and ached in his chest so that he thought he might die of it; and yet, such was the joy that accompanied it that he prayed it might be with him forever. His every waking thought was Carmelita. Daily he wrote notes and letters so full of love that they overflowed their envelopes, drawing clusters of hummingbirds to sip at their sweetness. He put little gifts where he knew she would find them, in their childhood hiding-place. He did everything he could to stay away from her, and everything he could to make sure their paths would cross so that they might speak and, if no one was present, kiss. Yes, gentlemen! Esteban was quite hopelessly in love."

Magdalena looked up and laughed. Her face was quite flushed from the telling of it.

"Finally the time came when Esteban knew he must declare himself or die from the pain which ached day and night in his chest. He told Carmelita that he would wait for her at the end of the row of stables after everyone had gone to bed. He arrived early, holding in his hands a small box which contained a gift; the symbol of the depth and sincerity of his love.

"It was a rosary which he had requested to be made by a famous Zuñi grandmother, a carver known for her skill and deep spirituality, which were reflected in her work. The beads were carved out of pearl-white shell, each bead in the shape of an animal, while the five larger beads, which marked the Mysteries, were all doves. They were strung together with links of silver, and the silver cross was set with five small rubies to represent the five wounds of Christ. A great love had flowed out of the old woman's heart and strong fingers into her creation, and when Esteban took the finished work from her, he felt the power of it course through him like a fire.

"'Take care not to let this fall into the wrong hands.' The old woman wrapped the tissue carefully around the gift. 'This is powerful medicine.'

"Now, as Esteban saw Carmelita walking towards him, his heart swelled with love for her. He reached out and drew her close to him, his whole body on fire with longing. With hearts beating as one, they embraced.

"'I have something for you.'

"Carmelita opened the package, and gave a cry of wonder. She lifted the carved beads until they hung suspended like so many tiny, gleaming moons.

"'Oh, Esteban!'

"Her fingers moved over the carved surfaces, touching each one, marveling at how skillfully the carver had managed to keep the beads so similar in size and shape.

"'It is beautiful, Esteban.'

"'So that your animals will be with you always; and that even in your prayers you will know my love,' he whispered. 'And the doves—las palomas—so that your spirit may always fly to me if ever we are apart.'

"But apart was the last thing on Esteban's mind. From his pocket he took out a plain gold ring and slipped it onto her finger.

"'I love you, Carmelita,' he whispered. 'Will you marry me?'"

"Well, gentlemen, what do you think should be done?"

Much discussion followed this. What on earth could the boy be thinking? He must have lost his senses! Some of the men thought it quite shocking: animals on a rosary. Was that not rather a heathen idea? Surely it was a sin? Others disagreed. How could true love, any aspect of it, ever be considered a sacrilege? And no fault could be found with the doves—las palomas—for was not the dove the symbol for the Holy Spirit? And we must never forget our beloved Saint Francis: for did he not hold all animals in high esteem, second only to God?

Eventually they reached consensus. Love was all very well, but it could not always call the tune. The boy should come to his senses, marry the girl his father had chosen, settle down and have many sons. The girl should keep her head down and get on with her work.

"Yes, well, gentlemen. But it gets a little complicated.

"It seems that, some time later, the weather became very hot. No rain had fallen for weeks, and the land ached with dryness. One night during this spell Esteban, unable to sleep for the heat, stepped outside to cool himself in the night air. A full moon hung over the hacienda, flooding it with light. The stars spread themselves across the velvet night sky like a veil of jeweled silk; there was no wind, not even the trace of a breeze. It was one of those slow, sultry evenings that invite our hidden lives to dare to fulfill their most secret dreams, a time that is ripe for romance, and when anything seems possible."

A flush appeared on the cheeks of the listening men.

"Esteban was about to turn and go back inside when suddenly he saw Carmelita across the courtyard. She had not seen him, and so it was with no self-consciousness that she lifted her long hair off her neck, reaching up so that the soft cotton of her night-dress fell against her body. Then, with her arms still raised, her eyes closed and her head thrown back so that the moon shone full upon her face and drew a line down the slender loveliness of her throat, she began a slow, almost dream-like dance, her long hair and the fine cotton gown floating about her as she danced, revealing the small, delightful breasts and the gently rounding curves of her slender body."

There was a groan of appreciation.

"Well! He could not help himself! What full-blooded, virile young man could? He was ignited by a fire of such passion that he felt it might consume him. Overcome by desire of such intensity, he threw aside all caution and surrendered himself to fate. It was as if the stars themselves had ordained it.

He felt himself lifted by the power of love and carried across the courtyard to her side.

"'Carmelita!' he cried."

Magdalena paused.

"Well, gentlemen, you can imagine! A handsome young man, a beautiful woman, a hot, sultry night, a full moon!"

The men laughed; yes, they could imagine!

"Well, things went on for a while, and Esteban and Carmelita managed to disguise their passion, but it was only a question of time before something would give them away. And then it happened.

"Carmelita discovered that she was going to have a child."

There was a sharp intake of breath from the men.

"Well, she was beside herself, of course. A part of her was filled with joy at the idea of bearing a child for her beloved Esteban. But she knew the rage that they would have to face from their families, the questions that would be asked, the shame and embarrassment her mother and father would feel.

"But surely things would work out. When she told Esteban about her condition, he was delighted. He kissed her and held her close and told her, now they would marry. Nothing could keep them apart. Nothing would stop them, not even his father.

"But Don Alonso Esteban Rodríguez Bautista did not come from a family with a pedigree over five hundred years long for nothing. And his name had not maintained its honorable standing through all that time by marrying young servant-girls, however beautiful! His bellow of rage was that of a fighting bull. His shoulders hunched, and one could quite easily imagine the lowered horns and the furious pawing of the dirt, the clouds of dust rising about him.

"No! Never! He would not hear of it! Would never hear of it, and that was final.

"'Look at those horses out there!' he exploded. Don Alonso ran a frantic hand through his hair. He glared at his son.

"'Do you think they arrived at such perfection through haphazard breeding? Through allowing a lesser animal to breed into the line? Do you think that just any mare and any stallion will produce such progeny? No! It is through careful choice that you achieve a line as fine as that. And that choice is made on blood; on form; on mettle; on achievement; on winning when pitted against the very best.'

"Don Alonso's hands worked feverishly, as if trying to grab hold of his fury and shake it in his son's face.

"'And your name? Do you think just anybody can trace their lineage back with honor through hundreds of years? Do you think that? And do you think I am going to permit you to bring disgrace to this proud name? This family? No! I will not allow it! Never!'"

Magdalena shifted her position slightly.

"Well, gentlemen, what do you think now?"

A very heated discussion followed. For some of the men nothing had changed. The lines were clear. It was unfortunate, but these things happen. The girl had been told to stay away, and she had chosen to disobey. She could not be allowed to ruin such an illustrious family name.

Others disagreed. It was not only the girl who should be held accountable. What about the boy? What kind of man, what manner of lover would even contemplate abandoning such a love? And what about honor? What honor was there in walking away from the consequences of your actions? And although she was not of noble birth, she seemed like a strong, healthy, hard-working woman.

This evoked a howl of protest from the first group. How could they even begin to consider the possibility of a man of Don Alonso's standing having his only son married to his groom's daughter? He would be the laughing-stock of the land. His life would be ruined. All that he had worked for, all that those of his line had struggled to achieve would be undone by a mere slip of a girl who had got herself pregnant. One must look at the big picture; at the principles and values. That, after all, was what life was about.

This, then, was challenged. Just what kind of principles and values were being protected here?

"Are we not really talking about pride and arrogance? These are surely not considered to be values of merit? And we must remember that the values of our ancestors are not necessarily the same as the values we honor today. We live in modern times. Things change."

The discussion went on until it became late, and Magdalena said she must close.

"We shall finish the story tomorrow, gentlemen. Perhaps Father Octavio could resolve this dilemma."

The Kiss of the Patriarchy

When Magdalena opened the salon the following day, she learned that the priest had gone away for a few days to administer the last rites to a woman who was dying. It was a condition she regularly contracted, and the poor priest was becoming weary of traveling the tortuous route, only to arrive and be told that a miracle had occurred and she had been spared.

In his absence Carmelita's erstwhile champions had reluctantly come to agree with the Mayor that the boy should obey his father, and that some arrangement should be made for Carmelita and the child.

"But go on, Magdalena! Tell us what happened."

"Well, it was a difficult time for Don Alonso. How was he going to handle this? On no account was his son going to be allowed to marry Carmelita, but how would he manage this and not lose the services of his groom, Miguel? Things were very delicate. He decided to make him an offer. Esteban would be sent away for a year to gain further experience of business management with his uncle. Carmelita would remain on the estate until the child was born. Once she was strong again, he, Don Alonso, would set her up in business, perhaps a dress-making business. He would buy whatever equipment she needed and find suitable premises, with a shop front for display, and he would open a bank account in her name and deposit money for the child's maintenance and education. There was a condition, however. She would have to leave the hacienda and promise to stay away from Esteban, and not reveal to anyone the name of the child's father.

"The two men reached agreement after some discussion about the amount of the settlement, and shook hands. Then they went to inform their wives, and finally to face the difficult task of telling their respective children what had been decided.

"Carmelita was distraught. She could not believe that this could happen to her. Her grief knew no bounds. She begged and pleaded with her father. She beseeched her mother to intervene. She wept so much and at such length that her mother held a basin to catch the tears that flowed from her eyes like rain. In a country where every drop of water is precious, no sensible woman of the soil would dare waste such an abundance of moisture.

"Things did not go quietly with the father and the son. There was a fierce and terrible fight. The family genes that had carried generations of Rodríguez men to safety through battle and through all manner and measure of adversity were much in evidence. Esteban said he would not think of leaving Carmelita; that he could not live without her. His father stood his ground; said that no child of a servant would ever be accepted into this family. Esteban called him an arrogant bigot. His father said if he was a bigot, at least he was a well-bred one.

"The argument raged back and forth, with neither giving ground. Esteban spoke of his love, and pleaded with his father. His father told him he would get over it.

"'And what about the child?' Esteban asked. 'It will be a part of your flesh and blood, a part of the blood-line you love so much. How can you turn your back on that? And what about Miguel? Is he not a fine man? A loyal friend? Have you no respect for him? For his daughter? For his grand-child? This is your grandchild too, father. Whether you like it or not, this child is of your line, your famous blood. How can you say no to your flesh and blood?'

"His father stared in disbelief. Obviously Esteban had not understood the finer points of his argument.

"'He is an excellent horseman, Esteban. But Miguel is mestizo: mixed blood. Do you not comprehend what that means? Are you unaware of the danger? Do you imagine for one minute that his blood could ever be considered suitable to breed into the Rodríguez line?' Don Alonso shook his head. 'Never!'

"'Perhaps you are afraid that this so-called mixed blood might prove stronger than the pure strain of which you are so proud! Perhaps you fear that your theories about blood-line breeding might be proved wrong; that this child will surpass you and all those hundreds of years of much-vaunted honor.'

"Don Alonso lunged at his son, but Esteban, as agile as a matador before a charging bull, stepped to one side.

"'So that is the truth of it,' he said triumphantly.

"Don Alonso, looking fit to murder him, turned on his heel and strode off toward the stables.

"Esteban appealed to his mother, Doña Corazón, to intervene, but she had long ago learned not to challenge her husband.

"'I'm so sorry, Esteban,' she said, 'but you must do as your father says. Carmelita is a sweet girl, but it really won't do, my dear. You must know that.'

"Esteban begged, pleaded, shouted, threatened, but his father remained uncompromisingly resolute in his decision. Finally, when it looked as if his son might walk out on him, he played his last card.

"'Marry Carmelita, and you are not my son! You shall inherit nothing!'

"There was silence. Esteban knew, though he hated to admit it, that he was defeated. He knew he had been raised as a gentleman's son. He knew that if he went against his father, doors would close on him. He knew he would never be able to make a living working on the land. He had no aptitude for it; no skills. His uncle in New York would not be able to offer him a position, and he had no training, and certainly not the hands or the physique for any rough work. Under the circumstances no one in the town would offer him employment. His father's influence reached far.

"Esteban knew that he was tied into the family system of ancestry and inheritance. He would not be able to provide for Carmelita and the child without it. For all his name and education, he was still dependent on his father. He hated this. He hated that it should be this way. And he despised himself that he could think of no practical solution.

"'I hate you, father!' he said.

"Reading his son's face, Don Alonso knew he had won. It was decided. He was content.

"Don Alonso knew nothing of the final meeting between Carmelita and his son. Nor would he have cared to know about it. Carmelita listened in silence to Esteban's explanation of why he could not marry her. She stood motionless, her face white as the bleached steer skulls that hung on the feed room wall behind her.

"She said nothing when he professed undying love for her. She stood like one frozen. With tears running down his cheeks, Esteban took her in his arms and kissed her farewell. She did not return the kiss, neither did she weep. She only stood there, staring into space.

"'Carmelita, say something. You do understand, don't you? Please, Carmelita.'

"But Carmelita did not speak. She stood with a look of terrible sadness on her face, her gaze directed at the series of images that flashed before her eyes. Esteban stood in front of her, uncertain what he should do.

"'Carmelita? Speak to me! Carmelita!' he beseeched, but to no avail. Wherever it was that Carmelita had gone, she was beyond his reach. Eventually, with a last touch to her arm, he turned and walked away into the night."

Magdalena stared at the men, an expression of sadness, or perhaps compassion, in her eyes.

"But for the rest of his life," she continued, "Esteban would be haunted by his acceptance of his father's ultimatum. Not immediately, but later, too late to make amends, he would examine his conscience, his soul, and curse himself for his cowardice; curse those famous genes for which this sacrifice had been made. The cure for such wounds is long and bitter."

"Well, it seems to have all worked out fairly satisfactorily in the end." This was the Mayor's opinion.

Sebastián, standing over at the bar, wrote the word "imbécil"—idiot— on the wet counter-top, turned his back and pretended to busy himself with some glasses.

Some of the men, who were shocked by the unhappy turn of events, uttered their protest at this callous remark. The argument was about to start up again, but Magdalena intervened.

"Wait, gentlemen, the story does not end there!"

"So what happened next?"

"Well, Esteban was sent to the uncle out east. Carmelita wept without ceasing for the next nine months. She wept so much that finally her mother set her to work in the garden, where at least the plants might benefit from so much moisture."

"Surely, Magdalena, salt water is not good for plants," one of the men interjected.

"This is a story, Carlos," she chided. "Do not be so literal. Tears are blessings. You must know this."

But she gave him her most charming smile.

"For just short of nine months, as her belly grew bigger and bigger, Carmelita wept over the beds of lavender. Once she had finished in the herb garden, she moved on to the paddocks, where she planted rows of lavender along the fences, her tears spilling over and filling the acequias, the canals that irrigated the lands, until every field was surrounded by the soft, purple blooms and the fragrance of the herb wafted over the whole area.

"Don Alonso was so delighted by this that he gave instructions for a two-acre field of lavender to be planted in front of the house. Carmelita duly planted this area, her tears flowing freely all the while. Those tears were remarkable, for scarcely were the plants in the soil than they grew at such a rate that, by the time she had planted the last row, the rest of the field was a mass of purple blooms. Never had the hacienda seen such a bounteous crop.

"Then, one day while she was harvesting the plump lavender heads in the middle of the two-acre field, she gave a cry. The canvas basket full of lavender fell from her arm, and the contents spilled out over the ground, furnishing a soft, thick carpet.

"Fortunately her father was nearby, but by the time he reached her, her waters had broken, and she was already in labor. He ran to call for help, and almost immediately Carmelita's mother, Josefa, and the old woman, Soledad, who worked in the hacienda kitchen and who had delivered more babies than she could remember, ran out carrying towels and sheets and jugs of boiling water."

What were the waters? Such details had always been kept from them. The men listened in fascination.

"Once they had made Carmelita comfortable, they requested more and more buckets of hot water, and more towels, and more bowls of boiling water to steep the herbs. Miguel was soon almost spent from running to and from the kitchen. Carmelita labored mightily. She panted and pushed and groaned, but in spite of her mother's herbs and Soledad's frequent prayers to the Blessed Virgin Mother and Saint Bartholomew it was only at sunset that the child was born and the cord was cut."

The men sat, wide-eyed with horror. Cut?

"It was at this precise moment, as the new-born infant opened wide his mouth to draw in his first breath, that a small, dark wind which had been floating its way languidly over the field of lavender, riffling the plump, purple heads, blew a black shadow down his wide-open throat.

"Soledad, who was about to wrap the babe, started and crossed herself.

"'Holy Mother, it is the Duende!' she cried, and turned to stare at Miguel and Josefa.

"'Be quiet, woman, with your foolish superstitions!' Miguel snapped at her, but he too crossed himself and shuddered, for he feared it might be true, and that the babe had indeed been blessed, or cursed, with that mysterious force that burns like fire in the blood and brings no peace."

Magdalena looked up inquiringly at the listening men. They nodded. Some of them had attended bullfights in Mexico. They had felt that shadow. They knew what it meant to be touched by the Duende, that dark wind that challenges the soul; that is both beautiful and terrifying.

No one knew why he selected certain people over others, but they had never heard of a new-born babe being touched by this dark power. They knew that some said it was a blessing, but that if indeed it was a gift, it was one that would exact a heavy price. For such a fate to make its appearance with your first breath—that was hard. The men shook their heads. They did not envy the boy his destiny.

"What Soledad did not see, what nobody saw, was the flash of brilliance that, for an instant, illuminated the crown of the infant's head. If the Duende was to have its say, even so would the Angels play their part in the life that lay ahead.

"Josefa paid no attention to their remarks, but straightway wrapped the babe in a soft cotton shawl and gave him to Carmelita, who for the first time in months stopped crying. She sat up, wiped the tears from her eyes, looked into the face of her son, gave a deep sigh, and smiled.

"So! There you are. Carmelita has a son, a strong, healthy boy, resembling his father and grandfather: the same striking good looks already clearly defined. He had inherited the undeniable, proud Spanish profile, the same set of the brow. Carmelita named him Hermoso, for he was surely the most beautiful child ever to be born on this earth: Hermoso Esteban Rodríguez Valdez, although she knew she would not be able to write his surname on any document.

"Miguel and Josefa were enchanted with the boy, which made their pain all the more acute. They knew that Carmelita had to leave, that an agreement had been made, but they were saddened that life should have dealt them such a cruel blow.

"Carmelita, however, seemed quite reconciled to her circumstances. In spite of her grief at the loss of her dream, she was seized by such passion for her child that when the time came for her to leave her mother and father, she gave them each a warm hug and her blessings. Her mother struggled to hold back the tears, but there was such an air of confidence about her daughter as she mounted the steps of the hired mule-cart that she felt a sudden rush of pride in her strength and the manner in which she had embraced her fate.

"Don Alonso never saw the child. Neither did Esteban. Carmelita left quietly one morning, babe in arms. Her parents stood just outside the entrance to the courtyard, waving. Carmelita turned and waved back to the two people who grew smaller and smaller as the mule and trap made its way along the narrow dirt driveway.

"She waved goodbye to her parents and her childhood all the way down the tree-lined avenue until it reached the place where, at last, it turned. And then she was gone."

Magdalena stared into the faces of the men.

"Carmelita never did see Esteban again."

The men were shocked.

"After all that? Are you sure?"

"I'm sure."

"Couldn't you tell it differently? Have them meet again later? Perhaps marry and be happy?"

"No."

The men were silent.

"She settled in the nearby town, and ran a successful dress-making business. Her customers were mostly men who wanted to buy something special for their wives. These dresses were often at such variance with the size and style of clothing favored by the women to whom they were married that Carmelita could only wonder at the fickle nature of men, and had to employ every scrap of diplomacy any time she met either the wives or the dresses, for they seldom if ever appeared together."

A number of the men could be seen to blush.

"Miguel and Josefa spoke frequently to their daughter on the telephone, but they saw her only occasionally, for it was some distance, and they found the travel arrangements difficult. Then one day she closed down her business, left the town, and nobody has heard of her since."

"Not even her parents?"

"I can't answer that."

"And what about Esteban?"

"Oh, Esteban. He came back from the east, married Perfilia, the girl his father had chosen for him, settled down and joined his father in the horse business."

"So it did all work out in the end?"

The Mayor was determined to have his happy ending.

"Well, yes and no."

In response to the look of inquiry she continued.

"Well, Esteban and his bride built a house on the property, and settled down. A year passed. Two years. There was no sign of a child.

"Don Alonso was getting impatient. He wanted to see a long line of grandsons, and maybe a few granddaughters too.

"Another year passed, and there was still no sign of a child. Doctors were consulted, specialists; even some midwives of good reputation were called in to give their opinion. But no one could find any reason for Perfilia's continued barrenness. It was suggested by doctors that Esteban should be examined.

"This, of course, enraged Don Alonso, but he could not speak out. He could not offer his reasons for objecting. No one had been told of Carmelita's child. But his every sense was outraged that a son of his seed, the product of his loins—and what more favored or potent loins could one hope to find?—should be questioned. But what could he do? Esteban was examined and pronounced in fine health.

"The years went by, and it became clear that Perfilia would not bear children. Esteban was disappointed. His life with Perfilia was quiet, respectful, tender even. But there was no fire in it. Perhaps a child would have made a difference. Perhaps a child would have woken some love, some passion in him; he was not sure. He could not help thinking about Carmelita; thinking about the child he had never seen, who must be ten, eleven now. He was not, however, truly aware of the utter depth of his grief or of his sense of failure; the fullness of his betrayal, not only of his love for Carmelita—that was bad enough—but of himself. He could not permit himself to know this, or to feel how much of himself he had lost when he walked away from her. No.

It would remain hidden from him. Perhaps, in this respect, the gods were merciful.

"For the first time in his life Don Alonso felt powerless. All his money, his position in society, the proud name, all his connections with people of influence, all meant nothing now. He had no grandson! He had no heir. This was the end of the Rodríguez line! So there you are, gentlemen. That is the story."

"But you can't end there! What happened? What about Carmelita's child? Surely he carries the genes, the name, the ancestral line into the next generation?"

"Ah! But gentlemen, I thought we had resolved that issue. He was just a farm girl's bastard—if you will forgive the term. He was not given even the name, if you remember. Are you saying now that the child, without the mother, of course, would be acceptable? Shame on you! Anyway, no one knows where Carmelita and her son went, so the question is quite academic."

"But you can't just leave it there! Stories have to have a good ending!"

"Gentlemen, you have been reading too many fairy-tales. Only fairy-tales end happily ever after. But real stories are not like that. There are no endings. There are only pauses. And sometimes it is not given to us to see the next chapter."

"But this is not a real story! Come, Magdalena, you are teasing us. You have made up the story, invented it if you will. You always leave it there. Tell us this time. How does it end?"

"You are wrong, gentlemen. No stories are invented, even if we mistakenly think that to be true. Stories are only remembered. As long as we live and breathe, the story continues. So if you ask me what Don Alonso will do about Carmelita's son, I might say I don't think he has decided yet. I might say I don't know."

The men were not happy with this situation. They felt sympathy for Don Alonso; for such a fine family to end like this, to have no heir. A worse tragedy they could not imagine.

Magdalena took pity on them.

"You want to know what happened? The haciendéa was sold. All the horses were auctioned. Don Alonso's wife died, and Esteban and Perfilia moved away. There is no telling what became of Don Alonso. There you are, gentlemen. I am afraid that you will have to be content with that."

"And Carmelita? And her son Hermoso? What happened to them?"

"Ah, gentlemen. All stories must have a mystery. Some unanswered questions. A thread hanging out at the end of the tale."

Father Octavio

He arrived in Las Madres by wagon towards the end of a hot day in summer, just as the purple shadows were starting to creep across the road and the sun was casting the first of its scarlet veils across the sky.

Looking about him, Father Octavio could see the magnificent Sangre de Cristo mountain range that formed the distant backdrop to the small town.

The two white mules, driven by an old man who, Father Octavio thought, must have been well into his nineties, slowed their pace and threw their weight into the harness to cover the remaining stage of the journey, the steep and dusty dirt road that wound its way up to the small plaza.

"Come quickly, Domingo. The baby! It is coming!"

The woman sat on the side of the bed, holding her back for the pains that gripped her. Her waters had broken, and there was nothing she could do but surrender to the will of her body and its implacable demand.

"I have been waiting, Domingo. I couldn't come to call you. The pains are coming fast now. The baby will be here soon."

"Three weeks early!"

But he didn't waste more time. He helped his wife undress, and made her as comfortable as he could on the bed. Next he put water on to boil and made her a drink of herbs to help with the pain. He boiled more water and gathered towels and a basin, and brought the soft birthing-blanket that she had washed and folded, ready for the new infant's arrival. Then he sat with her, rubbing her back and holding her hand, talking her gently through each pain.

"You're doing fine. Nearly there."

The labor was short; the birth uncomplicated. One last push, and the baby slid out into the work-roughened hands of his father: the same hands that had assisted the occasional troubled cow or horse in the delivery of its young and brought many a birth-mute lamb into the world. They knew, quite instinctively, what to do to make as gentle as possible this first separation of mother and child. He cut the cord, and the infant gave his first lusty wail.

"¡A bien hecho, mi querida! We have a fine boy. He looks like you. And he has a strong pair of lungs!"

This infant, who made his entry into the world in the early hours of a June morning in 1908, crying so lustily, was Octavio Ascensio Córdova, the eighth child to be born to that family.

His father wrapped him securely in the birthing-blanket and held him close to his chest, where the new-born could hear the strong, steady beat of his heart. He ceased his bawling and squinted out at the blurred world, which was for him the sky-blue denim of his father's work shirt.

It is perhaps significant that the first touch he ever knew, the first hands to hold and cradle him and the first heartbeat he was to hear immediately after his birth were those of a man, his father; for he too, in the fullness of time, would become a shepherd caring for the well-being of a flock, albeit of a different nature. His early arrival presented no real difficulty, as Octavio was their eighth child, and birthing was for them a part of the great round of natural experience.

Octavio's father worked as a stockman and shepherd for a wealthy patron on a large hacienda. His mother worked in the grand house as a cook.

From childhood Octavio showed evidence of a deeply caring, sensitive and spiritual nature. As early as he could remember, he had known that he would become a priest, doing whatever he could to alleviate the suffering that he saw all around him.

"What have you there in the box, Octavio?"

The small boy indicated to his mother that she should speak quietly, or the bird would frighten.

"It's a white dove; a pigeon, really. See! It has a silver band on one leg. It must belong to someone. I think it must have got hurt in last night's storm. Its wing is broken. I have made a splint. When it is healed, I will see if it remembers how to fly home."

The young boy peered into the box.

"It is quite comfortable now. I must go and find it some grain."

Following his ordination in 1932, and a period of advanced studies at the Seminary, where he had also lectured in Greek and Latin, Father Octavio packed his bags and made his way to Las Madres, a town about which he knew nothing. He was informed that he was to service both the town and the growing needs of the surrounding community.

In the late afternoon, as the wagon finally made its way through the ramshackle collection of small-holdings, shops and trading stores, adobe houses and barns that leaned at such precarious angles that it appeared that only Divine Providence kept them from collapse, Father Octavio took in the simplicity of the small town with appreciation.

Rangy-looking dogs ran out of dirt yards, barking as they passed, and a few small children ran to see who was coming along the road, and stood waving enthusiastically at the black-clothed figure. Father Octavio waved back. At intervals the road was crossed by the dry pathways of the arroyos, and he could see by the eroded banks and rows of exposed roots that, although everything was bone-dry at present, it was not always so.

Finally they gained the relatively level ground of a small plaza, and the wagon came to a halt in front of a modest adobe structure. Only the white cross perched on the roof-top signified that it was a church. A cluster of tamarisk trees sheltered the entrance, and a tall cottonwood cast shadows over the small graveyard. This latter, by contrast with the drab and dusty surroundings, was filled with clusters of brightly-colored artificial flowers. Wreathes and bunches of blooms tied with white ribbons adorned the old, weathered crosses that seemed to lean and tilt at every angle except the vertical.

Father Octavio climbed down from the wagon and stood for a moment, feeling the quiet atmosphere of the small town. He had prayed that he would be sent to some foreign place, Brazil perhaps or even Mexico. He felt a little disappointed when he was told of the need for a priest in the small northern town of New Mexico, and struggled to banish the unworthy feeling. People were in need of spiritual encouragement in every place, and no less here, he was sure, than in some equatorial jungle. Looking around the small, dusty square, he wondered what manner of challenges such a sleepy-looking little place might offer him.

Dong! Dong! Dong!

He was startled by the sound of the church-bell ringing.

"He's here! He's arrived!"

People poured out of every doorway, and hurried towards the building where the wagon had stopped.

"There they are, father. There's your flock, come baaing for you as ever a flock of sheep did for the shepherd. I'll just see to the mules."

While the old man unharnessed the mules and took them to drink from the trough, Father Octavio turned to meet the crowd that soon surrounded him, all welcoming him to their town, introducing themselves and their numerous children and explaining the many threads of relationship that existed in Las Madres.

"And this is my cousin Margarita, and her two children, Pedro and Lupe, and my brother's sister-in-law, Rosita."

Father Octavio gave up making any attempt to remember names or to unravel the extraordinarily complicated tangle of small-town genealogy, and just smiled and shook hands with everyone.

"I made you a bowl of chili and some guacamole and nachos, father. You must be hungry. Come, we can show you to your new home. It is right next door to the church."

The house was freshly plastered, inside and out. The door and window-frames were bright with a new coat of blue paint. Father Octavio stepped through the gate. The men followed, carrying his box of books and another crate containing the candle-holders, goblets and cloths for the altar and his vestments for communion and other services. The rest of the sum total of his worldly goods was contained in a brown leather suitcase.

At the entrance to his new home Father Octavio was introduced to Elena, a middle-aged unmarried woman who lived with her brother and his wife two doors down from the church.

"Welcome, father. It is so very good to have you here at last. I will be taking care of the church and any needs that you may have: you have just to let me know. Let me show you round your casita."

Proudly she led him through the few small rooms, opening cupboard doors and drawers in which she had placed lavender bags to add fragrance.

She showed him the tiny kitchen with its humble collection of mismatched plates and cups displayed on the home-made dresser; the horno, an oven in the yard for roasting, and the small, fenced kitchen garden beyond.

The townspeople had all contributed towards providing him with a supply of linen and blankets for, they told him, although it was hot now, when winter came the temperature could drop to well below freezing. They would make sure that he had a good supply of firewood stacked and dry before winter set in.

No welcome could have been warmer or more generous in spirit. Standing alone at last in the small kitchen, looking around at the simple gifts that the people had brought him, noticing the fresh shelf paper and the arrangement of wild flowers on the window-sill, Octavio offered a prayer of thanks for the blessing of such a welcome.

He unpacked his suitcase and hung his few items of clothing in the wardrobe in the corner of the bed-room. Next he put a white, hand-embroidered cloth, a gift from one of his sisters, over the kitchen table, set a candle in the silver candle-holder and lit it. He poured a little wine into the goblet, and then knelt on the beautiful, woven rug that covered the earthen floor to offer a prayer of thanks for a safe homecoming. After the last amen he stood and uttered a blessing for the house which was to be his home, thanking it for its sturdy beams and the comforting protection of its thick adobe walls. Finally he raised the goblet and drank the wine. He helped himself to some of the food left by the women, made a quick repast and then, tired from the long journey, retired to bed.

He lay for a long time, unable to sleep, listening to the silence of the gathering night, punctuated only by the occasional sound of a coyote howling, a dog barking in the distance and the gentle rustle of the leaves of the cottonwood. He watched the moonlight move slowly across the bed-room wall, wondering when it would touch the foot of the bed. Before it did, he fell asleep.

That night Octavio dreamed that he was riding a mule down a dusty road that meandered between the steep slopes of desert hills. Occasionally the dirt road crossed a dry arroyo, the slopes of which bore evidence of erosion from flood waters. Apart from the stunted junipers, some stands of rabbit-brush and wild sage, the land was barren.

The day was hot, throwing up a series of mirages, and giving from time to time the illusion of water flowing over the track in front of him.

He came to a bend in the road, and saw a narrow path leading off to the right. He felt himself being irresistibly drawn to follow this. At the same time he was overcome by a feeling of such intense love that he feared he might faint. His head swam with dizziness, brought on perhaps by the intensity of his feeling; perhaps by the heat. He thought he saw a figure walking towards him. He strained to see who it might be, but the form kept melting in the mirage. He gathered from the movement of the figure that it was a woman.

She passed by some little distance from him, and stooped to place something on the side of the path before melting away into the quivering waves of heat. Octavio found himself walking to this place. He noticed that his feet were bare. He saw a small, white cross, with next to it a red rose. He found himself on his knees, weeping, filled with an intensity of love and grief.

When he woke from the dream, Octavio found that his cheeks were wet with tears.

A Conspiracy

As much as the men enjoyed Magdalena's company, the women of Las Madres, particularly those of wealth and status, distrusted her. They did everything in their power to keep their men out of Magdalena's salon, but to no avail. Casa Magdalena had become both a secular sanctuary and the most popular place in town.

Although the women failed to uncover any impropriety, instinctively they felt Magdalena to be a threat. She was too free, too independent, too beautiful, and now far too successful with their men. Their individual and collective feelings of passionate attraction towards her son remained a hidden secret. They kept a vigilant eye on their husbands and their sons, for it was generally held that she had slept with every man in the town except the priest, but nothing they did, it seemed, could keep their men away from Casa Magdalena.

Eventually things came to a head. The Mayor's wife put pressure on the men, saying that anyone seen frequenting the salon would be struck off her list. When this had little effect—for her evenings were tediously protracted and infinitely dreary events comprising non-alcoholic beverages and polite conversation about nothing—she went to Father Octavio.

He, poor man, was put in a quandary. As a dutiful pastor he had to consider the women's feelings. At the same time he was aware that Magdalena offered something unique to the men; a way of relating that drew out of even the roughest of them, a new appreciation for the world. If the wives had not been so jealous, he thought, they might have been able to see the subtle changes that were taking place in their men. It was, he thought, the price of beauty. How few were able to see past these physical attributes to the qualities that lay within.

In Magdalena he sensed an extremely potent energy combined with a unique brand of wisdom. He too had enjoyed the occasional drink in the salon after a christening or a funeral. He enjoyed Magdalena's company immensely, and was charmed by her stories which, he had come to appreciate, were far more than mere entertainment. Now, with the women's demands, he failed to see what he could do. Magdalena had done no harm, committed no sin; she attended Mass regularly, although, he had to admit, her striking appearance did tend to draw men's attention away from the sermon and their concentration on spiritual matters. But surely she could not be charged for being beautiful.

Indeed, on some days, as he labored through the difficult task of making sense of the many injustices and evils that the world presented, to a congregation not given to introspection, he thought that perhaps to allow one's eye to rest on something of beauty might do more good than the total inadequacy of words or the illusion of understanding. He was as yet unaware of the intensity of hidden passion and subliminal guilt that was gathering in reaction to Sebastián's dark and sultry attractions, and the sense of outrage and jealousy that the women felt with regard to Magdalena.

When he confided in Elena she merely remarked that Magdalena was 'other' and that her energies would make it impossible for anyone who met her to ignore the response that arose in them. Such energies, Elena said, would amplify whatever was being experienced in the people she met. She was like a transformer and whether people liked it or not, they would be altered by contact with her.

"Like mother, like son!" she added, a remark that left Father Octavio perplexed, but he was in too much of a hurry at the time to ask for clarification.

Father Octavio informed the women that he could find nothing amiss with the Casa Magdalena or either of the people who ran it. Things remained the same.

On learning this, a small group of women decided to take matters into their own hands. It was agreed that they would stage a burglary and plant several supposedly stolen pieces of silver in Sebastián's room the following Friday, the idea being that Casa Magdalena was a front for other, less legitimate activities.

They decided that five of the women would each take one article of silver from their collections, so that the theft would not immediately be spotted by anyone in the family. It would then require the aid of some illegal migrant workers, who could be hired to plant the stolen items.

It was perhaps unfortunate that the women did not pay more attention to the finer details of the plan.

Over the days that followed, if anyone had been looking closely, they would have seen the extraordinary spectacle of women of the upper social echelons, heavily veiled, conversing with men from somewhere further south, all of whom wore large sombreros. If anyone had been looking even more closely, they would have seen money and some item of silver—a tray, a cigar-case, a wine-goblet—changing hands. The women would then leave as furtively as they had come, leaving a tobacco-stained peasant marveling at the eccentricities of rich women.

An unexpected flaw in the plan was the choice of silver for the goods to be planted. It had not been appreciated by the women that no self-respecting man of rich blood and meager finances, when handed a heavy piece of silver, would not consider how simple it would be to convert it into, perhaps a magnificent concho-belt and a matching bolo to replace his sweaty neckerchief;

would not, by the end of the day, have persuaded himself that this was what had been intended all along.

The local jewelry-makers from the nearby Indian village, a pueblo famous for its silversmiths, did a brisk and profitable trade over the next few days, whereafter an eye accustomed to observing detail and certain incongruities would have noticed the unfamiliar sight of several penurious migrant workers lounging around the plaza, smoking fat cigars under their large hats. All were sporting heavy silver concho-belts, rings of an alarming size and brilliance and, beneath their chins, large discs of turquoise mounted in hand-beaten silver, glinting with newness in the sun.

Such is the synchronicity, or perhaps limited opportunity, that exists in a small town that each man, independent of any discussion or even any knowledge of the other transactions, had decided to replace the silver item with a piece of new, shiny tin-ware that could be quite literally picked up from the local market-place. These items were disguised under chili ristras—those long strands of twine carrying copious red chili pods—yet another donation from the market, which had been most generous, although unaware of its support for this unusual venture.

Friday evening came; a hot evening. All the windows of Casa Magdalena were wide open to allow what little breeze there was to cool the interior of the house. The salon was filled with men and laughter and the sound of the piano being played by Santiago Fuentes, the music teacher, with some of the men singing along to their favorite mariachi songs.

Nobody noticed the furtive individuals, carrying arm-loads of chili, lurking in the shadows around the plaza, stealing surreptitious glances to left and to right from under their large hats. From time to time one or other of these slinking figures would make his stealthy way down the narrow lane that led to the back of the salon. There he would disappear through an open window, only to re-appear a few moments later, lightened of his load of both goods and conspiracy. The figure would then stroll away at a leisurely pace, whistling with that note of joy, satisfaction and light-heartedness that only those of full heart and quiet conscience can ever achieve.

It was an hour before closing time at Casa Magdalena when the sheriff, who was enjoying a quick and not strictly permitted on-duty drink with his friends, received an urgent call to return instantly to his office. There he was informed of a number of complaints that had been lodged throughout the afternoon, all from women, all curiously identical. They all reported the theft of a valuable item of silver, heirlooms that had been in their families for generations. All mentioned that they had seen the young man Sebastián, from Casa Magdalena, loitering near their premises the previous evening.

On being confronted by the sheriff, who returned with the charge sheets, Magdalena laughed and assured him that some mistake had been made. Yes—they were welcome to search anywhere they pleased.

The conversation that had become hushed started up again. Glasses were replenished, and the business of boasting about successful land deals and satisfactory trading in such and such merchandise continued.

They were interrupted again by the re-appearance of the sheriff and his men, their arms full of items of tin-ware and trailing behind them the long strings of red chili. Magdalena and Sebastián stared in amazement.

"And this is not the worst of it, ma'am. Come and see for yourself."

There was a rush for the door as all the occupants of the salon strained to see what the worst might be.

The worst was a tin hat on the head of Xavier Martínez' carving of the crucified Christ, which hung in the turquoise niche above Sebastián's bed.

In addition, there was a garland of red chili hanging around the Christ's neck, like an exotic chili boa, achieving a note of impiety that not even such an eccentric artist as Martínez, in his most irreverent moments, would have dared to imagine.

Magdalena began to laugh. So infectious was her laughter that soon loud guffaws could be heard erupting from the men.

The sheriff did not laugh.

Neither did Sebastián. He did not appreciate being the center of such mirth.

"What did you do with the silver?" The sheriff turned to confront Sebastián. "We have several reports of stolen silver, and you were seen loitering outside the houses from which the goods were removed."

"Are you accusing me of something, sheriff?"

"Come now. The evidence lies here in front of all of us."

He was unprepared for what happened next. Sebastián strode across the room. Seizing the tin hat and the chili boa from the crucifix and relieving the officers of their burdens of tin and chili ristras, he rolled them into a ball and threw them out of his room with such force that they flew across the salon, out the entrance door, down the steps and into the street, where they clattered and clanged so loudly that Perro Mestizo, who had been watching with interest, leaped into action.

With blood-curdling howls he hurled himself down the steps and attacked the ristras, shaking them as he would shake a rat, tearing the long garlands to shreds. Attracted by his snarls and growls all the town's dogs rushed to join in the attack. The scene was like a feeding frenzy. People appeared from around corners and out of stores, where they were preparing to close for the night. Seeing the snarling pack, now covered with copious amounts of red chili resembling blood, they thought that someone had been attacked, and they came running, bringing buckets of water which they threw over the dogs. Women screamed and men cursed. Tin-ware clanged and clattered. The volume of noise was tremendous.

And then someone fired a shot into the air, and all was suddenly silent. The dogs scattered, their red-stained mouths on fire. They ran to the stream that flowed past the town, where they lay all night, exhausted but triumphant, lapping the cooling water.

The sheriff was almost in tears. He wrung his hands and looked toward heaven.

"My evidence!" he wailed as he stared down at the remains. Apart from some very battered tin-ware that could have come from anywhere, there was nothing but some shredded rope, stained red, and some chili seeds that, even as he looked, were being blown across the street by the wind.

"I am arresting you, Sebastián Chávez, for the destruction of evidence," said the sheriff, regaining some semblance of authority.

It was Magdalena's turn to get angry. With an arm she restrained Sebastián, whose face was suffused with rage.

"Surely you cannot be serious? This is so obviously a ridiculous prank. You might just as soon arrest the dogs! And this evidence, as you call it, in no way matches your charge sheets. Unusual though my son's room appears, it could be of no interest to the women who reported the theft of silver. There is no silver here!"

She picked up one remaining tin goblet and presented it to the sheriff.

"And isn't it rather strange that so many pieces of silver should go missing, all from different houses, all on the same night? Why did this alleged thief take only one piece from each house? Surely you find this rather peculiar."

The sheriff scratched his head. He had never had a case like this. Fights over women. Stolen horses. That he could understand. But this? And strings of chili draped over Our Lord's suffering—here he crossed himself—this he did not understand. He was out of his depth.

The incident became exaggerated out of all proportion. A letter branding Magdalena as morally corrupt, an unhealthy influence on the people of Las Madres, a woman who had blasphemed against Our Lord and sold liquor under the very noses of the saints, whose son was also of questionable morals, was sent to the Bishop, bypassing the priest. It intimated that the priest too was at fault in that he had failed to chastise these two when requested.

The Bishop was a busy man. He was about to host a party of visiting dignitaries from Europe, and he did not want so much as a whisper of scandal reaching their ears. He wrote a letter to the priest suggesting in no uncertain terms that this woman, Magdalena—here he included a brief parenthesis hinting at the unfortunate tendencies that seem to infect women of that nomenclature—and her son should be suitably chastised or asked to leave Las Madres. He hoped he would not have to ask twice. He particularly hoped he would not have to make the rather long and tedious journey to ensure that his wishes were carried out. He signed off with the usual blessing and put the matter out of his mind.

Father Octavio spoke to Magdalena about the letter; told her that there was no obligation for her to leave either Casa Magdalena or Las Madres. She could decide what she wanted to do. She in turn discussed it with Sebastián, who was still outraged by the accusations.

"I know just who they are—those women. Don't think for a moment that they are paragons of virtue. They might do well to examine their motives. But they don't want us here. That's certain. I will be going to college soon, so their pettiness is of little interest to me. I am more concerned about you. Do you want to stay where you are not wanted?"

"But it's not the whole truth, Sebastián. There are many who want us to stay."

But in the end she decided that the two years in the salon was long enough. It had been fun for her, but she knew that this was only a stepping-stone. Her destiny lay elsewhere. She would take this as a sign.

"I don't know what comes next. We have to have somewhere to go, some place where I can earn a living. We can't just walk out into the desert."

But as it transpired, that is just what they did.

It was shortly after this conversation that one of the men, José Barela, the driver of the road grader and one of Magdalena's most devoted champions, having learned of her plight from Father Octavio, told her about the possibility of purchasing some land with a number of adobe buildings on it out in the desert, in a small valley several miles outside Las Madres. It had been on the market for many years and the buildings were in need of renovation, but the land was arable and fed by a constant spring. How did she feel about living on the land?

Magdalena said she would look at it. She and Sebastián were duly driven by José to inspect the property. The drive took them a little over two hours, not because of the vast distance from Las Madres, but on account of the condition of the road that took them there. It twisted and wound around the small hills and was crossed in a number of places by arroyos—deeply eroded, full of stones and uprooted sage and rabbit-brush. From time to time they passed small-holdings whose dilapidated houses, ramshackle sheds and poor fields spoke of poverty and struggle.

"How do people manage to live here? How do they get into town? And what about schools and clinics? I don't see anything of this nature anywhere."

"Their faith carries them through all trials and tribulations. They do not complain. There is a strong sense of community and people share their time and their skills. On very rare occasions a baby dies for lack of necessary medicine, but generally people rely on the old home remedies. The bigger children get lifts to town for schooling, and from time to time a truck is shared to take produce into market. Some of the women weave or make pots. The men find work in the chili season and part-time work in town from time to time. They live here because the land is cheap. They can keep a cow and chickens, grow some corn. They get along."

José negotiated a particularly rough stretch of road. "We are nearly there."

Ahead Magdalena saw a tall cottonwood and a small dirt road leading off to the right. They turned into this and bumped slowly up the narrow track.

She found herself looking into a small, protected valley, almost surrounded by steep hills. In the center there was an area of grassland and what must have once been fields under cultivation, overgrown now with rabbit-brush and grasses. It was bounded on the south side by a stream and a long line of cottonwoods. To the north of the property she saw a cluster of weathered adobe buildings. A pink hill, not as steep as the others, was distinguished by large fragments of weathered basalt on its west-facing slope. This marked the eastern boundary.

"Stop the car for a moment, please, José."

Magdalena got out and stood, eyes closed, beneath the tall cottonwoods, feeling the stillness. What flashed before her closed eyes were fields of lavender and chili. She heard children's laughter and the faint sound of women's voices chanting. She smelt piñón-scented smoke and the fragrance of wild herbs. She opened her eyes. Before her the whole valley shone with beauty. She knew instantly that she would buy it.

The sale of the salon was organized by the Mayor and three of the town's men who, angered by the Bishop's response to the letter sent by the women, wanted to make any amends possible. They managed to secure a good price for Casa Magdalena as a well-attended business, although they knew that the new owner would not have anything like the success that Magdalena had enjoyed.

It was on an overcast day towards the end of summer that Magdalena and Sebastián packed their possessions onto the pick-up. A truck with all the larger furniture had already departed.

In ones and twos the men who frequented the salon came by to say farewell, but they were for once tongue-tied and embarrassed, ashamed at this treatment of an extraordinary woman who had won her way into their hearts. They were not alone, for there were several women who came with small gifts to wish her well. They worked close to the salon, and had discovered in Magdalena a friend who had offered them much comfort and support in their various troubles.

In addition a hang-dog gathering of the town's yellow-eyed canines, picking up the feelings of depression and sensing an unwelcome change to their vicissitudes, sat in unusual silence and watched as the bundles were stacked and fastened securely. From his elevated position in the cab, Perro Mestizo looked down at them with blue eyes and an expression of satisfied superiority. By mid-morning the pick-up was loaded. A subdued crowd waved them goodbye, calling out blessings for good fortune.

"¡Adios, Magdalena! ¡Adios, Sebastián! ¡Buena suerte! ¡Dios le guarde! ¡Adios!"

They left Las Madres as they had arrived, with Magdalena driving, her arm in its familiar position, dangling out of the cab window, fingering the wind; and Sebastián and the ever-faithful Perro Mestizo beside her in the cab.

And so a chapter in the town's story came to a quiet end.

Life appeared to continue as it always had. But something had changed, and the people of Las Madres knew it. The young children no longer gathered outside the salon, waiting for candy, and the town's mongrels returned to their favorite pastime of scrapping amongst themselves and tipping over garbage-bins in search of food.

The sign, "Casa Magdalena", was removed and was replaced by a new one which said simply: "Saloon."

But it was the men who were most affected by her absence. They were restless. It was not just that Magdalena had left. Rather, her departure had made them aware that a whole dimension was missing from their lives, and although they could not begin to understand what had happened to them, they knew they would not find peace until they recovered it.

The lavender on either side of the saloon steps grew into a veritable hedge, and had to be clipped regularly. On those days when the fallen heads lay like a carpet on the dusty sidewalk, the strong scent would fill the street, and people passing would turn and look as if remembering the tall woman who had brought such energy and vitality into the town.

But everyone, even the women who had plotted to have Magdalena removed, knew that the town had lost something of value, although they were not able to articulate or even think very clearly just what that was.

The Adobe

The Morada, a small adobe chapel with its surrounding sheds and outhouses, and a building which might have served as a hall, was built in the late eighteen hundreds by a group of Penitente priests. It nestled between striated, pink hills, painted in some geological past by the flood waters of an ancient river and weathered now into round, sandy domes dotted with drought-stunted junipers that clung stubbornly to the slopes like persistent bonsai trees. The valley was chosen because of its remoteness and its seclusion, for it was not visible from any road. In addition, it was served by a constant spring and a hidden water-course. This ran alongside the row of cottonwoods which marked the southern boundary.

It was hoped by the priests who settled there that in this remote area they might be able to avoid the persecution of their faith and their religious practices, a harassment which was an unwelcome scourge, and which brought suffering to so many of their followers. They did not, however, manage to maintain the secrecy they sought, and the eventual raids by hooligans— bored, uneducated and intolerant young men from the nearby town, who thought it great sport to hunt down the priests and laugh at the rituals which they found barbaric—finally drove them further into the desert, leaving the chapel and the nearby barn and outhouses deserted. Over the years the dirt track that led into the small, protected valley became overgrown with disuse, and few people knew of its existence.

The priests had built well, and the thick adobe walls were still sound, although the paintwork on the doors had long since weathered away and there was no glass in the deeply recessed windows which stared out at the hills with vacant eyes. At the far end of the chapel a simple wooden altar still remained, above which there hung a retablo comprising four panels depicting the Annunciation, the Nativity, the Crucifixion and Resurrection of Christ. Although the paint had faded, there was no mistaking the excellence of the artistry.

Evidence of an old camposanto or graveyard, overgrown with chamisa and wild cosmos and recognizable by the presence of a few weathered crosses, was contained by a low fence of hand-cut saplings, almost hidden by a hedge of straggly lavender. Beyond this the silted trenches of an old acequia, with the remnants of its wooden gates fallen into disrepair, outlined the edges of what had once been irrigated fields.

Because of its situation the valley was protected from the worst storms, and the topsoil, that over the centuries had been leached from the surrounding mountains and trapped in this natural basin, had built up a deep and fertile loam, rich in minerals. The grove of olives which grew beside the hidden water-course had fared well over the years. This was adjoined by an orchard of apple trees, badly in need of pruning.

In spite of the weathering, the chapel retained a sense of dignity, as if something of the simplicity of those who had built it had survived the solitude. It stood as an eloquent voice of memory, a testament to an austere practice of worship and a deep-rooted spirituality which seemed to reside in the simple architecture and the rough-hewn timbers.

A curious feature, one most unusual for such a stark place, was the presence of several overgrown lilacs, their thick trunks attesting to many seasons of springtime bloom. They tumbled in rich profusion over the high walls which connected the chapel and outbuildings, and which enclosed the courtyard. Now, with summer almost over, it was the fragrance of their last blooms, mingled with that of earth and lavender that filled the air. Whoever had lived here over the years had left behind a deep-rooted sense of peace, and something else that moved lightly through the scented air and the rustle of the cottonwood leaves: a blessedness.

At the sight of it, as they moved up the narrow dirt path, Magdalena knew she had come home.

Magdalena had indeed come home. She was back to the land: to the huge stillness of the desert; to the familiar patterns of the seasons, both the subtle and the dramatic; back to the elemental simplicity of nature.

Her small-holding became known as The Adobe. She liked the earthy sense of history held in the mud bricks. She enjoyed the knowledge that the small chapel and outhouses had been built by men of strong conviction out of the ancient dirt and dust of the desert, and that these unknown builders would have blessed the labor of their hands. She liked to think of this as she ran her hands over the rough texture of the walls, the subtle contours, enjoying the shadow of the deep-set doorways and windows.

The restoration of The Adobe would have taken many months of hard work to make it even barely habitable had it not been for something that occurred a few days after their arrival.

On their first Saturday, just after sunrise, Magdalena was surprised by the clarion sound of hooting from what turned out to be a small convoy of pick-up trucks. They appeared to be laden with building materials. One truck carried a tractor and a plough.

Five trucks proceeded with all the gaiety of a carnival, led by the road grader driven by the faithful José Barela. Bringing up the rear was a pick-up pulling a cattle truck from which a pair of wide-eyed mules tossed their heads in protest at the noisy, lurching ride. A cacophony of baaing, bleating, crowing and cackling came from their fellow-passengers, namely two goats, several sheep and a three-tiered cage which contained a rooster and a dozen or more speckled chickens.

One by one the trucks pulled into the courtyard. The men, wearing sweat-stained leather hats, jeans, work shirts and wide smiles, jumped down from the cabs. Magdalena recognized with astonishment many of her regular clients from the Casa Magdalena, including Father Octavio who, with a glint of devilish delight in his eye, waved to her and Sebastián as the truck in which he was riding pulled in. He had dared to brave the outrage of the town's wives by supporting the idea that the townsmen make amends for the shocking treatment that Magdalena and Sebastián had suffered. The men had been appalled by the incident, and more than a little angry that their convivial end-of-day relaxation with friends had been terminated by a group of conniving women.

Although no names were ever mentioned, everyone knew who they were, and now it was their husbands who had arrived at the idea of organizing a work party to contribute whatever they could towards making sure that Magdalena was set up in fine style in her new home. There had been no protest from the women. They knew they had gone too far.

Magdalena and Sebastián stood in the yard, watching the procession roll in, mindless of the dust which was blowing over them.

The first to greet them was Father Octavio. He came striding across the courtyard as if this was a most natural, everyday occurrence.

"Good morning, Magdalena! Morning, Sebastián! Well, isn't this a fine day for a work party?"

He wiped his brow with a large, white handkerchief, for although still early, the day was hot.

The rest of the men gathered around Magdalena, shaking hands, laughing at her surprise. Perro Mestizo ran around, alternately barking and sniffing the myriad scent messages carried from town on the men's clothing.

"But what is all this?" Magdalena's hand indicated the loaded trucks. "Mules! And sheep, and goats! Whatever are you doing?"

"It is our way of saying thank you."

"But you can't possibly give me all of this!" But even as she spoke she was laughing and running from one to the other, throwing her arms around each man. "I don't know what to say!"

In response to their questions about her ideas for the future of the place, Magdalena sat down with Father Octavio and one of the men, a builder, explaining to them her plans and what she thought she might need in terms of renovation.

It was agreed that the immediate priority was to convert two of the small outhouses into comfortable dwellings for her and Sebastián. In addition, the barn needed to have separate stalls and pens for the livestock to keep them safe from coyotes and other night prowlers. She needed store rooms for crops and seed, and a section for the farm equipment.

The acequias that irrigated the fields would need to be freshly dug, and the old wooden gates that regulated the flow of water from the stream, now weathered and warped through long neglect, would need to be replaced.

There needed to be a fenced paddock for the mules and the small stock, and a henhouse for the chickens with an enclosure covered with chicken wire to protect them from buzzards. Without this protection, she was informed, the hens would all be gone in a week.

The animals being the priority, the men as a team set to work partitioning the barn and constructing the various pens and paddocks. Sebastián rolled up his sleeves and looked about for what he could do to help. He kept himself apart, concentrating on unloading the trucks and carrying timber to where it was needed, but slowly he felt himself drawn into the body of work, and he found himself enjoying the unfamiliar experience of working with a group of men.

By the end of the day the work on the barn was accomplished, and several paddocks had been strongly fenced. The hens' enclosure was secure, and a henhouse where they could roost for the night had been built.

They stood in the barn as the sun began to set, a group of tired and contented men and one woman, united by a bond of goodwill and respect.

Some wine was produced, and Father Octavio was requested to bless the day's labor. Magdalena brought glasses, and to the sound of contented animals settling in for the night, they said amen to the short blessing and sipped the wine. It was agreed that they would return early the next day to continue the work, and that the work parties would continue for as many weekends as it took to complete everything. Father Octavio would follow later, after Mass.

"How do I ever thank you enough for all this?" Magdalena walked with the men to their various pick-up trucks. A weary Perro Mestizo followed them.

"I can't begin to tell you how overwhelmed I am by all your generosity and kindness; and all your time! How will I ever repay you?"

"Ah! That's easy," one of the men replied. "We'll build you a new Casa Magdalena over there under the giant cottonwood, and then we will get you to tell us the end of that story at last!"

Magdalena laughed as she waved them goodbye.

When the last truck had rumbled out of sight, Magdalena joined Sebastián in the barn. They stood for a long time, neither one speaking. Finally it was Sebastián who broke the silence.

"This is truly your place," he said. "I can feel it." He was leaning against the barn wall, watching the mules that had crowded to the far side of the stall. "You are going to be happy here."

Magdalena looked at her son in surprise. "Did Father Octavio speak to you today?"

As she spoke she edged over to the new stable door and stood there with her back to the mules.

"He asked me if I had decided what I wanted to do next. It made me realize that I would be sad to leave."

"He told me that he would be happy to talk to you about your future. I think it would be helpful to talk things over with a man."

In spite of themselves, the mules could not resist coming forward to smell this new person who was ignoring them. Magdalena turned slowly and reached out a hand for them to nuzzle.

Sebastián watched this in wonder, distracted for a moment.

"But a priest! What does he know of the world?"

Talking nonsense to the mules, she ran her hand down the strong neck of one and reached up to rub the crown and the dark pricked ears of the other.

"Well, you have enjoyed some conversations with him, haven't you? Perhaps you should try to see him as a man who at some time in his life had to make the very choices that you are about to consider. He will be down here tomorrow after Mass. Why not speak to him then?"

As the weeks went by, The Adobe lost its deserted air and began to respond to all the work and attention it was receiving. The men replaced roofs and installed water tanks. They built a pair of hornos, outdoor ovens for baking bread and tortillas and roasting green chili and corn, and a lean-to shed next to the barn, with long rows of vigas for hanging and drying chili and medicinal herbs.

Magdalena, after living for so long in a town, was delighted by these rather primitive amenities. She found her mind going back to her childhood, remembering all that her mother had taught her about herbs and healing.

She was surprised at how much she remembered. Dear Mamá, she thought, did I ever really see you? How little she knew her mother. There had been so few opportunities to meet after she left home—just letters and the hopelessly inadequate phone calls; that last phone call to tell her that her mother was ill. She had arrived too late to say goodbye. Her father's unexpected death a week later had shocked her, leaving her feeling orphaned and vulnerable. The finality of it appalled her.

Monday to Friday, Magdalena and Sebastián plastered, fixed and painted the inside of the two cottages. They planted a vegetable garden with potatoes and carrots, onions, garlic, squash and corn, beans, chick peas and cow peas. Magdalena planted one corner with melons and water-melons, knowing how welcome the sweet fruit would be on hot days. Together they pruned the apple trees in the orchard and weeded around the olives. Magdalena had plans to extend the orchard, but that could wait a while.

With the help of a farmer from the other side of town, they learned how to work the tractor, and were delighted when Sebastián ploughed a creditable field for the planting of chili, which was to be their main crop.

The acequias had been freshly dug, and the new gates were in place so that water could be diverted from the stream into the fields and vegetable garden.

"I think you will be lucky if these grow," the farmer told her, looking at the straight rows of planting in her vegetable garden. "Wrong season."

"Oh, they will grow!" Magdalena replied with confidence. "You will see! You just have to know how to talk to them."

Six weeks after they made their first appearance, the men finally packed up their tools for the last time. The basic work was completed. Magdalena prepared a luncheon as a thank you to them. Standing at the head of the table that she had put together out of two planks of scaffold on a pair of trestles, with a sheet for a table-cloth, she raised her glass of wine to all of them.

"To all of you, for your incredible generosity! How can I ever thank you for this wonderful gift? Without your help we would have struggled to make this place even barely habitable before winter. Thank you all for making this such a rich home-coming for both of us."

She raised her glass and drank deeply.

Magdalena's Dream

The night following the men's final departure from The Adobe, Magdalena had a dream.

She was standing in the chapel doorway, looking out. Everything looked different. She saw four small casitas, and a long building with many doors and a walkway, and two additional buildings with children running and playing outside them. There was a garden in the middle of the courtyard, filled with herbs. Someone was singing.

A young woman was walking in the middle of the garden. It was she who was singing. She wore a long dress, her head covered with a scarf or some kind of veil. She walked a strangely circuitous path, as if she were in a dream. She was surrounded by a glow of light similar to those auras in paintings of the Santos in the store at Chimayó. She turned her head, looked right at Magdalena and smiled. Magdalena had never seen such a beautiful or serene face.

Sebastián was fascinated.

"I haven't seen any traces of the buildings you describe. Ask Father Octavio if he knows anything."

"As it happens, he has invited us to visit him this week when we go into town for groceries. We could go today. Would you like to come with me? Perhaps you could discuss your future plans with him while I do the shopping."

They arrived at Father Octavio's house by mid-morning, and found him working in his garden. Magdalena dropped Sebastián, saying that she would be back before lunch.

"Perhaps he can give you a hand with your work for a change," she said laughing.

"Have lunch with me, Magdalena, you and Sebastián. I have been asked by the men to give you something."

She returned later with the back of the pick-up filled to capacity with plants, bales of alfalfa, sacks of meal and all the necessities for country living.

Conversation during the meal was general. Father Octavio asked how they were doing out in the country; had they met any of the people yet? Magdalena informed him that their nearest neighbors, Emilio and Melita Villa, had dropped by to introduce themselves.

"They told me they heard that I was going to start a school and a clinic," she said and laughed. "It obviously does not take long for word to get around. Apparently there would be great support for both ventures, and there is a retired teacher who would be interested in teaching the little ones, so it looks as if I will soon be building a school."

She looked up at him, suddenly remembering her dream.

"I had this strange dream." She described the woman with the veil and the way she was walking. "It was almost as if she was lost in a maze, but she seemed so composed—not lost at all."

"She could have been walking a labyrinth," Father Octavio suggested, "although it would be unusual—extremely unlikely, actually, to find one in this part of the world."

Magdalena was fascinated.

"It is different from a maze in that, although the path winds and doubles back on itself, there are no blind alleys. Provided you stay the distance, you will reach the center—and find your way out again. There is only one path in a labyrinth."

Magdalena was thoughtful. "How very strange," she said.

As they were about to leave, Father Octavio produced an envelope which he gave to Magdalena.

"The men asked me to give this to you."

She opened the envelope.

"They have given us two season tickets to the opera! I can't believe it. This is the grand opening. Look, Sebastián! There is a photograph of the opera house. It is out in the desert, and it has no roof. 'DESERT OPERA BENEATH THE STARS,'" she read. "'A SEASON OF PUCCINI.' Madame Butterfly—La Boheme—Tosca—Turandot. What a program. How did they ever manage to get these seats? It has been booked out in advance since last year."

"It seems that you have some friends in high places," the priest said with a chuckle.

"We can go to all four operas, Sebastián! What a wonderful gift!"

Sebastián flashed an enthusiastic smile, and then appeared to change his mind.

"I think you should ask someone else to go with you, Mamá. It would be wasted on me."

He turned to address the priest.

"Father Octavio—do you like opera?"

And that was how it happened that Magdalena was escorted to all four operas that season by Father Octavio, and, as it transpired, because of their mutual enjoyment of opera, every season thereafter, providing the gossips with much fuel for their need to be shocked by something, as long as it was not of any real substance.

The Santa Fe Opera

The good-looking priest and the beautiful Magdalena Chávez made a striking couple at the opening night for "A SEASON OF PUCCINI." The only other woman who drew such admiring glances from the men was Catherine Luna de la Cruz. She was the wife of Señor Lorenzo de la Cruz—who enjoyed the conceit of being known as Don Lorenzo—the owner of the most prestigious hacienda in the district.

All of the wealthy from Las Madres were present, in spite of the long drive and irrespective of whether they actually enjoyed opera. It certainly would not do to miss being seen at such a prestigious event, and now they were making it their business to know just who was, and who wasn't present in the large crowd. Such things matter in certain circles.

Behind the sophisticated elegance and the polite conversations over glasses of wine, an activity not unlike the sniffing beneath one another's tails of a pack of dogs was being energetically if surreptitiously conducted. This was a time to learn all the "who and what" of the goings-on in their society. For the gossips it was a time for reaping, and no detail, however seemingly insignificant, escaped their predatory eyes. But it was the tall woman whose hand rested so lightly and elegantly on the arm of the priest, Father Octavio, who held their attention. What brazenness! Look at the way she moves: it is disgraceful.

"Good heavens! It is that woman from the salon! Whatever can Father Octavio be thinking?"

But they all came up and greeted Father Octavio and smiled most charmingly when he introduced Magdalena to them.

Magdalena and Father Octavio found a quiet corner away from the excited crowd, where they could enjoy their wine before the performance. They stood together, admiring the sunset and the desert skyline, watching the sky gradually change from crimson to indigo, seeing the desert grow dark until it was a low, black silhouette above which the solitary evening star hung suspended.

"What a dramatic setting for an opera house," Magdalena said. "To be surrounded by all this space, and this huge silence."

Just then Father Octavio was greeted in loud tones, and Magdalena, turning, saw that they were being approached by a handsome, powerfully built man. He was followed by the beautiful and elegant woman she had noticed earlier on account of her extraordinary red hair.

"Father Octavio! Good evening to you, sir. I didn't ever think to see you here. What brings you to the opera?" He managed to make the simple question sound insulting. "And who is your charming partner?"

He stared at Magdalena who, under his arrogant scrutiny, felt compelled to hold his gaze until he finally looked away.

Señor de la Cruz was an exceptionally good-looking man. He was dressed impeccably. His clothes had been skillfully tailored to bring elegance to his powerfully muscular body. He sported a large onyx and silver bolo in place of the more traditional black tie, and a scarlet cummerbund. When he moved, the scarlet lining to his flared opera-coat flashed dramatically. He wore his thick hair, which was just starting to go silver at the temples, cut long, which added a Dionysian touch to his appearance. His swarthy complexion was unlined. His eyes were his most startling feature, Magdalena thought. They were set beneath a straight and formidable brow that looked as if it was accustomed to being obeyed. The eyes were dark, almost black, and, she thought, frightening. They would be able to devour the will of anyone who was either unwary or unwarned. Although he was smiling, his eyes remained inscrutable. They permitted no entry into whatever secrets lay behind them. He allowed his penetrating gaze to pass over her in the manner in which one examines, critically, a piece of prime stock that one contemplates purchasing. Magdalena felt naked.

"Good evening, father," Catherine de la Cruz said quietly. "What a pleasure to see you on such a wonderful evening. I don't believe we have met," she said, turning to greet Magdalena.

"Ah! Lorenzo! Catherine! Good evening to you! Catherine, you look quite lovely! Let me introduce Magdalena Chávez, who has invited me to accompany me here tonight, for which I am most grateful. Yes, Lorenzo! I believe I am here to listen to Puccini's Madame Butterfly, to which I am looking forward immensely. What a triumph this is for Santa Fe, don't you think?"

Father Octavio smiled at them with his most friendly, most innocent and beguiling smile.

Magdalena stared at Catherine, wondering where she had seen her face before. When the couple moved away to greet other friends, she remarked to Father Octavio on the strong sense of recognition she had felt.

"And what a powerful man! I should not like to make an enemy of him. I don't think I would even want to risk being a friend; and his wife, so lovely and so sad. There is a story there."

"There are stories everywhere, Magdalena, aren't there?"

Magdalena smiled at him, but said nothing.

Their quiet conversation did not go unnoticed, but it was the sight of Father Octavio producing a handkerchief and tenderly wiping away the many tears that Magdalena shed during the love duet that got the women's tongues wagging; that, and the way he looked at her, that gave them much to talk about.

It would have been impossible not to notice the surreptitious glances that were cast in their direction, the heads that leaned together and the whispered conversations that took place behind hands and fans. Magdalena was concerned, not for herself but for Father Octavio's reputation.

"They are staring at us, Father Octavio," she said to him, almost under her breath.

"Well, good! Let them stare," he said.

For in truth it was a long time since he had experienced being looked at in this way. It was all very well to be a priest, but the admiration, or was it envy, he saw in the men's eyes made him feel quite unaccountably alive. Just let there be one word of criticism! The pulpit could be a powerful place, and Jesus Himself would furnish much material for a sermon to put an end to any stone-throwing. He almost hoped it would be necessary. In the meantime he was savoring his enjoyment of a memorable evening with a lovely woman.

"It is difficult being a priest, Magdalena," he confided to her as they were leaving. "They raise their eyebrows if you escort a man, and they are shocked if you are seen in the company of a woman. And I suppose it is almost unforgivable if that woman is as beautiful as you, Magdalena."

Magdalena blushed. She didn't know where to look, and pretended to be searching for a handkerchief.

"Am I, as a priest, forever doomed to accompany dull and stolid married couples, paragons of misplaced virtue, on such occasions—or perhaps some sufficiently plain spinster of advanced age, ascetic disposition and stern temperament? There is nothing in my vows that makes any such demand. It is not a requirement. No, Magdalena. I think that this will provide some much-needed exercise for their souls, and many opportunities for confession."

"Father Octavio!" Magdalena uttered in a tone of mock reprimand. "I am shocked!"

The Work

When Elena Trujillo said that Magdalena was 'other', she had spoken a truth that was soon to be felt by everyone in the district surrounding The Adobe.

Word of the prediction reached the isolated community via a mechanic who worked in Las Madres. He told his wife, and soon Magdalena was inundated with visits from locals curious to meet the newcomer and to learn what it was, precisely, that was 'other' about her. They were not to be disappointed. The rate of growth of her crops alone spoke of some unusual power, and the strong, sweet fragrance that hovered over the valley was felt by many to be a presence, of what they could not say. It was soon learned that she was a curandera, a healer, and before long Magdalena found herself treating a growing number of women and babies, and even some of the local men.

In her second year at The Adobe Magdalena invited Father Octavio and everyone in the surrounding area to attend a meeting. This was to be a turning-point in the lives of the members of the small community, providing them with a new way of seeing themselves and their circumstances. Magdalena stood in front of all of them, and offered her proposal.

"As isolated individuals, there is little we can achieve of any great impact. If we want a better life for ourselves and our children, it rests, not in the charity of others, but in our own hands. If we decide to come together and offer our various talents, I think we will make something happen here that will benefit all of us. This is an opportunity for us to find out who would be interested in pursuing this idea, to discover what skills we have to offer and to decide what we need to manifest here initially so that this community can thrive."

The meeting was a great success. The immediate needs, as Magdalena had anticipated, involved a clinic and a pre-school. In addition, they needed some form of regular transport to take the older children into Las Madres for school.

Their resources were many, the majority being in the area of craft work: sewing, weaving, ceramics, painting and wood-carving. There were also many women known for their traditional cooking and their family secrets of ways to prepare chili, which led to the idea of publishing a recipe book. There was a man who had once been a tinsmith, several men who played the guitar and one violinist. There was a young man who had almost drunk himself to death, but who was, when sober, a gifted artist whose designs could be seen spray-painted on the flashy lowriders, the renovated vintage cars with lowered suspension that occasionally cruised down the main street of Las Madres. All together it was an impressive list.

Father Octavio said he would be conducting Mass in the small chapel on alternate Sundays for those who were unable to travel in to Las Madres. In addition, he said he would speak to two people who lived in Las Madres who might be willing to offer their skills: the first, Alejandro Jaramillo, a santero, to help with instruction for those interested in wood-carving, and the other, Santiago Fuentes, a musician and teacher. Perhaps they could establish a church choir.

Work progressed speedily at The Adobe. Magdalena bought the building materials, but the community supplied all the labor to build a structure that would house the clinic, the pre-school and two rooms for the craft work. Men and women worked side by side, and at the end of eight weeks the building was complete.

It was not long before The Adobe became a busy center of activity. The lavender crop was harvested, and provided a range of products. In September fresh green chili and red chili tied into ristras was sent into town for the annual Chili Festival. The remainder of the chili crop was dried, ground and packaged.

Work parties were organized to assist local farmers in their work on the various small-holdings, the women set to work on a book of traditional recipes and Magdalena began to compile a book of medicinal plants of the area, providing illustrations, methods of preparation and their use as remedies.

Alejandro Jaramillo attracted a group of gifted men and women who were inspired to become santeros, having seen some of his work. The tinsmith gathered his tools, that had lain idle for many years, and set to work, and the young artist put an advertisement in the Las Madres weekly paper.

A new and industrious spirit entered into the community, which every day seemed to discover new ways of expressing its creativity. Even Magdalena was astonished at how much had been achieved in such a short time.

But it was the attendance of Mass in their own chapel that transformed the soul of the community. This small, humble chapel with its rough-hewn pews and faded altar-piece became a center for their spiritual lives. Soon the bare, whitewashed walls were hung with retablos painted by members of the community. Statues of the saints found places close to the altar, and white lace curtains softened the windows. Hand-woven rugs covered the bare earth floor, and bright kneeling-cushions hung from the backrests of the pews. The last act was to name the chapel. It was agreed by the community to call it after what they considered to be the new spirit which seemed to have resurrected itself in the valley, and which now enriched their lives. They painted the name onto a piece of ponderosa pine, and fixed it over the entrance.

Father Octavio, when he conducted the first service in the latest history of the morada, thought that no choir ever sang more sweetly than that of La Capilla de Nuestra Señora de Sofia.

In the evenings, when everyone had left to return to their homes, Magdalena would sit on her porch with Perro Mestizo at her side, enjoying the cool evening and watching the sunset's colors fade into night. Sometimes she would fancy that she heard the sound of men's voices floating over the hills, and at other times a woman's song seemed to haunt the trees beyond the graveyard. On these occasions the dog's ears would prick, and he would turn his head towards the hills as if he too heard those faint echoes blowing towards them on the evening breeze.

PART II
SEBASTIÁN

The Gift

"Come, Amigo! Come, Ladrido!"

The small boy called to his dogs as he went racing down the dusty street, swinging the empty shopping bag over his head the way a cowboy swings a lasso. Only one dog, Amigo, could be seen scampering after his young friend. Ladrido was invisible to everyone except Sebastián, who said that people just hadn't learned how to see him.

"You have to look sideways. He makes himself invisible when people stare at him. It makes him nervous."

From the front window Magdalena watched her son, and gave a sigh. He needed a playmate. She should spend more time with him, she knew, but her work load was heavy, and raising a son alone was no easy task. Every time she turned round there were more bills to pay. However, she did not regret her move to the small town.

Desterrado was, in fact, little more than a village. It lay some twenty miles south of Santa Fe, as the crow flies, and was hidden between the eroded slopes of an imposing mesa which overlooked it. It was originally, as its name suggested, a place of exile; a place where men and women outlawed by society sought refuge. And it was well-suited to those who chose to live, for whatever reason, outside the more conventionally accepted norms of small-town life.

In the early days, before the railroad put Desterrado on the map, many chose to move there to escape a too close scrutiny of their questionable business dealings, and much of the town's present affluence derived from these not strictly lawful practices.

In spite of its rough and rather undesirable beginnings, Desterrado had evolved into a peaceful town, but one which still upheld the rights of an individual to anonymity and privacy. Whatever the nature of its possibly ill-gotten gains, the community was now respectable, and enjoyed a degree of wealth and privilege unusual for those parts.

Magdalena arrived at Desterrado with her son on a late summer evening, thankful that the house was all that the agent had promised it would be; thankful that Sebastián had slept for most of the tiring journey; thankful to have arrived in a place where nobody knew her, and where no awkward questions would be asked about her past.

News of Magdalena's dress-making skills quickly spread through the small town, and soon a number of women were knocking at her door with requests for her unique creations. She became so busy that she had to employ two young women, sisters, Petronila and Sotera Ortega, to help with the sewing.

Sebastián loved their company, and waited each morning on the porch steps to greet them. They brought him small gifts, fashioned strange dolls out of scraps of fabric, and showed him how to draw houses and cats and dogs and trees and flowers. They taught him songs and rhymes and how to write numbers, and took him with them when they went on shopping errands for Magdalena. Sebastián enjoyed all of it. Best of all, they brought with them a small radio which played music constantly through the day, to the delight of the small boy.

Sebastián loved the songs, and would sit with his ear close to the speaker in order to learn the words. Soon his voice could be heard throughout the house, adding a child's high note to the day. There was one song he particularly loved, called 'The Wind in the Valley', that brought tears to his eyes.

"I would love to know this place," he told his mother. "I think it would be full of animals and birds and friends to play with."

Magdalena gave him a fierce hug.

He spent his days between the cutting-room, where his mother interviewed clients, conducted fittings and made the patterns, and the front room where Petronila and Sotera pinned and sewed and altered Magdalena's creations.

While their deft fingers worked on seams and fine pin-tucks, on ruched neck-lines and bodices, beaded and embroidered, they talked constantly, pausing only to respond to some request from Sebastián or to tune the radio to a new station.

"Look, Sebastián, we brought you a box for your 'pieces'."

Sebastián's 'pieces' were carefully chosen scraps of fabric from the cutting-room floor. He loved the way the light reflected off satin with a soft gleam, and the sound taffeta made when he crinkled it; how the white chiffon became a mist when he waved it through the air. He kept all the dark 'pieces', the dark blue and black shades, at the bottom of the box under a white tissue. These were his shadow pieces that he loved. They were his hidden things. He did not speak about these or play with them.

Instinctively, Sebastián knew that the ladies who came to the house for fittings were somehow different from Petronila and Sotera and his mother. These women, in their elegant clothes, their fine shoes, and smelling deliciously of fragrant perfumes, were careful to avoid the dusty little boy who played under the table, and although they occasionally asked politely how he was doing, they never thought to speak to him, far less bring any gift for him. Eventually Sebastián came to realize that if he sat very still when they came, even if he was in the center of the floor, he became invisible.

During these times, when the women came for dress fittings, Sebastián enjoyed this invisibility the most. It was at this early age that he began to develop a quality that he would become conscious of only much later in his life. This was his capacity to observe, to perceive, to intuit in the minutest detail, everything that was going on around him; a way of noticing; a habit that was entirely unselfconscious. For Sebastián this sensitive perception of his world, both its infinitely detailed physical appearance and the complex, interweaving threads of subtle innuendos that lay just beneath the surface of things, came as automatically as breathing. He was not even aware of its happening; not aware that he was gathering tens of thousands of multi-sensory images and storing them somewhere deep in his memory.

Only much later, when people began to remark on the depth of his perception and his grasp of what was really happening beneath the apparent reality of things, would he come to realize that he had a gift.

While the women stood in front of the long mirror, turning this way and that, he would sit unobserved while his mother fitted the bodices, adding a tuck here, taking in a dart there so that their slender bodies were shown to full advantage. He watched spellbound as they twirled about to test the fullness of the skirt, swishing it this way and that in the manner of a flamenco dancer. Then he would see their legs and their high heels and wonder how anyone could walk in such shoes.

He marveled at their long, red fingernails and, comparing them to his own grubby but functional set of short-nailed digits, wondered how they managed the simplest of tasks. His mother didn't have nails like that, nor did

Petronila or Sotera; nor did they wear such shoes. And although they made the most elegant dresses and costumes, they never wore such clothes. Sebastián decided that there must be two different types of women. Instinctively he preferred the short-nailed variety.

On the long summer evenings when he and his mother sat together on the porch steps, reviewing the day, he would show her all the pictures he had drawn and recount the stories that went with them.

"This is the lady who came to try on the red dress."

Magdalena had to hide a smile, for the picture captured the air of haughty sensuality perfectly. He had drawn her two hands pressing her breasts upward. Magdalena recalled that this was a habitual movement the woman made quite unconsciously every time she came for a fitting. She looked at her small son.

"She is not a very nice person, is she, Mamá?"

Magdalena looked surprised.

"What makes you think that?"

"It's the way she looks at me. I can see it in her eyes. She doesn't like herself very much either. I think she must be very unhappy. Perhaps somebody told her she was stupid. Perhaps her mother spanked her when she was small."

"Sebastián! Wherever do you get all these ideas? I'm sure that there is no truth in any of it."

"Yes, there is. Sometimes, when people don't talk to you, they tell you so much."

Magdalena was more than a little alarmed, and thought it best to turn the page and look at the next drawing.

When they finished looking at all the pictures, and his mother had heard every detail of his boy's-eye view of the day, Sebastián would close the scrap-book and curl his body up close to her for story-telling. He never tired of these stories, but listened with rapt attention as she told him about the ancient peoples of Mexico, the Aztecs and the Toltecs of Central America, and the even more ancient Mayans and the Olmecs.

"Your grandfather came from Mexico. He was a person of mixed Spanish and Indian blood, so we have strong blood in our bodies."

Sebastián was curious. "Indian?"

"Our family's Indian ancestors reach back to a time long before the Conquistadors arrived in South America."

"Were they the ones with the horses?"

"Yes. They were great horsemen."

Sebastián learned about the power of the gods who ruled the earth and the sky. On warm, sultry evenings they would sit and watch the great storm clouds gather, and marvel as lightning leapt out of the thunderheads to writhe a brilliant, jagged path across the heavens.

With so much of his time spent alone, to compensate for his lack of playmates, Sebastián developed a lively imagination. It was into this imaginary world that the small dog Ladrido wandered one day and thereafter accompanied him wherever he went. On a number of occasions Magdalena observed that her child appeared to be deep in conversation, apparently explaining the intricacies of some childhood game to an invisible entity.

"You see, Ladrido," he explained carefully, "most people cannot see this world of ours. They only see what they think is there—like their dining-room table or the tree in their garden. They don't know that if you close your eyes tight and long for something, with all your heart"—Sebastián bent down and repeated the words—"all your heart—it will come to you. Like you did, Ladrido. I wanted you so much. And here you are."

Ladrido, the subject under observation, was a dog possessed of almost supernatural intuitive qualities, immense patience and intelligence superior to that of most humans. Sebastián informed his mother that he was a real dog who knew how to make himself invisible.

Initially Magdalena did not pay too much attention to the part Ladrido played in her son's life. However, when Sebastián told her that he and Ladrido had mistakenly walked to the edge of 'the place where the light ends', she began to worry.

"There is a place," Sebastián said in a whisper, "that is so empty that the light can't go there." His eyes were huge with the terror of it. "And if you fall in," he shuddered, "you can't ever be found again. Ever! It is the place where the light ends."

Magdalena stared into her son's intense face.

"Sometimes humans can't see that they are right at the edge, and they do fall in."

Sebastián stared down as if he saw the dark place open up in front of him.

"But animals are much cleverer. They know when they come near to this place, and they give a warning. Ladrido barked!"—Sebastián slapped his hands together sharply—"and that is why we were both saved from falling in. That is why Ladrido has come to be with me. To make sure I am safe."

It was at this point that Magdalena decided that Sebastián was spending too much time in his imagination; that he needed something of flesh and blood that he could touch and hold and love, a real dog that would be a friend to him; a dog that ate and had fleas and made a noise and a mess: above all, a dog that she could see.

The last dog in the long row of cages was a creature with a large jug head, bright, intelligent eyes, a thick barrel of a body and short legs, as if the maker had suddenly run out of material when it came to this last detail. It was to this extraordinarily odd and ill-fashioned creature that Sebastián pointed.

"This is Amigo," he informed his mother with conviction as the kennel man struggled to slip a rope leash over the dog's huge head.

Amigo was a dog of the most uncommon coloring: white with odd spots of black and brown brindle, dotted randomly over his body. Black patches over both eyes added a rakish air of mystery to his appearance, and he had a very long brown tail possessed, it would seem, of a life of its own, for it drew energetic circles in the air regardless of what was occurring at the other end.

When he saw Sebastián, he did not waste time at the wire, but raced over to the gate as if knowing that he was being fetched at last, impatient to be gone, and perhaps mildly surprised that it had taken so long.

As they walked home with Amigo tugging against the rope, the tail working furiously, Sebastián turned to his mother and said:

"They seem to like each other. I think they will be good friends, Ladrido and Amigo."

Magdalena refrained from saying anything.

Sebastián and Amigo were inseparable and Magdalena, who loved all animals, was delighted with the new family member. She half hoped that Ladrido might slowly fade away into a forgotten invisibility, but it was not to be, and he remained an important part of Sebastián's world. It was to the shadow figure of Ladrido that Sebastián turned with his troubles, often sitting for long periods, deep in conversation with this strange entity while Amigo looked on with interest, his head cocked, his tail whirling and thumping in concert with the energies of the encounter.

Amigo was unquestionably real, and displayed his amiable temperament and good nature to everyone, with the exception of Magdalena's wealthy customers.

"This strange creature is yours, Magdalena?"

The woman stood frozen in the doorway, regarding the dog that was obstructing her path.

"Does he bite? He seems to have taken a dislike to me. Please take him away. I do not like his manner."

Accordingly, Sebastián had to forgo his game of being invisible, and when his mother expected such clients, at the first knock at the door he would take Amigo out the back and go to his secret place, a ring of junipers behind the house, and wait there, watching the two dogs wrestle in mock fights of terrible ferocity.

Only when he saw the women depart would they all rush back into the house with much noise, Amigo barking excitedly and generally rushing around in a frenzy of delight, his tail sending vases and books flying, making a huge mess, while he grabbed at scraps of fabric which he shook violently to their death.

Magdalena was so delighted with the influence he had on her son's life that she forgave him his less loveable attributes. He was real, he was alive, and there had been no more talk about 'the place where the light ends'.

It was Sebastián's seventh birthday. He had been in a fever of excitement since early dawn.

"When will they be here, Mamá?" he asked again.

He and Amigo were sitting inside the doorway, waiting for Petronila and Sotera to arrive.

Magdalena set the tea table and brought in the birthday cake she had baked. She placed it beside a large, wrapped gift in the center of the table.

Solemnly Sebastián placed pictures he had made next to the places at the table, together with a white bloom for each person, picked from the yuccas which grew behind the house. He tied a bright, red handkerchief around Amigo's neck.

Petronila and Sotera arrived, giggling like two young girls, with ribbons plaited into their hair to honor the occasion and carrying a large, oblong-shaped and brightly-wrapped present, tied with a satin bow.

"This is for you, Sebastián. Happy birthday!"

They placed their gift into his arms.

Sebastián sat on the floor, solemnly untied the bow and folded it carefully. Very slowly he unwrapped the parcel and looked inside.

"Look, Mamá! Look what I've got!"

Their gift was a dobbin horse which they had made out of shiny, black satin and a sawn-off broomstick. It had large, blue-button eyes, a long, black mane and a leather bridle, put together with tin rivets which shone like silver. A pair of slim-fitting black pants, a white shirt and black waistcoat, together with a scarlet neckerchief and a black hat, completed the gift.

Sebastián tore off his clothes and drew on the new garments. Setting the hat low on his forehead, he glanced at his observers sideways from beneath the dark brim and flashed them a dazzlingly wicked smile.

Suddenly he transformed from a dusty little boy into a young man, slender and powerfully elegant.

"Well! Just look at you, Sebastián!" Magdalena remarked, a little shocked at the sudden change.

He was tall for his age, she thought, but it was more than that. He seemed to have grown up all at once. He was no longer her little baby boy.

But when he mounted his black steed and ran prancing and bucking around the room, yelling encouragement to his pony, she relaxed. It was just the clothes that made him appear different. Just the clothes.

Tea was served. Everyone exclaimed how beautiful their pictures were. Sebastián ate slowly. He was saving the big parcel until last. The anticipation was as delicious as the large slab of chocolate cake that he was working his way through steadily. As he munched, he considered the parcel's size and shape. Finally it was time to open it.

Sebastián wiped his fingers one by one on the paper napkin, folded it and laid it next to his plate. He was delaying the actual opening of the present quite deliberately. He did not rip the paper, as many children would, for it was the not knowing that thrilled him. As long as he did not see what was inside the bright paper, it had the potential to be a thousand things. In this way he was receiving the joy of not one, but a thousand birthday gifts. When at last he did untie the bow, he folded it into a tidy loop and put it with the other ribbon. These would go into his box of treasures later. Piece by piece he removed the tape which held the paper in place, and put them all together. Only then did he slowly pull back one side of the shiny wrapping and peer inside.

"Oh, Mamá!" His eyes shone.

Carefully he lifted out the shiny, new radio.

It was the latest, most modern design that she had been able to find in the store. Its case was made out of polished wood; it had gold cloth over the circular speaker section in front, and a dial with colored numerals. It was beautiful. Sebastián ran his hands over its contours, examined all the buttons, and considered the small dial with its bright lines and mysterious numbers.

"Oh, Mamá—it's beautiful." He gave his mother a swift hug.

Sebastián carried it, with the utmost care, over to a corner of the room, set it down on a low table, plugged it in and turned the knobs until he found a station.

The powerful sound of a flamenco guitar being played fiercely, staccato clapping and the throaty voice of a vocalist filled the room. Sebastián stood absolutely still, listening. Then, to everyone's surprise, he removed his hat and climbed onto the dining-room table.

He stood erect, raised one slow arm, wrist turned back, fingers held tensely, as if he were aware of each small digit. His other arm moved into the position of a dancer's behind his arched back. His head, with its arrogant Castilian profile, turned to look over one shoulder, the gaze of his black eyes directed back into himself, listening.

Slowly he began to turn, as if taking in the whole world through his feet; a gentle, stroking movement, caressing the smooth table-top.

At first it was only his feet that moved—a slow stamping now, as the beat of the music entered into him. And then the energy moved upward, swiftly, and the onlookers witnessed the small body seized as if by the force of an unleashed storm.

The three women stared at the small figure, strung tight as a bow-string, possessed by the dark rhythm that flowed into him like a flame. The dark sounds of the song shuddered their way up from his feet, right through him to the top of his head and down his arms to each small fingertip.

Sebastián danced with an intensity that made their hearts beat faster. They felt a prickling on the back of their necks; tears sprang to their eyes.

Sebastián did not look at them. There was nothing beyond him and the music, and it appeared that the two were not separate. All the fire and fury of that passionate flamenco rhythm seized him. His bare feet stamped with the power and authority of that mix of Andalusian, Arab and Moorish intensity. His small fingers clicked: sharp, staccato, clean as castanets.

Petronila and Sotera stood up, clapping furiously in time to the music, shouting out, "¡Ole! ¡Ole! ¡Viva Sebastián!"

Magdalena stood staring, her eyes wide in shock.

The small feet drummed faster and faster till they became a blur of speed. The small figure whirled; the music reached a crescendo; there was one last stamp—"¡Ole!"—and the music ended.

Sotera reached over and turned the radio off. The room was silent.

Sebastián, his cheeks blazing, stood still, his chest heaving, his eyes still looking inward as if he were in some other world that dwelt deep within him.

At last Magdalena moved over to where he stood on the table. Very gently she put her arms around him and kissed the top of his head.

"Sebastián—mi querido."

Magdalena lifted the long, black hair that was saturated with sweat, out of his eyes. With a table napkin she wiped his scarlet face.

"Mi querido," she whispered.

And then Sebastián burst into tears.

The Wound

The seasons turned.

Nothing happened to break the comfortable security of Sebastián's world. He was growing fast. He had a head full of magnificent richness; the love of his mother; two young women who adored him, and two friends, both canine and one visible, who never left his side. His world was complete. The place where the light ends had retreated from his awareness into its empty shadows to await its time. It was in no hurry.

Magdalena had not spoken to Sebastián about his father, so it was only when he started school, shortly before his eighth birthday, and he heard the boys speak about their fathers, bragging about their qualities of strength and bravery, that he became aware of this absence in his life.

He asked his mother where his father was, and why he didn't live with them like the other boys' fathers did.

Magdalena hesitated, wondering how much she should tell. Finally she told him that his father had gone away on a long journey.

"He has work he has to do, and it is far away. We won't see him for a very long time."

In response to all his many requests for details she remained deliberately vague.

Sebastián digested this meager offering, and then constructed his own idea of the truth, which he told to his classmates at school. Although it was an unlikely tale, it impressed his eight-year-old friends.

It was on the day of his eighth birthday, however, as he stood before the class, invited to speak about any topic he wished, that he told them the whole story of his father.

"My father is a very great man, and very clever. He knows all about the ancient gods in South America."

Sebastián made sure everyone was listening.

"There is one very bad god. He stole a very important piece of light, and he has kept it hidden for thousands and thousands of years."

Sebastián stared intensely at the hushed class.

"He stole this piece of light, and now there is a terrible place of darkness. 'A place where the light ends.'"

Sebastián looked distraught with the telling of it.

"And so many people have fallen in and never been seen again!"

Sebastián held his hands in front of him, as if desperately trying to push away the darkness.

"And more and more will be lost if the light isn't found, and the terrible, dark place isn't filled with it."

Sebastián paused here for dramatic effect. The small boys stared at him in horror and fascination. Their fathers did nothing like this.

"Only a man with very great courage will be able to find the light and put it back where it belongs. My father has been chosen out of many, many men. He will have to travel a long way—a very long way. It may take years and years. He will have to face so many dangers to find the light and take it to the place where the light ends. But my father will not fail."

His story was met with silence.

The teacher, who had looked confused and then become angry, told Sebastián to come to the front of the class. Here she subjected him to a period of questioning, at the conclusion of which she announced to the class that the story was a lie.

Sebastián's world broke into pieces. It became known that he had never met his father, and indeed, did not even know his name. This hero did not exist. He stood before the whole class while his teacher, who felt strongly that boys should be punished for telling lies, continued to interrogate him.

Sebastián attempted to defend his imaginary world, fielding the questions with indignant denials, until it was apparent to everyone that he had invented the entire story.

He stood facing all of them, his eyes flashing, while the humiliation continued. He did not utter another word. Amigo stood at his side, and for the first time his tail was still.

"Perhaps you haven't got a father," one boy suggested.

Sebastián gave him a look, and the boy was silenced.

He ran all the way home from school, and refused to come out of his room for the birthday party Magdalena had arranged for him and a few friends.

"He won't come out because we know about his father," one youngster informed her. "He told lies at school, and the teacher found out."

Magdalena sent all the boys home with parcels of cake, and then went to her son's door. Hearing a muffled sob, she entered the room.

Sebastián was lying face down on the bed, with Amigo attempting to lick his face. Magdalena sat next to him and put a hand on the small, heaving shoulders. She sat without speaking, stroking his hair, until the weeping grew quieter and eventually stopped. Sebastián rolled over and looked up at his mother, his small boy's face red from the weeping. He wiped his sleeve across his face.

"Where is my father?" he asked.

Magdalena paused to reflect for a moment.

"Your father and I met when we were children. We grew up on the same rancho out in the country. Then he went away for a number of years to study, and when he returned, we fell in love. But there were difficulties. We were not allowed to marry. His father forbade it. And then you were born, and we had to leave. We came to live here. And here we are."

She simplified it as best she could. The truth of it was brutal, but Magdalena felt that it was the least he deserved.

"Why didn't he come with us?"

It was an obvious question.

"His father would not allow it. He was a very powerful man. He would have made life impossible for us. Your father would have been unable to find work anywhere."

Listening to her own words, she wondered now if this was indeed true; whether they shouldn't have made a greater effort to stay together, whatever the cost. Looking down at her son's face, she wondered what price could have been greater than the pain he was suffering right now. She thought that she had dealt with all her pain and anger, but now she felt it welling up again, only this time for her son.

"So who is my father—and my grandfather?"

"I promised I would not reveal his name. Not to anyone. I made that promise, Sebastián. I must keep it."

"I hate him!"

Magdalena said nothing.

"So I will never meet my father. He hasn't even seen me! He doesn't know who I am!"

There was a long pause.

"He will never know me. You told me he loved me. You told me a lie."

Sebastián jumped off the bed and, followed by Amigo, ran from the room and out to his place behind the house. There, in the small clearing, hidden from view, he sat in silence while the afternoon shadows gathered around him. The dog sat beside him.

The Man Who Wasn't

It is possible that some childhood pain never leaves us entirely; that it lives on behind that lonely wall we build to protect ourselves from further hurt, and that many unexplored gifts and talents, and all the unlived aspects of our lives, reside in this isolated place, finding perhaps, from time to time, a brief escape into another reality; into the passionate world of our dreams.

It is seldom recognized how much of our time and energy is spent in maintaining this wall, or that it is an area of bitter conflict between the longings of the spirit to fulfill itself and the determination of our numerous defense mechanisms to maintain it.

Sebastián's senior school years passed relatively uneventfully. He was a brilliant student, a stimulating and adventurous thinker, much sought after by his peers for his skill in discussion and debate and for his highly original view of the world.

"Hi, Sebastián—will you help me with this proposal? The subject is 'The world we see is not the only world.' I don't know how I got into this, and I don't have a clue about how to begin."

He tended to favor the least popular side of any argument, and invariably would win his point. Although he did not stand out in the ordinary course of events, his charismatic qualities became evident when he engaged in heated debate, and he could swing a group this way and that effortlessly.

From time to time he was approached to join his peers in their jaunts around town, for meetings with girls, weekend dances or illicit trips to the casinos; but he politely refused all invitations, steadfastly avoiding any form of intimacy, preferring the more predictable and unemotional realm of the intellect.

"Anyone got a few dollars to throw away?"

It was the weekend, and a group was gathering to visit the casinos. It was forbidden, which made the jaunt all the more exciting.

"You, Sebastián?"

Sebastián smiled and shook his head. He knew that the invitation was a polite formality. His peers had finally accepted that he was an oddball with an unusual mind, who did not want to socialize.

"Sorry. I have an essay to finish and it has to be in by Monday. Maybe next time."

At times like this he would feel all over again that he was on the outside of life looking in, envying other young men their sense of security in the world, their ease and decisiveness.

It was only when he was alone that he experienced his solitude as a blessing. He would take long walks out into the desert alone, or stand at night beneath the vast mystery of the heavens and feel the centuries blow their indifferent breath over him; sense with awe those other, more ancient gods, bowing their heads in reverence as they contemplated the immensity of time.

These times were the closest he came to feeling that he belonged in the world, and he would be deeply moved. He felt then that there was a place or a state that he had once known, that was beyond anything he could articulate.

And then the awareness of this loss would throw him back into his sense of shame, and he would feel all over again the haunting absence of his father, the anger towards his mother and the guilt: that he was in some way responsible for all the pain of it.

He would return from these experiences, his revolutionary spirit recharged but conflicted. He longed to march with those passionate gods who encompassed all of life and death and timeless history, yet there remained always the need to find some expiation in this world for his sense of alienation. He wondered if anything could ever resolve the struggle of two such opposing notions.

It was towards the end of his final year at school, as part of his literature examination final, that he wrote a play for which he was awarded a distinction and the prize for English. It was called 'The Man Who Wasn't', and it was produced and performed at the end of the year by the members of the school Dramatic Society.

Briefly, it told the story of a man who, wounded by life and finding the world a painful place, and his own affliction too much to bear, had consulted a shaman. The shaman agreed to treat him. His fee would be high because of the complexity of the undertaking. The shaman advised the man that he was unable to change the world, but that he could remove the wound that was causing him such distress. His ailment would become invisible and entirely imperceptible by all his senses, and therefore quite bearable. There might be some side effects, but nothing that would cause him any discomfort.

The man agreed to undergo a ritual, and duly endured the discomfort of having a large block of ice placed over his heart. When the ice block had completely melted away, the shaman proceeded to remove his heart. The operation was painless, but the sounds of his heart leaving him caused the man to lose consciousness. When he awoke, there was no trace of a wound on his chest. The man left, overjoyed at the new freedom he experienced: free from care, free from anger, free from pain, free from doubt and the paralyzing sense of powerlessness that had previously plagued him.

It was only on returning home that he realized that not only had his wounding become undetectable to him, but that he too could not be seen. In addition to this he found that he was mute, and could only speak through the mouths of others. He had become a man who, to all intents and purposes, wasn't there.

This caused him no discomfort, however, because all capacity to be disturbed had been removed. Because he no longer had any feeling function, his voice could not carry or express any trace of empathy or compassion, and, free from the encumbrance of having to consider others, problem-solving came effortlessly to him. The solutions he offered were swift and effective, and any unpleasant consequences, or the impact that such decisions might have on other people's lives, was their problem, not his.

This dispassionate voice became like a destructive plague that spread through the land, infecting it with all manner of accompanying atrocities.

The play explored most eloquently the impact that this voice has had on society, and how often it is heard, and many times revered, throughout the world today. It questioned the nature of what it is to be human, and the nature of human rights.

The play ended with a darkened stage. Under a spotlight stood an empty wire frame in the shape of a man, and a news reader sitting in front of a radio broadcast microphone, reading through a series of newspaper articles that Sebastián had selected over a period of six months to make his point.

As he read through the long list of accounts of the abuse of power and sanctioned atrocities, in a voice devoid of any emotion, the spotlight started to fade until the whole auditorium was in darkness. Only the voice remained, reading on and on and on.

The production of 'The Man Who Wasn't' was an outstanding success with all the parents, even if they didn't fully understand what was being said.

Sebastián was delighted. His teachers were proud of him, and told him he would go far. He won a scholarship to a university. He was on his way.

Early Manhood

"I think it is time for a change," his mother said over a breakfast of refried beans and chili. "How would you like to go and live in Las Madres?"

Sebastián looked up surprised. "I would love to. When?"

"As soon as I can find a place and make all the necessary arrangements."

"Do you really mean it?"

His mother nodded.

"I can't wait."

Now that school was behind him, he was clear that he did not want to stay in this small and rather suffocating village, so cut off from what was happening in the world. There were people in Desterrado who made a virtue of the fact that they had lived there their whole life, and were content. He would never be satisfied with that.

All his contemporaries knew exactly what they wanted to do—not that any of their plans held the slightest interest for Sebastián, but he envied them their clarity.

"It will become clear in time, Sebastián," his mother said. "I have made enquiries about the scholarship, and they have agreed to let it wait a while."

Magdalena, however, knew exactly what she wanted to do.

"I am going to open a salon in Las Madres."

Sebastián looked at his mother in amazement.

"Good heavens! What kind of salon?"

"A place where people can meet at the end of a busy day, where they can relax, be comfortable, surrounded by a pleasing décor; where they can unwind from the day's work. Sit and talk. Have something to drink, have some soft background music."

"It sounds a bit weird."

She thought for a minute.

"You can learn to be a barman. It is time we had some fun and it can start right now."

She gathered up the dishes and tidied the kitchen.

"Fetch your jacket. We are going to buy a car."

With great excitement they went to the local second-hand car dealer.

Sebastián made the final choice: an old, low-mileage 1941 Chevy pick-up that had been owned, but seldom driven, by a wealthy eccentric who thought he would like to be a farmer. His wife's sudden illness had put an end to his dream. It was bright red, the color of ripe chili, and appeared to have more than its share of shiny chrome trim.

Sebastián was thrilled with the purchase. This was not some ordinary car. This was a set of wheels with class.

They put their present house on the market, and while Sebastián stayed in Desterrado to pack all the smaller items into crates, Magdalena made a trip to Las Madres to look at property for sale. She returned with the exciting news that she had bought a house.

"I have found just the place for us, Sebastián. It has been on the market for a long time, and the price was low."

Sebastián, unexpectedly, found the final leave-taking oddly disturbing. He thought he would feel excited, even relieved when the time came. Instead he felt strangely numb.

He said goodbye to his classmates, most of whom had already settled their plans for the future. He felt uncomfortable admitting that he hadn't decided yet what he wanted to do with his life. The leave-taking, however, was not of an emotional nature. They chucked one another on the shoulder, saying things like, stay in touch, and, don't forget to write, but Sebastián knew that this was farewell, and that he would probably not see them again.

His lack of emotion dismayed him.

On the last evening he paid a visit to the place behind the house where the junipers grew. He hadn't been there for some years, and was surprised to see how small the clearing had become.

He laid some long stems of lavender on the little grave where Amigo slept the long, peaceful sleep of one who has served life faithfully.

For the first time in years, Sebastián found himself weeping. He sat down next to the grave, his head resting on his knees, and wept uncontrollably. When finally his tears were all shed, he re-arranged the stones that marked the grave, set the cross straight and said goodbye to his friend and thanked him for the years they had shared.

Then he sat in silence, watching the shadows lengthen, uncomfortably aware that his only true friend, his only confidant, had been a small, misshapen but entirely loveable dog.

Finally he bent over the grave and whispered a last farewell to his dog, his friend— and ultimately to his childhood.

The Trip to Las Madres

Magdalena and Sebastián set off for Las Madres early in spring, just as the Easter daisies were making their first appearance and the small blooms of the Russian olives filled the air with their spicy fragrance.

For Sebastián the road trip was exhilarating. To be setting out into the world, along this dusty road, made him feel like an explorer about to set foot in a foreign land.

"Tell me again what the house looks like."

Magdalena laughed.

"It hasn't changed since I told you only half an hour ago."

"Does it really have a painting of St Sebastián? Or are you kidding me?"

"No. It does have a painting of him—and very uncomfortable he looks, too, with all those arrows going through him."

"Yuck!"

The shiny, red pick-up with its load of boxes and chairs, and an upside-down table, rumbled over the corrugated road. The landscape had opened up and they were passing through dry, undulating grassland dotted with juniper bushes.

Sebastián, tired from his work of packing and loading up all their goods, fell asleep with his head against the window-frame, the warm wind blowing a stray lock of hair across his face.

Magdalena, looking at his sleeping face, smiled—then started. For the lock of hair suddenly looked like a shadow.

Sebastián stirred and yawned in his sleep, the lock of hair just brushing his lips.

With an exclamation, she reached over and smoothed the hair back off his face. For a moment she thought she heard a whisper:

"Duende!"

The road began its descent into the valley. Magdalena could see the small town of Las Madres ahead of her. She slowed down when they entered the main street, driving with her right hand on the wheel, the left out of the window, her fingers playing with the warm air.

She pulled over and stopped outside an adobe house with deep-set windows.

"Wake up, Sebastián. We've arrived."

A Conversation

It had not rained for several weeks.

The land baked in the dry heat. Sticks of corn, their leaves dry as parchment, stood bleaching in the small gardens. The leaves of the Russian olives hung down, white and shriveled, and even the cactus, usually so plump with moisture, looked wizened.

A blanket of heat, undisturbed by even a breath of wind, hung over the town, which was unusually quiet on account of the listless torpor that had overcome all who lived there.

In the plaza the dogs, that motley pack of belligerent mongrels, who customarily scrapped over any and every territorial preference, lay temporarily silenced and panting in whatever shade they could find. They stirred themselves only for frequent, languid trips to the water trough, where they lapped water with their eyes closed against the glare.

Father Octavio and Sebastián sat in the shade of the priest's back porch, which overlooked the small kitchen garden in the Las Madres rectory. They were enjoying a refreshing meal of sweet-melon which, Father Octavio proudly announced, he had grown himself.

"Somehow they always taste sweeter when you grow them yourself," the priest said appreciatively, in between mouthfuls of the juicy fruit.

Magdalena had left Sebastián with him while she went to buy things for the salon. She told him that Sebastián seemed to be preoccupied, and she wondered if there was not something other than the usual discussion about a career choice that he was needing; an approach that might offer some meaning into the choice of his future studies.

Sebastián was just eighteen, and as such was not required to register for military service. Magdalena hoped he would decide on a course and enter university before that time came.

Father Octavio spat out a pip and wiped his mouth with a large, white handkerchief.

"Well, Sebastián—what is on your mind today?"

Sebastián mopped his brow and looked around at the wilting trees.

"I was thinking how at times like this, when the land bakes and the rivers grow small, I feel a deep kind of fear: almost as if there isn't enough air. As if everything will just shrivel up and die. And all of us with it. Sometimes life feels to me—so tenuous; so transitory."

He looked at the priest for signs of disapproval, but Father Octavio was listening attentively.

"Almost as if our lives were at the mercy of the fickleness of nature. As if we lived,"—he pointed to a brightly-colored butterfly fluttering over the melon plant—"like butterflies. Such a brief life. And if a hard wind blows and the butterfly doesn't find a mate, well, that's just too bad."

"Your choice of the seemingly transitory life of the butterfly—and I think the moth, too—is a good one. I say, seemingly, because of course the butterfly, in a sense, transcends its own particular form, and lives on."

"You are not going to give me all that stuff about our meeting up in Heaven. I am sorry, father, but I just don't get it."

Octavio picked up a handful of hot, dry sand and allowed it to trickle out between his fingers.

"I think that the thirst that we see suffered by the land mirrors our own thirst for something eternal: something, perhaps, that will enable us to transcend this brief life; transcend the sense of who we are in this body, this life—we might call it this house of moths and butterflies."

Sebastián looked unimpressed.

"At school we were forbidden to ask such questions. What is the use of religious studies if you can't ask questions?"

Father Octavio raised an eyebrow.

"Tell me about your schooling, Sebastián—your favorite subjects, for instance."

Sebastián responded with some factual information about examination results.

Father Octavio noticed the young man's lack of confidence, even when speaking about such an achievement as the end-of-year play, 'The Man Who Wasn't,' which he had written and produced for an enthusiastic and appreciative audience.

"Do you have a copy of the play?" he asked. "I should like to read it if I may."

Father Octavio was less interested in the success of the play than he was in what it might tell him about Sebastián. From what he could gather from Sebastián's brief account of it, it was extremely insightful, but disturbing in the depth of its disillusionment with life, particularly in one so young.

Sebastián nodded, but he was obviously preoccupied.

"Last week at Mass," he said, "you read from Psalm 23. One line has stayed with me: 'For Thou art with me'. How wonderful to experience such surety, such conviction. What a great thing it must be, to know this. 'For Thou art with me'. I do not have such assurance. I have always felt alone. Always a stranger. Forever on the outside, looking in."

He thought for a minute.

"But what is the point, father? I am nobody, with nothing to show. So what if—'Thou art with me'? Am I then just a happy fool?"

He looked directly at Father Octavio.

"Perhaps you do not know this, father. I am illegitimate. I am mixed blood. I do not know who my father is. I have no connections. I have no great, wealthy family behind me with an irreproachable name. Nothing."

He gave a shrug.

"What will I ever amount to? As I see it, life is hugely weighted in favor of the wealthy: wealth with its trappings of education, ownership, power and social standing."

The words sounded dead, as if they had been repeated many times.

"If you have these things people respect you. If you have wealth, you can obtain the rest. It is not required, as far as I can see, that you be good, or even particularly pleasing. No punishment appears to follow acts of unkindness and dishonesty, even downright cruelty. If you have money, you have power. It is as simple as that."

He gave Father Octavio a glance. The priest remained silent. It sounded as if this had been a mantra of sorts for a long time. Let him get it all out.

"Only believe, and you shall be saved. But what if we cannot believe? What if we have eaten of that fruit; if we have seen good and evil—and we cannot return to that garden? What if we have lost our innocence forever? And why was the opportunity to disobey given? What if the act of disobedience in Eden is required by God; if the very act of disobedience is the beginning of autonomy? Is this not what is meant by: 'the Son of man has nowhere to lay his head'?"

Words were pouring out of Sebastián as if a dam wall had broken.

Father Octavio cut them each a fresh slice of melon. Never had he wanted so much to find the right words. Clearly Sebastián had given the matter a lot of thought, but, equally clearly, there was a short circuit somewhere. Was it his feeling of shame about his lack of a father that prevented him from moving forward into his life?

Octavio ate his slice of melon slowly. Finally he spoke.

"When people of the parish come to me with their troubles," he began slowly, "and some of their stories seem to be so complicated and convoluted—I ask them one question. Just one. I have found it most helpful in cutting through all the tangles. There really is only one question in the end; don't you think, Sebastián?"

"One question, father? What would that be?"

"Are you in love?"

Sebastián looked up, surprised; half wondering if the priest was joking. But there was no sign of jest on the older man's face.

"Am I in love?" Sebastián stared at Octavio. "Am I in love?"

"Yes."

Sebastián looked down at the ground, where a thin line of ants was making a pilgrimage from the vegetable garden to the damp patches where small fragments of fruit and juice from the melon had dripped off their fingers onto the porch floor.

"Am I in love?" He paused. "I don't think I can answer you." His eyes searched Octavio's face, perhaps for some clue to what was being asked. "I'm not sure that I even understand what the question means. I don't think that I am in love with anyone—or myself. I don't know, Father Octavio. I don't think I even know who I am!"

"Well, that's a relief. Most people do think they know who they are. They can recite family trees, long lists of accomplishments, titles, degrees and the details of their possessions and their material wealth. But what you have achieved, and what you own, has nothing to do with who you essentially are, although many people would argue this fiercely."

"What about: 'by their fruits shall ye know them'?" Sebastián asked.

Father Octavio was impressed. It was an intelligent question.

"It is a good question. But a lot depends on how we relate to these 'fruits.' Briefly, in response to your question, I would say that a healthy apple tree bears apples."

Sebastián looked bemused.

"It does this because this is what an apple tree does. Bearing apples is not separate from what an apple tree is. Bearing apples is not an achievement. It is the natural expression of its being-ness as an apple tree. It does not stand around all day, counting—how many today?—evaluating its merit. It bears apples, because it bears apples."

Sebastián was leaning forward. "Are you serious?"

Father Octavio ignored the question.

"I think the answer to the question—am I in love?—is synonymous with the answer to—who am I?—or possibly more correctly, what am I? And the answer to both is your destiny."

He thought for a moment.

"It almost seems that we are afraid that we may miss our destiny, as if it was a 'thing' and that, by some mischance, we may be asleep at that critical moment when it passes by, and the opportunity to grasp it will be lost forever."

Sebastián regarded Octavio quizzically.

"But our destiny, or fate, is who we are: our character. It does not exist in the future or the past."

Sebastián was listening closely.

"If a sense of yearning for..."—he paused to consider—"for something I can only call transcendent has no meaning for you, then you can go and immerse yourself in the world and live a comfortable, and by the world's standards a successful life. But if this won't satisfy you, you must 'labor to work out your salvation', as the Bible puts it.

"For example: let us say that there are two men. The one sees that he has a particular skill, let us say wood-carving. And so he decides to be a sculptor, and maybe even become famous. He is ambitious. He studies the craft, develops a style and promotes the work. At best he is driven to be the finest wood-carver alive, and perhaps by the recognition of this, he may earn a living. At worst he is driven only by the desire for wealth, fame and power."

Octavio looked up. Sebastián nodded.

"This man," he continued, "thinks that he is in control of his fate. He thinks he knows who he is. If you ask such a man who he is, or what he is, he will give you his name, and tell you he is a wood-carver or sculptor; that he has won awards, has become famous, is wealthy, and so on. He thinks about himself, observes himself and his reactions, as if he were an object. There is no other dimension to his life. This is not who we are."

"So who are we?"

"Our true identity shows up in quiet moments—if we are listening. It does not speak about itself. The awakening to this 'I' opens many questions in the heart. This awakening implies a kind of death to our exterior self: the famous, wealthy, important—and so on."

Sebastián looked at the priest.

"It sounds far less painful just to be a wood-carver."

Octavio ignored the remark.

"Another man, who lives out of this sense of self, may also be a wood-carver, but the carvings are an expression of who he is. He experiences himself as called in some way, and this is the way he expresses his response. Something is asked or required, and he responds. It is not the wood-carving that defines him. He brings the same attention to everything he does. He shows up in the way he responds."

He paused.

"You have not met Alejandro Jaramillo, I think?" He looked inquiringly at Sebastián.

The younger man shook his head.

Father Octavio cut another slice of melon with precision, and offered it to Sebastián.

"I will introduce you to him. Alejandro carves angels."

Sebastián looked surprised.

"He does not have ambition in a worldly sense. He is serving something else, and it would be painful for him not to honor this something. He was called to do this work at the age of ten, and he never questioned the calling."

"How do you mean?"

"He was commanded to carve as many angels as there are stars in the universe."

"But that's impossible. He'll never finish."

Father Octavio paused. He seemed to be considering whether to say something or not. Finally he was decided.

"There is a way into all of this. If you are curious, go and read Ezekiel 36. 26."

In response to Sebastián's look of inquiry he said:

"You see, Sebastián, you are thinking like a man of the world. Very reasonable. But Alejandro is in love, and he is carving angels: one by one by one. That is his calling, and that is his character—we might also call it his fate. No one can know the hour of his death, but this day, this hour, this now—this angel: this we have. To be in love, passionately in love, with this instant, makes time meaningless."

Sebastián could feel tears springing from his eyes, and he looked away. It did not go unnoticed by the priest.

"If you were to ask him who he is, what his identity is, he might give you his name, but further than that he would be unable to speak. He might give you an angel. From the outside the two men may, at a superficial glance, seem to be the same. Two men. Two carvers of wood. But one is a man of the world, and the other is—"

Octavio thought for a moment.

"The other is—an apple tree!"

Father Octavio gave a laugh.

"You are teasing me, father."

"I have never been more serious in my life, Sebastián," Octavio replied.

Later that evening Elena came into the priest's office to bolt the shutters.

Looking up from the notes he was preparing for his next sermon, Father Octavio asked her what she saw in Sebastián, and whether she had any clues to what path he should follow. He had noticed the two of them speaking together, not infrequently.

"Oh, he is 'other', father, just like Magdalena, only he has not come into it yet," she said with conviction. "More than that, he carries a curse and a blessing: they are in fact the same thing in the end."

Father Octavio looked at her questioningly.

"He is young to have such power locked up in him. All that thinking in his head going round and round. And his hands haven't woken up yet. Now, if he were a dancer or a musician ..."

Elena shuffled around the desk to the other window.

"Have you noticed, father, how the Duende sleeps behind his eyes? It is waiting for him to be ready."

Father Octavio gave an exclamation.

"What are you saying, Elena?"

"Only that his dilemma over what course to follow at college is not the true issue. Sebastián is bright, and anything he gives his mind to will benefit him. His real issue is with death, and what this means for him. He almost senses this, but he can't put his finger on it. He is still thinking too literally. That is why he is so angry."

She swung the heavy panel across the window.

"But it will find him, father," she said. "And beauty also."

She closed the last shutter. She was about to leave, but then turned and added thoughtfully:

"But first, perhaps you should introduce him to Raho."

Father Octavio raised an eyebrow, but she did not explain herself.

"Good night, father. Sweet dreams," she said as she quietly closed the door.

Father Octavio put down his pen and sat back in astonishment.

Raho

Raho lived in California.

He had driven his old '39 Chevy Coupe, which he had bought from a junkyard for $100.00, all the way across Arizona to visit Father Octavio.

He wore baggy, white cotton pants, a long, loose cotton shirt, also white, and a short bead necklace close to his throat. On his long and narrow brown feet he wore a pair of what looked like home-made sandals. His head was shaven.

Sebastián thought he must be way over six feet tall, this height accentuated by his lean frame. He had never seen such blue eyes ever in his life.

"Octavio! Good to see you, my friend. It has been too long. Far too long. When are you going to lay down that cross and follow me?"

This was followed by a bellow of laughter.

Octavio gave his friend a fierce hug.

"And when, my heretic friend, are you going to see the light at last, and the error of your ways?"

While the two men greeted each other, Sebastián walked around the car. He was impressed. Not even the rust and dents could disguise its elegant lines.

"Here, Sebastián. Let me introduce you. This is my very dear friend Raho. We have known each other—how many years is it?" He gave a shrug. "But I must warn you, he is a little mad—and not entirely harmless."

It was agreed that Raho and Sebastián would go off and have some coffee together, until Octavio came back from a visit to a sick man. They watched the priest rumble off in his old car, and then made their way up the main street.

"What made you decide to leave the priesthood and study Zen Buddhism?"

They were sitting at a table in a sidewalk café, enjoying some refreshing beverage that Raho had ordered.

Raho did not answer the question directly. Instead he asked another.

"Have you ever watched a crowd of pigeons on a roof—the way they push and jostle each other for what is considered, or so it would appear, the ultimate place of pigeon power, the prime position?"

He took a sip of the nectar before continuing.

Sebastián stared at him, wondering if he had not heard the question.

"I often wonder," Raho continued, "if they could think, whether they would realize in their specific acts, which possibly they believe they choose, that they are obeying the ancient law of pigeons, which is centuries upon centuries old, and which dictates just such behavior."

He smiled at Sebastián, who found himself thinking that a pigeon could fly through those eyes.

"The point I am making is, that while we are so busy choosing our life and planning our future, all unawares that great tide of life is choosing us, deciding us, and sweeping us and everything else along with it."

Sebastián forgot about the eyes.

"But surely you are not saying that we have as little say in our behavior, our acts, our fate—as pigeons?" Sebastián regarded him in astonishment.

"And," he continued, "you picked up that menu, and chose this rather strange flavored tea. How did you do that?"

Raho was smiling.

"And what about our God-given free will? Surely this is what separates mankind from nature: that we can choose our fate. We have a mind. We have knowledge that can be tested and proven. We can make an evaluated decision. We can say—yes, and we can say—no!"

"Of course, Sebastián! I am sure you are right. I was forgetting the God-given free will." He leant across the small table with the teapot in hand. "More tea?" he offered politely.

Sebastián was suddenly less sure of himself, and although the man's face was expressionless, he knew that Raho was laughing.

"You say I am right. How do you know? How do you know when you are right?"

"How do I know when I am right?" Raho threw back his head and gave a guffaw of laughter. "Oh, Sebastián!"

The words struggled through the laughter.

"How do I know I am right?" Laughter tears were running down his cheeks.

Sebastián flushed. "Well, what is the answer?"

Raho leant forward. "I'll let you into a little secret." His voice was a whisper.

Sebastián found himself leaning towards the man, the better to hear.

When they came, the words were scarcely more than a breath.

"The question is the answer!"

He was still laughing when they took leave of each other.

Leaving Las Madres

The salon was sold.

Sebastián wiped the bar counter till it shone. He arranged all the glasses in the overhead racks, and then proceeded to straighten the tables and chairs.

"Are you done, Sebastián?" Magdalena's voice called from the street, where she was waiting in the pick-up with a load of empties to take to the store yard.

Sebastián took off his apron and joined his mother in the cab. This was to be the last time he would have to offload the crates and stack them against the wall. He was not sad to be leaving Las Madres. Two years as a barman had provided him with an excellent opportunity to observe some of the finer points of human nature, especially when that nature had downed a couple of drinks—or more—but time was passing, and it was time to take up his scholarship option.

The news of the unfortunate incident at Casa Magdalena had spread through the town, and Sebastián felt eyes were looking at him whenever he went out the door.

Although television had recently come to the town, and there was a growing awareness of troubles in foreign countries, local affairs were still of far more concern to the majority of the population. The affair of the missing silver, the chili ristras, the woman who ran the salon—and her son, occupied people's minds and tongues for many a week. A war taking place in a part of the world that they would have been unable to pinpoint on a map had made little impression on most of the wealthy women of Las Madres. Only when one of their townsmen was named, singled out for distinction or awarded the Medal of Honor, did the outside world make itself felt in the community. To many, a war being fought in a distant land was no more real than a page of history. It had not come home to them. Yet.

The move to The Adobe, so called by Magdalena because of its many small adobe buildings and chapel, was a festive affair. The men who had been regulars at Casa Magdalena, spear-headed by Father Octavio, arrived with building material, fencing poles and all manner of agricultural implements, including a small tractor and plough. A wrong had been done in their eyes, and it must be put right.

But once the move to the place in the country was behind them and all the renovation and building work was complete, Sebastián began to feel restless.

Father Octavio was a frequent visitor, sometimes bringing one of the locals to help Magdalena with the work, sometimes coming alone.

Sebastián found as many opportunities as he could to speak to the priest. Never before had he enjoyed such penetrating discussion; such examination of ideas. Never before had he felt so challenged, but challenged in such a way that he felt invited and empowered to respond.

They had explored many topics of conversation, but inevitably their discussion came back to Father Octavio's original question: are you in love?

"If I am to live as an apple tree, father—and I am using the term in the way you say is a metaphor—how do I discover just what my apples are to be? Surely we are more complicated. Apples are what nature intends for the apple tree. But what does nature intend for me?"

"Well, that's the rub. It leaves us with the problem of answering the question—who am I? And the answer will not show up in some neat little phrase. It will show up when you get your worldly self out of the way. And your worldly self has a vested interest in holding on to its good opinion of itself. It will put up a fight. It does not want to—to die. Not everyone is willing to suffer the anguish and the many tears that such an internal battle will present."

It was late afternoon, and Father Octavio and Sebastián were sitting on the hill that overlooked The Adobe.

The priest glanced at Sebastián.

"If you do not have a kind of hunger—a hunger," he paused, "without a name, then you will never be an apple tree. The poet John Donne knew this, I think, when he wrote: 'Everything is at stake all of the time'. He knew this path."

Sebastián looked at Father Octavio. The priest thought he had never seen such an expression of mental anguish on so young a face, and he feared he had said too much.

It was at this point that they saw Magdalena waving to them to signal that supper was ready. Father Octavio was loath to leave matters on this note.

He returned the wave to let Magdalena know that they had seen her, and then turned back to Sebastián.

"A moment, Sebastián, before we go down. I would like to know what you are feeling."

Sebastián looked at him, and shook his head.

"You don't want to know, father." But the priest held his gaze, and he felt compelled to continue.

"From ever since I was a child, I have believed that God, if indeed God exists, was an impersonal force, that is either unaware of, powerless to prevent, or indifferent to, the suffering of the world." He made an exasperated gesture with his hands. "What I witness in the world fills me with such rage—and such a sense of hopelessness—that I cannot live my life if I stay connected to the pain of these feelings." He gave a shrug. "So, I banish them, as best I may. But I cannot banish what I see with my eyes; and then it all floods back again. I do hear you, father. I do long for that experience of something—something—I don't know what. I just don't believe it exists; not for me. But even if it did exist, and even if I did experience this—whatever-it-is, how would that make any difference to the millions who suffer? The pain of the world remains. It is unacceptable, and I cannot change it. That is my dilemma, father. That is my pain."

Sebastián looked away.

"I shouldn't be saying this to you when you have been so good to us— to me. But if we are to speak the truth, if only this one time, then that is my truth: and I can almost not bear it."

Sebastián was ashamed of the tears he felt brimming in his eyes, and he kept his glance averted until he was in command of himself once more. Turning back at last, he saw in Father Octavio's face an expression of such compassion that he had to look away again.

Father Octavio waited till Sebastián met his gaze.

"I was thinking how utterly inadequate words are; and I was resonating with the pain that you express. And you are right. The suffering of the world will continue, and you will continue to feel its huge pain. Perhaps what I am saying is that we find meaning when we walk truly among our common suffering—the suffering of humanity and all that it loves—in our own particular and personal way. When we offer our singular gift to the world, wholeheartedly—sparing nothing—we find a sense of belonging through our offering.

In biblical term this would read—'to love the Lord your God with all your heart and with all your soul and with all your strength and with all your mind—and your neighbor as yourself.'"

Father Octavio was praying as he spoke that his words would reach a corner of Sebastián's heart where he might feel, or intuit, some truth that he could hold onto.

"This is the critical moment, Sebastián. There is nothing more terrifying than to come to this point, having worked so hard, only to discover the abyss at our feet, and our utter emptiness. And yet—this is the threshold. Only if we can endure such pain, and such emptiness, is it possible for the love of God—or rather let me say a great love—to enter us. Possible, mind. There are no guarantees.

"You see, in spite of all the suffering that is experienced in the world, there are those times when we find ourselves in the presence of excellence—and by this I mean witnessing something that demonstrates the greatness of courage and the human heart—by someone who is faithful to his own truth, and who dares to challenge the accepted norm or a perceived limitation. Then we are moved to tears. We recognize that life is passionate and fierce. We say to ourselves—'Thank God! It is true! It does exist! This defiant spirit lives'.

"You are young, Sebastián, and this is usually experienced much later in life, if at all. But I think that this is what you seek, even if you are not aware of it yet; even if everything I am saying makes no sense to you. Whatever decision you make in your choice of a career, I would suggest that it include the opportunity for the examination of your convictions, for there is much to surrender. You have an excellent mind, but it is only a mind. When you come to the end of it, if you have the courage to dare this, then there is the possibility that you may find some kind of peace. I would wish it to be so."

"Only a mind? What else is there?"

"Aah."

Sebastián was silent as they made their way back to the cottage, and he was silent all through supper. Magdalena, wisely, asked no questions, and she and Father Octavio spoke about general matters and about her plans for a school and clinic until it was time for him to leave.

Sebastián walked him out to his car.

"Thank you, father, for your words. I don't know where I am with them right now, but there was one word that struck me, and that was—meaning. I can see no meaning in my life. I must think about this. I fear I am a slow pupil, father. Thank you for your patience. We will see you at Mass tomorrow."

Father Octavio shook his head in wonder.

"Slow?" he said with a smile, and he put an arm around Sebastián's shoulders. "Slow! That is not a word I would even consider using to describe any aspect of you, Sebastián. But there is one ingredient that is still to come into your life and the way you view the world, and I pray it may come soon."

Sebastián looked at the priest's face, but his expression was inscrutable.

"Laughter," Octavio said. "Sometimes it is only an unholy laughter that makes it possible for something in us to burst open like a flower from the bud, and we see how ludicrous, even insane our conventional mode of thinking is."

Sebastián Enters College

Sebastián enrolled at the nearby university for a four-year degree, majoring in philosophy, although he did not as yet have any clear idea of what he intended to do afterwards. But both his mother and Father Octavio encouraged him, saying that it was important to begin somewhere; that in the course of his studies many new doors would open through which he might find the road he was to follow.

A few weeks before he was to enroll, Sebastián asked for directions and went to visit Alejandro. He found him ankle-deep in wood chips and the clean smell of cedar. Angels hung everywhere in the small workroom. He introduced himself, and mentioned that Father Octavio had suggested they meet.

"Ah, yes. Octavio mentioned it to me. Good to meet you, Sebastián!"

Alejandro appeared to be staring past him at some distant galaxy. Sebastián later learned that those eyes, from gazing out into the night sky, could not focus on anything close to him, except when he was carving his angels.

Alejandro showed him how he worked; his tools, the small device he had fashioned to find the stars, and the large wall where he mapped their positions.

Sebastián was overwhelmed by the immensity of the man's undertaking, but there was such a sense of stillness and peace in the room, and such a sense of quietness about the man that he refrained from asking questions. He found himself remembering Raho when he looked into the distant gaze of Alejandro's eyes.

"I am still preparing myself for the next cluster of stars," Alejandro said, "so I am not carving at the moment. Would you like me to carve you an angel, Sebastián?"

Sebastián was taken aback.

"Oh, I couldn't expect you to do that," he said embarrassed. "I don't think I am an angel sort of person." And then he added, "But thank you."

"Well, let's wait and see what the wood tells me."

"What the wood tells you?"

"Yes. First I must go and find the piece of wood—or let it find me—and then I must wait until I can see the form in the wood. Sometimes it takes me by surprise."

Alejandro gave Sebastián a hug when he left, which threw him into confusion. But he knew they would meet again.

In the days that followed he kept visualizing those eyes.

————

Ten days later Alejandro drove down to The Adobe with Father Octavio. Over a glass of iced tea, he presented Sebastián with a box.

"I must explain that when I made it, I had no idea it would turn out this way," Alejandro said apologetically. "And I wasn't going to give it to you. But it has given me no peace."

Sebastián opened the box and lifted out the carved angel.

He gazed at the exquisitely carved face: a face both beautiful and terrifying.

"It is the Angel of Death!"

"Ah! You recognize it!"

Both men watched Sebastián examine the carving. He turned it to view every angle, marveling at the use of the natural grain of the wood, and its weathering, to fashion the robe.

"This is not the face of innocence," he muttered—and later he was surprised that he had said it—"but I know it. I know it well."

Sebastián paused, then looked straight into the eyes of Alejandro.

"Without this, there can be no beauty." He paused to study the angel's face closely. "I have a sense that my truth will be as terrifying and as beautiful as this face."

The tall man nodded.

"This is what waits; what awaits," he whispered. He did not finish the thought.

Alejandro did not ask him to explain.

"Thank you, Alejandro," he said simply. "I will treasure it."

Uncharacteristically, he rose and gave the man a hug.

Grenville Oakley, professor of philosophy, was of medium height, with a muscular build which revealed itself even in his rather shapeless tweed jacket, which housed a pipe, some pens, a notebook, peppermints and often a folded publication on the latest archaeological findings—his second passion after philosophy. He wore hiking boots and jeans with a surprisingly pristine, white open-necked shirt, and a silver chain around his neck with a small, silver disc on which a date was etched deeply into the metal. His reddish hair sprouted rather than grew from his head, and looked as if no brush or comb would ever tame it. He had freckles on hands and face.

Instantly, on their first meeting, Sebastián liked and trusted him.

"Ah! 'The Man Who Wasn't', I believe. I enjoyed reading the script immensely. I am interested to learn what prompted it."

"Thank you, sir." Sebastián blushed at the compliment.

To his delight he found himself included in a small and select group that met on Wednesday evenings in the study assigned to Oakley. These evenings were set aside for informal discussion, during which students were invited to offer their opinions, however unacceptable they might be elsewhere, in the hope of stimulating some original thought.

It was during his second year, when discussion turned to consider the relationship between philosophy and religion, to examine religion and the part that religious belief played in the formation of civilizations, that Sebastián's anger came to the surface.

With flushed cheeks, he began:

"I find it confusing. If there is such a God, as we are taught, then I cannot understand, when we are told that we are superior to animals, why it would appear that this same God has endowed us with animal instincts which we are told are bad; that to indulge them is sinful."

He paused.

"Go on", Oakley said.

"Well, I see religion, as it has been used throughout the centuries, as a device constructed by the priesthood, who held a position of power because they could read and write. They were a patriarchy, sorely lacking in wisdom to my mind, who wanted to control the people: wanted to hold onto power through filling simple minds with fear of punishment—for alleged sins—by a God they could not see. Rule by fear. I have no need of it. It would seem to me that religion does not approve of God's gift of free will."

Here he took a deep breath.

"It is a quite brilliant construct. To tell people that, before they take a step or say a word, they are born in sin, and that their nature is sinful, that they will have to ask for forgiveness for the very qualities, the very nature they have been given by, if we are to believe it, the Creator himself. That is a master stroke. What audacity. But how else were they going to justify or explain the injustice; the suffering in the world?"

Here he made a gesture with a wave of his hand to include his fellow-students.

"We may dare to ask some uncomfortable questions, but for someone unlettered the authority of that voice is formidable. You encourage us to think. But what does religion encourage? Certainly not free thought. I do not want to believe something,"—he emphasized the word—'believe'—"I want to know."

Sebastián paused and looked around the group to see how he was being received.

"So you think everyone who claims to be religious has been hood-winked?"

It was Oakley who put the question.

"No, I do not say that. It is possible that a person could have an experience that is so powerful that he might feel that he has been divinely inspired. But that is not the same as being told to believe, literally, a whole lot of dogma.

"If we ask what influence religion has had on philosophy, I would say: religion has not permitted the asking of searching questions. Some individuals may have asked them and benefited from their questions, but orthodoxy remains the same."

"Go on."

"Well, perhaps the only way to talk about the experience would be in some form of poetic speech. Maybe that is why so much of Biblical writing is so poetic."

"Well, Sebastián! What is poetry?" Grenville Oakley interjected, enjoying the young man's argument; aware of its arrogance, but enjoying the abundance of passionate energy which would make working with him a challenge and a pleasure.

Sebastián thought he might be mocked for his ideas, but there was nothing spurious in the professor's tone.

"Well, sir, I think poetry is the language of the soul."

He waited for the laughter. None came.

"Most importantly," he continued, "it is the language of metaphor. That which apparently is being said is not ultimately, at depth, what is most truly being said. It is not meant to be taken literally. When it is used literally to support some convenient dogma, it makes a mockery of its essential message. The message is lost as soon as it is circumscribed by a literal interpretation or understanding."

He was becoming embarrassed. He realized that he was arguing rationally for something that was beyond rational thought: something he didn't understand. Perhaps he had gone too far. He felt confused.

"I'm sorry," he muttered to his professor and fellow-students. "I must apologize."

"Not at all. Do not apologize. I find your argument extremely interesting."

He turned to address the others.

"You see, Sebastián—all of you." He glanced around the group. "It is of no interest to me what you believe, or don't believe—and let me add that there is many a belief that is life-affirming and offers much good: faith is not the product of rational thought. But it is critical that you arrive at your conclusion through a process of rigorous questioning and self-examination, with an integrity that will permit no lie; an integrity that insists, at whatever price, on exposing all the flaws that are used to conceal bigotry."

Here he took a peppermint from his pocket, removed the twist of paper and put the mint in his mouth. He rolled the paper into a ball, and with a deft flick of the finger shot it into a nearby waste-paper basket.

"To continue. It is essential to examine not only what you think, but how you think; out of what—'system of beliefs'—you think, and how you arrived at that thought.

"We think that we are the thinkers of our thoughts. But if we are committed to this process of self-inquiry, we find that they are not our own thoughts, newly sprung from our pristine minds. No. They are thoughts we have heard, have been told, been taught, read in books. What makes them ours is that we believe them."

Looking up, he noticed their look of inquiry.

"Oh, yes! I am sure all of you have brilliant minds. And many beliefs. Beliefs that, when examined, are no more or less substantiated than the belief in God, which so many antagonists of faith take such exception to."

Sebastián was about to intervene, but his professor waved him back.

"You say you don't want a belief—you want to know. May the angels protect you from such hubris!"

He turned to the group.

"Your work will be to question. And I must warn you, you will never do any work more demanding, more challenging, and in some respects more terrifying than this. We use these beliefs to instill a sense of security. We long for certainty and meaning. We yearn for the comfort they provide, and to hide from the awareness of our essential solitude. Unless we risk facing this aloneness, this emptiness, we cannot leave what and who we thought we were, and step out into our mysterious and utterly uncertain future.

"I am not here to tell you what to think. I am here to see that you challenge yourselves; the very process of your thinking; particularly your beliefs. If there is only one thing you take away with you when you leave this course, I would ask that it be this: that each day you ask yourself, 'What do I know?'—and, 'How do I think I know this?' And when you come up against the mystery of human darkness, dare to make it known to you.

"You see, Sebastián," he said as he turned to address him directly, "in spite of yourself you already have a belief, and it is of a particularly dangerous kind."

Sebastián looked up with an expression of surprise.

"It is dangerous because you don't know what it is. You don't even know that you have it. One day you will discover what it is; and then the one that lies beneath it; and then the one beneath that."

Again, Sebastián was about to intervene, but his professor held up a hand.

"Not all, but most of the thoughts that we think—or that think us—are old and tired. They lack the vitality, the brilliance of those flashes of creative insight that can only happen when you do not think you know; when you no longer have all the answers.

"These are the truly sacred moments."

He smiled at the group.

"You need to let your imagination play like a child. You see, children don't know, and they know they don't know. They are not busy trying to protect their ideas. They want more and more. They ask endless questions. They are open to everything, and they are happy just to play with ideas. They have no difficulty holding what seem to be two mutually exclusive statements. They have no difficulty with paradox because they are still filled with wonder, and their minds are innocent.

"You say you don't want a belief—you want to know. Well, this is what your work will be. And beware of generalizations, gentlemen, for this is where your arguments begin to lose integrity. Beware of the comfort of absolute formulas for living. Reach out rather into the insecurity of questions, for a stammering question is worth more than a thousand packaged answers.

"You come here so full of knowledge, gentlemen. It is my task to see to it that you leave empty."

Grenville Oakley

Sebastián and Grenville Oakley were to have many lengthy discussions alone in the course of the following years.

As their respect for each other's insight and intellectual honesty grew, so did a mutual sense of trust and intimacy. Sebastián's only male mentor to date had been Father Octavio. He had seen the priest over the three-year period after coming to Las Madres and visited him regularly between semesters, during which time the two men had forged a bond that, while intellectually stimulating, was more about matters of the heart than the head.

This new relationship with Grenville Oakley was more in the nature of an initiation, for he would spare Sebastián nothing in his commitment to intellectual excellence. Sebastián recognized the value of these daily battles. He considered this a friendship beyond price, and he treasured the occasional hours they spent alone together.

"My father was a priest—an Anglican priest. Did I ever tell you that?"

They were walking slowly across the lawns that separated the college buildings.

Sebastián shook his head, and he continued.

"Yes. And it was always assumed that I would follow in his footsteps."

He gave a wry sideways glance.

"He was a good man—kind, loyal; a man who did not question his beliefs. He took the words of the Gospels as they came, as they were written. He never questioned his God, never questioned his goodness. His faith was so strong that the sheer power of it comforted those in his flock who were in need. It was astonishing to watch him. He was simple, but he had that human touch that could lift suffering into a place where it became transformed; where it became almost hallowed.

"All through my childhood I felt guilty because I did not share this simple faith. I wanted to believe, but I just couldn't accept the literal explanations that he offered. I was born asking questions, questions that no one could answer, questions that I now realize are not meant to be answered, only explored."

He gave Sebastián a brief, almost shy smile. He was unaccustomed to this level of intimacy with a student. But he sensed in Sebastián some very special quality: that attribute which is born out of pain and suffering, and which, if it does not become cynical and embittered, carves a depth of compassion, deeper and more insightful than that which may be found in those who may have had gentler, more comfortable lives.

"Still, I enrolled at the seminary and began my studies. I was a thorn in the flesh of all my tutors. I think you would have recognized the beast! I was constantly frustrated in class discussions, and no doubt very taxing to the other students who did not share my views and were not interested in my perceptions. The truth of it was that I just wasn't designed for the priesthood.

"And then, quite by accident, I stumbled on philosophy. There was an open lecture, a debate really, at a nearby college, which, having some space between classes, I attended. The subject being debated was the nature of reality. At some stage in the proceedings, when the debate had been opened to the floor, I stood up to refute something that the previous speaker had stated. Somehow I ended up in a lengthy and heated debate with him.

"I don't know how long it lasted. I felt I had been transported into the realm of the gods. Never had I seen an issue with greater clarity. I took pleasure in peeling back all the layers of defective thought, exposing all the contradictions, the assumptions on which his argument rested. I know only that after I had said my last word and once more taken my seat, there was a silence. I wasn't sure that I hadn't just made a fool of myself.

"After the debate was concluded and we had all voted for or against the motion, I was approached by a man who looked to be in his late fifties. He introduced himself as the professor of ethics, Julian Salazar—at this very university. He asked me what I was studying, and out it all poured: my discomfort with the career that had been mapped out for me; the difficulty I was experiencing with my lecturers; my feelings of alienation from my peers. The long and the short of it was that the following year, after discussing things with my generous but disappointed father, I enrolled in his course. As you can see, I never left."

He paused. "I married the year after I graduated."

He touched the silver disc at his throat.

"She gave me this on the day we married. I treasure it." He paused and cleared his throat. "She died a week before our first anniversary."

Sebastián didn't know what to say. He almost reached out a hand to touch Oakley.

Grenville Oakley looked up at the familiar buildings.

"You might say that this is my home. I enjoy the work I do. I learn more and more each year from my students; maybe more than they learn from me. Many of them are already ahead of me in brilliance. All I have to offer them is a tempering, so that this very brilliance does not call up an equal darkness before they are ready to deal with it.

"It can be a sobering task, one I am sure that many a parent must know. In their first year the students are eager to learn anything that is offered. But by the third year they know it all, and I have become just another, perhaps rather foolish individual in their eyes, and easily dismissed. They do not recognize the painful allowances that are being made—even then.

"But this is the pathos of the human condition. It is not the young adult who is growing old; not he who is suddenly aware of his mortality. He is not the one who longs for tenderness; compassion. No. For him it is the taste of power, and like all life it is ruthless."

Sebastián had not considered before that the adults in his life all had their own insecurities. It came as a shock.

"Now is the time," Oakley continued, "for the parent, whose mortality comes rushing up to meet him, to bow out gracefully and retreat. It is appropriate it should be this way—and painful. Very painful. I often think of my father; how gracious he was, and how little I knew it at the time."

Sebastián thought of his mother, seeing her perhaps for the first time from a new perspective. He had never thought to ask her about her life, her pain. It had been all about him. He felt ashamed. He was about to say something, but Oakley had changed the subject.

"The most profound lecture I ever attended," he said, turning back to Sebastián, "was given by my professor, and was titled 'The Son of Man Has Nowhere to Lay His Head'. It was a brilliant and daring interpretation of Christ's words, which he connected to the study of ethics.

"The main thrust of his argument was that there is no such thing as truth. The operative word was 'thing'."

Oakley offered Sebastián a peppermint.

"He understood the concept of truth to be a verb that, like the movement of the wind, in order to remain true to its definition or essence, could never take a form and be still—could never be defined, just as God cannot be defined."

Sebastián was about to say something but Oakley continued.

"That desire is what lies behind the golden calf and other idols. They are things. As soon as you define God, God becomes a thing. That is why some religions do not permit you even to speak the name.

"'The Son of Man' was, in his eyes, a metaphor for truth; but such a truth as could never be known, owned, held or described by anyone. Although it might be touched in a transcendent or revelatory moment, it could never be held. There was indeed nowhere that this truth could—lay its head. This, of course, is the same argument put forward for defining, or rather not defining God. You, of course, are familiar with this argument?"

Sebastián nodded.

"He went on to argue that those persons who claimed to know the truth were misguided, and did much harm; that it was people such as these who constructed the dogma of a religion, which then excludes all those of any other faith. It is the language of exclusivity and separation, a dangerous language which ultimately leads to war, as history has attested over and over again.

"I will never forget the uproar it caused. People were incensed, enraged. For a while it looked as if a holy war was going to be fought right there in the lecture hall. People were yelling at each other—at him; chairs were being smashed and punches were being thrown left and right. These halls had never seen the like of it.

"When finally some order was restored, he offered his closing statement:

"'Indeed, gentlemen, your behavior has confirmed all that I have been saying. Unless you are willing to live with the mystery, unless you are happy to live with the absence of final answers, as long as you subscribe to a world of right and wrong and are not willing to surrender this destructive, polarizing view of life, you should leave this course and go out into the world and do something useful, basic and concrete: philosophy is not for you.'

"It shook us all up. Some left at the end of that year. Their reason? He was losing his edge." Oakley gave a rueful smile. "But for the rest of us, it opened a door into a world of infinite possibility. He was a remarkable man."

He smiled at Sebastián.

"'Always keep the door open', he used to say. 'As soon as you think you have an answer, the door will close. The mind will go back to sleep.'"

They entered the college building, and at the steps they parted, each going his separate way.

Georgia

Sebastián was in love.

He met her in the first week of his third year at college. She was an art student in her final year.

For the first time in his life, he was seized by an emotion so over-whelmingly powerful, and so utterly irresistible that he was helpless to even consider what might be happening to him, or where this might lead him. For the first time in his life, he didn't care.

He was caught in the magic of an eternal moment in which there was no future and no past. He was bewitched, enchanted, enthralled; longing only to be with her, and barely able to endure the brief partings that their respective studies demanded. While they were together, he could scarcely take his eyes off her. He constantly found excuses to touch her, thrilling as he did so at the unfamiliar closeness. When he was with her, he knew he would never feel alone again; when she had to leave, he felt bereft. She was his last thought at night, after which she filled his dreams, and she was his first thought the moment he opened his eyes in the morning.

During lectures he found his mind wandering, remembering the last time they were together—what she wore, what she had said—or daydreaming about what they would do when next he saw her.

He repeated to himself sentences that she had spoken, remembering the particular lilt of her voice; that distinctive intonation that belonged only to her, the sound of which held him mesmerized. He whispered her name out loud, loving the soft breathiness it held. He had never heard a name more beautiful, more filled with secrets and whispers.

He was amazed and grateful that she, mysteriously and quite miraculously, loved him. She, who could have had any man she wanted, had chosen him. He could almost not believe it.

And then he would remember how she had kissed him and whispered his name, and he would be filled all over again with the wonder of it. He loved everything about her: how she laughed, the way she spoke, her slow smile.

Especially her smile.

Georgia Fitzgerald was her name, and she was the daughter of wealthy parents, third generation Irish Protestants who lived in San Francisco. Her father was a lawyer and her mother a psychologist. She had three brothers, all younger than her, whose peers, from a freckle-nosed distance, had one by one, over the years, fallen hopelessly in love with her.

Georgia and a friend from school had come to New Mexico five years before to study art. They had chosen New Mexico because they wanted to see just what it was that had drawn so many artists and writers to this one particular location. They had heard that the landscape was a painter's heaven, and that Santa Fe was well known as a center for the arts that attracted visitors from far and wide.

The landscape with its many moods, its wide sky and dramatic storms, its palette of every shade of earth and sky imaginable, had not disappointed them.

They hoped that after graduation they might find some way of staying there for at least a few years. This was their final year of tuition and they were due to graduate, each with a Master's degree, at the end of it.

Sebastián and Georgia met at a student gathering, and had been instantly attracted to each other. She was tall and fair, having the golden look of an outdoor girl who glowed with health and vitality. She was everything that Sebastián wasn't. She was essentially an extrovert, of an exceptionally generous and spontaneous disposition. She drew her life in bold, bright brush strokes that were startling, and yet showed a depth of sensitivity unusual in one so young.

Where Sebastián analyzed and planned and considered, she acted, trusting her intuitive and instinctive qualities to see her through her various ventures. They seldom let her down, and she seemed to walk a charmed path. Doors opened for her, opportunities presented themselves, chance meetings brought with them benefits that no amount of planning could ever have devised.

A lesser character might have become arrogant or self-opinionated, for she seemed to have everything: wealth, looks, charm, intelligence, success and abundant good luck. But she never took her good fortune for granted. She worked hard, determined to succeed in the extremely difficult and competitive world of art.

Next to her, Sebastián's mix of Spanish and Indian blood, his swarthy handsomeness and dark, brooding introspection became more noticeable.

"How did you ever get to be so wise, so serene about life, Georgia?"

It was during a period of study in the library, while she was showing him some of the works of her favorite painters—Cézanne, Picasso, Rousseau and Matisse—that Sebastián first became uncomfortably aware not only of the different ways in which she and he perceived things, but the different ways they responded to these perceptions.

She seemed to thrive on challenge, leaping out to embrace life, whereas he found himself caught in a web of endless questions and argument.

"Are you telling me that this is truly how he saw these women?"

He was responding to some illustrations of Picasso's famous 'Les Demoiselles d'Avignon'.

"When Picasso painted it, he called it 'Le Bordel d'Avignon'—you know, The Brothel. But when it was exhibited, the gallery changed the name."

"Why did they do that?"

"There was a lot of controversy. Even his close friends were incensed. They thought the softer title might diffuse people's anger somewhat."

Sebastián studied the picture closely.

"I wonder what he was trying to say. The face on the right looks like a baboon. And they all look broken. Fragmented. All those angles. Was it a comment on prostitution?"

"No. I don't think so. He called it his first exorcism painting. His contemporaries, and some critics, thought it was a fake; that he had copied the idea from African carvings. In any event, it was later considered a pivotal work and a precursor to cubism."

"How can you tell whether something is art, and not just a massive hoax?"

Sebastián was having difficulty finding anything to like in a painting which he found ugly, and somehow aggressive. "Do you think he wanted to shock people, or did he hate women?"

"No, I don't think so. I think he was wrestling with a new way of seeing—or painting. He is quoted as having said that—intentions have no value in art. The only business of the painter is to paint, and the work of art will take him by surprise. He said that the appeal of great art lies in that it arises out of unconscious regions."

"What do you mean by 'unconscious'?"

"Well, you have to surrender yourself to what wants to come through." She turned and smiled up at him. "For me it is rather like allowing ourselves to know or recognize something: perhaps some very deep memory, something that we have always known or intuited. To let it have a face or a voice."

"But how are we to understand a painting like this one?"

"Well, many people will put forward their theories, and these may even be interesting: one is that his paintings reflected the fragmentation that was occurring in society, which may or may not be true. But theories do not replace the actual experience of standing in front of the work. Everyone will have a different experience. The appreciation of art is destroyed by understanding. All we have is our perception of it, right now. How then can we say that this painting means exactly this or that?"

"I thought I was the one studying philosophy," he said with a laugh. "So there is no certainty, and we cannot say what anything means! Is that what you are saying?"

"I am suggesting that the only certainty is in the experience, in the instant. The very next instant it is memory of the experience. Not the same thing at all. And when you speak about it, it is your account—of the memory—of your experience."

Sebastián grimaced.

"Please don't repeat that."

She turned to a double page representation of 'Guernica' and placed it in front of him.

"Don't tell me what you think; tell me what you feel," she said, sitting back in her chair.

Sebastián stared at the painting, at the extremity of horror, in wonder. Far from finding it a fearful image, he felt an instant connection with the artist and a sense of relief that someone else had visited these terrifying places. It was the first time in his life that he felt that perhaps there were others who knew that alone place that so often visited him. He knew nothing of the painting's background. Today was in fact the first time he had seen any of Picasso's work. Instantly he was taken back to his childhood, to the feelings he had endured as a small boy.

"This is like 'the place where the light isn't—where the light ends'," he told her.

"Tell me about it."

Sebastián blushed.

"When I was a child I had a sense of a place that was so empty, so full of pain, so evil if you like, that I called it—'the place where the light isn't'."

He gave a laugh, embarrassed at the childish title.

"The painting is like that. I wonder if it is possible for the beings caught in such a place to ever escape. It is worse than death. It is like Hell. An endless horror. Why would he paint such a picture?"

"He was commissioned by the official Spanish Republican government to contribute a painting for their national pavilion at the World Exhibition in Paris. Shortly after this he heard of the bombing of Guernica, which took exactly three quarters of an hour, during which time the entire town was destroyed. He decided to record in the painting, not the actual events, but the feelings that they evoked in him. He was painting a different kind of truth. It is this, the suffering and horror that he felt in himself, that gives authenticity to the pain we see depicted."

"How wonderful it must be to be able to express such feeling creatively, like this."

He gave a laugh.

"I am no artist, but sometimes I feel as if I were pregnant with something that longs to be birthed. It has been with me since I was a child. I don't know if everyone feels this way."

He gave a deprecatory laugh.

"You laugh, Sebastián. But perhaps you are right."

Seeing his look of anguish, she added: "Maybe you should change your course."

"Oh! So what would you suggest?"

"Wait here."

Georgia crossed the room, and after searching a shelf she removed a book which she took to the librarian for stamping.

"Here, Sebastián. I took it on a month's lease."

"The Selected Poetry of Rainer Maria Rilke."

"Yes. Read it. Pay particular attention to 'The Duino Elegies'."

It was not long after this conversation that Sebastián asked Georgia if he might see what she was working on for her Master's degree.

Sebastián stepped inside the large, square room.

With its two skylights, the large, north-facing windows and its space and silence, he felt as if he had stepped into some kind of temple. All around him light-filled paintings covered the walls, their transcendent translucency radiating out of the canvases into the stillness of the room.

He turned slowly, taking in one canvas after another.

In one painting, a huge canvas, she had captured the quality of light that is seen so often in the New Mexico sky just before a storm breaks over the land. Storm energy seemed to break out of the confines of the canvas and fill the room, leaving the viewer dwarfed by its towering power.

Below the storm clouds stood a tree lit by a shaft of sun.

She had captured both the quality of pregnant silence and the almost unbearable electric tension that never fails to evoke an ancient, superstitious awe; an almost Biblical dread. Looking at the painting Sebastián could even hear that shrill electric sound that fills the ear at such times, and feel the current of electric energy fill his body.

He had the sense that Georgia was intimating that the gods were merely playing at such times, even though death and destruction might follow. He found this disturbing.

She had painted with passion, not the form, but the energy of storm, the purples, grays and black—so heavy, so saturated with moisture—and the sudden areas through which brilliant shafts of light slanted down to illuminate the land.

How many people, he wondered, think that artists and writers just copy what life sets in front of them; what they see, what they hear—that they copy life. Looking at Georgia's work he realized that they do not copy it: they invent it. They create it out of or through themselves. At what price, he wondered. He recalled the many times he had seen Georgia drained by the effort of birthing these elusive energies, and knew that the delivery was not the peaceful process that many imagined it to be. He knew that for something to be born, something must always die, and the artist must be willing to experience that death personally.

Sebastián was profoundly aware of Georgia's presence in the room, and that this experience of seeing her paintings, with her watching him, was the most intimate moment he had ever shared with her. In showing him her work she was showing him the most naked part of herself, and he was moved and humbly grateful that it was he whom she had chosen for this intimacy.

Georgia did not have to ask him what he thought of her work. She could see that he was deeply moved.

Sebastián was not only moved. He was shocked.

He had been told by her friends that Georgia was in a class of her own, but he had been unprepared for the power of her work. These were not just beautiful paintings. They were profound. In them Georgia was daring to look beyond form to that which gives it meaning—space, and silence.

He realized then that what he was struggling to grasp in his life, Georgia had managed to reveal through the absence of form. It fascinated him to think that what we most want to know, to hold, lies forever beyond our grasp; that although less tangible than a chair or a mountain, thought and its product, ideas, was no less form for being invisible. It made him realize that for most of his life he had lived in the world of form, wanting to hold it, own it, subdue it—to understand it, thinking that this would lead him to the mystery. He saw now the futility of such endeavor; that even as we stand with our hands filled with all our acquisitions, power, knowledge, certainty—the idols turn to dust and we find we are empty of what we long for. He saw that Georgia had dared to allow this emptiness.

He had not fully appreciated, until now, that she would go on to be an artist of reputation; that she would have a career that would take her out into the world, and possibly into a life that would not include him.

"They are quite wonderful, Georgia," Sebastián said, turning to her. "Quite, quite wonderful."

The words were inadequate, but he had no others.

Sebastián pulled a chair over to the painting that he found the most haunting. It was entitled Where the Pink Hill Waits.

It was a large canvas, about four feet across, of soft, diffused color suggesting early morning sunlight burning through a mist. Sebastián could sense the presence of something, something that was not form, but perhaps the longing for form, a quality of eternal waiting.

"If you ever sell your work, Georgia, I want to buy this one," Sebastián said. "I don't know why, but there is something so familiar about it. It is almost as if I have stood and looked at precisely this, this…" The words failed him. "I have been here," he said. "What were you feeling when you worked on it?"

Georgia looked at him.

"It is strange that you should be drawn to it. I felt so powerfully drawn to paint it. I had a dream that I would visit a place where the pink hill waits. I have no idea what it means. I have only a sense of this place, and this pink hill—not the sight of it, but something that I could only conceive of as a pink hill, waiting, for what I cannot say."

Sebastián looked at her in wonder.

"You are the most extraordinary person I have ever met, Georgia," he said.

Suddenly he felt very separate from her. He felt, only for an instant, a cold wind blowing between them. And then she crossed the floor and stood behind him where he sat on the paint-streaked chair. She put her hands on his shoulders and kissed the top of his head.

"It is yours, Sebastián. I would love you to have it."

Summer Vacation

At the end of his third year, partly because of the influence of his many discussions with Georgia, and partly because he could feel the old longing to be creative in some way clamoring to be heard, he decided to extend his degree and include English as a second major.

Georgia had awakened the sleeping creative energy in him, and he was eager to explore the pile of books that was growing daily next to his bed. He could feel a sudden and new excitement about his life. He had found a book by Herbert Read, and was in the middle of a chapter on Art and Religion. He began to realize how simplistic his arguments had been in the past, a realization accompanied by a mixture of embarrassment and joy. He felt the world opening up to him, and it was full of challenging ideas.

But it was only on his reading of Walt Whitman's—When I Heard the Learn'd Astronomer that he realized how little he had allowed the gifts of wonder and mystery to have a significant influence on his convictions. As he read, he thought that perhaps there might be some future for him in writing. That he might dare to dream this spurred him on, and he was hungry to throw himself into the thoughts of as many writers and poets as he could lay his hands on.

He was delighted that Georgia had decided not to go home immediately after graduation. She and her friend Samantha had decided to take a painting holiday, traveling around the country, stopping to paint wherever the fancy took them. They would visit as many galleries, and talk to as many artists as they could find along the way.

"Why don't you come with us, Sebastián?"

"Do you mean it?"

Sebastián felt breathless. He said he would love to come along with them. He would take all his books. They would spend long, lazy days together. He visualized her in front of an easel, painting the bright light and strong colors of Mexico—for Mexico was to be their first destination—while he lay in the shade, reading poetry to her. They would spend weeks and weeks together: they would sleep together. Sebastián closed his eyes. He could hardly believe that this was happening—to him.

Samantha's boyfriend would be coming as well. They would all share the expenses of hiring a small van which would accommodate all their books and equipment. They arranged to borrow two old tents, sleeping bags and some camping gear. They would take a few provisions which they would supplement along the way, as and when necessary.

It was agreed that they would begin by going south, crossing the border into Mexico, and then gradually make their way northward again until they reached Taos. Here they would spend some time with friends. They would then pay a short visit to The Adobe, where Sebastián could introduce Georgia to his mother, before returning to the university in time for the first semester. With these general plans in place, and the few personal arrangements taken care of, they were eager for term to finish and the long vacation to begin.

Sebastián was excited about the trip. At the same time, he could feel a growing anxiety which had to do with his relationship with Georgia. The first issue that worried him was that she had not yet decided on her plans for the following year. He feared that she would leave New Mexico, and that he would lose her. Neither of them had raised the subject of the future, and he felt stupid about doing so, knowing that he had nothing to offer her.

The second concern was more immediate. In all the time they had known each other, they had not become lovers. Sebastián knew that the time was approaching when they would consummate their love, and he wondered how he would ever be able to tell her that he was still a virgin. He knew nothing about making love to a woman. He had had no father, no older brother or cousin with whom he had been able to speak of such things. He had never been part of that system whereby boys spoke freely about their sexual exploits. He had thought it vulgar and insensitive.

Now he realized that much of it was the bravado of young men, terrified that they would not meet their girl's expectations. He was overcome by doubts, feeling how awful it was to be a man, always expected to know how, when and where to act; always expected to take the lead, to be confident.

He wondered if he should find some book that might explain a few dos and don'ts, and immediately dismissed the idea as ridiculous. He fantasized the bizarre scenario of Georgia and him, both naked in a tent in the middle of nowhere, and he thumbing the pages of some dreary little sex manual for beginners, trying to read by the light of a flickering candle what the next move should be, while she patiently gave little moans of encouragement.

He was sure that Picasso would never have done that. What would Picasso have done? Sebastián considered the question. One thing was certain: Picasso would not have sat around agonizing about it. He would have allowed the experience to seize him. Was that enough? Did people just know how to make love the way animals know how to copulate? He thought it was surely very different. Or was it?

Georgia noticed that Sebastián was preoccupied, and wondered what might be on his mind. She knew that very soon they would become lovers, and she longed for the time to arrive when they would make this intimate commitment to each other. Could this be why he was so distracted?

For the first time she considered what he might be feeling. She knew he was sensitive and very shy. It was one of the things that had attracted her to him. He had told her a bit about his background: the absence of his father, his rather lonely childhood and the feeling of always being on the outside of things. Could it be that he had no sexual experience? She was a virgin, but then she was a girl. Somehow boys were expected to know all these things, although where they were supposed to get all their knowledge was another matter. How much did he know? Did he know about contraception? He was a Catholic, so perhaps it was not allowed. Should she do something about it? That would look very forward. How silly it was to know about things and have to pretend innocence. She decided to talk it over with Samantha.

Samantha had been around. She quickly summed up Sebastián as being ignorant on matters of lovemaking, and told Georgia that she had better take charge of some of the necessities, at least in the beginning. She accompanied her on a visit to a gynecologist. Georgia's face was flushed with embarrassment by the time she had learned what was needed, but Samantha told her that she was doing just fine.

The last few days of the second semester flew by. Results were announced. Sebastián attended Georgia's graduation ceremony, where he met and was introduced to her parents. He did not think that he was exactly what they had expected, or that he was all that they would have wished for their daughter, but they were polite, shook his hand and inquired after his studies. He thought he sensed some relief in their faces when they learned that he still had at least three years of studying ahead of him, and probably more.

Georgia's exhibition was a triumph. Sebastián noticed that the small card beneath Where the Pink Hill Waits informed the viewer that the painting was owned by Sebastián Chávez. He felt humble and guilty when he saw the prices of the rest of the work. He would never have been able to afford to buy one. How naïve of him! By the end of the opening night, more than half of the canvases had been bought.

"I can't accept it, Georgia. I'm a fool to have thought I could ever afford the painting."

But Georgia was adamant that the painting was his.

"It's not about money, Sebastián. There is something about this place that is struggling to manifest itself out of, or through the mist, that has to do with you. There is something so gentle waiting to be born. The painting was yours before I ever painted it."

The day after the opening, he sat with Georgia, reading what the art critics had to say about it. All praised the work, one going as far as saying that serious art collectors should not miss the opportunity of buying this early work of a most original young artist.

Although Sebastián was thrilled for her sake, he felt his heart sink.

The many farewells were said, the usual end-of-year celebrations were observed, and then there was nothing but the long summer vacation ahead of them. They packed their bags, gathered their books, paints, canvases, easels and all the equipment they might need, stashed it all into the back of the small van and, finally, they were ready to leave. They set off on their trip, heading south, feeling footloose and free, ready for anything.

All through the long drive of that first day, Sebastián was aware that this would be his first night alone with Georgia, and he participated distractedly in the general conversation as he drove along the long, straight road south down the Interstate. They stopped at a roadhouse for a quick lunch, and then were on their way again. They hoped to reach Las Cruces before dark and spend the first night there. They had given their respective parents the vague outline of their route, which was to follow the old Camino Real to Chihuahua, but they said that they had no idea how long they might spend along the way.

Georgia said that she wanted to visit the White Sands National Monument, so they would do this before crossing the border. Magdalena had suggested that they call home from time to time, just to let her, and through her the other parents know that all was well with them. This they agreed to do.

Sebastián had his eyes focused on the road, but in his mind he saw Georgia in his arms, the two of them alone together under the vast summer night sky, with the air so clean, so clear, and the heavens, with those millions of brilliant stars, close enough to touch, and a fat moon climbing up over the horizon.

He played the images of the night ahead over and over in his mind's eye. He watched her undress; saw the slim and lovely length of her body, the golden hair spilling over her breasts; watched his hand move out for that first touch; felt, even now, the thrill in his body as she looked up at him from where she lay, her arms reaching up to receive him; felt his body trembling, alive as it had never been before, and ready, ready for her, to love her, to enter her, never to leave her again.

He imagined her face turning towards him as he lay down beside her, and her smile, that smile which would kindle somewhere deep within her and move across her face, bringing a glow to her cheeks, lighting up the astonishing clarity of her eyes. He had never known eyes that so held the gaze of the other. They were eyes that listened. At times he thought she could see right into the depths of him; that the light from her gaze would bring light to his darkness. In such a way he longed to be taken by her; longed to be penetrated by her clarity; to find completion, fulfillment; to be made whole by her love.

He was brought back to the present by Georgia saying that they should take the next off-ramp. They had arrived at Las Cruces.

The Telephone Call

"Is there someone here called Georgia?"

The desk clerk put his head around the corner of the small dining-room. Georgia looked round in surprise.

"I'm Georgia."

"Telephone for you."

She left the breakfast table and went to take the call. She was away for barely five minutes. When she returned, her face was flushed.

Sebastián looked at her inquiringly.

"It was my father. I have been offered a three-year bursary to study art in Paris with Henri le Noir—you saw him at my exhibition. He bought two of my paintings. I have to return immediately. I am to take a taxi to the airport, where a ticket is waiting. My parents will send for all my equipment."

Her cheeks were pink with excitement. Sebastián looked at her in disbelief.

"So you're going?"

"Of course I'm going. Oh, Sebastián, I know we had plans, but don't you see? This is the opportunity of a lifetime."

Seeing his face, she leant forward and put an arm around him.

"It's only three years. And then I'll be back, and you'll be qualified, and we can go to Mexico then."

"It's not Mexico that concerns me."

"Then what?"

"Oh, it's nothing. It's great, Georgia. I'm happy for you."

Had the previous night meant so little to her?

So they never did go camping. Nor did they go to El Paso or Mexico or anywhere that they had planned. Sebastián could not believe that life could change so dramatically overnight. His reason told him she had not rejected him, but his feelings were not interested in such a rational assessment. He felt abandoned.

Suddenly he was a boy again: a boy with no father; a boy who was still trying to find a life for himself. And Georgia seemed now so distant. She was successful; she was stepping out into the world, embracing her life with eagerness and enthusiasm.

He was hurt that she had not consulted him. But why would she? Had he really expected her to turn the offer down and hang around waiting for him to make up his mind about his future? No. Of course not. But what then? He could not say. His emotions threw him this way and that like a small boat in a storm. He did not know what he was feeling; only that something had died. It was as if Georgia had died, and something, so new and wondrous in him, had died with her.

She left twenty minutes later. The parting was brutal.

For Sebastián the journey back home seemed endless; and yet when he finally turned the familiar corner at the bottom of the row of cottonwoods and made his way up to The Adobe, he wished that it could continue forever: that he would not have to face the reality of his life, but rather stay forever on an endless road of transition, somewhere between his dreams of the past and the emptiness of the future.

All that long, hot summer, Sebastián stayed at The Adobe. He saw no one other than the people who had business with his mother, and Father Octavio. The priest made frequent visits on the pretext of having pastoral work to attend to, but really to try to find some way past the wall of silence that Sebastián had built up around himself.

But Sebastián was back in that familiar, safe place that had carried him through much of his childhood pain. He seemed unaware of the attempts made by both his mother and Father Octavio to find a way to make contact with him.

Sebastián threw himself into hard physical work, rising early in the morning, driving himself through the day, barely pausing, even in the extreme heat of midday, to eat the lunch that Magdalena brought out to him.

"I want to plant a herb garden inside the path of a labyrinth. Will you lay the path for me, Sebastián? I have ordered a load of river stones to be delivered."

She spent a day drawing the shape in the dirt with a stick, scuffing the line out with her bare feet and drawing it again and again until the curve was true and the space for the path and the beds of herbs was sufficient.

The load of stones was duly delivered, and Sebastián began to apply himself to the laborious task of laying them, very precisely, into the dirt, following the lines Magdalena had drawn.

Every day, he carted stones from the pile by the gate and bent over the work. It seemed to him that no matter how many wheelbarrow-loads he carted up the incline, the original pile remained the same. It was, he thought, a new version of the fruitless efforts of Sisyphus, and he wondered if it would ever come to an end.

Magdalena, as she watched him toiling through the heat, pausing only to take long draughts of cooling spring water and dunk his entire head into the overflow bucket, was concerned that he was pushing himself too hard, punishing his body, taking no rest from his labor.

When Father Octavio arrived the following week, she asked him what he thought she should do about this.

"I think you must leave him be, Magdalena. He needs to feel his pain in some way; to make his suffering tangible. He has chosen this work, and what more powerful healing practice could he have found than this: to feel himself so close to the earth, and even through the pain of his loss, be able to create something of beauty that will serve many others in the future?"

"Do you think he sees it this way?"

"We do not always have to understand our symbolic rituals of healing for them to work their power in us. We make the connection at a far greater depth than mere understanding. But you know this, Magdalena. I have seen you working with the people who come here. No! I think this is exactly what he needs."

The weeks passed. Day by day the narrow path grew in length and intricacy, and the pile of stones beside the barn grew smaller. Sebastián, however, did not pause to admire or contemplate his work, but kept his back bent to the task, determined that it should be completed before he went back to college.

Magdalena watched him load the stones; watched him stagger with the effort of dragging the heavy load from the barn up through the soft sand to the open area of the courtyard. His chest was bare and covered in sweat that ran in rivulets down to the stained waist-band of his jeans. She was reminded of a painting she had seen of 'Christ on his way to Golgotha', and her heart went out to him.

It was on a late afternoon towards the end of the summer vacation that he did, however, complete the last stretch. As he knelt in the dust, holding the last stone in his hand, he paused, reluctant to set it into its space, for then the task would be finished and he would have to pick up his life and return to his place in the world once more.

The placing of this last stone, therefore, carried a special significance, and he looked at it, amazed that this small stone, essentially the same as the many thousand others that he had set in the pathway, should be the one to carry such meaning for him.

He placed it carefully into the small remaining space, and then walked to the center, where he sat for a while, eyes closed, not thinking or feeling anything in particular, but aware of the intricate path twisting and curving about him and the cool of evening bringing its relief and its shadows to the dry landscape.

When at last he stood and prepared to step directly across the intricacy of the path, the way he had while working, he found that he was unable to do so. He felt pulled back onto the path by the sheer power of the design. With some wonderment, and a certain amount of curiosity, he began the indirect journey leading outward, pausing only to remove his boots so that he might feel the smoothness of the path beneath his feet.

As he moved slowly around the wide curves, changing direction at the sharp turns that sent him back, seemingly the way he had come, he felt a huge sense of peace come over him. The fading light, the cool of evening and the warmth of the stones beneath his feet all contributed to an unfamiliar sense of place; an appreciation of the enduring quality of the land that he had never felt so powerfully before.

He was taken completely by surprise, therefore, on reaching a certain place on the path, to find himself unable to take another step. Try as he might, his feet refused to move, and he felt something huge and heavy enter his chest; felt the swelling ache of loss fill his heart until he thought that he must surely suffocate from the pain of it.

Unable to find any way of escaping the panic that he felt overtaking him, Sebastián sank to his knees on the path, consumed by such anguish that he was left bawling out his pain in a hoarse voice, a raw cry that sounded like that of a wounded animal. He sobbed uncontrollably, unable to do anything but surrender himself completely to the upwelling flood of grief and sorrow that engulfed him.

When finally it was done and the storm of emotion, so long confined, was released, he remained on his knees, emotionally drained, washed clean and empty. And it was there, on his knees, that he felt the earth, the night, the silence, put its arms around him: watched the last of the sun's afterglow move through that strange transition which is neither light nor color, until finally the dark indigo had faded into night.

Only then did he stand, and feeling his way along the path by the smooth warmth beneath his feet, he completed the journey from the center back into the world.

That night Sebastián dreamed.

He was sitting on the hill overlooking The Adobe. On the hill beyond him Georgia stood, dressed in a painter's smock and wearing a small French beret. She was pointing to something at his feet. A book. The book opened and the pages turned, but he could not read the words. When he looked again, Georgia had vanished. A mist descended, blotting out all sight of her. He was alone.

Sebastián woke with a beating heart and the sharp pain of loss filling his chest. He lay watching the daylight slowly define the shape of his room, his mind going over his last moments with Georgia: he, standing on the pavement as the car pulled away, full of disbelief that this could be happening; Georgia, hanging out of the window, waving and blowing kisses. How could she look so beautiful when his whole life was falling around him?

"I'll write and tell you all about it."

"Don't write, Georgia. I don't think I could bear it."

He saw the look of hurt on her face, and felt a momentary flash of satisfaction. He too had the power to inflict pain.

The day before he left for college, Sebastián made a cross out of an old piece of cedar and painted it white. In the late afternoon, when the paint was dry, he made his way to his favorite place on the nearer of the two hills, carrying the cross under one arm and the small book of Rilke's poetry under the other. There, next to a lump of basalt which had weathered into a comfortable seat and which was surrounded by a protective grove of yuccas, he built a pile of rocks and stones and placed the white cross in their midst. He filled up the hollows, packing small stones into every crack until the cross was secure. When he was satisfied with his handiwork, he picked up the book and turned the pages.

Since the dream he had read the book many times over, and while it had not removed the pain he felt, it brought a perverse sense of satisfaction into his suffering. Georgia knew what she was about when she gave him Rilke to read. Sebastián read the poems with a profound admiration for the poet, mixed with a sense of hopelessness that he could ever achieve anything worthy of such respect. Here was a man who dared to visit the very depths of human darkness; who expressed, so exactly, the painful thoughts that had always haunted him. He resonated with the pain of this man.

All he wanted now was to be a poet; to be able to go to those depths, and bring back the words and images for all those unanswerable questions that had been with him since ever he could remember. He needed to find, not answers, but the questions that never could be answered—to live, or die, by their truth. Above all, he needed to find his voice. If he was never to love again, or be happy, so be it. He would celebrate his darkness and grief in poetry. He began to read out loud:

"Who, if I cried out, would hear me...?"

Oh, how he knew this! His eyes moved down a few lines.

"...every angel is terrifying."

Sebastián sat watching the sun set.

Three Days

It was a long weekend towards the end of October.

Sebastián came home to spend it away from friends and fellow-students; away from all the reminders of Georgia. All but one.

He had kept the book of Rilke's poetry, and paid the library the fine for lost books. He could easily have bought a new copy, but this was the book Georgia had touched, had given to him, and he wanted no other. He had not read it at the time: now it became his Bible.

He could not bear to be in that place, so filled with memories of her. Everywhere his glance happened to fall, he was confronted by her absence. She was waiting for him in every walkway, around every corner. He would turn his head, certain that she must step out of the shadows of the trees and walk towards him. He would hear her laughter in a crowd, and strain to see her.

He could not bring himself to revisit their favorite eating-places, but there was no avoiding the pedestrian lanes and corridors around the college where so often they had walked, arm in arm, she chatting about study matters, and he so breathlessly enchanted that such a miracle as her friendship and her love should be granted him.

And so he came home, like an injured animal, seeking a familiar refuge in which to hide, away from the demanding world and all its hungers. He had nothing to give to it, especially to those well-meaning friends who sought to help him: especially to them.

He had, however, confided in Father Octavio, who had taken supper with them the night before.

"I feel cold, father. Sometimes I think that none of it happened and I will wake from an insane dream and find that I and the world will still be gloriously drunk with fullness. And then I know that it is true; that it is over; that all that is left is dust, and there is no substance to my life: nothing left of me. I feel like a shadow moving over a wall, and the wind blows through me. And still..." Sebastián's voice wavered. "Still I cannot lose the pain of it."

He had not spoken to Magdalena, and she was worried about his continued withdrawn state.

"He is not ready to deal with all of it just yet, Magdalena," Father Octavio said. "But I must warn you. He is going to be very angry when the time comes."

The small, white cross stood high on the hill like a humble beacon. It was a reminder: a signal that entreated all those whose eyes lit on it to offer a prayer for the soul of one whose life had been abruptly taken. At the same time, it reminded the faithful of their duty on earth and the reward that awaited them in Heaven.

It kept watch over the valley, bravely etched against the sky like a guardian angel, embracing all of heaven and earth within its outstretched arms, beckoning to all who sought redemption, that they might hold this image in their hearts.

It was the first thing that anyone noticed turning into the narrow road that led to The Adobe. For all its small size and the simplicity of its stark, white form, it dominated the landscape. It had a presence more powerful than the triangle of sky framed by the two hills, or even the steep hills themselves with their scars of fallen scree and dark, stunted junipers, or the sprawling acres below, with the long rows of cottonwoods reaching their pale, bony arms up towards it.

These two crossed pieces of wood, painted white, were a testament to many centuries of faith in the goodness and mercy of God: a faith stoically held even in the face of extreme testing, almost unendurable suffering and violent, seemingly incidental acts of God that often, with dispassionate equanimity and no apparent moral or other discrimination, destroyed the lives of the innocent and the evil alike.

This cross on the hill did not mark a literal death, as descansos crosses more conventionally do. It marked for Sebastián, not the belief in a hereafter or any kind of a reward in Heaven, but an end; a cut-off point to the possibility of any kind of future with Georgia. It marked the end of a time and a dream that, paradoxically, he could not, and did not want to forget.

It was an overcast October day. Sebastián had just arrived at The Adobe, and was paying a late-afternoon visit to Georgia's cross.

The land was dark and shadowed—a mix of drab, brown earth and dry grasses, the fading yellow and grey of the chamisa and sage bush and the shriveled, silver-green leaves of the Russian olives. But for the occasional burst of radiant yellow and gold, where the sun just caught the turning leaves of the cottonwoods along the river, the darkness of the juniper and the pine-clad hill was oppressive. There had been a drought, and many of the low-lying piñón had died that year.

The small stream had, against all odds, defied the aridity of the summer drought.

He brought with him a white river stone. It was an oval-shaped piece of quartz, worn smooth as polished marble by centuries of flowing water. It reminded him of Georgia's paintings, for it held a soft glow of light in its translucency. He positioned it among the pile of stones that he noticed had been placed around the base, stones that Magdalena must have carried up, one by one, and left there each time she visited the small shrine, and he felt grateful for this tangible expression of his mother's compassion.

He noticed that she had planted a second grove of yuccas close by; a plant known by the locals as Our Lord's Candles on account of its tall shafts of creamy, white blooms. They stood some distance away from the solitary white cross, silent witnesses to a memory, offering a mix of stark and tender beauty to the loneliness of the arid and rocky stretch of hill with its poignant legacy.

He had this, he thought to himself. At least he had this. Somehow this cross on the hill made him feel less alone.

It was pre-dawn, and a storm was brewing. Sebastián, who had awakened an hour earlier from a shallow and wretched sleep, made his way across the valley, along the line of ghosting cottonwoods to the familiar path that led to his place on the hill behind The Adobe.

He could just make out a faint trail of footprints in the powdery dirt, tracks made by four or perhaps five coyotes. It would appear that they had climbed the path, perhaps to pay some kind of feral homage to the foreign structure. He had heard them howling just after midnight, a lonely, disembodied sound which made him think of a documentary he had seen. It was shot somewhere in Africa, and featured starving children with swollen bellies reaching up skeletal and urgent arms to a famine-relief truck. The insubstantiality of the coyotes' cries was as thin and tenuous as the desperate cries of those starving children who held up, in supplication, small tin mugs for a scoop of some milled grain which might sustain their fragile hold on life for one more day.

On the horizon a thin slit of light was visible. The day was struggling to open its shivering eyelids before the storm obliterated the land from its sight. The dark clouds were gathering, and could be felt as an ominous and oppressive heaviness leaning into the day.

Sebastián shuddered.

As the slow, red light squinted through the narrow wound and the dark, brooding masses of storm cloud crowded in, pressing their heads against the low-raftered sky, he felt the first cold rushes of air. He watched the spiraling eddies of dust whirl away like thin smoke, signaling that the storm would come his way.

The mass of black, saturated cloud thickened. Sebastián could feel an equal electric energy gathering inside his body. The storm was about to break. He didn't care. Let it come. He neither welcomed it nor feared it. Let the day be blotted out.

He was close to the highest point of the hill just as the first huge drops of rain began to fall. A few minutes later the entire hill was stained red. Above him Georgia's white cross stood, white and stark against the black sky. He knew that soon he would be soaked through, but what could the storm rain do to him that made any difference now? He had no requests, no urgent prayer. What could it offer him? He did not even ask to be spared its fierceness.

The storm was directly over him when a flash of blue light lit the valley and left him blinded. Simultaneously, thunder cracked above him, so loud it seemed to split his head, and he felt himself falling into darkness. A second flash followed, illuminating the fallen figure, its arms thrown outwards by the power of the electrical charge. He lay on the red-stained earth in the out-stretched position of one who has fallen from the skies. He did not move. The rain sliced down on him, and the storm raged above.

When at last he lifted his head out of the rushing, muddy water that was dragging small rocks and bushes down the flooding hillside, the storm had moved on. Slowly he raised himself and stood unsteadily, looking around him. Everywhere water was rushing, carving out small fissures in the hillside, converting the normally dry arroyo at the base of the hill into a raging river.

Sebastián looked up to where Georgia's cross stood beside the yuccas. He could see nothing. With great slipping and scrambling strides he made his way up to the shrine. He arrived at the place to find the small grove of yuccas uprooted and broken, many washed away. He searched for the white cross, but it was no longer there. All that was left was a short, charred piece of wood surrounded by blackened stones.

Sebastián stared at it. All around him the sounds of wetness filled the after-storm quiet. He felt a rage flood into him, a fury which arose from beyond those shadowy depths he knew; an old anger that lay hidden and not visited inside him.

"Why?" he yelled. He reached down, tore out clod after clod of wet earth and hurled them into the sky. Streaks of earth-blood stained his bare arms.

"Look at me!" He spread his arms wide and threw back his head to face the sky. "See me! I am a man! I am not a thing that you can treat me so!"

He snatched at a clod of wet earth and raised it over his head in a gesture of defiance.

"You may do what you will to me! You can take my miserable life! But I will never bend a knee to you! I will never bow to you! Never!"

He did not bow or kneel. He fell onto the streaming earth, his hands gripping hold of the charred shaft of what had been Georgia's cross, while the sobs welled up out of him. A small, charred stump of wood was all that anchored him. He lay as still as death, utterly spent, unaware of the wet, the cold, the wind. He lay, small and broken beneath the low, dark sky. He did not pray for death, but he would have welcomed it. He did not pray at all.

Hours later, Magdalena found him there, chilled and white, almost unconscious. He was lying where he had fallen, his one arm stretched out towards Georgia's cross, and the streams of pink and red earth-water flowing around him like blood.

For three days Sebastián lay in a state of delirious fever. Magdalena never left his side, but bathed him with cool water to which she had added an infusion of herbs. She managed to coax her special tea between his dry, cracked lips, giving him as much as he would take many times throughout each hour. She applied her special compresses to his burning head and held them in place, even as he tossed and wrestled wildly with such angels or demons as were visiting him. Over and over she heard him mutter the same words—'...the world is within us...'

She would speak softly to him to calm him, but he would not be calmed. He would sit up and stare through her with wild, unfocused eyes.

"It is just the way it is. The cross is gone. Do you see that? It is the way it is! That is all. Rilke knew this! Tell them! The rest is lies."

And then he would fall back onto the sheets, muttering urgent words that she could not grasp.

On the third day, Father Octavio drove down to sit at the bedside so that Magdalena might rest.

A little after midnight on the third day, the fever broke. He wakened her, and together they bathed Sebastián and changed the sheets that were drenched with sweat. They gave him fluids and settled him back on the pillows, where he fell into a quiet sleep. Eventually, after sharing a few thoughts, they too fell asleep in their chairs, exhausted and relieved that the crisis had passed.

Outside all was still. The night was clear, lit by a dazzling multitude of stars. A numinous moon, with its waif-like crescent of virginal light, slipped between the two pink hills and hung for a while over the valley. Beyond, the desert, dark and inscrutable, slept in the depths of its untold millennia and remembered itself in silence.

It was just as the first light of dawn slipped its wraith-like fingers through the east-facing window, touching the strong face that lay so peacefully on the white linen pillow, that Sebastián, rising out of a dream the way mist rises and dissolves into light at the onset of day, opened his eyes. He lay for a moment, somewhere between two worlds, remembering his dream.

He could see himself as a boy of maybe fifteen, standing beside a man. He had a notion that the man might be himself. He felt safe. He felt both serene and exhilarated. They stood together, looking out of the windowed flight-deck of a spacecraft which, without the benefit of any controls, was flying effortlessly over a vast plateau that seemed to reach into forever. Ahead he saw a large, brown rock that stood directly in the center of their flight-path. He saw by a slit of light that it had a crack, a narrow fissure that ran diagonally through it. With consummate ease they flew through this slim opening and on, and on, and on into blue and distance. And now there was no man and no boy. Just an ever-expanding, open and outward gaze. Just light. And clarity.

Coming slowly back to the room now, his eyes were clear and calm. He watched the pale light move slowly across the room, touching the shapes and textures of the walls and the furnishings, caressing rough and smooth alike.

He saw his mother and Father Octavio, asleep in their chairs on either side of the bed, the light slanting in from the side window falling on their sleeping faces. He noticed something he had not been aware of before now: that these two faces had moved well past their youth. Unanimated and relaxed as they were, he could see the slight hollowing of the cheeks, the deepening lines around the mouth and a hint of looseness in the line of the jaw. He realized with a shock that he could see now how they would look when they were old. He had never thought of his mother as someone who would ever grow old.

He turned his head slightly so that he might more easily see Father Octavio. He looked older than his mother. In sleep the face was gentle, almost sad. He noticed, with a pang, the priest's hands that rested loosely in his lap; the swollen, arthritic joints. Quite suddenly he was filled with an overwhelming feeling of gratitude to these two people who, he realized, loved him.

He recalled the time when Father Octavio challenged his curiosity; how he never told the priest that he had found the lines in Ezekiel. At the time they meant nothing to him.

'A new heart also will I give you, and a new spirit will I put within you; and I will take away the stony heart out of your flesh, and I will give you a heart of flesh.'

The words felt like a blessing: like a gift.

"Father," he said, almost inaudibly.

Although he surely could not have heard the whispered words, Father Octavio opened his eyes and, meeting Sebastián's clear-eyed gaze, sat up, filled with relief, and leant forward.

"Ah! Well now! Sebastián. This is a good day. Welcome back to the world!"

Sebastián smiled and murmured some reply.

Their voices woke Magdalena. Throwing off the exhaustion and sleep, she rose quickly out of her chair, prepared for whatever was needed, but seeing her son's quiet face, she sank back into the cushions again and smiled at him.

"Well, look at you!" she said. Although she spoke calmly, she could feel herself about to give way to tears of relief. She rose again and began to busy herself with the bedclothes and the pillows.

"Shall I pull the curtain a little? Is the light too bright for you?"

Magdalena moved about the room, finding some relief in her fussing and the distraction of the small, domestic activities.

"How long have I been in bed?" he asked.

"Three days," his mother said as she poured fresh spring water into the glass on the bedside table. She drew her chair a little closer and resumed her seat.

The sun, just cresting the hills, cast spokes of sunlight in through the window. They could hear the small, bright notes of the birds outside as they went about their morning rituals, seeking out the last unfortunate insects and sipping the remaining drops of dew that still lay caught in the plant foliage.

"I will bring you a little food shortly, and then you must sleep," Magdalena said. "Sleep is what you need for the next little while."

Father Octavio stood up, and eased his stiff legs and his bent back. He too had uttered a silent prayer of thanks to God for bringing Sebastián through his ordeal.

"I need to be getting along. I'll just freshen up quickly if I may, and then I'll be on my way. Good to have you back, Sebastián."

He looked at the young man fondly and bent down, almost as if he might touch him, but patted the bed instead. "I'll see you at the weekend."

"Thank you," Sebastián said. "Father."

Father Octavio stood still. Never before had he heard the word—Father—spoken in just such a way. He turned. Sebastián's face had just the palest flush to it. Magdalena, who was standing in the doorway, felt her throat constrict. She saw Sebastián reach out a hand, which was soon clasped in the two rough hands of Father Octavio.

"Even so, Sebastián," he said. "Even so."

Poetry

Laurence Mann, the professor of English poetry, strode into the Poetry I class and put the small book he was carrying down on the desk. He was a thick-set, burly man. He wore jeans, a pair of boots with soles that resembled the tread of car tires and an old denim shirt. Over these he wore a faded poncho. It had obviously seen much sun and weather. The color and detail of whatever its earlier woven design might have been was now little more than a memory. He was not at all the image one carried of a disciple of poetry.

It was understood by the students that he was a lover of nature and hiking; that he spent as much time as he could climbing the remote peaks of those forbidding mountains that ran down the west coast of South America. He was studying the fierce lives of the Aztecs who used to inhabit those sacred reaches and breathe that high, thin, rarefied air.

With scant introduction, he launched into the first lecture.

"Poetry, whether you are reading it or writing it, demands that we pay attention. To pay attention we need to get ourselves, and all our fiercely held opinions, out of the way. You cannot add anything to a pot that is full."

Laurence Mann strode up and down, staring into the faces of the students, his right fist hitting into his cupped left palm, rather like a boxer's, as if wishing to drive each point home.

The students stared back at him. What on earth did he mean?

"However—and it may surprise you to learn this—you can get anything out of a pot that is empty."

He glared at the mystified students. Those who thought he might be making a joke, on meeting his fierce, blue stare decided not to laugh.

"Poetry is the voice of the soul sounding its own depths: it calls us into the deepest places in ourselves. It is the work of the poet to surrender himself to this ruthless, insistent and demanding energy, which will take him right to the edge of what he can bear—and further."

He paced to the window and stood looking out at the sky.

"Few people know at what cost you give yourself to this discipline. There are poets who cannot bear what they see."

He turned back to face the class.

"If you fail to serve the voice that wants to come through you, you will have to suffer the extreme frustration of your failure. If you succeed, you will be changed. There will be no way back to your previous, comfortable existence. It can be wondrous—and terrifying. Poetry is not for sissies."

There was a titter in the lecture hall.

"And if you are to be any kind of a poet, you will discover this to be true."

The room became quiet.

"And don't think that you will be able to escape this by writing about seemingly impersonal topics—ecology, the stock exchange, political matters."

He resumed his pacing.

"Poetry, if it is worth a damn, will always bear the signature of the poet. It will always reveal something that comes as a surprise or a shock. However noble the topic, there will always be that personal element: but it is personal in a way that will touch a nerve in all of us; personal in a way that is universal. It is this that we long for—and dread."

The class was quiet and attentive.

"In a sense, poetry is a matter of how you approach the world: one might say—how you revere it. Whether you are writing, reading or teaching poetry, if you do not bring this fierce integrity, this passion to it, you betray it. And if you try to be original, poetry will find you out. You will discover that the oldest truths are the most revolutionary."

He thought for a moment.

"I would say, to be a poet, you have to be in love with the world. That is what qualifies you. You can be a poet, and never write a single line."

He picked up the small book and began to read from it. His voice was clear and strong, free of sentiment or any attempt to offer interpretive expression to the stark, powerful lines. The students listened, held by the clarity of the imagery and the unfolding drama of the poem.

"Men!"

The word was like a pistol shot.

"... the only animal in the world to fear!"

He was reading from the poem Mountain Lion by D. H. Lawrence. The reading was more like an account of one of his mountain trips, with the short, explosive statements that seemed to incise themselves into each listener's brain. Sebastián could feel the cold of the dark canyon—and the fear.

"Lift up her face ..."

Sebastián could hear death in the reader's voice.

"...bright face ..."

Sebastián stared at the reader.

"...bright as frost ..."

Sebastián was about to make a note when, all unexpectedly, he felt a rush of tears as the memory of Georgia, turning to him in the car on that last day, came back to him, clear and vivid.

"We're there, Sebastián! Take the next off-ramp."

The image of her face, lit from within by such radiant light, left him feeling breathless. The golden mane of her hair now filled his seeing to the exclusion of everything else in the room.

Two lines kept repeating in his thoughts—'The light has gone now. I shall not see her again.' Sebastián made a note of them in his note pad.

"...she will never leap that way again..."

In just such a way, Sebastián thought, Georgia had leapt out into the world, into the great experiment which is life, with the clear brilliance of her personal vision.

"Our first response to reading or hearing a poem is to fully receive it; to allow it to be; to let it sink into some deep, empathic place inside us."

Laurence Mann shed the poncho and threw it over the back of his chair. Sebastián brought his attention back to the room.

"Is there a particular line, one thought, to which we feel drawn? We need to allow ourselves time to sense, to intuit what the poem is telling us, for it is here that we may find resonance. What are we being called to know, to recognize?"

He stared at the students. Not waiting for an answer, he continued:

"First, the inference that we are animal. There are many who would take exception to such a suggestion. Then, by what right do we kill this creature? Is it that we cannot bear to see an animal living so free, so unbound, when we know, if only subliminally, that we have killed that wildness in ourselves?"

Laurence Mann scribbled brief notes in point form on the blackboard. His handwriting was large and energetic.

"If we attempt to analyze—"

He continued pacing energetically back and forth in front of the class. The students scribbled urgent notes in the margins of their textbooks.

"—if we try to grab hold of understanding before we allow the poem and its rhythms to speak to us, we are likely to find ourselves with a handful of words and little else. Only after we have to some degree made the poem our own, only then may we ask some questions."

He strode up and down in silence for a minute, then turned to stare once more at the class.

"Are there any questions?"

There were none. He continued.

"For instance, with Lawrence's poem we may ask ourselves: who is it states that men are the only animal in the world to fear?"

Laurence Mann frowned down at the page. The students, who by now had found the poem in their own books, frowned down too.

"This is not just a poem about two Mexicans who shoot a mountain lion." He gave the class a fierce look. "This is about, among other things, a rage at such stupid brutality. It speaks to the arrogance of men who seek to dominate nature and all its creatures. We can feel the poet's rage resonate in us."

He paused.

"And it is about loss. Loss of that place: that gap in the world. That absence in the hole in the blood-orange rock, and—"

He stabbed his chest with an urgent finger.

"And the loss of something fine and wild within ourselves."

Sebastián could endure it no longer. He gathered up his books, and keeping his head down, he muttered some excuse and left the room.

The pain was not the same as it had been in those first weeks after her departure. Now there was just the awareness of absence. And yet, with it there was now a gratitude that he could feel this; that his heart had awakened from that dreadful, cold sleep; from that place of ash and shadows.

He made his way to his car and sat in it, in the shaded parking lot, still holding the books to his chest, the tears streaming down his face.

"Lift up her face…"

Oh, God! He held a hand over his mouth and shut his eyes.

'So she will never leap that way again…'

He opened his note pad where he had written the lines that had come to him, and sat staring at the page, not at the words, but at the whiteness of the paper. How could she not be here?

Finally, he wrote four more lines and closed the pad.

He sat for a long time, looking up at the fluttering leaves of the cottonwood in whose shade he had parked, until, almost hypnotized by the green blur, he fell asleep.

When he awoke the sun had already moved past the midday angle, and he noted from his watch that he had missed his afternoon lecture. He went back to his rooms, washed his face, made a cup of coffee, and only then did he sit down with his note pad to read what he had written.

'No argument can comprehend such finality
When the absence of her is everywhere:
Memory will not permit this departure
Nor my soul accept its loss.'

He felt a thrill that this had come to him. He had never experienced this kind of excitement in his life before. What if this could be a poem: the start of a poem? He felt exultant. He held the page up to his chest. He did not know whether these painful words could be considered poetry or not; whether they had any merit. And he did not care. All he knew was that the words expressed all his grief and pain, all of his loss. And in so doing they had, in some extraordinary way, transformed that loss into something unutterably sacred.

He didn't know what to do with the feelings that were flooding through him. Laugh? Cry? Dance?

That night he was woken by the sound of the wind.

He got up and went to sit outside. The night was warm with the wind blowing in from the desert. There was no moon. The only light he could see was the faint glow of lights from the town.

His thoughts went back to Georgia, and he felt a painful constriction in his chest. He closed his eyes to breathe his way through it.

As if they were spoken out loud, two lines came to him. Muttering them under his breath, he went inside hurriedly to fetch pen and paper. He was terrified that he would lose them. He turned on a small night light and wrote—

A dark wind is eating me
I feel it in my bones

He picked up the pen and paper, and went back to sit outside.

He sat for a long time, gazing out into the dark night, listening. What was happening to him? It felt as if a great wall had burst open. He could feel something, like a huge tide gathering its waters, inside him; a flood of words and feelings that had been held back for so long, now seeking their own river.

He took up the pen and wrote the rest of the verse:

This fierce communion
This shuddering black song

A wave of relief flooded him. He felt he wanted to say—thank you—but to whom? He read the four lines over and over. They so exactly expressed what he was feeling that he felt tears come to his eyes. Apart from his love for Georgia, nothing in his life had ever felt so strangely precious before.

He wrote another four lines, as if some invisible hand held his.

Oh what rapture, what rapture
This night without a moon
This fierce communion
This shuddering black song

Sebastián sat for a long time, tears of gratitude running down his face.

When at last the tears were over and the night wind had dried his cheeks, he went back to his room, put the sheet of paper into his note pad with the other writing and turned off the light. He got into bed and fell into a deep sleep.

The Dig

Grenville Oakley learned of Georgia's sudden departure from Sebastián on one of their evening rambles.

It was their custom to meet from time to time after classes were over. They would take a walk to free their minds of cobwebs, pick up a meal at the local restaurant and end the evening with a glass of wine in Grenville's study.

The two of them had grown as close as a shy, middle-aged professor and an introverted young student, whose youth had been painful, could be. It was the level of trust that Sebastián felt in Grenville, and the mutual respect they had for each other's intellectual integrity, that made it a friendship they both valued immensely.

Sebastián had attempted to make the announcement sound casual, but his drawn face showed that he was barely holding himself together.

Although a shy and not very demonstrative man, Grenville Oakley was extremely sensitive and compassionate. He knew full well all that Sebastián was suffering. He knew how it felt to have such a sudden loss. He also knew, from his own experience, that the last thing Sebastián wanted was to discuss it.

Instead he suggested that Sebastián join him at the weekend on a visit to an archaeological dig. He had been following the progress since work began more than a year ago. Just recently a level had been reached which called for the most delicate removal of soil.

"As you know, things are uncovered in specific layers of silt," he said as he strode along the edges of the dig and down a series of steps cut out of the hard soil. Sebastián followed until they came to the deepest place, where there was a platform with buckets of soil waiting to be carried away.

Grenville took out some peppermints, gave one to Sebastián and unwrapped another for himself. He stuffed the twist of paper absent-mindedly into a shapeless pocket.

They were standing at the edge of a section of the dig which was roped off to prevent people from accidentally stepping on the sensitive work site. All around them, men and women were working with quiet concentration.

"Sometimes one layer carries nothing: it might be the build-up of sediment after a long period of flood water. But under that, and this is the case here, we find a layer rich in fossils. This is a comparatively new discovery, not far from where they found a whole graveyard of fossils in 1947."

Sebastián was fascinated.

"Why so many, all in one place?"

"Probably this was a smallish water-hole—all the water that was left owing to the elevated temperatures at the time. They must have died of thirst, or been buried in a flash-flood which drowned them."

He moved to another part of the dig where a young man was lying close to the earth. He was clearing soil away slowly and with great care, using a small brush.

"This is the part I love." He gave Sebastián his shy smile. "You have to be wholeheartedly dedicated to the work to be this patient. It makes me think that all of life is like this—most especially our own lives. So much of who we are lies under layers and layers of our own particular mud. But still, you must work sensitively. You must take care in your eagerness to get results, not to overlook something which may be the key to the whole story."

He nodded to the young man who was working below them.

"Come and take a look at this," he said excitedly. "They were just beginning this the last time I came."

Sebastián bent down to see better. He saw the fossilized bones of a creature, lying almost fully uncovered. The young man was brushing the soil away from its skull. Most of it was now clear. It was perfect. There was not a single break.

"Just to put things into perspective," Grenville said as he too bent down to examine the fossil, "that is probably a Coelophysis, and this 'sleeping beauty' has been lying there, exactly as you see it, for close on two hundred and forty million years."

Sebastián stared at him.

Grenville nodded. "Makes you think, doesn't it?"

Rafaél

"Who gave you the retablo?"

The five-year-old Rafaél and his father were sitting at the kitchen table while his mother attempted to remove a mix of dried beans, flour and red chili from his thick curls.

"I painted it."

"You painted it?"

"Yes, father."

"And who showed you how to paint like this?"

"Jesus, father."

"Jesus?"

"Yes, father."

"And just how did Jesus show you this?"

"He speaks to me, father."

With his eyes half closed, almost dreamily the young boy made a strange, knuckling gesture in the vicinity of his temple with his small, brown, loosely curled fingers.

"He speaks to me here." The small hand rotated slowly. "He speaks to me—in my imagination." He had difficulty with the word, imaginación. The boy opened his eyes again.

"He tells me what I must paint, and I paint it."

Rafaél smiled, remembering the incident as if it were only yesterday.

It was his mother, Dolores, who first discovered the small retablo, the painting of Christ Crucified, executed with masterly skill upon a small plank of ponderosa pine, which Rafaél had hung over his bed. Alarmed, she called to Ignacio, her husband, to come and see what she had found. The two of them stood and stared, dumbstruck, at the image on the wall. Earlier Rafaél had been sent to the shop for his mother, and had not yet returned, so they would have to wait to ask who had given him such a painting. In the meantime they both felt anxious about the retablo's presence in their house. What on earth could it mean?

What should they do? Whom should they consult? They could see only trouble coming out of this. Rafaél had never been told about his grandfather, and therefore had no knowledge of what had happened to him, and how the tragic circumstances of his life had affected his son, Rafaél's father. Now it would appear that the grandson was drawn in some way to the grandfather's gift—or curse: it all depended on how you looked at it. Now, after all this time, when it was to be hoped that the past would stay right there, in the past, this had occurred. Now, they feared, it would all have to be told after all.

"The curse is in the blood. I always knew it."

Standing in front of the painting, both Rafaél's parents crossed themselves. They were appalled. They felt they should do something. As they stood gazing at it, their initial feeling of shock and uneasiness began to turn into something else. Dolores, in an effort to deny the beginnings of the new sensation in her body, ran to the kitchen and brought back a cloth to drape over the offending image. She fixed it in place with a couple of clothes pegs.

"There. We will ask him when he comes home."

"We certainly shall."

She pursed her lips and patted her apron smooth. It was utterly outrageous. She was about to say as much to her husband when she caught sight of the gleam in his eye. Before she knew what she was about, she was completely overcome by a sense of how ridiculous her dish towel looked pegged over a painting of Jesus, and burst out laughing.

Her husband, through a sense of propriety, struggled to contain the wave that began to swell inside him. It made its way from his belly up to his throat, and emerged in a guffaw so loud that it startled the dog sleeping in the doorway.

This rather large canine in turn shot out of the house and straight into the legs of the small boy who was returning, laden with bags of groceries. All the packets went flying. Beans, red chili and flour exploded out of their brown paper packets and flew into the air, covering both boy and dog.

When he had sat himself up and wiped some of the flour out of his eyes, Rafaél was startled to observe his two parents, clutching hold of each other in a manner entirely out of keeping with their usual, dignified composure, and weeping with laughter. It was too much for him. He didn't know what had caused such hilarity. He didn't stop to ask. It was just too infectious.

Without stopping to brush off the chili or the beans, he too threw his small head back, and laughed until the tears streaked their way down his floury cheeks.

The object of their concern, the retablo, was truly astonishing in its degree of artistry. It would have been considered a work of superior execution had an adult painted it, but, as they subsequently learned, coming from a child who was barely five years old, it was extraordinary. That alone might have caused them a certain amount of concern considering the family history, but it would not have caused this degree of disquiet. It was the young boy's interpretation of the subject-matter, so far removed from traditional portrayals, that shocked them and resurrected painful memories of the past.

The subject of the retablo was Christ on the Cross, Cristo Crucificado. This much was obvious. The nailed hands and feet, the wound in the right side of the chest, the crown of thorns—although here he had substituted a garland of pink roses—all spoke to this.

The cross stood on a three-tiered pedestal, traditionally a base-form used by santeros to symbolize the Trinity. The bottom tier was painted with a wide, wavy blue line to represent water, in which there were four scarlet fish. On each side of the cross the artist had painted a tall, flowering yucca, the blossoms of which were large, creamy-white and voluptuous. The figure's hands were nailed to the cross, with blood flowing down the arms in the time-honored manner, but the palms had somehow turned to face upward, and showed a company of white doves flying out of them and up to Heaven.

At the apex of the painting, which was framed by two pillars, there was a small arch in which one white dove, painted in the familiar and orthodox position to represent the Holy Spirit, was surrounded by a golden halo. The entire background comprised an indigo sky filled with stars.

None of this strayed too far from what was considered, if not conventional, at least acceptable. Only a purist might have argued this.

But it was the figure of Christ Himself that was so disturbing. For a start, the figure of Christ was dark, almost black. In place of the more customary, discreet loin-cloth, which frequently was painted to resemble a Jewish prayer shawl—white, with blue or black bands and a fringe—there was a Mexican serape, flamboyantly striped in brilliant primary colors. Even this, although it would have found criticism, did not offend unduly. It was the face and the hair that so alarmed Rafaél's parents.

The hair was long and flowing, and red. It streamed about the body like a halo of fire, with tendrils flying up to touch the stars. The head did not hang forward and to one side to denote Christ's suffering for the sins of the world, as was held to be doctrinally correct. No! This Christ had his head thrown back. Tears streamed from the outer corners of his eyes. His mouth was stretched open in a wide grimace—not out of the agony of His betrayal, nor for the pain of His tortured flesh; not out of the extreme suffering of this most terrible of ordeals, but—in laughter.

Cristo Risueño. The Crucified Christ was laughing!

This was the story that Rafaél was recounting to Sebastián as they sat, drinking coffee and sharing a plate of 'guacamole grande' in a small café frequented by students, just down the road from the university. Rafaél had approached Sebastián a few weeks earlier, the day following the lecture on D. H. Lawrence's Mountain Lion. Sebastián's hasty departure from the poetry lecture had certainly not escaped Rafaél's notice. But it was more than that: for Rafaél, from the moment he laid eyes on Sebastián, knew beyond any shadow of a doubt that their paths were, had always been, and would be forever linked. He would have been unable to explain this certainty to anyone, least of all himself, but it did not matter. All he knew was that destiny had tapped him on the shoulder, and he did not wait for explanations or proof. In a sense, it was the moment he first truly stepped into and embraced his fate, and he knew it.

For both of them the meeting was like that of good friends who have been separated for many years and are eager to catch up on all that has passed in the interim. Rafaél had heard all about Georgia. It was the obvious starting-point. And then Sebastián back-tracked, giving an overview of his life, ending up with how he and his mother came to move out to The Adobe.

Rafaél showed extreme interest in this last piece of information.

"Where exactly is The Adobe?" he asked.

Sebastián furnished the details.

"Of course that area has many old moradas tucked away in remote places. Many of them were abandoned and have weathered beyond repair, but some of them have been saved from the vandalism they suffered, and renovated most beautifully. I only ask because my grandfather was a Penitente, one of the Brotherhood who built a morada in that very vicinity. It is probably just coincidental."

"Your grandfather was a Penitente?"

"Yes. It's the hidden family secret. A long story."

"I'll order more coffee."

Felipe Montdragón was twenty in 1870 when he moved to northern New Mexico to join the Penitente Brotherhood. As a result of constant raids by local hooligans, the Brotherhood had found and bought a piece of land far out in the desert, in a small valley which held a spring that ran summer and winter, and with a small stream on the southern boundary. Here they built a morada.

Felipe was a devout worshipper and a gifted artist. He painted the exquisite retablo for the altar—four panels depicting the Annunciation, the

Nativity, the Crucifixion and the Resurrection—a work which shone with the passion of his devotion to Christ and His suffering.

And then, in 1908, Felipe changed. It was as if he were seized by some intractable spirit that demanded he give it expression. Obediently, he set to work on a painting. When it was finished and he saw what he had painted, it is told that he became afraid of the strange power that had entered him, and he underwent the most extreme form of self-mortification in an attempt to exorcise the demon. His fellow-hermanos, on seeing the latest retablo of the Christ Crucified, were shocked to note that the artist had given Christ the head of a ram with horns. When questioned, he muttered something about 'take Isaac, your only son'—'the sins of the world' and 'sacrifice'. He was so weak from his excessive flagellations that he could barely speak.

It was at this same time that the morada suffered a terrible raid by a gang of young men, who came in pick-up trucks, with a pack of savage dogs. Many of the hermanos, including Felipe, were bitten and badly beaten up, and one of the barns was set on fire. When finally the louts were tired of their sport, they departed, saying they would be back. And it was no empty threat, for they returned again and again until it was decided by the members that they should move further out into wilderness. It was suggested that the 'Cristo Carnero' had brought the evil to them, and that Felipe should examine his heart.

"Apparently my grandfather left that same night. He moved out and lived the life of a hermit in the desert, where he was found, very nearly dead, by a woman, a curandera who had been gathering medicinal plants. She managed to get him to her small cottage, where she nursed him and took care of his festering wounds.

"She healed his body, but it seems that nothing could heal his spirit. He was unable to make sense of, or integrate, his experience, and a month later he died. But not before the last spark in his passionate body had made that impossible and completely unknowable leap, from his body into hers. Nine months later my father was born."

Sebastián stared his amazement.

"Yes, well, the story doesn't end there. My grandmother took great care that my father never saw a painting—or even a picture of a painting. He was not allowed into a church. She taught him everything herself. When the time came for his confirmation, she managed to have a priest come to her. It was all extremely bizarre."

"And what does your father do now? Obviously he grew up and married. He must have seen paintings and churches and the like."

"Oh, yes, but it seems she was successful—well, partly successful. He has never painted a santo or anything at all religious; he has never painted a picture at all. But painting must be in the blood. Today my father is a sign-writer; he paints signs for advertising: words and logos. I don't think he has ever painted anything more imaginative than an arrow."

"And you?"

"After seeing my painting of the laughing Christ, my parents consulted our priest, who said I should keep away from any artistic career. He suggested I pick up on the other passion which my grandfather unfortunately—betrayed, I think was the word he used, and become a priest. So here I am.

"I have completed my studies, but I don't feel ready for the responsibility: not yet. Sometimes I wonder if I ever will be. That is why I am taking this course: to gain a wider sense of the world through the eyes of writers and poets. I am tired of doctrinal matters. I discussed my feelings with my supervisor, and he agreed that I am not ready to be ordained. Not yet."

"Do you still have the retablo—the Cristo Risueño?"

"Yes."

"I should like to see it. When did you last look at it?"

"Not for years. I think I am a little afraid of it; what it might do to me, to my life."

Sebastián said nothing. He tried to visualize the painting in the chapel at home.

"Do you have any idea of the subject of the altar piece your grandfather painted before all the trouble started?"

"Not really. I know it had four panels. But apparently he had a style that was almost like a signature."

"In what way?"

"He loved stars, and he would always include them in his paintings: the decoration on a plinth, or on a santo's clothing, or a small band in one corner of the sky. Things like that. Why?"

"When I go home next time, I am going to take a close look. The altar painting was there when we bought the place, faded but not damaged in any way. Wouldn't it be strange if it was your grandfather's?"

"Very strange."

The Message

Ten a.m. Father, one of the parents called from The Adobe to leave a message from Magdalena. She asks if you could come down as soon as possible. I have taken the parcels over to the school hall, and will be working there tonight. Elena.

Father Octavio drove as fast as the road and his old car would permit. It was late afternoon. His day had taken him to Santa Fe for a long and tedious discussion with the Bishop, and he had arrived home to find the note.

Magdalena wouldn't send such a message unless it was urgent.

He cursed the bumps and the sharp bends in the road that hindered his progress. He eased his car over the stony place where the dirt road crossed an arroyo. A rain-storm had played havoc with the road, and this was not one that received much attention. Still, someone would have to come and shore up the one side, or it would be washed away entirely. The pink earth had been carved away by the storm-water, and the roots of the junipers that clung to the steep sides had been exposed and hung down into the ravines. They would, however, cling to life by the few remaining roots. The growth would be stunted, but they would survive. He always marveled at the tenacity of these desert shrubs. It must be terrible to be a tree in this land; to stand there and take what comes. And what goes.

He turned into the familiar road which ran alongside the row of cottonwoods. The slight trace of evening moisture and the coolness of the air, now that the sun had set, carried the sweetness of the garden to him.

When he arrived, he found the door to her small casita open. Inside the room was dark. She had not lit the lamps yet, and at first he did not see her in the gloom. The bed was pulled into the front room to face out through the doorway and down the narrow track up which he had just driven. She was lying there, looking out at the last traces of the sunset.

"I am so glad you have come."

There was something in her voice that made his heart skip a beat. He had heard that note so many times before.

"What is it, Magdalena?"

He made a move as if to go and light the lamps, but she raised a hand.

"Please, father, let us enjoy the last few minutes of dusk. The darkness will be here soon enough. Then we can light them. Come, pull up a chair and sit by me."

He fetched one of the chairs from the corner and placed it close to the bed.

"What is it, Magdalena?" he asked again.

She waited until he had settled himself beside her.

"I have been feeling very tired lately. I thought perhaps it was the heat, or that I had overdone it a little; but it is not like me to feel so depleted. Two months ago I went to visit my doctor, and he sent me for some tests. The results were not good. It seems that there is nothing they can do. It has gone too far. The cancer has spread right through my body. I am dying, Octavio."

He did not hear her statement. He did not want to hear it. All he heard was his name. She had never called him by his name before. He heard his name from her lips, repeating over and over in his heart. He was filled with a rush of joy such as he had never experienced before—not in prayer, not in worship, not in all the years of his priesthood. He was lifted out of the ordinary world by the intimacy of it; of hearing his name spoken, by this woman; of being seen by her, not as a priest, but as a man. Hearing his name, Octavio, from her lips filled him with such sweet pain that he felt his heart might break. In that moment, that seemed to last forever— that was forever— in that instant he knew that he loved her: that he had always loved her.

He stared at Magdalena. All his life he had reached out to God, in prayer, in supplication, seeking always to know that grace, to feel that love enfold him; and now this woman, by simply speaking his name, had opened the door to his heart, and the joy of it filled him like a tide at the full, rolling in to shore.

Very gently he leant forward and kissed her on the lips.

Outside the world was still, but it was nothing to the stillness that now filled the small room, stillness so absolute that it felt as if time itself had been arrested.

Octavio took Magdalena's hand and together, in silence, they watched the last of the sunset's after-light fade into blue: that shade of blue that steals in with the approach of night; a blue that is somehow less color than a quality of light; a blue that reveals nothing but the dark silhouette of the hills; that seems to grow and grow in depth and intensity until, at last, the darkness claims it.

"Are the doctors certain?" he asked at last. "Perhaps they have made a mistake. We can arrange for another opinion."

The terrible truth of what she had told him was beginning to sink in.

"I have received the same diagnosis from three specialists. There is no doubt."

"How long did they say...?" He couldn't finish the question.

"They said a few months: three months at the most. Maybe less."

Octavio stared at her.

"No, my dear. It can't be."

But already his heart was admitting the truth of it. She looked suddenly so frail, the usual glow of health replaced by a pale translucency. How had he not noticed this before?

"What is it about this life, Octavio—with its pain and its beauty—that is almost unbearable? Sometimes I wish that I could make a single moment last forever; that I could enfold myself in the perfection of an instant and never leave it."

She glanced up at his face. He was glad of the darkness. He did not want her to see his tears. But she had seen them. She reached out and took his hand.

"Octavio." Her voice was soft. "No man has ever wept for me. Please do not turn away."

He looked at her, helplessly, the tears streaming down his weathered cheeks. Within his heart was such a confusion of emotion. Nothing like this had ever happened to him. He had loved so many people, had been with them through all the many and varied vicissitudes of life, been with them in their passion and their suffering: but he had never known the tumultuous mix of feelings that filled him now. What was he doing, weeping? He was a priest. It was his duty to comfort and console; to pray for strength for those who suffered. And here he was, weeping like a child. With an arthritic hand he wiped away the tears.

Magdalena tried to raise herself a little, and he bent to arrange the pillows for her and help her to light the lamp on the bedside table.

"I have spoken to Sebastián. He will be here tomorrow with Rafaél, a friend of his—I think you know him. I have much that I need to arrange, Octavio, and something I need to tell you. There is not much time. And there is something I am going to ask you to do for me. We can speak about it later. Can you come down tomorrow? I have made a will, but I am so worried about the work here. I am hoping Sebastián can help until we make new arrangements."

———————

Sebastián duly arrived. He had obtained leave on compassionate grounds, and now stepped into the role of running The Adobe. He spent as much time with his mother as the work-load permitted, fearing each time he left the room that he might not see her alive again. He could not believe that she was dying; that one morning, soon, she would just not be there. It was utterly incomprehensible.

He had been so busy, attending lectures and working on a book of poems that would be ready for publication as soon as he could decide on the title, that he had hardly noticed the passing of the months—and the years.

Since Georgia's departure, apart from his studies and some brief visits to The Adobe during his vacations, he had been obsessed with the poetry that was pouring out of him as if some lid had been lifted, or, with Georgia's departure, a dam wall had broken, allowing him free access to a dark and painful world of experience and feeling.

His room at the college was stacked with books and papers; folders of poems he had written, waiting to be selected and edited, and some that he considered to be complete, waiting for remarks from Laurence Mann.

He and Rafaél spent as much time together as they could manage. Rafaél was still continuing his studies at the seminary as well as his poetry course, and in addition doing some pastoral work to help an elderly priest who was struggling to meet the needs of his many parishioners. His visits to his family in California were, of necessity, brief.

Now Sebastián cursed himself for not spending more time at The Adobe, helping his mother: just being there with her.

"I should never have taken this course. I should have been here with you, helping with all the work."

"But Sebastián, my dearest, nothing could give me more pleasure than to see you moving into your life. This is what parents long for: to see their children succeed, find their path in life. You bring me great joy. And to think that I have a son who is a poet—what more could I wish for?"

"Are you sure that you won't see another doctor? I can take you. The school and the clinic can wait. The whole world can wait. Please, Mamá! Doctors have been wrong before now."

"Read the reports, Sebastián. Three separate doctors all say the same thing. There is nothing to be done, my dear, so let us not spoil what time is left by getting agitated. Just having you here like this is all I could wish."

Father Octavio moved into the cottage he always used when he stayed overnight. He arranged for a young priest to stand in for him in Las Madres, and told Elena to phone if there were any difficulties.

Sebastián observed Father Octavio's attentiveness and the care he gave to Magdalena, and was struck by the familiarity and comfortableness of their relationship. For the first time he became aware that they had a bond that had nothing to do with him, and it left him feeling oddly alone.

This feeling was compounded by his witnessing a moment of intimacy between the two of them. He had entered his mother's cottage late one evening, just as Father Octavio bent down to kiss Magdalena goodnight. It was a tender kiss, on the forehead, but nevertheless a kiss. They had not seen him, and he departed feeling confused, aware that he should knock on the door in future. But what future was there?

The farm work continued apace. The community, hearing that Magdalena was not well, volunteered to help with the packaging and invoicing of the goods to be delivered, making sure that a clear record was kept of the various farm products and items from the craft workshops. Sebastián and Rafaél were to take some of the goods to Las Madres, but the majority of the output was destined for Santa Fe. They planned to leave early on Monday morning, make the deliveries and then purchase the numerous items needed by The Adobe before returning home late the same evening.

Early that Monday morning Sebastián knocked on the door of his mother's cottage. He entered softly, tip-toed over to the bed and bent down to give her a kiss.

"I hope I didn't wake you."

Magdalena shook her head.

"We are about to take the goods now, Mamá, but I just wanted to tell you the news. Rafaél is so excited. Of course we can't be sure, but he thinks he has found, on the retablo in the chapel, some faded stars in the Virgin's hair. And, would you believe it, in 'The Crucifixion' Christ has on his head—not a crown of thorns—but a circlet of stars."

Magdalena took his hand.

"How simply wonderful." She smiled up at him. "How wonderful that we can't be sure."

He nodded. "Anyway, we're off. We'll be home this evening. If it's not too late, I'll pop in to say goodnight; otherwise I'll see you tomorrow morning. Is there anything you need from Santa Fe?"

Magdalena shook her head and blew him a kiss. He was pleased to note that she was looking a little better than she had for the past few days. He blew a kiss in return, and then joined Rafaél in the pick-up.

The truck pulled away slowly for the heavy load and the unevenness of the track, the various crates and boxes rattling and banging beneath the large, protective tarpaulin. From her bed Magdalena watched its progress all the way down to the turn-off. She saw the familiar cloud of pink dust rise and hang in the air; and drift slowly over towards the fields. She heard the brief pause as the truck negotiated the sharp turn at the bottom of the row of cottonwoods; heard the engine rev as the truck pulled onto the road; listened for the last, faint noise of it. Then it was gone.

Don Diego's Last Word

"Are you there, Octavio?"

The priest left his chair and came over to the bedside.

"Octavio?" Magdalena called again. He took her hand.

"I am right here, Magdalena." He pulled up a chair, sat down, and held her hand in both of his. "Right here." He tried to hide from his voice the dread he was feeling.

It was early evening. The Adobe was quiet. All the workers had gone home, and Sebastián and Rafaél had not yet returned from Santa Fe. Father Octavio sat in a chair in Magdalena's room, alternately reading and dozing. He and Magdalena had spent the morning talking about matters relating to the work at The Adobe. They took lunch together, and then Magdalena, exhausted from the mental activity, had fallen into a deep sleep. She woke just as the sun was setting.

"Oh, Octavio! I dreamed that I was on a train. It was pulling out of the station, and I saw that I had a letter in my hand that was meant for you, and I had forgotten to give it to you."

Octavio pulled the chair closer to the bed.

"I am right here, Magdalena, and if there is a letter you need to give me, you can do so. But, my dear," he said as he took her hand again, "I think it was just a dream."

Magdalena was suddenly fully awake.

"I need to tell you something that I have never told anyone. It concerns Sebastián. I must tell you before it is too late. I don't think I have long, Octavio."

With difficulty, for her breathing was shallow, Magdalena told the priest her story.

"I was born Rosalia Magdalena Chávez. My parents worked on one of the ranchos not far from Las Madres. The owner, a horse breeder, had a son a year older than me. We grew up together. In our early twenties we fell in love, and I became pregnant."

Magdalena closed her eyes, waiting to regain her breath.

"We were not permitted to marry. My son's grandfather was a very proud man. He would never permit the daughter of his horse trainer, a half-breed into the bargain, to marry his son. Antonio was sent away. I stayed on the rancho until Sebastián was born. I was issued an ultimatum: either, I accept a financial settlement, agree never to see Antonio again and move into town, where he would set me up in a small business or, my whole family would have to leave the rancho. And I had to promise never to reveal the name of my son's father.

"Antonio fought him, tried to fight for me, but he was young: he was no match for his father."

She paused for a moment.

"I stayed in the village, but I always felt I was in hiding. I was afraid every time I went out that I might see Antonio. So when Sebastián was four, we left. I settled in a small town south of here. Nobody knew me there. I made a new start. My business was very successful, and I managed to save money which I put aside for Sebastián's education. There is still a little bit left. I would like you to see that he gets it."

"Of course." He nodded his assent.

"I came back to Las Madres when Sebastián finished school. I used my second name, Magdalena. People didn't connect me with the young woman, Rosalia, who had left fifteen years earlier."

He thought this might be all she needed to say. She was exhausted from the telling of it, and this time, when she closed her eyes, she kept them shut for so long that Octavio thought she had slipped away; but finally she opened them and continued.

"I learned a short while ago that Antonio's father had died, and that he and his wife were living in New York. I wanted to ask you if you thought it would be correct to tell Sebastián who his father is, and if so, would you be willing to baptize him properly when he returns? Could you do that for me? He need not use the name publicly, but one day it will not matter to anyone who his father was, and then his certificate will tell the truth. My son's full name is Sebastián Antonio Felipe Merejildo Chávez."

She glanced up at him. Father Octavio stared back at her, a look of shock and disbelief on his face.

"What is it?"

Octavio shook his head. "Some coincidences are so extraordinary as to appear ordained by Heaven. No human mind—no human faculty would leave a matter of such importance to chance. I was called out last year to attend to an old man who was dying. He was living with his daughter, having sold his estate after his wife died in 1944. He said he had no son to take over from him, and that he was old and tired. He was a little confused: he kept going round and round; the details became more and more muddled and difficult to follow. And then he gripped my arm.

"'I have something on my heart, father, something I must confess before I die.'

"I nodded and said I would hear his confession.

"'I have a grandson, father. I don't know where he is, and I don't know his name.'"

Magdalena was looking at him intently.

"He asked me to try and find out what happened to him, a task I thought well-nigh impossible. He wanted to make amends, he said. He asked me to be custodian of a quite large sum of money, to keep it for a period of fifteen years, after which, if I had not found the grandson, I should see that it was divided between his four daughters."

He took Magdalena's hand once more.

"My dear, his name was Merejildo. Don Diego Felipe Merejildo Baca."

Octavio paused. "'Tell him his grandfather regrets never having met him. Tell him he has fine blood in his veins: from his mother's family, Chávez; and from his father's family, Merejildo. Tell him—tell him that his foolish old grandfather begs his forgiveness.'

"He died an hour later. He left Sebastián close to a million dollars."

Magdalena stared at him. She didn't know if she was angry or sad, or whether the whole saga, with its twists and turns, was not in the end quite ludicrous, farcical, and hilariously funny. All that drama—the love, the tears, the pain; all the humanity of it; all the desperate prayers, the agonizing over the lost love of youth; all the moments of triumph and despair—everything was like a Mardi Gras; a carnival; a pantomime.

She thought of the long, lonely years, the hard work and the people who came and went, adding to the complexity of it all. And even now, even as she lay dying, life couldn't resist throwing in one last card. That stubborn old man, obsessed with breeding and blood-lines, right to the end, had had the last word. Through the most extraordinary coincidence and a seemingly random, circuitous route, he had managed to pass his message on to his grandson. Maybe there was something in the blood and the genes after all;

some invincible will there that not even the forces of life dared to oppose.

And just what is this thing we call life? Certainly it has no respect: not for the living; not for the dying. Just when you think you can rest, it says: "Look, the story never ends! It goes on and around like those painted ponies on a carousel, going round and around and around, and up and down and around; turning, turning, turning—and then turning once more!"

Magdalena began to laugh.

"Do you ever have the feeling that God is playing with us, Octavio?"

Her dark eyes were bright. Her face was flushed with—with what? Was it joy he saw there? No. It was not joy. He was startled to recognize on the face of this dying woman—ecstasy!

"Oh, the absurdity! The absolute, utter absurdity of it all!"

Magdalena threw back her head and laughed. She laughed in waves that rose and fell; torrents of laughter that seemed to fly out the door and into the night, where they floated through the cottonwoods, over the small hills and up the mountains, to stream through the forests of piñón and ponderosa.

Octavio was appalled.

"Lie back, Magdalena," he begged. "You will feel better in a little while."

He tried to help her back onto the pillows, but she resisted.

"Oh, Octavio!" His name dissolved into a fresh wave of laughter. "Bless you, my dear, but I am fine. Surely the angels in Heaven must be laughing at us! Do not grieve on my account, dear, dear Octavio."

She reached out and took his hand.

"Oh, how I love you—Octavio! How I love you! God bless you, my dearest! I have never felt better in my whole life!"

Magdalena fell back on the pillows.

Octavio stood stunned. She was gone. He could not believe it.

Painfully he took his seat on the chair once more. He was devastated. This was not the way people died. He wasn't quite sure that it was respectful to meet death this way. But then Magdalena had never been one to mind too much about matters of convention.

"Oh, how I love you—Octavio!"

It kept repeating in his mind; in his whole body.

He bent down and kissed her. He took her hands in his, these hands that had been so slender and beautiful, elegant and expressive, like the hands of a dancer; hands, he remembered, that he loved to watch when she told one of her many stories; these hands that were still beautiful, but roughened now by hard work and burnt a dark brown by the desert sun. They were honest hands that had comforted many an ailing infant and healed many a wound to body and soul. He placed her hands on her heart, and offered a short prayer of thanks.

"Oh, how I love you—Octavio!"

Reaching for his prayer-book, he read the Last Rites. Then, with difficulty, he knelt down on his swollen, arthritic knees, close to the bedside, and prayed for the soul of this dear, courageous, extraordinary woman.

And he prayed for her forgiveness; for the time he felt he had failed her. It made no difference that things had worked out well for her. He should have taken a stand for her; for himself; for truth and integrity; for what he knew was being asked of him by God, no less. And now it was too late.

"Forgive me, Magdalena," he whispered. "I would do anything to have that time over again."

Octavio wept.

How was it possible that he had not seen this love when it was right in front of him? Was it from the success or the failure of his vows that he had not questioned his role as a priest? What makes a man whole—the denial of a full life or the embracing of it, no matter the cost? Huge sobs shook his body.

"Magdalena, I should have seen: I should have known."

He wept until he had no more tears.

And then he prayed.

He remained in prayer for a long time, until he felt his heart grow quiet again.

With difficulty Octavio stood up, and taking one of Magdalena's hands, he kissed it.

"Goodbye, sweet Magdalena," he whispered. "Forgive this stupid old fool who has loved you—long, if not always as well as he might have."

He looked with awe at the still face; watched the years fall away from it, leaving it with a look of such peace that he could not refrain from reaching out and touching one shining cheek.

"I love you, Magdalena."

The simple statement was a profound vow.

And then the tears came again; tears that rolled down his flushed cheeks, leaving them cool, the way summer rain blesses and refreshes a parched land.

He bowed his head.

"Oh, Magdalena! How little we ever know the nature of what is right in front of us."

He remained in prayer for a long time, until the candle she had lit guttered out.

The Cold and the Quickening

There would be three days before the funeral.

Sebastián stood on the pink hill overlooking the valley. He remembered his mother's words—words that she had spoken some months ago: slowly, as if the whole valley was speaking through her. He remembered the sweet smell of the hay he had been offloading, and the faint trace of lavender on the crisp morning air.

"You know, Sebastián," she said, "yesterday morning I was out here, next to the barn. The earth was still cool and damp from the night. I put the mules out into their paddock and I was leaning on the fence, watching them race up and down the line of the cottonwoods."

She paused, as if listening again to the sounds of early morning.

"The sun had just moved over the pink hill, and slow fingers of light were picking their way into the crevices between the basalt. I saw the wind blow through the grasses, and I watched a raven define the space between the hills, and I smelt the damp earth that the mules had kicked up in their frolic, and the early-morning scent of juniper and piñón; and I knew a moment of such perfection that I found myself weeping."

She paused again.

"This world, in spite of everything, has so much beauty. I became aware that I would leave it all one day, never see and feel the wondrous gift of all its richness again, and I realized how immeasurably precious the very ordinariness of each moment is."

"I should never have gone into town." Sebastián was distraught. "Not to be there when she died—when we all knew she was dying. And for what? A few boxes of goods. They could have waited. How could I be so stupid? And couldn't God have waited just a few hours?"

Father Octavio put an arm around the young man's shoulders, but Sebastián shrugged it off.

"Better not come too close, father. I think, after all, I must have the curse of darkness. You might catch it."

"None of us could know when it would be, Sebastián—and darkness is not a curse. Do not berate yourself for this. Maybe it was what she needed: to know that the work was being taken care of; that she was free to leave."

Father Octavio studied Sebastián's face. He had never seen him look so lost—so cold.

"I hope I have not acted out of turn, Sebastián, but I have asked someone I know to come down and help us with the clinic until we know what is going to happen here. Sister Piadosa. I hope that is all right with you. She will be here at the weekend. I have explained to her what has happened."

Sebastián nodded. "Thank you. That was very thoughtful of you," he said mechanically.

"I have known her for many years. She is a wonderful person; extremely practical, but also compassionate. I am sure you will like her. She worked for many years in a home for abandoned children: she has the touch. She can turn a hand to almost anything."

He replaced his arm and gave Sebastián a brief hug.

"And no one was ever less cursed than you, Sebastián. Rather, you are your mother's one true blessing. I think one day you will be surprised to realize how blessed you are, and how much you have to give to the world."

Sebastián left him and went to the empty office. He stood in the doorway, looking in. This room had always been the hub of The Adobe, always full of boxes and people and the sound of voices. He kept thinking how unreal it all felt; that he would look up and see his mother walking through the doorway with a bunch of lavender, saying what a good crop they had this year.

Now the reality of his loss confronted him from the silence—and Magdalena's empty chair.

Sebastián, together with Father Octavio, decided on the service, made arrangements for the vigil in the chapel and the digging of the grave.

All through the following day, through the funeral service and during that final moment when the coffin was lowered into the grave and the earth began to cover it, Rafaél stayed close to his friend. Sebastián was silent for the most part. He had no tears. He looked as if he had disappeared into some place inside himself. He managed to make appropriate remarks to all who came to offer their condolences, but it all felt like a dream to him. He could feel a screaming place in the back of his head; a place where an image kept flashing across a screen: 'the place where the light isn't'.

As a child, his imaginary dog Ladrido had saved him from falling into that dark hole. Where was Ladrido now?

He felt that he was being torn apart, and he struggled to stay with what was happening around him.

Father Octavio was moved to see how many people came to pay their last respects to this woman who had dedicated the past ten years to taking care of the community. All the families that Magdalena had served through her small school, the clinic and the men and women's craft-work center arrived in cars and trucks, with many, not having any means of transport, having arranged lifts with friends. Soon the grave was bright with flowers and little prayers painted on wood.

Alejandro brought a beautiful angel that he had carved, to stand watch over her. In a distracted way Sebastián noticed how different it was from his angel, which now stood in a niche in his bed-room. He gave Sebastián a hug, noticed the strained, white face and was wise enough not to say anything.

Many people had driven out from town: the men who knew her from the Casa Magdalena days—that was not surprising. But that so many of the town's women had come along was a surprise.

Now that, thought Father Octavio, casting his mind back to the bizarre debacle that had thrown the town into an uproar all those years ago, that was very close to a miracle. Now, the presence of so many of those very women at the funeral said a lot for Magdalena—and the women: and it said much about the essential goodwill of the community.

His mother was dead. He could not believe it.

Sebastián looked down over the valley. She was there in everything he saw. How could she be gone? Was he fated to lose everything that he loved? What did God—or life—have against him that he should lose both of these women?

He positioned the new, white cross he had made for his mother on the hill, close to the pile of stones which was all that remained of his tribute to Georgia.

From here, Mamá, you will be able to see every part of the valley. I will come and plant a circle of yuccas so that you can listen to the ringing of their bells: and they will be like candles in the dark, so that everyone will be able to look up, even at night, and know that you are watching over us and that all is well.

But was it?

He wanted to say more: something like a prayer. But he had no words. He felt the darkness calling to him, and the phrase that he had heard so often as a child, when he went to take communion with his mother—'the Body and Blood of Christ...'

What was happening to him?

He stood, trying to hold on to her image; to feel her close to him; but he couldn't.

He felt only his own emptiness.

Finally he bent down, touched the cross and whispered, "Goodbye, Mamá."

The air was like champagne.

Sebastián stood on a rock close to the timber-line on the Sangre de Cristo mountain range, catching his breath, watching the sun set over the distant mountains. He could see the dark cutting of the gorge winding across the sage flats, and in the distance, dimly, the rocky outcroppings at Tres Piedras.

'The Body and Blood of Christ...'

The whole world was scarlet, as if truly the blood of Christ had flowed out of the mountain range on which he stood and down over the land, staining all of its hills and plains. He turned to look upwards. He wanted to reach the summit before nightfall. It would be cold.

And then he saw it.

It was a tree: unlike the others. Its trunk, old and gnarled, sprang from roots that twisted tortuously over the rocks in their struggle to reach the stony soil.

Sebastián climbed the steep incline in order to examine it more closely. To his horror he saw that there was a man nailed to it.

The sunset had painted the naked body blood-red.

The tree was growing. Small, green leaves sprouted from the ends of the branches which, even as he looked, were spreading further apart.

The man struggled to pull himself free of the nails, for the tree's growth was tearing him apart. And then, suddenly, the flesh tore away from the nails. Sebastián saw the naked body leap forward and out over the ledge into emptiness.

With a pounding heart he ran forward and looked down. He could see nothing. In the darkness he could make out neither the cliff-side nor the ground far below.

Suddenly a huge bird rose up out of the gloom. It was colossal: a raptor, its wing-span all of ten feet. It circled and flew right at Sebastián, who pressed himself back against the tree. But the bird came on: the fierce eye, filled with the rage of wildness, stared straight into him. He thought it would take him, but at the last moment it banked away, so that its wing-tip just brushed his cheek. With the sound of rushing air, and a harsh, dark cry—a sound Sebastián would never forget—it rose and disappeared into the darkness.

He did not move. His heart pounded in his chest. At last, when there was no sign of the bird returning, he stood up. His whole body shook uncontrollably. He tried to think what he should do, but even that faculty seemed to be paralyzed. The night was black. There was no moon. There was no light at all. He had never been so cold.

He was aware of her the instant she entered the room. He did not rise from the bed, but remained curled into himself, his shoulders hunched, his fists knuckled up to his chin, facing the wall. Although he was expecting it, the first touch of her hand shocked him. He closed his eyes.

She removed his boots and thick socks, and set them down beneath the foot of the bed. He made no utterance, nor did he offer any resistance when her hands reached over to unbutton his shirt. He allowed himself to be rolled back while she drew the shirt-sleeves down his arms and slipped the garment out from under him. He felt a quickening when she loosened the belt and undid the buttoned fly. Only when she drew the rough cloth of his jeans down over his knees and feet did an involuntary groan pass his lips. He kept his eyes closed. She said nothing.

When he was naked, she drew the blanket over him. Her hand rested on his chest for the briefest instant, and he felt his body tremble.

She crossed the room with the bundle of folded clothing and placed it on the chair.

And then she proceeded to undress.

Light from the candle which burned on the bedside table softened the whiteness of her body, and cast a shadow on the wall behind her. She returned to the bed and slipped her soft, warm nakedness in under the cover, pressing herself close to the young man. His body was like ice.

Sebastián did not move. He wanted to reach out to the woman in the bed beside him, but instead he lay frozen into himself, his hands refusing to act on the impulse. He felt the warmth from her body spread through him. Still he did not move.

Now he felt the touch of her hands. He felt them move over him, touching the contours and planes of his body, a caress so gentle, so intimate that he felt tears spring up beneath his closed eyelids. He longed to touch her, to respond in some way to this tender courtship of his body, but something old and heavy deep within him held him back.

Only his love for Georgia had ever made it possible for him to open that long-closed door to his desire; had allowed him to dare to feel to the very depths of it. He would not be hurt again: not ever.

Across the room he saw that Alejandro's angel had left the niche in the wall and was standing, tall as a man, in the doorway.

It was a slow awakening, as if every inch of his body had to be touched back into life; had to kindle itself back from the cold place that had held it captive for so long. She did not hurry, but lingered over her caresses until she could feel in his body's response a new urgency; an involuntary, straining tension as he turned towards her.

Sebastián became aware of an ache reaching from his groin down his legs and into his feet. His heart pounded. He felt his hands unclench and open, palms upwards, his fingers spread taut and wide. He could feel part of himself being drawn irresistibly into the sensations that were flooding into him like streams of fire, coursing through every inch of his body. Another part of him struggled to hold onto that familiar place of safety; to refuse the demand that his body's desire was making on the mechanism that had grafted itself into his consciousness since ever he could remember.

He felt her mouth just barely touch his; felt her breath move into him. She kissed him again, harder now, so that his lips parted. Sebastián shuddered. His eyes opened wide. His face contorted. His mouth pulled back in a rictus of agony, and a cry escaped his lips; a raw, inarticulate utterance that tore at his throat and struggled out of him like the snarl of a wild beast, tearing at flesh and bone to free itself from the snare. It was a primal, inhuman cry such as women give in childbirth, and it split the darkness the way lightning cleaves a storm sky, creating a huge, jagged tear into which the candle-light streamed like a river of flame. And then the dark shadow that had inhabited him since the day of his birth was delivered out of him, to vanish, like a moth to the flame, into the stream of light.

Sebastián lay spent, dragging in deep, sobbing breaths of air. He almost woke, but another voice held him.

The woman raised herself until her face was over his. Their eyes met. With trembling hands Sebastián reached up and touched her cheek, her brow and her lips. He moved his hands down the column of her throat. He stroked the crisp curls of her short-cropped hair. His breathing became quieter. Then his hands fell to his side, and he was still. He held her gaze until he felt himself melt into her; until he could no longer see her eyes; until he could make no distinction between seeing and being seen.

When at last he entered her, he lost all sense of otherness. All thought abandoned him. There was only this union; only this miraculous sense of return. And then even that awareness left him.

He awoke at first light. He was alone in the bed. He looked across the room to the chair. It was empty. His clothes lay in a heap on the floor near the foot of the bed. On the table the candle had burnt down to nothing.

His first thought was of Georgia. In the dim light he could just make out the colors of her painting, which hung on the wall opposite the window. Had he betrayed her? Which voice could he trust? What is a dream? Was it a dream?

He sat up and swung his legs over the side of the bed. The air was cold, and he pulled the blanket around him like a shawl. He sat gazing out of the window, at the silhouette of the hills and the dawn sky gathering its slow, pink colors in readiness for sunrise.

He looked again at the painting. Where the Pink Hill Waits. Waits for what? To be seen? To be heard? He listened for its voice.

He looked down at his hands, as if inviting them to speak. They looked different. He felt that he had never truly seen them before. It was almost as if they belonged to someone else. On an impulse, he rose and crossed the room. The blanket fell to the floor.

He went over to his desk, took a fresh sheet of paper and fed it into his typewriter. He typed a heading: A New Voice.

He sat waiting.

Just as the sun was breaking over the pink hill, he reached for a pencil and scribbled some notes on a piece of scrap paper. He wrote lines, crossed them out, wrote others. He worked feverishly, as if on fire. Over an hour passed. He did not feel the cold.

Finally he turned back to the typewriter and began to type what he had written.

> To know at last this voice
> Breaking within me
> Passionate and sacred
> And the earth
> Rushing up to meet me
> And the dark bird overhead
> Sounding his harsh cry
> Calling out to me to follow

He would never forget that cry.

Sebastián crossed the room and stood in the open doorway, looking out. All the sky was on fire. Naked, he walked outside, listening to the sounds of early morning, feeling the coolness of it. He could smell the mix of lavender, herbs and juniper, and the fragrance of damp earth that had not yet been touched by the sun. He looked up at the painted sky above him. Georgia would have said that it was a perfect O'Keefe.

Suddenly it came to him that he was part of it, and that his wounding was a part of him. It was his, and in some way it had become a gift of incalculable worth. In his mind he saw the surface of 'the place where the light isn't' fracture and split open, and all the darkness pour out into the light.

He returned to his desk and typed the remainder of the poem.

And I on fire
With life's discordant symmetry
Turn my face
With its old scars
And its new bright edge
Into the uncertainty of that great wheel
Into that hard and fractured light
Into the dark wind

Sebastián stood up. He felt ecstatic. He knew in that instant that he was alive as he had never been alive in his life before.

He crossed the room and stood staring at himself in the long mirror: the naked length of him, and then his face.

He reached out and touched the face in the glass. Then he touched his own face; touched the glowing warmth of it.

The Letters

Father Octavio, Sebastián and Rafaél were sitting together on the porch outside Magdalena's small cottage, enjoying the cool evening air. The hour was late. It had been an emotionally exhausting time for all of them, and they were savoring a glass of Magdalena's sweet, home-made wine which Sister Piadosa brought from the kitchen and poured for them.

"Sebastián, I must introduce you." Father Octavio stood up. "You were away when Sister Piadosa arrived."

Sebastián stood to shake hands with the nun. His face flushed.

"Good evening, sister, and welcome to The Adobe." He tried to think of something else to say. He felt tongue-tied.

Their eyes met.

"Good evening, Sebastián. How very good it is to meet you."

"Your mother asked me to give this to you."

Father Octavio handed Sebastián the cedar box with the recently polished silver heart inlay on the top of it, inscribed with the name Rosalia. On the front there was a catch, fastened with a small, silver padlock, which had a key tied to it with a pink silk ribbon.

Before opening it, Sebastián turned to face the priest.

"You have been such a father to me, Octavio." He took the priest's hand.

Octavio grasped the hand in both of his. He struggled to contain his emotion.

"I mean it. I would like to think of you as—my father."

Octavio could not speak.

"And the most wonderful friend and—" he searched for the word—"and very dear friend to my mother. How would we ever have managed without you? I cannot begin to say what it means to me that you are here. That you always were there for us. I know she must have loved you so much."

Octavio looked down at the ground.

"I am sorry. That was thoughtless of me. It is none of my business."

"But it is your business, Sebastián."

Octavio lifted his head to look at Sebastián. He looked like a young boy.

"The times I spent at The Adobe, sometimes with both of you, sometimes with Magdalena alone, just talking of this and that, are the happiest times of my life. I would reach the bend down where the cottonwoods begin, and turning off the road and up the track I would have this overwhelming sense of coming home. Your mother was like a cool stream at the end of a very long journey in an arid land. She was water for the soul. I have so much love for her. I am going to miss her so much."

It was Sebastián's turn to look away. Such a naked admission of love. He touched the priest on the shoulder.

Father Octavio rose and embraced Sebastián.

"And you are my family. No one could have had better. I am blessed to know both of you."

The small cedar casket sat on the table between them.

"Why Rosalia?" Sebastián pointed to the small engraved heart. "It is her first name, I know, but I never heard anyone call her by it."

"She changed to her second name after you were born, but for all of her childhood, and until the time she left her home, she went by that name. I think the casket contains some letters from your father, and some of the gifts he gave her when she was young. They met when the old man bought the hacienda in 1920. He employed her father, a horse trainer, as his head man. Your mother must have been barely seven years old at the time, and your father a few years older. They grew up together."

Father Octavio repeated to Sebastián everything Magdalena had told him, and everything he had learned from the old, dying man, Sebastián's grandfather: where his father lived, his name, why he was forced to leave Rosalia; the repentance that the old man felt before he died, and the inheritance that he left to his grandson, should Father Octavio be able to trace him. He did not tell Sebastián how his mother had died laughing at the farcical nature of the whole tragic mess.

"My name is Merejildo?"

"Yes, if you should choose it. The old man left all the documentation, should you be willing to take it."

"And my father?"

"It shouldn't be difficult to trace him. His name is Antonio. Antonio Felipe Merejildo Juarez. I think he lives somewhere outside New York. When it was discovered that your mother was pregnant, there were terrible arguments, but your father was little more than a boy, and his father was a powerful man. Antonio was sent away to an uncle who had a business out east. He returned to the hacienda after you were born; after you and your mother had left.

"He married the woman his father chose for him; a woman of suitable breeding, with all the right genes to carry on his proud family line. The irony of it all—well, it would have been ironic had it not been so tragic—is that it seems that she was barren; certainly they had no children. It broke the old man's heart. He had no other sons, so it was the end of a family that could trace its ancestors back many hundreds of years. When his wife died, he sold the rancho. You may know it: El Rancho de Las Palomas."

"You mean the de la Cruz place?"

"The same."

"Good heavens!"

Father Octavio looked at him quizzically. He wondered what he would do under such circumstances. He was not prepared, however, for Sebastián's sudden burst of laughter.

"Don't you see, father?" he said when he had regained his composure. "That story she used to tell at the Casa Magdalena, the one that upset everyone because they wanted to know how it ended—that was her story. She just changed the names. What was the name she gave the old man?" He thought for a moment. "Yes! Rodríguez. Don Alonso Esteban Rodríguez Bautista. And Hermoso, the beautiful infant who was born in a field of lavender—that was me. What an impossible woman."

Sebastián, in spite of himself and the circumstances, was impressed. The nerve of it!

"It certainly was a very original and creative way to manage her anger—and her grief," Octavio ventured.

"My other grandparents died when I was young. My mother said that she took me to see them when I was small, but I have no memory of the meeting. I will ask around if there are some people who knew them."

The two men were silent. Octavio finished his wine.

"I think I will turn in. I must make an early start in the morning. I'll speak to you before I leave."

Before leaving the room, he turned round and added, almost as an afterthought:

"Oh, by the way, I mentioned the inheritance your grandfather left you. He said he wanted to make amends—should you be interested. "

He left the young man standing speechless.

"Dear God," thought Octavio as he walked towards the small cottage he always used when he stayed overnight. "Do you amuse yourself with the intricate games you play with the hearts of your poor servants?"

He touched his forehead with a finger in salute, and gave a little bow to the new moon that had just risen like a slither of light over the mountains.

He wished Magdalena was there to see it with him.

Instead of going straight to his cottage, he turned and made his way to the small graveyard with its fresh grave. The yuccas she had planted were still in full bloom, the faint moonlight falling on the tall shafts of creamy bells. He remembered being there when she planted them.

"One day when I am dead I want to know that they will stand guard and ring their bells for me from time to time," she laughed.

Death was far away then. There was so much still to be done. But it had not been so very far away after all.

"Why, God, did she have to die so soon?" Octavio stood there for a long time, his head bowed in prayer.

Sebastián turned his attention to the casket on the table, untied the silk ribbon and placed the small key in the lock. He felt a little uncomfortable looking through his mother's letters, letters written by his father. What a strange way to meet your father, after all these years. But then, she had left them to him, inviting him to read them.

He lifted the lid. Inside there were perhaps forty letters, some filling the envelopes, some little more than a folded note; the larger ones tied up with ribbon. The paper on some of them had turned brown, and one or two looked as if they had been read and re-read more frequently, for the folds were worn and the pages were beginning to fall apart.

At the bottom of the box there were several small drawstring pouches made of elk hide, and a larger bag made of purple velvet. That was all. Was this all that was left of their love?

He took the letters out carefully, and placed the pile on the table. He was shocked to notice that the strong handwriting on some of the envelopes was identical to his own. How was that possible?

His mother had numbered and dated each envelope. He picked up the one with the earliest date and, with fingers that trembled, drew out the folded pages. He realized that he was holding his breath. He tried to relax, but he felt himself shaking. He unfolded the letter and began to read the careful, young-boy handwriting.

28 July 1922

Dear Rosalia,

Father is taking me to Taos today. I wish you could come, but he says it is a day for men. We are going to fetch a bridle that has been custom-made for the stallion. I am going to find something special for your birthday next month. Father says if there is time we will hike up into the mountains. I am told that if you are lucky you could find one of those stones that look like crosses. I think they are called Lagrimas de Cristo, Christ's tears. If I find one I will bring it for you. Please say hello to Animado for me and tell him I'll take him out tomorrow. Tonio.

The utter simplicity of the letter touched Sebastián, and he felt tears spring to his eyes for this boy, the boy of the man who was his father; the father towards whom he had felt such bitter anger during his childhood. He felt confused.

He opened the next letter.

23 December 1922

Dear Rosalia,

We are going to Midnight Mass on Christmas Eve. I know that you are going too with your parents and Hermano and Ramona. Won't you come and sit next to me in church? I didn't get a chance to give you the present I made for you. It is quite small, so I can pass it without anyone seeing us.

Thank you for plaiting Animado's mane for the show.

Leave me a note in the usual place.

Tonio.

Sebastián read several more in the same vein; innocent letters of childhood, with all the precious intimacy of two young people who are entirely comfortable with each other. He wondered what had happened to his mother's letters to "Tonio." He found it strangely moving to think of his mother as this little girl. He had never thought of her as anything other than his mother, and here she was in some other reality: young, carefree, unaware of what lay around the bend in the road.

June 1924
Mexico City.

Dear Rosalia,

What an amazing city! I wish you could be here to see it! We are back at the hotel, and will be leaving tomorrow—and I thought the hacienda was grand.

Father has found the Arab stallion he wants. Wait till you see him. He is pure white, with a dark muzzle and so much dark around his eyes that he looks as if he is wearing mascara. His name is Sueño Mistico, and when he gallops he just floats above the ground. You are going to love him! He truly is like a dream.

Speaking of which, I had a dream about you last night. You were standing next to a priest in a huge field of lavender, and you were both laughing. Isn't that strange? It definitely wasn't Father Fernandez! He would never laugh like that! Anyway, you looked very happy.

I send you a blessing. Tonio. xx

Sebastián was thoughtful. He read several more letters written between 1925 and 1927, all in a similar style. He had a sense of the young Rosalia staying at home on the rancho, in the small, safe, familiar world of walls and routines, no doubt helping her mother and father with the work, while

Tonio traveled the world with his father, tasting life, seeing so many new things and doing his best to bring it all back to Rosalia. No doubt there were frequent opportunities for meetings; perhaps at the tree which seemed to be a favorite place for them, judging by the many times it was mentioned in the letters.

30 August 1928

Dear Rosalia,
¡Felicidades! Happy Birthday!
I found this fetish necklace of white doves in Santa Fe, and I just knew it was meant for you. It was brought in by one of the carvers from Zuñi, and it is an authentic piece. If you look carefully you will see the initials of the carver on the wing of the larger dove in the middle of the longest strand. I think these must be las palomas come back to the hacienda— unless you count the ceramic pigeons on the wall, and surely the place wasn't named after them!
Meet me after supper at the tree. I have something important to tell you.
Love—Tonio. xx

It did not escape Sebastián's attention that for the first time he had signed the letter with 'love'. He wondered what the—something important—might have been. He did a rough calculation. His father would have been about sixteen. He wondered if the sixteen-year-old boy realized that he was falling in love. He guessed not. How could he see something that had always been there? It needed to be lifted from its frame. It is often only when someone leaves, or in some way is taken from us, that we discover how deeply we are connected to them; how manifestly our lives have shaped and been shaped by the other. Either way, it was a very sweet, very tender romance.

Sebastián read all but the last bundle of letters. Through the language, the choice of words and the subjects under discussion he had a sense of the growing young man.

Father has invited some men to come and view the new stallion. Perhaps you would be willing to lead him round the lunging-paddock. You know how calm he is when you're around. We want him to make a good impression. I'll come by later to tell you times and so on.

Again he wished that he could have read the replies. There were so many questions, and references made to matters that would probably remain forever unexplained, small intimacies that might have spoken so eloquently of the secret life of these two young people.

Sebastián untied the last bundle. These letters were significantly different. Here was the handwriting that so resembled his own. Even the paper was different. The first letter was dated June 1934.

21 June 1934
My bed-room. Full moon. Can't sleep.

My darling Rosalia,

Sebastián put the letter down. This must have been written after his father had come back from college. He had been away from home for three years, studying and working for his uncle in the vacations.

My darling Rosalia,

I close my eyes, and all I see is you.
If I have lived for nothing else but this love for you, which has so filled me that I cannot eat or sleep—nor do I have need of either, for you fill every part of me with your beauty and your sweetness—then my life has been rich beyond my wildest imaginings.
Oh mi amante. I cannot wait to hold you. My arms ache for you. Meet me tomorrow evening at the tree. Until then, I am breathless.

I hold you in my throbbing heart.

Your love—Antonio.

Sebastián put the letter down again. He put his head in his hands and sobbed.

It was a long time before he was quiet again.

He read every letter, some two or three times, to make sure he could feel the lives of these two people.

At last there was only one left; a letter that bore evidence of having been opened and refolded many times.

What he read told him of the deep, true and passionate love that his mother and father felt for each other, and the impossibility of that love ever being blessed, or even contemplated. He heard his father's pain as slowly he became aware that theirs was a love that could never be consummated in marriage; that his family and the inflexible mores and strictures of their society would never sanction such a breaking of faith.

He read of the painful struggle to keep their love hidden, and the ultimate impossibility of hiding such intensity of feeling.

And he read of the night when Antonio had taken Rosalia into his trembling arms and made love to her. He read the lines over and over, for it was in those moments that the spark that was to become the infant Sebastián flew into his mother's womb.

30 September 1935

My darling,

When you told me that you were expecting our child, I felt such joy. I felt that nothing in the world could possibly separate us; that the miracle of this child was a sign that our love would overcome all adversity—even my father's obsession and bigotry.

Your silence since last we met is almost unendurable. Will you ever be able to forgive me? How painful to discover that there are forces in the world that can prohibit even such love from achieving fruition. I am loathe to acknowledge it, but I know that if we dared to challenge him, my father would make our life together impossible. He is a man of far-reaching power and influence—and he can and would be ruthless. He would rather see us ruined and destroyed than lose what he sees to be his legacy. I cannot allow this to happen to you.

Oh, my darling heart—how I ache for you.

I cannot bear to know that you are to be sent away as soon as our child is born. I cannot bear to think this, and imagine what will become of you. I cannot bear my impotence in this matter, the sense of failure that I feel; that I cannot find some way to overcome the circumstances, or find some way through this. It shames me that I am unable to provide for you and the child, and it is a pain I will have with me always.

I understand that you will be made financially comfortable, but I will not insult either of us by suggesting that this makes the future any less bleak. I cannot begin to understand why God should send such pain to both of us and also, inevitably, to that sweet life that already lies so full of mystery within you. I do so long to hold our child in my arms. To think that I will not be there with you at his birth; that he will not know me, his father; that he will most surely think that I do not love him. Oh! If only I could tell him the pain of such loss, of not seeing him grow; of not being part of those years. To know that I have a child in the world and will not see him—I cannot bear to think of this. I only hope that one day I may make some reparation; may in some way become a part of his life and yours.

And you, my dearest heart. I keep thinking that this is a bad dream, and that I shall wake and see you standing under the old cottonwood, waiting for me, and that we shall love each other and be together forever. Oh, Rosalia.

I swear to you that as long as I draw breath, and no matter what else may happen in either of our lives, I will love you, and I will offer prayers of gratitude, knowing that in that place where our love dwells, we will never be separated. Maybe God will find it in His plan to bless us, so that in some miraculous way that I cannot imagine, we may all be together again in the future.

I want you to tell our child out of what love he—or she—was conceived, so that he may find it one day, blossoming in his heart.

I want you to tell him how much I love him. How very much I love him. There is not a day shall pass that I will not send him a blessing of love and a prayer to wherever he may be.

I leave tomorrow morning.

I carry you with me always in my heart, my sweet beloved, my only Rosalia.

I kiss your name.

I am your love always—Antonio.

Sebastián laid the open letter down on the table and stared past the soft light of the lamp, out into the night. Finally he rose and went to stand in the doorway. There was no wind. Somewhere he heard a coyote howl. The thought that he had a father out there in the world who thought about him, who loved him, was not comforting: it was indescribably painful.

He turned, went back to the table and sat down. Carefully he opened the small leather pouches, one by one, placing the contents of each in a row on the table: a set of silver Mexican button covers, a large turquoise bead on a leather thong, the Lagrimas de Cristo that his father had mentioned in an early letter—he must have gone hiking after all.

The next pouch was a little larger than the rest. Out of it Sebastián drew an exquisitely carved, leaping mountain lion fetish, made out of the palest yellow, almost white Mexican onyx. He stared at it in astonishment. The artist had captured perfectly the tension of its lithe, tautly-muscled leanness. The eyes were of some deep blue stone, set into the onyx. Sebastián could not believe it. He felt a lump form in his throat. There was a note accompanying it.

There is a writer who has a place just outside Taos. Remind me to read you a poem he wrote about a mountain lion—Tonio.

It was too much. It was not possible.
He picked up the mountain lion and held it close to his heart.
"Oh, Georgia," he murmured. "I kiss your name."
He repeated the words.
"I kiss your name."
Slowly he opened the remainder of the pouches. They contained a pair of coral and turquoise earrings, a miniature set of Zuñi fetishes showing the six animals which traditionally represent the six directions, and a small,

carved doll covered with tiny beads set into what he took to be beeswax. It was covered with intricate patterns of rainbows and lightning, bright flowers and corn. He found the bear-claw bracelet that he had seen his mother wear whenever she and Father Octavio went to the opera. From the last, the velvet bag, he drew out two strings of beads, a double-strand necklace of small, white doves and a rosary of hand-carved, pearl-white shell beads. At the bottom of the bag he found a gold ring. It was the ring his mother had always worn. He held it close to the light and read the inscription engraved on the inside.

Rosalia Beloved of Antonio August 1935.

The ring fitted his small finger perfectly. He kissed it.

He recognized the rosary. It had always hung close to his mother's bed. He had never paid it any close attention, seeing such aid to prayer as a rather artificial, mechanical device. Now he examined the masterful carving of the small beads, recognizing all the totem animals of the south-west. It was exquisitely made.

Sebastián closed his eyes; his fingers moved over the beads, feeling the contour of each one, as no doubt his mother's had done so many times. He examined the necklace of carved doves and found the carver's signature on the dove's wing. He placed it on the open letter and sat staring down at it: white doves, flying over the black ink writing; white doves flying against a black storm sky.

Don Diego's Legacy

"Cows!"

"Yes, cows. I am going to look at them later this morning. Perhaps you would like to come along."

Rafaél admired the newly-planted bed of lavender, which was almost completed. While he spoke, Sebastián bent over the task, pressing the soil down firmly around the last small plant in the row. Rafaél had never seen him with his hands in the dirt: ever.

"Is this some kind of family ritual that you are engaged in?" He meant it in jest. Sebastián's reply was thoughtful.

"As a matter of fact, it is. I have only now realized why my mother planted lavender whenever we made a move. The fragrance is wonderfully calming to the soul, and it feels so good to be engaged in something physical that requires so little cerebral activity. This, and the fact that we will be able to use the lavender in our products and bring in extra revenue, adds a certain virtuous sense of satisfaction to the whole operation. Actually, Rafaél, apart from all of that, I like the feel of my hands in the earth and dirt under my finger-nails."

It was then that he mentioned the cows.

"I'm going to stay, Raf. There is so much that we can do here. I have thought a lot about whether I would accept the inheritance, I mean after how shockingly the old man treated my mother. But right at the end it seems that he did want to put things right, even if it is only because I carry those famous genes of his. So I am going to give both of us the benefit of the doubt: for him that he meant well, and for me that I am not just taking the easy way out. I am going to use the money to develop The Adobe. Let's think of it as Don Diego's legacy."

"But why cows?"

"It came to me last night. I need cows." Sebastián laughed. "There is nothing I want more than to write poetry. But I can't sit in some ivory tower and write about life, people and the world. I need to be in the world. I need to be in it right up to my elbows."

He examined his hands with satisfaction.

"Yes, indeed. But why cows?"

"You don't give up, do you? Why cows? Well—because they're big, and warm, and slow. There is something so calming about watching cows chew the cud. And then, there's all that milk. And they have calves. They are such bountiful creatures. We can use the milk for the children in the school, and for the nuns. We can make cheese."

"Oh. There are going to be cows and nuns. Tell me about the nuns. I must say, you have been doing some thinking. I suppose you have given some thought to a bull as well?"

"I have already discussed some of this with Father Octavio. He thinks that it is a wonderful idea. I am going to ask Sister Piadosa"—Sebastián blushed—"if she would stay, and whether she could arrange for some nuns to come and work here. We will of course have to build rooms, and whatever else is needed. I thought we might run a retreat, for people who wanted to get away for a while, or people who were convalescing. After all, we have the clinic already. We could extend it. And perhaps we could do more with the parents. There is so much talent here: perhaps an art center of some kind. Who knows where that might take us?"

"And the bull?"

"How are you ever going to be a priest with such a one-track mind? Joe Gonzalez has a bull. There. Are you satisfied?"

Building commenced in mid-September and by early November all the roofs were on and doors and windows had been fitted. Because of the rapid progress, it was arranged that Sister Piadosa and the nuns would come in time for Christmas.

And so it was that The Adobe made ready to enter a new phase in its history.

PART III
MARÍA

María's Birth

María Teresa de la Cruz Luna was born just as the sun, burning its way into the rim of dawn, lifted itself over the Sangre de Cristo Mountains.

It was a long and difficult labor for Catherine, her mother, who in spite of having given birth to five children already—five daughters, to be precise—was no longer young. Her youngest daughter was already ten, and she had not expected to have any increase to her family after so long an interval. Don Lorenzo, her husband, longed for a son, and was accustomed to getting his way. He had hoped throughout the pregnancy that she would give birth to a fine boy who would, once he was grown, help him in the business and inherit it when he died.

He sat outside the door all through the long night, not primarily out of concern for his wife, but in anticipation of holding his son in his arms at last.

"It has been a long time, nurse. How are things progressing?"

De la Cruz stood outside the closed door, for once powerless to bend things to his will.

"It will take its own time, sir," was the reply.

The dark, powerful man returned to his chair.

As the labor dragged on and on, he did begin to experience some fear that his wife might not have the strength to deliver, and that the babe would be harmed in some way. It had happened to Señor Torres' wife. She too was not young, and the child, when it finally came, was not right. The doctors said it would have been better if he had not lived. But in spite of his many physical disabilities, he had clung to life and had grown to be constitutionally very strong, although mentally he would always be a child.

As his wife's cries grew weaker and weaker he became increasingly alarmed, and, although he was not a religious man, he prayed to the Holy Mother to bring his son—and his wife—safely through their ordeal.

When the babe was finally born and the nurse called to him through the door: "Come in, Don Lorenzo, you have a beautiful baby girl," his initial reaction was one of extreme disappointment. Before going in to his wife, he walked over to the corner cabinet and poured himself a neat whisky, which he downed in a gulp.

"So it is not to be," he muttered. He allowed himself some time to erase the look of disappointment from his face, and then, placing the glass on the sideboard, he rubbed his tired eyes and turned to enter his wife's room.

Catherine de la Cruz, her face pale from exhaustion and loss of blood, her eyes heavy-lidded, turned her head wearily towards him when he entered.

"I am sorry, Lorenzo," she said in a tired voice. "I know how you longed for a son."

Don Lorenzo went over to the bassinette in the corner where the babe lay, warmly wrapped in a shawl. With one finger he moved aside the lacy fringe and looked at his latest daughter. He was completely unprepared for the upwelling of emotion that engulfed him.

All his previous daughters favored him in appearance. They had his olive complexion and black hair, and the same dark, almost black eyes. They inherited the same sturdy build, which was evident even from birth. As they grew older, they blossomed into the kind of voluptuous beauty, almost animal in its quality that is shown off to advantage by bright colors and provocatively flamboyant clothing. They exuded the same quality of sensuality and health as their father, but lacked his powerful intensity.

This child was different from her sisters. As he looked down into the perfect little face with its blue eyes and fair skin, pale as alabaster, he was reminded of the paintings of angels that hung in the vestry of the church. Her eyebrows were very fair, almost invisible, but he detected a hint of gold in them, a promise of what her hair would be when she was older.

As he bent over her, noticing all of this, aware of a new softness in himself, to his utter amazement she stretched out her two little arms as if reaching up to him.

"Will you look at that?" the nurse exclaimed. "I never did see anything like it in all my days!"

Don Lorenzo's response was to reach down, lift the little bundle out of the bassinette and fit her into the crook of his arm. He walked over to his wife, a look of unfamiliar gentleness on his face.

"You did well, Catherine," he said, smiling down at the babe. "You did very well."

He did not see the tear that his wife shed. He only had eyes for the child.

"We will call her María," he said, his voice soft and husky, "after her grandmother. María."

In the days that followed María's birth, Don Lorenzo was a frequent visitor to the nursery. This was an unusual practice, for with his five other daughters he had not wanted to be bothered by what he considered to be women's matters. But this child was different. From the moment he set eyes on her, María, tiny though she was, had captured his heart. Catherine and the nurse were amazed at his forbearance when, late at night or in the early hours of the morning, the little one cried. He would hasten into the room and scold them for being neglectful.

"What are you women about? The child is crying!"

Then he would lift the babe tenderly and whisper soothing words to her. She would respond with smiles, and Don Lorenzo would walk up and down, holding his precious bundle, tickling her under her chin and conversing in baby talk the while.

Watching him, Catherine thought, not without a pang, that it appeared that he did have a vulnerable corner in his heart after all. She had never been able to find it for herself, but she was pleased that indirectly she had brought him joy.

There was something so compelling, she thought, about a handsome man, no longer young but still virile, taking such delight in an infant. She cast her mind back to the day they had met: how he had taken her breath away. Of course, she was very young and inexperienced then. Would she have done it again? Surprisingly, she found this difficult to answer.

Catherine was very weak after the birth, and she spent many hours on the shaded porch overlooking the garden. For a number of days she had been aware of the sound of sawing and banging coming from the direction of the stables. However, as this was not an entirely unfamiliar noise, she had not thought to enquire what task was underway. So it was a complete surprise when Lorenzo led her out to the day bed himself one morning, and pointed to the new structure that had been erected at the far side of the garden. At first she didn't know what it was. She looked up at him, questioningly.

"Wait! Wait! You will soon see," he said excitedly, and he nodded to Roberto, the gardener, who was standing in front of it.

Roberto stepped forward, lifted a latch on the shuttered door and threw it open. For a moment nothing happened, and then, one by one, white doves emerged through the opening, and after some hesitation, flew up onto the roof. To Catherine's astonishment more and more birds poured out of the doorway. They jostled for position, pushing each other aside, fluttering up and down before settling further along the roof-pole.

"They are my gift to you and María," Don Lorenzo said to his wife. "I thought that you might both enjoy watching them. Roberto will let them out to fly in the morning when you are resting here, and again in the evening when it is cool."

"Oh, Lorenzo!"

She was afraid she might cry, and she knew he would not like that. She did not want to spoil this moment. She controlled her emotion.

"What a simply wonderful surprise! How many are there? I can't begin to count: there are so many, and they move so. Oh, I absolutely love them. And María will love them too, when she is a little bigger. Thank you so very much, my dear."

She spoke formally. She knew he would not want any demonstration of affection in front of the gardener.

"There are fifty birds," he said. "I had them brought from a man who breeds them in Albuquerque. Roberto is going to build some breeding-boxes, so that we will always have them to remind us of this happy time." He beamed with pride at the originality of the gift, and the surprise it had been for her.

So the white doves came to stay, and when María was not very much older, she would lie in her pram in a shady corner of the garden, hearing the soft, muted sounds of contented cooing coming from the shady dove-house. And when Roberto opened the door and the cloud of birds flew low over her pram, she would wave her hands and kick her feet with excitement, watching them as they flew over her, and round and round again.

María Looks Back

"My father bought this Hacienda, with its thousands of acres, in 1945, the year the atomic bomb was dropped on the cities of Hiroshima and Nagasaki in Japan: the year before I was born. I still remember the day when my father took me to Los Alamos to see the photographs. He was very proud of what our country had achieved. It was only later that I came to know the horror of it.

"I think my arrival, the youngest of six daughters, must have been something of a surprise to my mother. She suffered from delicate health, and was already forty years old at the time of my birth, with her fifth daughter, Bonita, entering her eleventh year.

"I grew up hardly knowing my sisters: I was only six when Bonita, barely sixteen and the last to wed, married a man almost twice her age, and moved with her husband to California. My sisters have been more like aunts to me, with their own children closer to me in age and outlook than they ever were.

"After my birth my mother's health took a turn for the worse. Never very robust, she began to suffer dreadfully from a wearisome fatigue for which the doctors could find no cure. They insisted that this late pregnancy, far from having caused her ill-health, should have helped her through the next period of what people sometimes call 'those difficult years.' I think it might have been that she was just worn out by my father's volatile spirit, his rages and temper tantrums. More often than not, it was she who bore the brunt of these long tirades: how the politicians were robbing him with some new tax; how ungrateful the mine workers were, sowing division in the ranks and threatening to break labor unity; how he was being pestered to make a donation to Boys Ranch, and why should he do that when he was a man with no sons?

"'But Lorenzo, dear, don't you think we perhaps have a social responsibility to help those not as privileged as ourselves?'

"'Please, Catherine. Don't argue with me. Women know nothing of such matters.'

"His voice would grow loud, angry at having his decisions questioned.

"'If I thought for one moment that you were capable of understanding how society works, we could discuss it. I make these decisions. You have no training for this. Apart from which, these boys and their parents are just lazy.'

"After he had unleashed his fury he would depart, relieved of his tension, whistling his favorite mariachi tune of the moment. My mother would be left exhausted and with a migraine headache; often in such a nervous state that she would have to lie down until the pain had left her.

"As a result of these frequent altercations, my mother spent long periods resting in her room, with the shutters closed against the bright light which hurt her eyes. Sometimes, on better days, she would have the hammock hung on the porch, close to the lilacs. From this slightly elevated position she could look out over the neat rows of lavender and the beds of herbs and small shrubs that made up the herb garden, and on over this, to the two fields of lavender that had been planted by a previous owner and beyond this to the foothills of the Sangre de Cristo Mountains.

"In the afternoons, when I was older, I used to join her on the porch. My grandmother on my mother's side, after whom I am named, used to come and stay with us at the Hacienda at times when my mother was not well. I think that she was the only woman my father feared, for when she was there he would manage to keep his tantrums to himself, or at least throw them somewhere out of our hearing.

"My grandmother began to teach me how to embroider, using brightly-colored silks and small glass beads. She started me on a sampler, a piece of linen on which she was teaching me the many different embroidery stitches. It was a tradition that was not widely known in New Mexico, but she told me that where her family came from, every little girl was required to complete at least one sampler, preferably before adolescence. The addition of beads into the design was the influence of the local Indian beadwork.

"'Do not be in a hurry, María. Each bead is special. Each bead is a tiny prayer. You will only stitch each bead into its place once. Make sure you do it with care.'

"I loved these times. They were the only times I saw my mother relaxed and happy, especially if my father was away on business in Mexico. Then she would seem to gather her spirits, and we would get up to all manner of enjoyable games, and laugh together at the silliest things. These were the only times she laughed. And some nights, if she was not too tired, she would sing for us. When she was young she had had her voice trained, and it was thought that she would make singing her career. My father, however, would have none of it.

"'If you think my wife is going to stand up and sing for a lot of drunken louts in some seedy dance hall, you have another thought coming. Never!'

"'But Lorenzo, these would be classical concerts. There is a vast difference.'

"'You will not be singing in public! And that's the end of it!'

"My grandmother said that this was the beginning of my mother's illness. She said that if we have a gift, we must use it, or we do ourselves terrible damage. I think my mother began to die from that time, little by little, so slowly that most people didn't notice. But Mercedes, who was my nanny when I was small, and who had become our housekeeper, she knew; and Encarnación, who helped in the house, and Roberto, Encarnación's husband, who was our gardener: they all knew that you cannot close the door on spirit without incurring much suffering.

"'Spirit will always out, María, you will see: if not in this place, then in that.'

"They said that my mother's voice was waiting for someone to carry it; and then I was born, and it chose me. It is true that I love to sing.

"With my father away the Hacienda would be so peaceful. Mercedes and Encarnación would be noticeably brighter, and would sing while they worked, enjoying the relaxed atmosphere.

"Encarnación was a powerful woman. She came from what she called 'the old country', and had brought all of its songs with her. One in particular was my favorite. It was the song the women used to sing when they made the long and hard journey from the old country up to New Mexico. They sang it for birth and for death, both of which, she told me, were so much a part of those arduous months, traveling through rough territory, at the mercy of the elements and in constant fear of raiding Indians.

"My grandmother grew up under the watchful eye of a young Indian woman who was the daughter of parents released from slavery in 1867. In 1889, at the age of fifteen, she applied to work in the house as a nanny to the new-born baby.

"It was from this woman that my grandmother learned the old stories of the Native American people, and gained an insight into their deep spirituality. She learned from this woman how the Great Spirit watches over all things; how, before the life of an animal is taken from it, permission must be asked, and gratitude expressed for the food it will provide. She learned of a world so different from the French and Spanish Catholic world of her parents that she had great difficulty fitting the two together.

"The most precious gift that my grandmother ever received from this woman was the gift of dreaming, and how to listen to dreams. It was a gift she later gave to me.

"'Dreams are not just imaginings,' my grandmother would say to me. 'Not just things our minds invent in our sleep. Dreams are not just silly notions that we may dismiss when we wake up. No. Dreams are—rememberings.

"'Do you know that we are millions of years old; that the stuff of our bodies comes from stars? Do you know that when we breathe, we are breathing the air that a second ago was breathed out by a wild bear or a coyote, or an eagle? Our breath will blow away and be breathed by forests and bears and wolves; and whales. And then it will be breathed by someone on the other side of the world.'

"'Am I breathing that air, right now?'

"'Certainly. This breath breathes all things, like the dreams that dream us, like the Great Spirit that inspires us.'

"At the time that she told this to me, I was very young, and I could only dimly follow the sense in her words. It was when I grew older, long after she died, and my life had begun to present its challenges, that I truly began to understand what she had been trying to tell me.

"My grandmother never spoke to the members of her family about these things. Even as a child she had known that such thoughts would invite stern disapproval from her family and the Church. But she lived her life as true to it as she could manage within the constricting norms of her time. And now she was giving all of it to me. She never had to tell me to keep it to myself. I knew that.

"For the rest, my grandmother was an immensely practical woman. She would busy herself with things in the house while I spent time sitting beside my mother, or bending over my work, struggling, clumsily I am sure, to keep the rows of beads straight, while she told me stories about France, and how her grandfather had left that country, where the family had lived for centuries.

"My mother's grandfather, Henri Jacques Latour, left France in 1869 to seek his fortune. He was the youngest of eight sons, and having no expectations of inheriting any part of the family estate, decided to come out to New Mexico. He had heard that land was being given to settlers who intended to become citizens. He acquired one hundred and sixty acres of land, and with his small savings he bought cattle. It was a wise step, for the cattle industry began to boom some years later, and he was able to buy more land.

"His second marriage—his first wife having died in childbirth along with the infant—was in 1886 to a Spanish woman of great beauty. She was the youngest daughter of a certain Señor José Montoya, who left Mexico in 1846 to escape the war. He arrived in New Mexico with his meager savings, which he sank into a mining venture. It proved to be only moderately successful. And so, my great-grandmother, María Juliana Montoya, brought into her marriage only her beauty.

"In 1889 my grandmother, María Jacqueline Latour, was born. She was an only child, something very unusual in those days, and a matter of great disappointment to her father, who had wanted sons to help him with the ranch. It turned out well for my grandmother, however, because on her parents' death she inherited everything, which by then was a very successful farming enterprise with interests in mining. She married my grandfather, Luis Armijo Luna, in January 1906, when she was just seventeen, and my mother, Catherine, was born on the last day of that same year, the only one of all the siblings to inherit the famous red hair.

"'And you take after the French side of the family in looks and coloring,' my mother told me, touching my braids. 'Your great-grandfather had blue eyes and flaming red hair.' She smiled. 'And I believe a very strong will, and quite a temper!'

"She told me this story so many times, each time filling in a little more detail, telling me some of the customs that had been passed down to her, and which seemed so foreign to the people of New Mexico. The strangest of these, it seemed, was French cooking. Her idea of a dinner party was a strangely exotic experience to people who had little or no contact with European customs. Still, people used to love to be invited to one of these affairs, and even my father seemed proud to be able to offer something which was unique in this part of the world.

"But the happiest memories I have of my mother are of the two of us sitting in the cool shade and the fragrance of the lilacs, hearing the lazy droning of the bees and the soft, murmuring sounds of the doves in the shade of their latticed dove-coop nearby. We would take our tea out there, and then wait until it was cool, when Roberto would come and release the doves for their evening flight.

"I loved this time. Both my mother and I would lie back on our cushions and watch the pattern of the doves' flight, a loose figure of eight design that rose and fell, lifting as they flew over the house and outbuildings, then swooping down, barely clearing the low adobe walls and the row of cottonwoods and Russian olive trees that separated the garden from the farm land and the large paddocks. Then they would gain height and spread out over that wide expanse of open range, with its grass, chamisa and small junipers that stretched out and upwards towards the hills and the distant mesa.

"It was as if they wanted to imprint their souls on that whole vast dome of sky. I loved the rushing sound they made as they passed, almost directly over us. It made me think of the stories of angels that Father Octavio told when we attended Mass; that heavenly host that lived somewhere up there beyond the clouds, beyond the blue veil that separates us from Heaven. I would close my eyes and fancy that the angels were coming to gather me up and fly with me right through that blue light, clear up to God.

"And then I would open my eyes again and watch the birds turn, vanishing for that surprising moment as they turned into the light; and then see the sudden, white flash as the light struck their wings once more: and then they would rise, high into the blue sky, and round and round and back again.

"'Your papá gave them to me as a present after you were born,' my mother told me the first time I ever watched them with her. 'Nothing, no other gift, has ever given me greater pleasure. I love to see them fly against a dark storm sky, with the black clouds piling up on each other like huge, black castles, getting so dark, and the sun slanting through those few spaces left before the storm closes in; and that electric tension in the air, when everything seems to vibrate; and that strange, yellow light on the trees, and the feeling that the earth is about to sing, and the distant rolls of thunder, and then the whiteness of them as they turn… I love to see them fly up there, so free, so…so unbound, so…'

"She didn't finish the sentence. She just let it hang there, as if words were inadequate to express what she was feeling. Young as I was, I could feel her huge, unfulfilled longing. And her sadness."

María leaned back against the trunk of the crooked, old cottonwood that stood on the hill behind the stables. She had been there for an hour, recalling all the vivid memories of her years at the Rancho de Las Palomas.

Now, very carefully she attached a tiny note to the leg of the white clay dove with the blue eyes. Standing, she held it high, released it, and watched it fly out into the vast, endless blue of the New Mexico sky.

Lorenzo

His earliest memory of his mother was of her standing next to a horse from which she had just dismounted.

She must have been wearing riding clothes, but this he did not remember. It was the black hat that he recalled so vividly, and the laughing face beneath it. It was their first official meeting. He was four years old.

He had spent those four years in the sheltering arms of a wet-nurse who, when he was weaned, became his nanny. His father, unwilling to share his wife with his new-born son, had engaged the woman, telling his wife that she was not to ruin her breasts by having some lusty boy-child tugging away at them day and night.

It was his father who decided that on his fourth birthday his son, Lorenzo, should be formally introduced to his mother.

The birthday tea was set on tables in the garden. It was late afternoon. The day had begun to cool, and in the shade of the giant tree it was most pleasant. The horses were led away, and the woman in the hat took a seat on one of the chairs set beside the tea-table.

Lorenzo held on to his nursemaid's skirt and stared at his mother.

"I have brought you a birthday present, Lorenzo."

She held out a brightly wrapped gift. "Come here, and let me kiss you happy birthday."

The nurse gave him a shove, and he found himself standing in front of her.

For the rest of his life he would remember the perfume she wore that day: how soft her lips were against his cheek. He fell in love with her, right there and then.

Lorenzo de la Cruz was sitting out in the garden with his wife Catherine. They were taking tea together; iced tea from a tall jug which Mercedes brought out to them. The day was hot, and Catherine's usually immaculate hair had begun to slip loose from its silver comb. She removed the comb and shook her long, red-gold hair free, threading her fingers through it for coolness.

It was at this instant that an image from his childhood flashed through Don Lorenzo's brain: a memory of his father, with his legs spread wide, standing in the bed-room doorway. He was holding a thick, plaited cattle whip. A woman was screaming. And then his mother, with her long hair loose, and blood running down her face, ran past his father and down the long, tiled passage, sobbing as she ran and calling out for Consuela, her maid. For years, repeatedly, he would dream of this: and as the years passed, the passage down which his mother ran grew longer and longer, and he saw a row of doorways open, one after the other, all down the length of it, and in each doorway there stood a small, terrified, six-year-old boy whom he knew to be himself.

The event in itself was horrifying enough, but it was exacerbated by Lorenzo's feeling of impotence, and his consequent shame at his inability to protect his mother.

From the time of this incident he took to lying awake at night, often until the early hours of the morning, waiting for his parents to finally enter their bed-room. He would lie still, listening for the familiar sounds of their night-time routine, waiting until he could be sure they were in bed. When the pool of light that was cast from their bed-room window into the patio vanished, and he was sure that all was quiet, he would leave his room, opening and closing his bed-room door slowly so as not to make the slightest sound.

Silently he would steal down the passage towards his parents' room. Once outside their door he would crouch down in the shadows, almost holding his breath for fear that it might be heard. He would listen for their whispers, and the early sounds of their love-making; the rustle of bedclothes and the bed's creaking. And then he would hear what he so dreaded: the sound of slaps, and his mother's cries of pain. "Please, Carlos, no... Please don't... No! No! No!"

There would follow the sounds of a struggle, and more slaps and blows, and his father's raised voice—"Slut! What makes you think you are any better than a cheap whore?"—Until the small boy could bear it no longer, and he would press his fingers into his ears to blot out all hearing.

He would stay like this, eyes tight shut, crouched over, cold and frightened, angry and ashamed, wanting to enter the room, to fight his father, to drive him away, once and for all; to hold his mother, to kiss away her tears, so that all the pain would disappear.

But he could do none of these things. His only resort was to believe that just by sharing her pain in the only way he knew how, by forcing himself to stay awake and by enduring the solitary vigil outside her door he was in some magical way preventing anything more terrible from happening.

Lorenzo loved his mother with a passion. He spent more time with her than with his young friends. Even as an adolescent, he would love to sit and chat to her when she was dressing for one of the many grand functions that she and his father attended. He loved the nose-tingling smell of the dark, red nail-varnish and the fragrance of her perfume. He would watch with fascination as she applied her make-up; gaze at the transformation that took place. But it was always that moment, when this was completed; when she reached up to loosen the bandana that secured her hair, and released the shining, black, perfumed mass of it, so that it fell almost to her waist, that stopped his heart.

It was an image that became so etched into his brain that at night, alone in his room, when he felt himself harden; or when he was older, and making rough and violent love to a prostitute, it was that image which superimposed itself over all others.

Sometimes his passion would overtake him while he was in her presence. He would feel his blood begin to gather, and he knew how he longed to hold her. Somehow he would contain his desire and would watch, breathless, as slowly she piled coil upon coil of glossy, black hair up on her head, smoothing away every last tendril, patting it into place before securing it with the heavy silver comb.

She would sit for a moment, regarding her image in the mirror, and he, sitting behind her, would feel his heart break for the sadness in her eyes. But then she would pull herself together, take down the scarlet evening gown and step into it. She would draw it up over her silk petticoat and close the top fastenings before turning to him, revealing to him the inviting shadow between the perfection of her wondrous breasts, and the heart-stopping curve of her waist.

"Help me with the fastenings, Lorenzo, there's a dear," she would say, turning her back to him once more so that he might assist her.

Lorenzo would feel faint, and his hand would stray, and all but touch the sensuous curve of her neck. He longed to lean forward and kiss the smoothness of her back. Somehow he would manage to fasten the small, covered buttons slowly, one by one, but his heart would pound so that he feared she might hear it. And then the door would be flung open, and his father would stride into the room.

"Aren't you ready yet?" He would turn and scowl at his son. "And what are you doing, hanging around here? Don't you have better things to do?"

Lorenzo, with heightened color in his cheeks and all his body on fire, would stammer some reply, and leave the room.

Lorenzo had not confided in Catherine about his past; how he had been bullied and ridiculed by his father, or how he had witnessed the violence being done to his mother, over and over again: how powerless he had felt in the presence of it. Indeed, he had told no one. He told no one of his promiscuity; how each new conquest would fill the emptiness he felt inside him—for a brief spell—before he would be forced to find some fresh erotic indulgence.

Instead, he constructed a story of grand family life, full of dignity and honor, and could regale his guests with many delightful stories of his wonderful youth in Mexico.

But the effects of his childhood trauma remained, and now he was only capable of feeling aroused in the presence of submission.

The arrival of Mercedes to collect the tea tray brought de la Cruz back to the present. As soon as the servant had departed, he turned on Catherine.

"Tidy your hair, Catherine, for God's sake! You look like a slut!"

And Catherine would hasten to gather up the thick tresses, her face white.

María Receives a Dream

"Just before she died, my grandmother told me a dream.

"She told it with her eyes closed, almost as if she was dreaming it right then and there; as if she could see it; as if it had become a part of her. She told me that she had dreamed it many times. She told me that she thought it was my dream.

"This is the dream she gave to me.

"'I am sitting on a rock at the top of a mountain. Above me there is only blue sky. I am alone. The air is bright and clean and cold. I am warmly wrapped in my sheepskin jacket.

"'I see an elk stag, standing motionless not far from where I sit. He gives no sign that he has scented me. I sit very still, hardly breathing. The sun falls on him in such a way that it appears his coat is on fire. He turns to look directly at me. A light, so dazzling that it blinds me, surrounds his head and antlers. I am forced to look away. When next I open my eyes the stag, the fire and the radiance have gone. I feel that in some way I have lost an opportunity to know something. I feel that I am being called. I must not turn away.

"'And yet in each subsequent dreaming I am once again blinded, and once again I turn away. It seems that I am not able to bear this light.

"'When I wake I feel a fire in my chest, in my heart. Tears sting my eyes. I am breathless with the beauty of it.'

"That is the dream my grandmother gave to me when I was just seven years old."

The Elk Calf

It was a spring morning with champagne air and a sky so full of blue, it made the eyes ache to look at it. The unusually early April rains had transformed the countryside, resurrecting it into a rich tapestry of vivid color, vibrant with the energy of new life. Shoots of the season's grasses pushed their urgent and indomitable spears through the warm earth crust, and on the mountain-sides one could see broad, horizontal bands of brilliant green where the quaking aspens opened their spring buds. Higher up, the deepest gullies still held the last blue-shadowed drifts of winter snow, but for the rest, snow-melt filled the many streams, and rushed clean and cold to join the swollen rivers that were the life-blood of the arid land.

It had been a long, hard winter, and the search for food had brought many wild creatures closer to human habitation than was customary. It was reported that a herd of elk cows had been spotted on the low hills, foraging close to some small stands of woodland. Ranchers in the district were concerned that they had come for a hand-out from the last of their winter supplies of alfalfa, which was still being fed to the cattle to tide them over until the grazing was more abundant.

It was the time of annual transition for the elk. Soon they would turn and begin the slow migration to their summer habitat, up in the mountains. Now that the snows had melted, they would become restless. The cows, heavily pregnant, were in need of the extra food, and it was known that not even a barbed-wire fence could keep them away from a supply of alfalfa. Soon they would drop their calves, and not long thereafter they would leave their wintering-places, setting off on that long, slow march up into the mountains to follow the retreating snow-line, browsing and grazing on the season's new growth.

At the Rancho de Las Palomas it was time for the spring ritual of inspecting the lands and the stock, making decisions for the coming year. This was an occurrence that took place every year, and continued on a weekly basis until early summer. Celebrating the first day of it had become something of an occasion.

María was excited. Her eighth birthday was a few months away, and her father had decided that she was old enough to accompany him.

All the family and staff members stood in the courtyard, waiting for Diego Sanchez, the foreman, to lead Don Lorenzo's fine Arab stallion Fuego, so named because of his fiery color, and the old black mare Amiga Negra up to the front door. Both horses carried the finest saddles Mexico had to offer over brightly-woven Navajo saddle blankets, with colored tassels which hung down below the length of the long stirrups. Diego had sat up late the night before, polishing the silver medallions that adorned both saddles and bridles so that they winked and shone and flashed in the bright sunlight. Ciprianita his wife had made rosettes out of spring flowers, and these were attached to the cheek-straps of the bridles with long, flowing ribbons, giving both mounts a festive appearance.

The group standing by the house cheered as the small procession rounded the corner of the stables. Both horses, sensing the excitement of the moment, tossed their heads and held their tails high, dancing in small, side-stepping strides, showing all the grace and carriage for which they were well-known.

The ultimate purpose of this small ceremony was to bless the coming year and the land that supported them, and pray for good rains. Don Lorenzo would say a few words to this effect, and then the two men would mount their horses and ride out through the grand gates to the enthusiastic cheering of the small group of spectators.

They would examine the state of the ditches and the gates in the acequias that irrigated the fields. Each year de la Cruz increased his acreage under cultivation, and he would communicate this to the mayordomo, who would make the arrangements for the ditch-digging and make adjustments to the previous year's financial agreement.

They discussed the pruning of the fruit trees in the orchard, the state of the grazing and how much extra alfalfa they might need to buy in. They checked the fencing, inspected the cattle and made decisions about which to keep for breeding purposes, and which to sell. The stock was not a serious financial venture, but Don Lorenzo took pleasure from the air of authenticity that the presence of a well-bred herd of prime and pedigree cattle lent to the Hacienda. It was a vanity that he enjoyed.

This year María was to accompany her father.

She was dressed in a white cotton dress that was embroidered with scarlet rosebuds and had little blue satin bows, the color of her eyes, and blue ribbons that fluttered gaily when she ran. Her red-gold hair had been brushed until it sparkled with fire in the sunlight. Looking down from his seat on the stallion at the perfection of her small, oval face with its alabaster complexion, her cheeks flushed with excited anticipation, Don Lorenzo thought he had never seen anything in all his life so fair, and his heart swelled with a love, almost painful in its intensity.

And so, that spring it became perhaps María's greatest pleasure to be lifted up to her father where he sat astride the red stallion; to sit on the soft cushion that was fixed for her comfort to the heavy Mexican saddle, and to feel his strong arm around her, holding her safe. She would sit like a little princess, resting her small, soft hands on the dark, powerful one that held the reins and lean back into his chest, resting her head with its long, red-gold tresses, as fiery as the stallion's own glossy mane, close to his throat.

She would love it when the stallion galloped, and would urge her father to make him go faster, and faster. The stallion's mane would ripple in the wind, and her own long hair would be flung up and out, wind-whipping her father's cheeks. And then, with her mouth just slightly open to taste the rushing air, she would give herself over to the rhythmic rise and fall of the stallion's stride; until those gentian eyes, that mirrored Heaven, closed, and she would be transported into the ecstasy of that expansive realm, floating on the wind like a soaring bird.

Perhaps it might not have been too fanciful to imagine that Beauty and the Beast had reincarnated, for there were those among the simple country folk who looked up at them when they rode by and who, for reasons that they would not have been able to articulate, crossed themselves and prayed to the Holy Mother to take care of the little one. For just as María was the epitome of the fairest of fairy-tale princesses, even so it could be felt that there was something cruel about the dark man whose strong arm held her so tightly. De la Cruz, in all his swarthiness, was a powerfully handsome man, but one in whom there seemed to burn a barely-contained, animal rage. There was a hint of something violent in the flashing smile that showed so many of his strong, white teeth and the full, red lips that looked as if surely they were painted; and the ardent flame that blazed out of the black eyes signaled a sensuality that would enjoy the outermost reaches of pleasure and passion—and pain.

It was on one such bright morning that María was lifted up to join her father for, as it would turn out, the last time. She wore a white sun-dress with all manner of strange creatures, fish and birds and bright flowers, appliquéd around the border of the skirt. Her father had bought it for her as a gift on his last visit to Mexico City, and it was her favorite dress.

Just as they were about to ride off, de la Cruz called out to Roberto, the gardener, to fetch the Winchester and shot belt that he had left in his study. This was brought and duly fastened to the saddle, and then the two horses with their riders, and the one small passenger, set off for the furthest grazing pastures that were bounded along the north side of the rancho by the river, and in the east by the tall pole-fence that ran for almost a mile just short of, and parallel to, the wooded foothills.

As they cantered over the open range, de la Cruz saw with satisfaction that all the work that he had ordered to be done was well underway. He raised his hat to Paco Castillo, the mayordomo, and the line of sweating ditch-diggers.

"How's it going, Paco?" he called out, reining in the restless stallion.

"Going well. We should be finished by the end of the week."

Paco removed his hat and mopped his sweating forehead. The men in the ditch did not look up.

De la Cruz was one of the parciantes, a member shareholder of the governing body, and he was not popular. Often he would overrule the mayordomo's authority, and the men would be made to go over a day's work with no extra remuneration. It was always difficult finding a work team for the Rancho de Las Palomas.

"Make sure they clear all the willow and grass in the bottom section. Last year it clogged up and broke the bank in the lower pasture."

Paco raised a hand, as if in acknowledgement, but he did not look up. The two riders moved on.

Continuing up the rise in the direction of the foothills, they stopped in the nearby grazing lands for de la Cruz to admire the herd of prize Herefords. He had been the first in the district to replace the more conventional Longhorns with the sturdy, white-faced breed, and already their progeny were taking all the awards in the local shows. The more conservative ranchers had been doubtful about his decision, but now had to admit that what they had thought to be a risky venture had paid off.

"Never be afraid of the future, Diego. She is like a young mistress: fresh, fertile and full of energy, challenging us to visit places we have never known. With such a woman we do not grow old. We feel the stirring in our loins. Our blood is young again. We are invincible. We go forward again, challenging life like young men, only stronger. We go forward like warriors: like gods."

Diego Sanchez said nothing. He was a devout Catholic, a faithful husband, and he worked long and hard during the day. He didn't want anyone to disturb his night's rest, not even a beautiful woman, and especially not anyone with all that energy, and he had no desire to visit 'those places', whatever or wherever they might be. His wife's ample and extremely comfortable body was what he enjoyed after a hard day's work. But he did not want to seem rude, and so to sidestep the issue he pointed to a young heifer, a yearling, who was attempting to lock her small, stubby horns with those of a young bull calf.

"Now, that one we must keep. She's a beauty! Just look at that conformation! Look at the depth of chest! She will take all the prizes from north to south."

They turned their horses and headed towards the foothills. The stallion was eager to run, and kept snatching at the bit. De la Cruz kept him tightly reined, and rebuked him with the spurs.

"We'll run when I say so." The stallion flicked back an ear at the sound of his voice, but gave obedience to his rider.

"Oh, please, Papá! Can't we let him run?" María pleaded. "There is just so much space, and wind, and light. It is just the right sort of place to let him out. Please, Papá!"

And so de la Cruz gave the stallion his head.

"Meet us in the north corner!" he shouted to Diego, as the red stallion leapt forward like a flame driven by a strong gust of wind.

He galloped as if trying to outrun his shadow. The strong hooves reached out, slashing at the earth and reaching out again, leaving in their wake a trail of dust and the sound of thunder. His head, with its flaring nostrils, thrust forward into the space that opened up in front of him; his muscled neck strained forward, his ears flattened against his skull and the long, red mane and tail streamed out behind him.

María could hardly breathe for the wind that snatched her breath away.

Wind-tears sprang from the corners of her eyes, streaked swiftly across her cheeks and were instantly gone. She reached up both her little-girl arms like an Indian warrior riding into battle, secure in the knowledge that her father held her fast, and let out long, high-pitched war-cries that were torn out of her mouth by the wind and floated away over the hills. Her soul, like a wild bird, flew across the land.

It was just as they cleared the last rise that de la Cruz saw the elk.

She had heard the sound of hooves, and her head was up and turned in their direction: alert. When she saw the horse and rider, she took off towards the river, trotting with a long, springy stride that was deceptively fast, circling around and away from them. De la Cruz saw that she would be in gun range for only a few more seconds.

He reined the stallion in to a brutal halt; reached for the rifle; brought it swiftly around, raised and cocked it in one swift and practiced action; took careful aim, made difficult by the impatient dance of the stallion, whose blood was up—and fired.

María would never forget that moment, or the following sequence of events.

Everything happened so fast, and yet it was for her as if someone had stretched time out, like a rubber band, into a line of slow, frame-by-frame pictures, sharply focused and minutely detailed.

She saw the long, dark length of the rifle's barrel lift past her right cheek; saw the sun glinting off the polished smoothness of it. She heard the deafening explosion of the one shot, and simultaneously felt the stallion rear and wheel away to the left.

She saw the gun fall: out and away from them.

She felt her father's arm about her tighten, and saw the other hand pull the stallion's head around sharply to the right, until she thought the neck might break.

She saw the running elk give a strange leap, even as it ran; saw it hang, motionless, in mid-air—for an instant: an eternity.

And then she saw it go down.

She felt her father kick the stallion's sides; the sudden leap forward. She saw the distance between them and the elk compact as the place where she had fallen rushed towards them. She saw the stallion's head drawn back, and felt the short, muscle-wrenching jolts as her father reined him to a violent halt. She felt the arm around her release its hold as he swung down from the saddle. Then she felt herself being lifted, her hand just touching the bright blood from the spurs on the stallion's heaving flank as she was lowered to the ground.

Without waiting, she set off at a run towards the place where the elk had gone down. She heard her father call out to her, but she paid no heed, and ran swiftly through the tall grass until she came to the fallen creature.

The elk was attempting to rise. Her head strained forward over the one front leg as if, by some invincible act of will, she could make the body ignore what had occurred, and answer the urgent and instinctual command to survive.

But the death was already in her. Already all the signals that had directed her vital life were shutting down. As María approached, she turned her dark face with the large, soft eyes towards her: and grew still. Pink foam bubbled from mouth and nostrils as she struggled to breathe.

María saw the wound in her side, and the scarlet blood pumping out onto the earth. Without thinking, she sank down into the grass next to the elk cow, and as the slow head began to fall, she caught it in her arms and moved closer to hold it in her lap. She felt the head go limp, suddenly heavy, and watched the light glaze out of the large, liquid eyes. She had never witnessed death before; had never seen how one moment there could be a presence, an intelligence, a being-ness, lit from within, and the next moment, only an unholy stillness: and dense form.

She stared down, willing the wound to close; willing the light to return to the eyes, but it had gone. Tears streamed down her face as she leant forward, holding and rocking the beautiful, dead head in her lap. She did not make a sound. Only the silent tears fell down her cheeks and onto the face that lay cradled in her arms.

It was at this point that she heard her father's voice.

"Stand away, María!" he shouted as he came running up. "She may be dangerous!"

She did not give any sign that she had heard him, and he was about to repeat the command when he was distracted by the arrival of Diego on the black mare. The foreman dismounted and walked over to the small group. He stood in silence, looking down at the dead elk and the small, weeping girl.

He looked at de la Cruz, and raised an eyebrow.

No one spoke. The world withdrew, leaving a strange silence. Only the hypnotic rocking of the child, and the soft wind sighing through the grasses.

It was de la Cruz who broke the spell.

"Come away, María," he said, and reached out to take her arm. She did not turn her head, or even appear to notice the outstretched hand.

"Don't touch me!" was all she said.

For the first time in his adult life, de la Cruz was completely at a loss. He glanced towards Diego, but the foreman had his eyes fixed on the ground, and was not about to offer any advice.

What a mess, Diego thought. What a completely unnecessary, brutal, barbaric act. Stupid!

He stepped forward, and bent down close to María.

"It's all right, María," he said gently. "I just want to take a look."

It was as he had suspected: the cow's udder was full. Looking more closely, he ascertained that she had recently calved. It was an early birthing, and she had become separated from the herd. She would have to wait some days before the young one was strong enough to follow her on the steep migration, up into the mountains. This explained why she hadn't headed off into the shelter of the wooded area. She had been leading them away from her calf.

Diego stood up.

"There is a calf somewhere, over there; probably only a day or two old."

He indicated with his arm an area some distance away.

"We won't see it unless we search for it. It will keep its head down, and it won't move, even if we step right up to it."

He turned to address María.

"When the mother sets them, they don't move until she returns. If predators come, she will draw them away from the calf; run them right off their feet, and then circle back to her young. And it won't have moved a whisker."

Hearing this, María gently released the elk's head, and laid it to rest in the soft grass. She stood up. The scarlet stain on the white, little-girl dress shocked the men. They stared at her. She ignored her father, but turned to Diego, her hands held out beseechingly.

"Will you help me find him, Diego?" she asked.

"What nonsense, María," her father blustered, trying to regain command of the moment. "We could walk about all day, and never find him. It is far better not to interfere in these matters. Let nature sort it out."

María whirled around to face her father: two spots of scarlet flushed her cheeks, her small face was white with anger and her entire body quivered with rage.

"Oh no, father! It is you who have interfered! It is you who killed the mother. And I am going to find the calf and take him home and raise him, and Diego is going to help me!"

She was about to turn away when, as an afterthought, she added,

"And I will not tell Mamá what has happened today!"

De la Cruz was silenced.

Diego turned away to hide the flash of admiration that he knew would be evident in his eyes.

He looked at the small, furious child with respect and wonder: that such extraordinary authority should rest in one so young; that such a little chit of a thing should stand up to this powerful man. And who could not feel some measure of satisfaction in seeing a ruthless man so neatly checked—especially one who was accustomed to wield his power to the detriment of others; one so accustomed to getting his own way? And here was a little girl, who in an elegant thrust had revealed his Achilles heel, and had negotiated her own way with such accomplished mastery.

¡Viva María! he thought.

De la Cruz was beaten, and he knew it, but he didn't know quite what he was feeling: pride at his small daughter's power of command, for he was enough of a sharp negotiator to recognize the skill when he saw it; amazement that one so young could be so sly; or anger that his decision had been thwarted. To regain the upper hand, he began directing the operation to find the young calf.

"Diego, you go to the far corner where the fences meet. I will go across to the hillside."

The two men remounted, each taking opposite sides of a wide area in which they thought the calf might be hidden.

María said she would like to walk. She didn't move in the same methodical path, sideways and back, chosen by the men. She walked in a straight line towards the trees, trying to sense where the cow might have hidden her calf.

Just short of the grove of junipers and small piñón she stopped. In front of her the hills rose up towards the mountains like soft, green waves. María stood still and waited.

Nothing moved: there was no interruption in the evenness of the grasses, or in the flowing undulations caused by the wind. She stood quietly for a while, not moving, and then, as quietly, she sank down until little more than the crown of her head showed above the heads of tall grass. Very softly, she began to sing.

It was the lullaby that she had heard Encarnación, Roberto's wife, sing to her infant son.

It was a song that had come from the old country, Mexico, hundreds of years before, and had remained unchanged, handed down from mother to daughter, across the generations. It had made that long, painful journey, with its many challenges and dangers, to New Mexico in the late fifteen hundreds. It had been the first and last resource of those women of long ago. It was both a lullaby and a lament; a comfort to a fretful infant, and a source of solace for a mother grieving the loss of a child. It was a song that called on the Holy Mother to bring her strength, compassion and comfort to all who had need of it. It was this song that María now sang, over and over, until her voice merged with the wind.

About twenty paces away from where María sat, an ear flicked.

The song did not falter, but very slowly María moved toward the calf. Moved, and sat still. Moved again, and again waited. She made no sound. Only the song grew softer, until it was little more than a breath.

And then she saw him. He was watching her. Neither of them moved.

María was in no hurry to attract the attention of the men. Slowly she wriggled her way down into the grass until she was lying on her stomach, facing the calf, entirely hidden from view.

Diego

It became a familiar sight on the Rancho de Las Palomas to see María, followed by a goat and a small, spotted elk calf, walking around the stables and the nearby paddocks. Diego had managed to acquire the goat from a nearby farmer. She was a rangy, white creature with particularly satanic, yellow eyes, whose kid had been born dead. She arrived at the rancho with udders so engorged with milk that she was more than willing to nurse the small orphan.

Diego had asked the farmer to bring the still-born kid with the goat, and now María watched as he removed the pelt and fixed it over the neck and back of the elk calf.

"He doesn't look at all like a baby goat," she said.

"She needs to nurse somebody soon with all that milk. She won't mind how he looks," Diego chuckled. "It's what he smells like to her that matters. This way she will pick up the scent of the kid, and she will accept the calf as her own. Tomorrow we can remove the pelt. By then they will have bonded."

María watched in fascination as the introduction was made. The goat's tail did a few rapid twitches as she strained forward to sniff this odd, oversize, spotted progeny, her eyes wide, nostrils distended. But there was no such hesitation from the hungry calf. He could smell the milk, and he moved directly to the udder, pushing his head up to nurse, only to find fresh air. He made another attempt, butting with his head, only to meet with the same result.

Watching this, Diego realized that the goat's udder was too low for the calf. The elk cow's udder would have been considerably higher. Asking María to keep an eye on them, he went round to the feed room and returned with a bale of hay and a small dish of oats. He placed the bale of hay close to the stable wall, and with the oats held out as an incentive, he contrived to have the goat jump onto the bale. Once she was there, he nudged the calf into position for nursing. Then they waited to see what would happen.

"It's working! Oh! Look, Diego! He's drinking."

María jumped up and down with delight, and even Diego had a broad grin on his face.

"They're going to do just fine," he said, and turned to go back to his work.

"Wait, Diego! I must name him."

María ran and dipped her hand in the water-trough. She came back and solemnly marked his forehead with the sign of the cross, and gave him his name.

"Santo."

Privately, de la Cruz had taken Diego aside and demanded to know what plan he had in mind for the elk's future. Diego told him that he had a friend who worked on a large estate up in the Jémez Mountains. He would ask if he could get permission to leave the young stag there in September, as soon as the herd came down from the mountains to winter in the valley. During the rut all the youngsters formed their own small bands, and this presented the best possible chance of his joining one of these groups. No hunting was allowed up there, so he would have time to reclaim his wild instinct and, hopefully, forget his human family.

"We can't set him loose here. He would just come back to the rancho whenever he felt like a hand-out. We have to take him away."

"Better tell her soon, Diego. Give her time to get used to the idea. The sooner the wretch is gone, the better."

De la Cruz turned and walked away, hitting at his boot with his riding-crop; small, angry, staccato blows that seemed to be punctuating his venomous thoughts. How could he tell this man, this peasant who worked for him, that he was jealous of the relationship he had with his eight-year-old daughter? Had he not seen María look up at Diego with an expression of such love and admiration, a look that previously she gave to him? This illiterate farm-hand was taking his daughter away from him. It was all he could do to refrain from hitting the man. Again the stick came down on the riding-boot. He would never have shot the wretched elk if he had known it was going to cause so much trouble. De la Cruz hit out at a clump of rabbit-brush with his riding-crop, sending a shower of bright, yellow flowers flying into the air.

Well, let him break the news to María. Let him be the one to take her to the mountains, and have her watch as her beloved calf is left behind. Maybe that will bring a little disenchantment into the balance. Yes, he thought. That will take care of the elk, and this infatuation with Diego. Feeling suddenly much lighter, he went off to his study, whistling his favorite mariachi tune and swinging the riding crop in front of him like a conductor's baton.

Over the following weeks Diego told María, little by little, his plan for the elk's future. María was distraught.

"But why, Diego? Why can't we build him a big paddock with trees and water, everything he needs?"

Patiently he explained to her that the best they could do for the young stag was to offer him an opportunity to live the life he was intended to live. The shooting of his mother had robbed him of his best chance to do this. Now, as reparation, he and she were going to offer him the very best they could devise, to make up for that.

"The wilderness is in his blood, María. It is imprinted in his brain. He might be happy here for a while, but as soon as he becomes a mature elk, that wilderness will call to him, and he will leave. He must leave. But we would have tamed him. We would have taken away so much of that fine instinct, and his chances out in the wild would not be good."

María's large, blue eyes filled with tears. She said nothing.

"We can't keep him here, María. Sooner or later he would be shot, the way his mother was shot. Ranchers do not like elk coming onto their lands and stealing their fodder. We have to take him far enough away so that he will stay there."

"Where will we take him?"

"There is a place I know, a valley, high up in the Jémez Mountains. There is sweet grazing for the herds who return there each fall. A stream runs through it summer and winter. This is the place where the elk come to spend the winter, protected from the worst of the winter storms. Best of all, no hunting is allowed up there, so the elk are safe from that danger. For the rest, he has with him the only gift his mother could give him, but it is a fine one: his instinct to survive."

And so it was decided. Santo and the goat were turned loose in one of the pastures close to the stables. Diego forbade María to take any food for him or even to call him over to her.

"He has to forget us, María. If you love him, you will do this for him."

So every day María climbed up the rails and hung over the top pole, her chin cupped in her two small hands, dreaming big dreams for the calf; seeing him, brown and sleek, with majestic antlers, running with his herd in this beautiful valley that Diego had described to her. Reluctantly, she would tear herself away when she heard Mercedes call to say that her tutor had arrived for her morning classes.

The advent of a tutor for María was one of the many ways in which de la Cruz sought to keep her close to home, where no unwanted influences would interfere with his plans for her. In time he would choose a suitable husband for his daughter: someone who would live on the estate and help him with its running; someone who would be easy to manipulate.

All María's sisters had attended the local school, but de la Cruz had decided that this would not be satisfactory for his youngest daughter, and so, after much searching and many interviews, a serious young scholar, who needed to earn some money to further his studies, had been employed. María thought he was very stuffy, and she found the mornings under his dry tutelage long and tedious.

As he had promised, Diego took María to the valley. They left early one morning in the old jeep, with a picnic lunch prepared by Mercedes packed into the back. They took the Interstate, and turned off onto the route which took them through the reservations and on up the tortuous, winding climb through thick forest, to the high valley. There they stopped at the look-out point and got out of the car. María stood, breathing in the clean air, feeling her way into the space that opened up in front of her.

Perhaps it is only when we are presented with the magnificence of truly pristine wilderness, that vast space and solitude that turns its fearless gaze ever outward, that we become fully aware of how much we long for it. As María stood looking out over the valley that seemed to stretch itself out, ever wider and further beneath her gaze, she understood fully why they could never keep the young stag on the rancho. What she had always thought of at home as wide-open space she now saw, through comparison with the magnificent vista before her, was small, contained; circumscribed by roads and walls and fences. She knew in that instant, not in any way that she would have been able to articulate, that she had left the safe, familiar world of her childhood forever.

They ate their lunch there, looking out over the wide expanse of grassland, punctuated by small, dome-like hills, each with a fringe of dark trees, and the narrow stream that cut across it.

"There was a volcano here over a million years ago," Diego informed María. "One day it erupted with such force that it blew itself and all the surrounding mountains into the sky, throwing rock and ash for hundreds of miles. We can't see the rim from here, but it lies beyond those domes. It is all that is left of the volcano. The valley is actually a caldera, a vast, volcanic basin."

"Will there be other elk there when Santo arrives?" María asked Diego on their return journey, as he negotiated the sharp curves of the steep road.

"It will be the start of the rutting season, when all the bulls compete for the right to breed, and you can hear their bugling echoing about the mountains. It is the most thrilling mating call you can imagine, and it carries for miles and miles on the wind; a challenge to other bulls in the area. The mountains ring with the sound of it.

"This is a good time to take Santo there. It is the time when all the young calves leave their mothers and form themselves into small bands. What we must hope for is that Santo will join one of these bands, because he will be able to learn from the others, all about the new terrain."

They drove back in silence. María, tired from the long day, fell asleep, her head resting on Diego's arm. He pulled her closer and placed his arm in its rough, leather sleeve around her, holding her safely against his chest. Now and then, as he drove through the late afternoon, he would look down at the little-girl form curled up against him and the wild, unruly mass of red, wind-blown hair that fell over her sleeping face, and wonder just what the future held, not only for the elk, but also for this passionate child.

The Valley

Snow had been falling in the mountains all morning.

As the jeep and horse-box pulled off the road and onto the rough track that ran along one side of the caldera, the clouds cleared, and bright autumn sunlight slanted across the snow-covered valley. In places the wind had blown the snow into thick drifts, deep banks that lay snow upon snow, still carrying the memory of sky in the blue shadows that defined them. With the exception of the dark line that the stream carved through the blanket of whiteness as it threaded its way across the valley, there was no mark or footprint anywhere to be seen.

As the jeep wound its way around one of the hillsides, gaining a little in elevation, Diego, who was searching the blank vista in front of them through binoculars, caught sight of an irregularity in the whiteness. As they cleared the small rise, a slight movement alerted him: an antlered head had turned fractionally, causing the covering snow to fall, and simultaneously the irregularity became a small herd, less than half a mile away. The elk had heard the sound of the vehicle, and now they could see it. They rose, shedding the covering of camouflaging snow, and stood, all heads turned to face them. Diego drove on a few hundred yards to where the ground leveled out, and there he brought the vehicle to a halt.

He turned to face María.

"Well! This is it."

María, her small face white and tense, nodded, unable to speak.

"Do up your sheepskin, then. It will be very cold outside."

He got out of the jeep and went to open the side door of the horse-box for José.

"Everything all right?"

The boy nodded. "I've put the collar on the goat and clipped on the lunging-rein," he said. "I think we should let them out as soon as possible now that we have stopped. The calf is getting restless."

María joined them. Even with the sheepskin buttoned and the hood pulled snugly around her face, the cold was making her eyes water and the tip of her nose turn pink. She tucked her hands deep into the sleeves.

José entered the horse-box through the side door. He removed the pole that they had slid behind the elk's rump, and then sat back, holding onto the goat. Diego went round to the back, released the bolts that held the ramp in place and lowered it to the ground. Then he stepped away and walked back to stand beside María.

The elk didn't move.

The goat, feeling the stream of cold air pour in and sensing an escape close at hand, began to bleat noisily and butt the walls with her head. Receiving no satisfaction from this activity, she pulled against the restraining collar in an effort to leave her small prison, so that José was hard-pressed to hold her. All her frantic bleating, and the thrashing and scrabbling of her hooves on the metal floor, caused the elk to start and to try and turn around, but the box had been made purposely too narrow for this.

He reared and plunged, kicking out at the padded sides until, eventually, with all the beating and battering, he managed to back himself down the ramp and stood, at last, outside on the snow, his flanks heaving, legs trembling, snorting his white breath into the cold air. He stood with his head raised, searching the wind, his whole body tense, quivering, surveying the unfamiliar, open space all around him. Then he lowered his head, pawed at the snow and smelt it. Raising his head once more, he took a few steps forward, facing down the valley. He stood motionless, his nostrils flared, receiving the scents carried on the wind. His ears flicked forward. He had picked up the scent of the elk herd. Then he saw them.

Now!—thought Diego. What happened now would determine the elk's future.

He folded his arms across his chest, feeling the sudden quickening of his heartbeat.

The young elk turned his head to where the goat was still bleating in the horse-box. He stood as if undecided. Diego could feel María's grip on his hand tighten.

"Will he go, Diego?" she whispered.

"Shh. Wait."

Quite suddenly the elk turned, and set off at a brisk trot in the direction of the herd. They watched him make his way across the vast expanse of snow until he was some small distance from it. There he paused before turning and moving away in a westerly direction, heading for the safety of the wooded slopes on one of the small domes.

"He's going to keep his distance," said Diego. "Wise decision. He's not looking for trouble, but he knows he needs them."

María glanced up at him questioningly. To allay her fears he replied:

"The season has just begun. Soon there will be more elk, and more bulls, and then the youngsters will leave the herd to get away from the frenzy of the rut. Then he may join one of their groups."

He looked down into María's face.

"He's going to be fine."

The young elk was still just in sight. María strained her eyes, as if wanting through her looking to hold on to him, but then he entered a patch of forest and was gone. Only then, only when she was perfectly sure that she could not see him anywhere on the small hillside, did she turn to Diego, bury her face in his rough leather jacket and burst into sobbing tears. He picked her up and, cradling her head on his shoulder, he took her over to the jeep and climbed in beside her. He reached for the sheepskin cover, wrapped it around her and sat holding her close until the sobbing stopped.

"There, María," he said drawing away. "We'll have some of the tea that Mercedes packed for us."

He poured two steaming cups, and gave one to her.

"I'm going to take this to José, who must be half frozen. I'll be back soon, and we can all have something to eat. You get yourself warm."

María sipped the tea. She suddenly felt very tired. She had woken early, not wanting the day to start: wanting to think up some alternative to releasing Santo into a place where she knew she would never see him again. She tip-toed into the kitchen and found that Mercedes was already in the kitchen, was busy filling a picnic basket with thermoses of tea and cocoa and food for lunch. She had made all María's favorite sandwiches.

When Mercedes saw the tense, little face, she went to her and folded her big, warm arms around her.

"He is going to grow big and strong in that beautiful valley, mi querida; there is no better place for him. And you are giving this to him. Write that into your heart, María. You may think he knows nothing about this, but there are places where all our acts are written. He will grow to be a beautiful elk, and live the way he is destined to live; and somewhere you will be carried along with him in his life."

Diego found José being led about by a rather disgruntled goat. He took the lunging-rein from him and suggested that he go and sit with María. He loaded the goat into the horse-box, gave her the uneaten alfalfa and locked the door securely before joining the others in the jeep. They drank and ate in silence. When they were done, Diego stowed the picnic basket, started the engine, turned the jeep carefully and began the slow drive out of the valley.

María turned to kneel on the seat so that she might see out of the window, wanting to fill her eyes with the memory of the day. Snow was starting to fall once more, soft flurries lighter than breath. As she looked out, they began to grow heavier and thicker.

It was when the landscape was all but obscured by the swirling, white flakes that she saw him.

He was running on an elevated stretch of ground where, miraculously, a ray of light, shining through the falling snow, lit him like a spotlight. Her eyes hurt with the brightness of it, but she didn't blink. She knew for certain it was Santo, although he seemed to have become much bigger, and she noticed with delight that he had grown a full rack of antlers. Something in the way that the light struck these twin branches made them look like gold, and indeed his whole head seemed to be illuminated by a golden halo.

She was about to draw Diego's attention to this when the snow closed in once more, and the vision vanished. She said nothing, but sat for the whole return journey, leaning against Diego's arm with her eyes closed.

The Bullfight

On the frequent occasions when Don Lorenzo and Catherine entertained guests at the Hacienda, it was customary, after dinner, for Don Lorenzo to regale them with stories of places he had visited and events he had witnessed on his many travels through South America.

On one such evening a heated discussion developed about beauty. One of the guests had stated that beauty and death could never be reconciled; that death, in all its forms, was ugly and abhorrent. The argument had moved this way and that, in spite of Catherine's attempts to bring the conversation round to more comfortable subjects. Finally de la Cruz protested that his guest's perception of death was extremely limited; that it failed to take into account that it was death, and death alone, that brought beauty and meaning into life; that it was in fact the awareness of the presence of death in every moment, the awareness of its utter finality, that created beauty.

"I challenge you to illustrate your point, sir!"

"Very well," de la Cruz replied. "I shall tell you about a bullfight."

He lit a cigar, and puffed on it to make sure it drew well. When he was satisfied that it was evenly lit, and that he had the attention of everyone in the room, he began his story.

"I have been to many bullfights in Mexico," he disclosed, "but the greatest bullfight I ever saw was in Mexico City in the late thirties. What a magnificent fight! Unforgettable!"

Quite deliberately, he avoided meeting Catherine's eyes.

"It was late afternoon, hot and sultry: unusual for that time of year. The heat hung thickly in the air. There was no wind; not a breath. It was as if the evening, the night, the very air was waiting for that other landscape to open and offer itself up to us."

He paused to take a long, slow draw on his cigar.

"The sun was low on the horizon. Soon it would begin to stain the sky crimson above us. There must have been a garden close by, for a sweet fragrance filled our nostrils. We could feel the tension mounting, the way it does before a storm; and something else, something over and above the usual sense of excitement. There was a feeling of—expectancy: an electric charge that was palpable, flowing like a river through the spectators.

"We had managed to obtain the best seats, close to the ring, so close we would be able to see the sweat on the men's faces; smell the blood. The trumpets sounded. The matador, a Mexican of barely twenty years, well-known for his artistry, his audacity and recklessness, was to fight a young bull."

He turned to address one of the guests.

"One is fortunate to find such courage, elegance and skill in a bull-fighter, more so in one so young, for many work only for the money. But not this one! He was in love, you see: in love with the bull. That is what makes for greatness. What a brilliant display of art and courage the young man gave us that day."

De la Cruz ignored the anxious glances his wife was giving him.

"Bullfighting is not a sport—you must know this. It alters the way you view it. It has its roots in a dark and ancient religion."

He looked slowly round the table at each guest as if to add emphasis to the statement.

"The bull entered the ring with a rush. The crowd rose to its feet, shouting '¡Toro! ¡Toro!' The bull was swift.

"There are stages to a bullfight." He looked around the table. "First the picadors must do their work to weaken the bull's neck muscles. They are the men on horseback. The horses must wear protective padding and be blind-folded, you know. Then the banderillero, the matador's assistant, must place the dowels high in the bull's withers until the morillo, that great hump of muscle rising from his neck, is weakened further, and his head lowers. This is the key to bullfighting."

He saw the look of inquiry.

"Oh, yes. This muscle guards the place between the shoulders where the sword must go in. If the muscle is raised—as it is when the bull is aroused—then this will not be possible." He paused.

"And then, with the blood streaming down the bull's powerful shoulders, it is time for the matador."

There was not a sound in the room. Catherine's face was very pale. One of the ladies had a hand over her mouth.

De la Cruz was enjoying the horror of his audience.

"The young man was beautiful: tall, lean and so proud; so magnificently arrogant. A face and a body made for love—yes! All the ladies adored him."

He smiled at the women, who were looking nervous.

"They threw blood-red roses to him, until a carpet of scarlet ringed the arena. And he loved it! From time to time he would turn his back on the bull, pick up a rose, lift it to his lips and bow to some fetching señorita. And the crowd would scream. He seemed not to know the meaning of fear. That is irresistible to a woman, you know."

His eyes flashed again at the ladies.

"But not a fool, this one. He knew what he was about. He knew about the shadows that haunt the bullring."

His audience was fascinated in spite of themselves.

"There are two shadows that the matador must learn about, and learn well."

He paused for dramatic effect.

"The one that throws a wall of shade across the bright sand, and which is the undoing of many a bullfighter; the other," he drew on his cigar, "the other is that dark wind that lifts the coleta, the black pigtail, and caresses the nape of the matador's neck."

The guests shuddered. They could feel the hair stand up on their arms. Noticing their reaction, de la Cruz nodded.

"You can feel it too? Even now? Ah, yes! This tells us that death is possible. The Duende's breath is cold.

"And didn't he watch his father die for the very lack of respect for the power of such shadows? He learned on that day, as his father's lifeless body was carried from the ring, how unforgiving the shadow is of an instant of carelessness.

"There is geometry to a bullfight, a pattern: did you know that? The matador, before he does anything dramatic, must learn the bull's orbit, and establish his own. Night and day lie at his feet. He must know where he must make the crossing. And so it was not through foolhardiness that time and time again he had the crowd on their feet—some shouting for him not to take such risks; the rest urging him on."

He paused to remove the ash very carefully from the end of his cigar.

"But what measured elegance. What skill! Such artistry is not taught; can never be taught. It is in the blood. Such matadors are born with the greatness already in them."

He turned to regard his challenger.

"There's the beauty, sir."

He took a deep draught of wine.

"But the young bull was quick and brave; learning fast! Ah!" he said, noting their astonishment. "You did not know that! He is not the blood-enraged brute you may think him to be. He is bred, from an aristocracy of bulls; a long, pedigreed line of bulls famous for their bravery and endurance. He is bred for one purpose only: to fight with courage. It is, if you will, his destiny. And he only has this one chance. One chance! There is beauty in that, don't you think? All his life and centuries of breeding for this one day, this hour, when he enters the bullring. Even if he was to win—and occasionally a courageous bull will wound or kill—he will never fight again."

The faces looked at him in surprise.

"He will never fight again, because he will have learned too much."

He smiled at their disbelief.

"Oh, yes! He will be far too dangerous for even the finest matador to fight. So this is his hour. He must learn quickly the nature of his opponent. He must learn the nature of this fight. He must learn not to be predictable."

He paused again, as if visualizing the bull.

"But there you have it!" He smacked his free hand down on the table. "That is where instinct is so magnificent. It is innate. He does not have to think; nothing so slow; so imperfect. Thought distracts us. But instinct! It is so swift! It is not separate from the act. He is not fighting. He is the fight! God! It is magnificent to witness it!"

De la Cruz deliberately refused to acknowledge the desperate signals Catherine was sending him.

"He was a fine bull; one of the bravest I have seen. You would not believe the speed of those charges, the agility of his turns; the restrained beauty of his moves; like a dancer. He seemed not to notice the punishment he received, but came back, again and again, driven by a superb rage.

"And then there was the stillness of the man. You could hear the gasps of indrawn breath at the beauty of those slow veronicas; that slow, sculpted cape, the muleta, lifting and turning, with all the elegance and grace of a flamenco dancer, and the straight, proud posture of the young man; the arrogant fearlessness, as if he were challenging not only the bull, but death itself."

De la Cruz turned to his challenger again. "There you are, sir. Death and beauty in the ring together. Inseparable."

The man returned his stare, but said nothing.

"This image of artistry, set against the huge instinctual force of the enraged creature—that moment when time is arrested—that is what brings one back, again and again, to the bullring."

With his eyes half-closed he turned his head slightly, as if looking back into that day, again revisiting the scene.

"If there is fear in the matador, you can smell it. Did you know that?"

The silent faces stared back at him.

"Ah! You see, the matador must fight not only the bull, but himself. He cannot escape the knowledge of his mortality. He must fight his fear of death, and overcome it: for it is that fear which will kill him, as surely as the bull will. There's the shadow! It is this that lends such pathos to the proceedings. For the bull does not know that he will die. That is what separates us from animals. The bull is free of the burden of such knowledge. He remains focused in the moment. All his energy is fixed on his intent to kill."

He drew on his cigar again, letting the smoke drift slowly out of his mouth.

"But that day there was something else," he continued. "We felt—how can I say it?—a passion I can only describe as reverence. We knew we were witnessing not only a fight to the death, but the essence of life itself. We were lifted out of the world, resurrected into a place, a place inside ourselves. A place we long for."

He paused.

"What an extraordinary evening. I have never felt so alive!"

He flushed and looked around the room, embarrassed that such an admission should have slipped out. He reached for the wine and offered it to each guest before refilling his own glass. Then, back in his chair once more, he drew on his cigar, fussing a little with the evenness of the burn to give himself time to regain his composure.

"He played the bull so close to his body that we saw the blood stain his brocade. And slowly, so slowly the bull, with blood and death in his eye, passed him, brushing against him. I felt the world disappear."

He broke off. Looking up at the attentive faces, he met the eyes of each guest in turn, visiting upon them a look of such intensity that they felt themselves disappear into his fierce world.

Catherine sat stiffly upright in her chair, her body turned away from her husband. The blood had drained from her face. She was so pale that the two spots of rouge with which she had high-lighted her elegant cheek-bones stood out unnaturally against the whiteness, giving her face the look of a painted mask. In her lap, out of sight, her hands twisted the white table napkin into a knot.

De la Cruz did not look at her, but seeing the guests' attentiveness, he took another deep swallow of the heavy after-dinner wine and leaned back in his chair. He had recovered himself, and was feeling expansive. The hand that held the cigar rested languidly on the arm of the chair, the pungent smoke rising lazily, drawn upward by the heat of the candles that stood in the center of the table. His eyes burned as if something within him were on fire. He was enjoying himself immensely.

"It was a dance, you see, a ritual dance to evoke that presence, that spirit if you will, that we might truly feel the mystery of death. It is said that the Duende haunts the bullring. They say that the poet Lorca—a strange young man by all accounts, but he knew this—the poet Lorca tells us that the Duende loves the rim of the wound and that it will not come unless it knows that death is possible."

At this point Catherine rose to pour herself a glass of water from the jug on the dresser. De la Cruz frowned his irritation at this interruption.

"Yes. Well, we all could feel that dark wind blowing over us, waiting for that moment, waiting for that landscape to open and offer up its dead. And all the time the young matador was pulling the bull toward him, winding him around him like a belt until the bull fell to his knees. And he just walked away! Such audacity! Proud, you know! Young and proud."

He paused.

"But we knew death was waiting. It was there, you see, in the wings; waiting. We could feel it. Of course, it was certain that we would see death that afternoon, but we could not be certain—whose death—it would be. The suspense was tangible, like a presence hanging over all of us. It is at times like this, when the black wind blows over the bull's horns, that we know what it means to shudder."

He puffed for a while in silence.

"It is an art, you see." He looked at the silent array of guests.

"And it is an art where the artist must risk his life, and it is a risk not taken lightly. If a matador—anyone, for that matter—has been touched by the Duende, if only once, then he must forever engage his shadow. There are many who do not have the heart for it. Many matadors die; or if they do not die, they suffer horrible wounds, and lose their nerve. Then they are finished. For a fight to be worth seeing, both the bull and the matador must be brave. If the matador has not learned to put aside his fear and fight out of a cool, detached space, he will be clumsy; make mistakes, and kill badly. If the bull is cowardly, he will not take the punishment, and he will be reluctant to fight. Then it is just a business of drawing him out of his querencia, away from that place in the ring where he feels most secure; of forcing him to his death. It is not artistic, and it is really not worth the time it takes."

Seeing the look of shock on their faces, he added:

"Oh, yes. There are bad kills, which end up as little more than butchery; but there are also artists, matadors who have perfected the art of killing, where the sword will enter cleanly, and come out slowly as the bull, dead on his feet, passes by, his horns only inches from the man's body.

"A matador must love to kill, you see, or he will never be great. He must love to kill, the way a fine musician loves his music."

He nodded as if in full recognition of this fact. All around the table, with the exception of Catherine, horrified eyes were fixed on him.

"And then there is the agony of the bull, just before death. This is the moment when he is most dangerous. He is tired. The picas and the banderillas have done their work, and that great neck muscle is weakened by the punishment it has taken. His head is low. There is a cold rage in the bloodshot eye which is fixed on the man. Nothing will distract him now. Now he knows who he must kill. The blood that stains his shoulder is no less scarlet than the matador's cape.

"And there is something else: something that brings tears to the eyes. There is beauty, you see. And an arrogance that takes your breath away. And something sacred. It is the stillness of that small figure. He is alone now. Alone with the bull. And then there is the splendid courage of the bull, thundering in to meet his death like some kind of pagan god. It is as if we were being shown how to die—magnificently."

He paused.

"But on this day, when the matador took up his position for the kill, we felt a thrill, as if something else had entered the ring; a presence. '¡Duende!' We all felt it."

Fascination was printed on the rapt faces of the listeners.

"I was on my feet. The young man, little more than a boy, had placed himself so close to the bull that we could feel the intimacy between them; an intimacy, a fusion of wills in the presence of death.

"It seemed to me that time collapsed: the passage of it became slow, like a film shown in slow motion, frame by frame; and haunting, as if the moment was drawn out, the way it sometimes is in a dream, where in that slowness there is both movement and stillness, time and no time. And silence. Just the perfect grace and elegance of the man, and the deadly intention of the bull. I will never forget that day."

Catherine had shut her eyes. Her back was stiff and straight.

"It is possible that the banderillas were not correctly placed, or that the picadors had not weakened the neck muscle sufficiently; but the young bull had not wasted his time in the ring either. He too had been learning. In the final suerte, that final manoeuver as the matador moved in to position himself for the kill, the crowd, unusually silent, rose to its feet.

"Surely he was too close. We held our breath.

"We watched the sword go in, perfectly placed. It was an act of unsurpassable beauty."

Seeing the look of relief on the faces of the guests, de la Cruz raised his hand to indicate that this was not the end of the story. He continued.

"But the matador had not reckoned with the depth of the bull's instinct to kill, or with his stamina. It was the last chance the young man would take in the ring. At that crucial moment, as he reached over the horns and slid the sword in cleanly, the bull raised his left horn, up and outwards, and through the young man's bowels. The bull went down, dead, even as his horn penetrated the man's body. The crowd went wild."

There was a flush on de la Cruz' face. Seeing the look on his listeners' faces, he read their question.

"Oh, yes. The boy died a few hours later," he confirmed. "But what a magnificent display of courage!"

No one spoke. They stared at the man at the head of the table. One of the candle flames dipped and guttered out.

Finally de la Cruz turned to address his challenger.

"Is not that, sir, truly the marriage of death and beauty?"

There was no reply. His audience was shocked. The telling had been so vivid, so passionate: it was as if they had been there. They could almost smell the blood. The ladies looked pale enough to faint.

Not long afterwards all the guests left.

As the last guest departed and the great door closed, Catherine turned to her husband with a look of disgust, unusual for her.

"You have ruined the evening with your blood-thirsty story," she said vehemently. "You and your love of killing, and death! Brute!" She spat out the last word, and turning abruptly, she left the room.

De la Cruz poured himself a whisky. He sat for a long time, sipping the strong drink, reviewing the events of the evening and in particular his account of the bullfight. Something had come alive in him in the telling. He could see the bullring, as clearly as if he were there; smell the heat and sweat of that sultry evening—and the blood.

"God!" The thought, if it was a thought, just hung there.

He reached for a cigar and then, changing his mind, put it back in the humidor. He did not understand what was happening to him; the huge frustration that had suddenly seized him: but he felt, deep inside himself, some kind of desperate rage that brought him to the edge of tears.

He dismissed the weakness almost immediately, gulped down the last of the whisky, and placing the glass very precisely back on the silver tray, he left the room and went to bed.

Salvador's Muse

It was Wednesday afternoon. Santiago Fuentes, musician and music teacher, was sitting in the front pew of the church, sorting through sheets of music.

He and his son Salvador met the children of the Las Madres school choir in Father Octavio's church every Wednesday at three o'clock for an hour's choir practice, in preparation for the following Sunday's service.

Salvador, at the age of twelve years, was a handsome youth with deep-set eyes and a full, sensual mouth which spoke eloquently of his passionate nature. His mother had died giving birth to him, and he had grown up an only child, very close to his father. As such he had known music from the cradle, and was already a proficient musician. On Friday afternoons he would play the organ while his father led the children through the verses, giving the descant parts to a few of the older children whose voices were strong enough to hold the harmony.

In addition to being a gifted musician, Salvador was especially skilled in the making of musical instruments, violins in particular—a craft that was being taught to him by New Mexico's most famous santero, Alejandro Jaramillo, his godfather and his father's closest friend. He was a natural.

"You have an instinct for wood, Salvador."

The boy smiled.

Alejandro often noted how, when God saw fit to rob an individual of one blessing, he compensated by sending some other talent. Salvador had never known his mother. His father and Alejandro did their very best to make up for this loss, but of course they could never replace a mother's touch. However, he had known a closer relationship with his father than many sons ever experience. In addition, he had been held in the extraordinary embrace of his godfather's very unique brand of eccentric spirituality.

Both men had devoted themselves to encouraging the development of Salvador's many talents, teaching him everything they knew. By the time the boy was twelve years old, Santiago had to concede that his son had overtaken him in musical excellence. He hoped that when Salvador finished school, he might be able to afford to send him away to study further, under the tutelage of one of the country's great teachers. In the meantime, he and Salvador worked together in all matters musical, one weekly appointment being with the children's choir in Father Octavio's church.

It was on just such an occasion that María de la Cruz, now nine years of age, made her first appearance at choir practice.

She was brought by her mother, who had long been aware of her daughter's extraordinary voice. She hoped that perhaps María might have the opportunity to develop this gift, an opportunity which had not been afforded her. In some way she felt that if María were to be able to live the life she herself had been denied, it would make up for the painful disappointments to which she had been forced to submit, and finally accept. This would be a beginning, an innocent way in which María might receive, and benefit from, some musical instruction.

Catherine did not inform her husband of this decision—an unusually independent act. Instead she managed to rationalize to herself that she should not trouble him with such small, mundane matters, matters that could be of no consequence to him.

With an unusual show of physical strength and determination she chose to drive María to choir practice herself, a decision which left Roberto speechless.

"Are you sure you don't want me to take you?" he asked her as she climbed into the car, which he had brought round to the front door for her. "It would be a pleasure for me."

She thanked him, but assured him that she was looking forward to having the time alone with María.

They arrived early, and Catherine had a word with Father Octavio, who was attending that day's choir practice because of an upcoming festival in which the choir would be singing.

"How wonderful to see you, Catherine!"

The priest was alarmed to see how pale she had become. He wondered if there was any truth to the rumors he had heard, that there was something not quite right at the Rancho de Las Palomas. Still, it was good to see Catherine out and about for a change, and he invited her to stay and listen to the choir practice.

"I will bring you a cushion. I have never been able to understand why sitting in church should be quite such an ordeal for the buttocks."

He settled Catherine in one of the back pews, where her presence would not distract María from her singing.

It was customary for any newcomer to be asked to sing a short solo portion of a simple and well-known hymn, so that Santiago could assess their voice and decide where they should stand, and where they would sing to best advantage. María was not to be an exception to this, and when the time came for her test she dutifully stepped forward to sing her solo part.

Salvador, having been told that a little girl would be singing, and expecting a small, shy child, played the introductory bars to the hymn very softly and struck the opening chord for the voice.

It was then that María de la Cruz' extraordinary voice was heard in public for the first time.

At the sound of the first pure notes of this voice, a voice that lifted and soared upward as if on wings to fill the chapel, all faces turned towards her and stared.

Santiago froze with his arms raised, unable to believe that the sound that he was hearing was coming from a little nine-year-old girl.

His son Salvador managed to keep playing, although his fingers, and his feet on the pedals, were working almost automatically; for he was leaning out from the organ-bench, straining to see the owner of this wondrous and entirely phenomenal voice that sounded with all the clarity of a silver bell, and which had flown, as if carried by Cupid's arrow, straight into his heart.

He saw a small, fair child with hair that reached down to her waist, a burning mass of reddish-gold locks from which he fancied he saw small, blue sparks leap out and upward like the sparks that fly up from a log fire when it is stirred; a little girl singing her heart out with such passion that her voice filled the church, right up to the rafters, to where the pigeons roosted in the heat of the day. These same began to fly about the church, swooping down to skim the backs of the rough pews, hovering before the altar and then soaring up to the high beams as if carried on the power of her song.

It was in that moment that María turned her head, and saw Salvador staring at her: and it was in that instant, when their eyes met, that the nine-year-old María de la Cruz and Salvador Fuentes, all of twelve, fell in love, and all of Heaven knew it.

From the very first time Salvador heard María sing, he knew that she was to be a part of his destiny. Within a few moments of hearing her extraordinary voice he recognized that she was the muse who would inspire the soul of his music. Although she was still a little girl, barely nine years old, he recognized that she possessed a soul of great radiance, and was gifted with a voice of power and beauty that would have been considered exceptional in an adult, but which in a child was haunting.

In the first instant that their eyes met in the small church, he fell irrevocably in love, not only with the little nine-year-old girl, but with the purity of the soul that dwelt within her.

He became seized with a desire to capture in music the feeling of awe that her singing evoked in him. He began to work like one possessed, often through the night, only falling into bed, exhausted, in the early hours of morning, just as the stars began to fade. He composed a collection of love songs and hymns celebrating the beauty and longing that her singing awakened in him.

At school his teachers complained that he was distracted, but no amount of punishment, or keeping him in after school, seemed to have any effect. They doubted that he even noticed their efforts. He seemed to be living in another world. On every possible occasion that he could, he would find a place where he would not be disturbed, and there would sit for hours with pencil and paper, humming to himself and making furious marks and notes on the page, which later he transposed into his book of music manuscripts.

Santiago, not knowing what had sparked this sudden torrent of creative work, was astonished, and not a little concerned about this passionate, almost obsessive change that had occurred in his son; for the boy scarcely took the time to eat, and had become pale from lack of sleep. He was, however, enough of a musician himself to recognize that there was the beginning of something very fine; signs of an exceptional talent, in his son's compositions.

He heard María, who now attended choir practice regularly, sing some of the songs, but he had certainly not connected his son's new passion to the little girl herself. It would never have entered his head. While acknowledging her extraordinary voice, he had not been struck in the heart the way his son had been. He saw an exceptionally gifted and very beautiful little nine-year-old girl with startling hair.

As the weeks passed by, Salvador grew paler and thinner. He seemed to be consumed by some flame, a fire that allowed him no rest.

"I like what you are doing, son. Like is not the word. This new work of yours is very fine: very original. But what is this frantic haste? Look at you. You must have lost twenty pounds."

But Salvador just muttered, "There is very little time, father; very little time."

"Why do you say this? You are not yet thirteen years old. You have a whole life ahead of you."

"I don't really know, father. I just know there is very little time."

Wednesday afternoon choir practice became a regular part of María's week. When Catherine felt strong enough she drove María there herself, and then went to take tea with friends and to catch up on the latest gossip. Living at the Hacienda, a fair distance from Las Madres, and with her frequent bouts of illness, she was out of touch with all the latest happenings. She enjoyed these afternoons, the intimacy of the conversation with women of her own class who, all too often, experienced the same constraints placed upon them by their autocratic husbands as she endured from de la Cruz. She was hugely grateful for these afternoon teas, for without them she would have had to divulge the real purpose of her weekly visits to town: and she certainly didn't want to bother her husband with all the details of her life, or María's.

On those days when she was indisposed, Diego's son, José, would drive María to the church, drop her there and go visiting. As the years slipped by and Catherine's health deteriorated, it became increasingly José's duty to escort María, one with which he had no argument. He loved the opportunity to escape his other chores and meet with the young bloods of the town.

It was extraordinary that de la Cruz should have remained ignorant of María's weekly attendance of choir practice. It was only when she turned sixteen that it was brought to his attention, when she took part in a church concert.

Salvador had just turned nineteen. His father decided that the time had come for his son to present an evening of sacred music and love ballads, all of his own composition, in the chapel in Santa Fe.

This produced great excitement, for it was the first time that the school choir would be included to sing with the adult choir members. Nothing of this magnitude had ever been suggested, and for a little country church choir to perform in Santa Fe itself was a great honor. Santiago had given his son free rein in deciding what the program should contain.

"Come to me if you feel you need my opinion, but you know more about music than I do these days: certainly this kind of music."

Salvador spent many hours planning the program for the concert. He had to work within the time-frame that he was given and decide who should sing solo parts, and how to vary the evening so that the audience would remain engaged.

At first he felt shy about directing the senior members, telling them what he wanted to achieve; but as work progressed and he felt their admiration for the music he had composed, he relaxed.

The only inclusion in the program that required no decision on his part was the last offering of the evening, a sacred love ballad. This was a duet, unaccompanied by any musical instrument, but which used the choir as a background of sound without words; a rich tapestry of voices that held a steady note at its center, from which two individual voices reached out, seeking to unite above that unwavering central note. María, of course, would sing the female solo voice, and he would sing the tenor.

It would be explained in the program that the love song, although written in the passionate language of love between a man and a woman, was in fact a metaphor for the longing for spiritual union.

Salvador wrote it one Wednesday evening after choir practice.

José was late in fetching María. All the other members had left, and Santiago had gone to prepare for an evening function. Salvador and María were alone for the first time. They were both very aware of this.

"You really don't have to wait, Salvador. I will be quite all right by myself." María knew she was blushing and looked down, trying to hide this fact.

Salvador wanted to tell her that he would wait until the end of time for her. He wanted to say that just standing there, alone with her, was the most wonderful experience of his whole life. He wanted to tell her all the thoughts, all the feelings that were surging inside of him; feelings that he had kept secret from everyone; secrets he had not shared with the other boys when they spoke of their conquests.

Most of all he desperately wanted to touch her.

As it was, when he spoke his voice was hoarse, and he had to clear his throat. He managed only to stutter out a few mundane words.

"It's really no trouble, María."

Inwardly he cursed himself for his clumsiness. What kind of a fool was he? He tried again.

"If you are feeling cold, we could wait inside."

The day was hot. The sun had not yet set. There was no evening breeze. María, although three years younger than Salvador, was just beginning to take the first steps into womanhood. Already she had a woman's intuitive awareness that the intimacy of this moment had thrown Salvador into confusion.

Just as she saw the car, with José driving, turn the corner, she reached out and took Salvador's hand, throwing the young man into a state of rapturous bliss.

"Thank you, Salvador, but I see José coming now. Thank you for waiting with me." She gave his hand a soft squeeze. "I will see you next week?" She looked up at him enquiringly.

Poor Salvador was completely undone. He felt his knees go weak, and was aware of the heat in his face. He was aware that his hand was on fire from her touch; that his heart was beating so hard that she must surely hear it.

And he was aware of something else. He was aware, as they stood there in the doorway of the empty church, that all about them, and above them, and filling the church behind them, angels were singing a glorious music.

"Till next week, then." María smiled at him.

"Till next week," he managed to reply.

Later Salvador couldn't remember how long he stood there, or just when he re-entered the church. Somehow he found his way to the organ, picked up his pen and, while one hand played the first few notes, his other began to write down the words and the notations for the music that filled his head. He worked feverishly until the light faded and he could no longer see the marks on the page.

He raised his head in surprise, but wasting not a moment, lit one of the candles and continued with his labor. At midnight he had completed both words and music for the duet.

He sat in silence, his head bowed. At last he reached out and struck the opening chord. Then, while he held this center chord with his left hand, he introduced the two voices of this ecstatic song of love. He played the whole piece to the end. When the last remnants of sound had faded into the night, he sat motionless with the silence folding itself around him.

A moment or an age later he felt a hand rest on his shoulder. Turning around, he looked up into the astonished face of his father.

The Concert

The advertising for the concert was extensive, and well before opening night tickets for the entire week were sold out. Word spread quickly of the young composer and of the even younger soprano who, it was said, had the voice of an angel.

María's father hastened, as soon as the date was announced, to book the entire two front rows for opening night. It came as a surprise, of course, to hear about María's singing lessons and choir practice, but he fancied no harm could come from singing in a children's church choir. He felt very proud when he heard that she had been picked to sing a solo part.

"Why did you not tell me, Catherine? I might have had some influence with that musician—what is his name again?"

"Santiago Fuentes."

She did not tell him that his patronizing attitude was insulting, or that María was considered to be a gifted child. Let him find out for himself, she thought.

The concert was to be a grand, black tie affair with champagne and especially catered snacks and delicacies, generously donated by Don Lorenzo, and an opening speech by the Governor in the courtyard half an hour before the concert was to begin.

Father Octavio spoke of the concert every Sunday in church, urging all to attend what he promised would be an unforgettable evening of music. He invited Magdalena and Sebastián to accompany him on opening night. There would be a few raised eyebrows, but let them be raised, Father Octavio thought impishly.

The weeks before the opening saw a flurry of activity in the small community. María and Salvador, because they would sing the love duet, were to be dressed as Romeo and Juliet. And so, with much blushing, Salvador had suggested to María that she speak to her mother and see if it would be possible to have a long, white dress of some soft fabric: and would she leave her hair unbraided? He would wear a Romeo shirt and black pants, and carry a red rose.

María had promptly arranged with Roberto, the gardener, to make sure they had a week's supply of perfect blooms.

Eventually the evening of the concert opening arrived. The day had been hot, but the rain that had been threatening to fall all day held off, and the evening was fine, if a little humid.

Just before they left the Hacienda Catherine came to María's room, carrying a piece of jewelry.

"This belonged to my great-grandmother. She gave it to my grandfather when he left France, to come out here. It was all he ever inherited. I want you to have it."

She fixed the dainty, heart-shaped locket around María's slender throat. It was made of silver with a filigree of gold work, a delicate tracery representing two intertwining rose stems that wound their way to the apex, where they united in a single bloom; a crimson ruby set into the gold. The heart-shaped outline of the locket was set with tiny seed pearls, and it hung on a very fine gold chain.

"Oh, Mamá!" María kissed her mother's cheek. "I love it."

Catherine looked at her daughter, aware that María was on the brink of becoming a woman. How beautiful she was. She touched the mass of auburn hair that was identical to her own hair when she was younger, but which, from the time of her marriage, she had not been permitted to wear unbound outside her bed-room. Her husband said only women of questionable breeding, or dubious occupation, let their hair fall loose in public.

It was Catherine who, on looking at her lovely daughter with the long, unbraided hair falling like a shower of fire about her shoulders, suggested that María wear the blue cloak for the drive in to Santa Fe.

"Just in case it should turn cold," she said.

They dropped María off at the vestry, where Señor Fuentes, the choir master, was taking care of things. María, her eyes bright and her cheeks flushed with nerves and excitement, wore the hooded cloak of blue velvet over her long dress. De la Cruz thought she looked very seemly. Both her parents offered her their good wishes and blessings for the evening.

The small courtyard was crowded to capacity when Don Lorenzo and Catherine arrived.

Don Lorenzo made his entrance dramatically, as was his custom, calling out in his rich voice over the heads of the throng of guests to an acquaintance standing across the courtyard.

There was something about his arrogant self-confidence, Catherine thought as she observed the reactions his behavior elicited; something about such a profound sense of entitlement: an authority that demands respect. People are attracted to such virile power, in spite of themselves. They might disapprove of, or dislike, such an ostentatious display of personal power, but they certainly cannot ignore it: nor, in many instances, resist it. Catherine still felt a thrill at the power of it.

All heads turned to look at them, as well they might, when he and Catherine entered the room. They made an extraordinarily handsome couple: he with his steely hair and black eyes, magnificently dressed for the occasion in a dinner jacket, a finely pin-tucked shirt, a scarlet cummerbund of some rich brocade and splendidly tailored trousers with a fine scarlet trim down the leg; and over this he wore an exquisite, black theatre coat that flared open as he walked, showing flashes of a scarlet silk lining. As always, in place of a tie, he wore one of his bolos; a magnificently wrought piece comprising a center of onyx set about with diamonds in a traditional conch setting with scarlet, plaited leather thongs, tipped with heavy silver.

Catherine wore a simple raw silk dress of French design, a shade of indigo that set off her eyes to perfection. It was long to the ankle and close-fitting, revealing, for all her years and the many children she had born, an elegantly slim figure. Her hair was braided, and held in a coil by the heavy silver comb which her husband had given to her for their wedding day, a comb which ever since that time she had worn daily to confine that shining fire, tucking away even the smallest tendril, making sure that no hint of the electricity it held was visible.

How strange it was, Catherine thought to herself, that the silver comb, an object of such beauty, such exquisite craftsmanship, should become a symbol of tyranny. Although her hair was showing a trace of grey and her frequent attacks of nervous illness had removed the bloom from her cheeks, with her delicate bone structure, her high cheek-bones and deep-set eyes, together with her very fine, creamy complexion, she was still far and away the most striking woman in the room.

Don Lorenzo moved through the guests, greeting his friends and acquaintances, immensely proud to be sharing this moment of his life with them.

"Yes, yes, María does have an exceptional voice. Yes, Señor Fuentes is a gifted teacher. The music? The young boy? His son, I believe. Well, it will be interesting to hear what he has to offer. Always did love choral music. Expect we'll all have a grand evening. So pleased you could come. My dear, you look ravishing! Takes the breath away. Evening, Arturo. Glad you could come."

Catherine followed him, observing how, in his usual proprietary manner, he had taken over the whole evening as if it had all been his idea.

Embarrassed a little by the attention he was attracting, she looked for some avenue of escape. Seeing Father Octavio standing quietly in a corner, she left her husband's side and went over to speak to him.

"A proud day for you too, father," she said after she had greeted him. "We have all been so looking forward to this evening. Do tell me: is the music as wondrous as they say it is?"

She smiled at Magdalena and Sebastián.

"My dear, I think you will find it more than inspirational," Father Octavio said, and then turned to introduce Sebastián. "Of course you have already met Magdalena."

Catherine greeted them both warmly. She had not been privy to all the town gossip, and although she had heard about the famous Casa Magdalena, she did not associate this very lovely woman with the stories she had been told of 'that Jezebel'.

After hearing from Father Octavio and Magdalena about her work at The Adobe, Catherine turned to Sebastián.

"Are you a lover of music, Sebastián?"

Sebastián regarded the handsome woman before him. He thought he had never seen such loneliness in a face before, or eyes more filled with shadows. He wanted to look away, but he was mesmerized by her sadness. He knew he was staring.

She is lost, he thought to himself. This is what happens if you fall into 'the place where the light isn't'.

He felt afraid for her. He knew that her question, and whatever answer she would receive to it, would be of no real interest to her. It was something else she was asking. He wondered if she knew this herself.

"I have recently enrolled for a degree in literature, and I am just beginning to be acquainted with poetry and the arts: and yes, I do believe you might call me a music-lover in training." He smiled.

"What brought you to study poetry? Have you always been interested in it, or is this a new venture?"

It was Sebastián's turn to dissemble. He attempted a light-hearted reply.

"Perhaps it is all those desert sunsets. We live out of town, and I have a favorite place on a hill where I like to sit when I am at home." He paused. "Or perhaps there is poetry buried in the desert hills. Perhaps it is carried by the dust, or the souls of the dead, or the black night wind; and it has crept into my bones."

Where did all that come from? he thought. He tried again. "Perhaps it was always there, waiting for me to find it."

Catherine stared at him. What an extraordinary reply. Still, she was fascinated by it.

"No. It is deeper than that," she said. She had been seized by a sudden excitement. Two spots of scarlet appeared on her cheeks.

"It is what is given if ever we would save ourselves. It is a hunger for that dark touch. It is the only way we can come through. If we lose this, we are lost—but of course, you know this."

She was about to continue when a man pushed his way through the crowd and made his way towards them. Sebastián noticed the sudden change in Catherine's face. In disbelief he watched the presence of her flicker out and slide back into the shadows, right before his eyes. He was shocked.

"Evening, father."

It was not a greeting. It was a dismissal. De la Cruz nodded his head abruptly in the priest's direction and then, muttering something about "someone I want you to meet," he literally pulled Catherine after him.

She turned briefly towards Sebastián.

"Don't ever lose that hunger. It is all we have in the end."

Sebastián almost reached out a hand to her, but meeting the furious eyes of the dark man who had turned briefly to scowl at him, he allowed his arm to fall.

When de la Cruz considered that they had moved a safe distance away from Father Octavio, and that their conversation would not be overheard, he turned and glowered at his wife.

"Don't you know who that woman is?" He managed to keep his voice down. "She is that dreadful woman who ran that salon in town. How could you be seen standing there, talking to her? Have you no sense of propriety? What do you suppose the Governor will think of you? I can't imagine what she is doing here this evening."

"I believe she came with Father Octavio," Catherine said coolly, trying to keep her composure. "Señor Fuentes gives music instruction at the small school she has started, somewhere outside of town; out in the desert, I believe. Father Octavio was telling me about it, and I had just begun an interesting conversation with her son Sebastián when you came and pulled me away. Father Octavio must think you very rude not to have spoken to him."

It was at this moment that it was announced that the Governor would make a speech, and so the subject of Magdalena was dropped.

The Governor was not a particularly eloquent man. He made up for this by way of his overwhelming sincerity.

He spoke at length, and with many superlatives, about how gratifying it was to have a young talent—two young talents—emerge from Father Octavio's diocese; a not very accurate description of the small country church, run by a simple priest and serving what was little more than a village. "It is a privilege—an honor—for all of us here tonight to be present at this, the very first performance of work by a young composer—a young man who will, I am sure, soon attract the attention of music-lovers far and wide."

He went on to say that Santa Fe could be proud of whatever greatness might come to him in the future, but this chapel, and these people, the people of this community were proud to be present tonight, when it all began. There was more in this vein and finally, on a flourish, he declared the concert officially ready to begin. Would people please move through to the chapel and take their seats.

There was some enthusiastic clapping, and several cries of "Here! Here!" Then, with much fanning and mopping of brows for the heat, everyone filed through the doors into the small chapel and seated themselves in the dark wooden pews.

All conversation ceased when Señor Santiago Fuentes stepped into the small space next to the lectern to introduce the evening's music, and speak a little about the choir, the soloists and the composer of the music that they would be listening to that evening.

When María's name was mentioned, Don Lorenzo glanced from side to side at his invited guests, as if acknowledging his part in the program. Catherine, with a sudden lump in her throat, held back a sting of tears— tears of pride that her daughter should have achieved such public acknowl-edgment.

"… and so I would like you to welcome Salvador Fuentes, composer of the music we shall hear tonight, and the voices of Our Lady of Compas-sion Church choir. Ladies and gentlemen!—Salvador Fuentes!"

There was loud applause.

As the choir began to file in, Catherine dropped her handbag behind their pew. In a whisper she asked her husband to see if he could reach it for her.

By the time this was achieved, the choir was in place. María stood in the center of the back row, and so her white dress was not particularly notice-able. However, nothing could hide the glory of her hair. Salvador entered and bowed to the audience. There was another round of applause.

All became quiet, and Salvador turned to face the choir.

All eyes were on him: everyone's in the choir; everyone's in the audience; everyone's, that is, except de la Cruz, for he was staring in shock at María's unbraided hair. Catherine kept her eyes fixed on the choir, paying no attention to the nudges she was receiving.

"Catherine!" he whispered. She ignored him.

"Catherine!" he whispered louder.

"Shhh, Lorenzo. This is a concert."

Her words were drowned out by the organ's opening chord. The choir came in low and very softly at first, but gradually, through the subtle intro-duction of solo tenor and soprano voices and a vibrant descant, it increased in strength and volume until it reached a crescendo of praise; wave upon wave of voices that filled the chapel, right up to the high rafters, with glory.

A stunned silence followed the last amen. The audience was shocked. No one moved. Catherine, who had listened throughout with both hands up to her face, the tips of her fingers just touching her lips, made no move to lower them. Her cheeks were wet.

De la Cruz sat still, staring up at the group before him. On his face there was an expression of shock; or perhaps it was some kind of recognition. After several moments he shook his head and looked down at his hands. He was breathing heavily.

There was a stillness in the chapel; a hush.

Salvador was a little taken aback by the silence. He was not sure whether to continue. From his position at the organ his father gestured to him to proceed.

As the evening progressed, the audience became aware that they were indeed witnessing the debut of a serious talent. Salvador had their complete attention. There were songs of elegant simplicity and songs so sensuous and erotic that they stirred the blood. There was a lament that Salvador had composed in memory of his mother; a lament of such low and haunting intensity that many of the listeners were thrown back to moments of grieving in their own lives, and some silent and unabashed tears were shed.

Finally it was time for the last song, the love duet. Salvador informed the audience that he would be joined in the duet by the wonderfully talented María de la Cruz, who would sing the soprano voice. He walked over to the step where María was standing, and offered her his hand.

María stepped down and moved lightly across the small space, the white dress floating softly about her. She took her place opposite Salvador, some small distance away. All lights were dimmed. Two spotlights, one on María and one on Salvador, shone through the darkness. There was the sound of an intake of breath from the audience.

Catherine heard a choking sound come from her husband, and kept her gaze steadfastly on the young couple. This was such an unforgettable moment for María, and she was not going to let him spoil her enjoyment of it. In another world it might have been her standing up there. As it was, she felt a profound gratitude that her daughter would achieve that which she had longed for and dreamed about, knowing that it was not in her destiny to make it a reality. Her heart swelled with a mixture of grief and pride as she looked at her youngest daughter standing there, so beautiful, so utterly composed that it was hard to believe she was barely sixteen years old.

Santiago was waiting for Salvador to give him the sign to start. Salvador looked at María enquiringly, and at her smile nodded to his father.

Santiago struck the center note. It was picked up and held by the choir.

The organ became silent. No single voice could be heard above another, so skillfully did they weave into each other. It was out of this chord that the two solo voices emerged.

Salvador's voice was vibrant and earthy; but it was the purity of María's voice that lifted the longing of the two lovers, out of this world into a sublime realm.

In the audience hands grasped other hands. The intensity of the passion grew and grew, until those listening could almost not breathe for the ache they felt inside their bodies. The small chapel had become extraordinarily hot. Some of the ladies retrieved their hands and began to fan themselves with their programs. Father Octavio had, unknowingly taken hold of Magdalena's hand in both of his, holding it up as if in prayer.

And still the river held its note, until finally the two voices touched and became one: and María was in Salvador's arms. The two lovers, clasping the single scarlet rose, stood together in a pool of light, surrounded by the brilliant fire of María's hair.

There was a silence. Then, from the audience, there came a deep sigh.

It seemed as if the echoes of the song still moved above their heads in the high rafters, waiting perhaps for angels to carry this music out into the night, even up to the stars.

A thunderous applause broke the spell, and Salvador and María, as if only then noticing the intimacy of their embrace, stepped apart and moved forward to make their bows. Salvador acknowledged the choir and his father, standing at the back of the stage, and then he and María bowed again.

The applause went on and on. One by one members of the audience stood to acknowledge the artists, their arms raised, hands clapping above their heads.

Catherine was unashamedly sobbing. She had forgotten Lorenzo. All her attention was directed towards those two radiant figures standing in front of her, transfigured by the light of their love.

She recognized, beyond any shadow of a doubt, that María and Salvador had found, each in the other, a twin soul; that they were united by a love that few find in a lifetime. She thanked God for his grace that she should have lived to see this day. In some way it cancelled all the disappointments of her life. If that was the price for this night, she would gladly pay it many times over. If life had not permitted her to express that passion that lived, now so respectably contained within her, then that same life had seen fit to bestow on her the gift of this extraordinarily talented child. What a destiny!

Such dreams Catherine forged, while the applause continued around her.

She was brought back to herself by her husband's painful grip on her arm. She looked into his face, and was shocked to see that it was flushed almost purple. He appeared to be struggling for breath, and she feared he might be having a seizure.

"Lorenzo," she asked, "are you all right?"

"You will answer for this later, Catherine," was the only reply she received, for at that moment a group of acquaintances came up to congratulate them.

"Well, Lorenzo! Catherine! What an exceptional evening. You are to be congratulated. What a voice! Your daughter sings like an angel. Where have you been keeping her all this time? Well, the secret's out now! You must be so proud of her—so very proud—eh, Lorenzo? Lucky man! Such a voice! And such a beauty, too! That hair!"

Lorenzo and Catherine did not speak on the long drive home. María chattered away excitedly about the evening; about the press, who had taken photographs of her standing next to Salvador. There was to be a column in the Santa Fe newspaper about the concert; about how nervous she had been until they started to sing, and then all her nervousness had just flown away.

"Was it not the most splendid evening, Mamá, Papá?"

Lorenzo was barely able to respond, but Catherine assured her that the evening had been perfect. Everyone she had spoken to had nothing but praise to offer for the music and the singing. She tried to keep her voice light, but María, as her excitement started to settle down, became aware of the tension between her two parents.

"Is there something wrong, Mamá?" she asked. "Papá, did you perhaps not enjoy the concert?"

De la Cruz was torn between his need to express his rage and his desire not to upset María. This was not her fault. She was a little girl. What had Catherine been thinking to dress a little girl up like that?

"My sweetheart," he said with difficulty, "you were wonderful."

None of them spoke after that, and María, exhausted from all the excitement, fell asleep in the car.

An Arrangement

Two years had passed since the Santa Fe concert.

The sudden omission from the program of the young soprano, María de la Cruz, owing to her unfortunate illness, caused much disappointment in the audiences of the ensuing performances, for they had heard of the magic of the finale on opening night.

De la Cruz had wasted no time in taking steps to shore up the damage that, in his estimation, had been done that night. He put an end to all singing lessons, and all choir practice. María was a young woman now, and it was time she began to learn how well-brought-up young women behaved.

He and Catherine engaged in bitter arguments. He rebuked her for deliberately encouraging María in behavior that was most unseemly. His reaction to María's unbraided hair at the concert was so violent that she began to think that her husband was really more than a little deranged.

"But all the girls wore their hair loose, Lorenzo."

"María is not 'all the girls'. She is María."

A visit from Santiago Fuentes some weeks after the concert, inquiring whether María was ill and saying that they were looking forward to seeing her at choir practice soon, did nothing to placate de la Cruz' anger.

"And if that common little musician calls again, do not encourage him, Catherine. I told him that he, and his son, should leave María alone. I told him—'things happen'. He knew what I meant."

Catherine felt a chill run through her. She heard the sound of a door that had recently opened, closing.

It was José who informed a devastated Salvador of the planned engagement party to announce María's forthcoming marriage to Javier Francisco Otero.

Javier was the son of a wealthy merchant. He was short in stature, slightly corpulent, with a pasty complexion given to acne: not a figure likely to arouse romantic yearnings in a young woman. Nor did the fact that he was devoted to his mother; that not a day passed when he did not find some reason, some little excuse to visit her or speak with her on the telephone, count in his favor.

With his father away so much on business trips, it became Javier's duty, and pleasure, to accompany his mother to concerts, art galleries and numerous other functions, and even to partner her to dinner parties if they were of a formal nature and required a male partner.

Although good-natured, he was a tedious bore, inducing in his listeners a state of stupefied torpor in the face of which many thought death might be preferable. He had none of his father's drive when it came to business. He was content to take life as it came, happy to do his father's, and indeed almost anyone else's will, secure in the knowledge that he, as the only son, would inherit his father's very considerable wealth one day.

It was for these very reasons that de la Cruz had chosen him as a husband for María. He would be easy to manage. He would take the boy under his wing, introduce him to his business affairs and keep him occupied at the Hacienda. That way he would not have to lose his daughter. He was well-pleased with the arrangement.

The engagement was to be a sumptuous affair. All the rooms were being redecorated. Mercedes engaged three extra cooks to help her prepare all the dishes that de la Cruz had requested for the event. A maríachi band was booked for the evening, and Diego had been set the task of building a special dance floor in the courtyard. This was to have a canopy which would protect it in the event of rain. De la Cruz was taking no chances. This would be an event that everyone would remember; an evening worthy of his beautiful María.

The wedding was to be held eight days after the engagement. Father Octavio was informed, and the church was booked for the ceremony. It would have been customary for him to speak to the young couple, to advise them of the seriousness of the step they were about to take, and the obligations each would have to the other when they were married. It was his duty to prepare them for entry into the holy state of wedlock. He was startled, therefore, to be informed by de la Cruz that this would not be necessary; that he himself had had lengthy talks with María, and that she fully understood her duties to her future husband.

Father Octavio felt uncomfortable. Ever since the Santa Fe concert, after which María had ceased to attend choir practice, he had an uneasy feeling that all was not well with María. When finally he asked where she was, and why she no longer attended the Wednesday practices, de la Cruz said that her health would not permit it; that the concert had left her weakened, and that it was better she stayed quietly at home with her mother.

Father Octavio found this difficult to believe, for on the occasions when he saw her in church with her parents she appeared to be in radiant health. In addition to this, the surreptitious glances that passed between her and Salvador, and the heightened color in both these two young people's cheeks, had not escaped his notice. He wondered whether there was not perhaps much more than met the eye to de la Cruz' concern for his daughter. On the few occasions when he tried to have a private word with María her father materialized, seemingly out of thin air, to take charge of the conversation, and Father Octavio could learn nothing of María's state of mind, nor of her wishes.

Finally he decided to have a word with Santiago, Salvador's father. He strolled into the church one late Wednesday afternoon, just as choir practice was coming to an end. While Salvador was collecting the sheet music and tidying away the hymn books, Father Octavio asked Santiago if he had noticed anything out of the ordinary about his son.

"Well, he has seemed rather preoccupied of late, but other than that, no, I can't say that I have noticed much." Santiago thought for a moment and then added, "But then, I have been rather distracted myself of late. Our band has been booked to play at the engagement party of María de la Cruz. It is to be a very grand affair. He has invited hundreds of guests. You know Don Lorenzo, father. Nothing in half measure."

He was thoughtful for a moment.

"Now that you mention it, I did find it strange that our band was booked for the engagement party. De la Cruz has not shown any interest in it or our music since Salvador's concert: in fact, quite the reverse. And I did wonder that my son refused to play with us that night. He always does, you know, but he said he had other commitments. I didn't give it much attention. Perhaps he is the one you should be asking. What is on your mind, father?"

Father Octavio waved a hand dismissively.

"Oh, just wondering."

He had heard all he needed to know. Just what he was going to do about it was another matter. The wedding was little over a month away. Perhaps it was none of his business.

"Perhaps I am becoming a sentimental old fool," he thought, but he couldn't get the matter out of his mind.

It was the custom with all Catherine's daughters that when they turned thirteen, they should begin working on their trousseau in preparation for the day they would marry. As such, María was no exception, and she had spent many years stitching and embroidering the various items which, on completion, her mother packed away between bags of fragrant lavender in a large cedar chest.

As the years passed, the chest gradually filled with beautifully handcrafted items of linen and table-wear.

Seeing his daughter bending over her work, noticing the graceful curve of her neck and the shadowed cleavage, glimpses of which the cut of her dress permitted when she bent to reach for the reel of thread, de la Cruz was forced to acknowledge that his little girl was indeed growing into a woman.

It was this realization, together with his uneasy sense that he might already be too late, that had driven him to approach Señor Otero about his son. Señor Otero was delighted, and more than a little surprised that his son should have been selected, but he was most agreeable to the arrangement.

Unaware of these schemes, María, dreaming of Salvador, was working on the final article, one that her mother had kept until last: the wedding veil. María had been working on it for many months, embroidering hundreds of tiny rosebuds, scattered over the long train that was more than six feet in length. So fine was this work, that at the end of an hour she would have to rest and massage her fingers that were stiff from securing all the tight little French knots. But even as she did so she smiled, dreaming of the day when Salvador would lift it over her head, and they would share their first married kiss.

It was one evening after dinner, while María sat bent over such work, that her father informed her of his plans for her marriage.

"I think he will make an admirable son-in-law, and I could use some help with the business side of things."

"You can hire someone to do the work for you, father. It is not necessary for me to marry the man."

María thought for a moment.

"And when I marry, I shall choose my husband. Not you."

Catherine kept her head down, in case her husband read her face correctly. Silently she applauded María's courage.

"I could never marry a man I did not love, father." She smiled up at him, certain that he would understand.

Her father, not wanting to upset his daughter, decided to leave the matter for a day or two. He would let her digest the idea before he pressed any harder.

It was a few days later that he raised the matter again, and told María of Javier's agreement to the arrangement. She was appalled that matters should have gone so far.

"How could you, father? Without even consulting me! I could have saved you the trouble. You will just have to go back to him and tell him that you made a mistake. Or tell him the truth, if you like. Tell him your daughter does not wish to marry him. No! Tell him I refuse to marry him."

María slammed the pair of scissors she was holding down on the table.

De la Cruz could feel his temper start to rise. María, although always high-spirited, had never given him any indication of such outright defiance.

With difficulty he kept his voice light. He attempted to placate her with promises: gifts he would present to her. He would build her the house of her dreams, right here on the rancho. She could have anything she wanted. She and Javier could have a trip to Europe; anything that would make her happy.

He told her how happy she would make her mother if she did this. Surely, if not to please him, then to help her mother, who after all was not strong, and could not take care of her forever. He asked her to name what it was she wanted, and it would be hers. He only wanted her to be happy.

María became increasingly rebellious.

"How can you say this, father? What about my singing? Did you stop that to make me happy too? How can you believe that marrying this man, whom I do not love, that this is going to make me happy? I won't do it, father! You cannot make me do this!"

María threw down her sewing and left the room in tears.

With an effort de la Cruz managed to hold onto his temper.

"Catherine, you must make María see sense. Javier is a good man. She will always be looked after. We will not always be here to take care of her. This way she will never want for anything. The Hacienda will be hers. Whatever happens, she will always have that. She will be a woman with her own means. She will be able to command respect through that."

"Well, Lorenzo, she is still young. I wouldn't push her too hard. She isn't ready. It's not as if she needs to marry yet."

Privately she knew very well why María was determined not to marry, not just this man, but any man her father chose for her. She knew, or at least suspected, that her husband knew that María was in love with Salvador Fuentes.

María had always been an obedient child, but Catherine knew there was a wild spirit beneath that sweetness. She would not be coerced or bribed into any act, whatever the cost, if it was one that compromised her integrity, or went against her deepest desires. In this respect she was very different from her mother. Catherine took consolation from this knowledge.

"How like you, Catherine! You have never had to make plans for the future; direct the course of things towards the greatest benefit. You just take luxury for granted."

Catherine remained silent.

Lorenzo paid no attention to his wife's silence, but raged on at her for being a foolish woman who didn't understand what would be best for María in the long run.

"She needs someone solid, and dependable. She doesn't know what the world is like."

"And whose fault is that?" snapped Catherine with unusual spirit.

"María is too delicate for all the games the world plays," said de la Cruz. "That is why we kept her home and hired a tutor."

"You mean you! You decided she should stay home. You ordered that."

Catherine's face was scarlet with rage. De la Cruz could not believe he was hearing this: from his wife.

"How dare you speak to me in this rude manner? You will do as I say for a change, and make María see some sense."

He went on and on with his argument, bullying her to agree with him until she too left the room in tears, locked herself into her bed-room and collapsed onto the bed in a state of nervous exhaustion.

The arguments continued for over a week. De la Cruz put forward all the good reasons why María should agree to his wishes. María steadfastly refused to even consider them.

Catherine, who was caught in the middle of this intense altercation, became ill and took to her bed.

It was this that finally decided de la Cruz who, at the end of his tether, told his daughter that it was not a request that she marry Javier, it was a command. He knew better than she did what was in her best interests. She had better pull herself together. Her mother was going to need her assistance with all the preparations for the wedding.

María sobbed and begged, and pleaded; all to no avail. The date was set. She would do as she was told.

"And finish that veil!" he commanded. "You have a month to make yourself ready!"

So María stayed in her room, stitching the little diamonds that were her tears in between the rosebuds on the veil.

Before the Party

The day of the engagement party dawned with a faint mist hanging over the low hills, soon to be burnt away by the sun. The day promised to be clear and hot.

De la Cruz was the first to rise. He strolled at a leisurely pace up and down the covered porch, breathing in the early morning air. In the end, notwithstanding the various objections and suggestions, he had managed to orchestrate all the arrangements for the party to his entire satisfaction.

He made out the guest lists, posted the invitations and decided on the various dishes they would offer their guests: something for every taste; a veritable feast. He spent considerable time in the wine-cellar, selecting the very finest wines for the occasion. It was his idea to have dancing, and a mariachi band to lend an air of festivity to the events of the evening. He arranged for lanterns to hang in the garden, to add just that touch of romance, and bonfires to be lit in case it turned cold.

In short, he took care of everything.

The extra cooks arrived, and were given clear instructions for the many dishes they were to prepare. The dance floor was complete, but the pillars supporting the canopy would be adorned with flowers after midday, so that they would be fresh for the evening.

It had all turned out well in the end. He gave a deep sigh of pleasure.

Catherine thought the arrangements vulgar. The traditional engagement party was a more solemn affair, where only the families, and perhaps very close friends of the families, would attend. It was a way in which the one family could introduce themselves to and be included in the other, each embracing, through this meeting, a wider sense of kinship. It was thought that the exchange of promises and gifts of a symbolic nature, gold rings or rosaries, should be a quiet ceremony that would be more suited to the seriousness of the commitment each was making to the other. This was the way things were done. She felt that her husband was turning the whole evening into a carnival with his feasting and dancing. Whoever heard of a mariachi band at an engagement?

She did not interfere, however, knowing through bitter experience that any efforts to influence her husband would prove fruitless. The less she had to do with the evening, the better. All her thoughts were for María. It had surprised her not a little that after her initial outbursts, María seemed to have accepted her father's plans with fortitude, for she made no further complaint, but worked busily to complete the veil so that it should be ready for the wedding.

Catherine was not aware of José's many excursions into town, and even if she had been, her suspicions would not have been raised, for he would have been able to show her legitimate reasons for all his trips: to collect goods for her husband and to return or exchange others. All this he did to the entire satisfaction of de la Cruz.

What was not known was that José was also the willing emissary, the carrier of perfumed notes that contained declarations of undying love, between Salvador and María. They also carried information of the plans

Salvador had devised for their elopement. As the only one privy to these plans, José felt hugely privileged to be chosen for this mission, and was enjoying the drama and the secrecy of it immensely.

Salvador arranged to borrow a friend's car for the elopement. He would fetch María shortly before the celebrations were due to commence, at a time when she would certainly be in her room, dressing for the party. She was to have a small bag of necessities packed and hidden discreetly underneath the bed.

He would somehow contrive to be at her bed-room window at this time, and have the car parked a little distance away. Hopefully, they would make their way to it unobserved. It would be a while, they hoped at least a half-hour, before María's absence was noticed, and perhaps another hour or more while they searched the property for her. This would give them ample time to disappear.

Salvador had made arrangements with his godfather, Alejandro Jaramillo, to witness their marriage. He was an honorary justice of the peace, and was permitted to perform civil marriages. But Salvador wanted more than this. He had discovered, in a book from the library, a text on old marriage customs. This spoke of the ways in which marriages were once conducted, where a couple could be married by exchanging consent, without having a priest or witness present. He was sure that if this had once been considered legitimate, it must still apply.

"Would we be truly married, Alejandro?"

"Your marriage would be legal, but I am not sure that the Church still recognizes the validity of the ceremony you are contemplating."

"But we would be married?"

"Yes."

Alejandro scrutinized the text that Salvador brought to him. Although it was outdated and, in the present times, probably unnecessary, there was nothing in the account of the ceremony that intimated that it was not valid.

For Salvador the only detail that still remained unresolved was how he would gain access to María's window without being noticed. He sat up half the night, turning the matter over and over in his mind, before he arrived at the solution, stunning in its simplicity.

Such were the plans that ran parallel to each other: the one set manifest in the form of food, flowers and party details; the other invisible, but perceptible, perhaps, should anyone have been paying close attention, in the form of an electric tension that simmered beneath the surface of things.

De la Cruz was so filled with the flamboyant music of the ritual he was orchestrating, that he could not, or certainly did not, detect the presence of the counter-voice that filled the more subtle realms of the operatic drama that was being played out at the Hacienda. De la Cruz, with his extraordinary mix of bombast and sensitivity, in the ordinary course of events would have sensed some artifice in María's rather sudden and inexplicable compliance. As it was, when he watched her with her mother, checking the table-linen, the cutlery, the positioning of the flowers, taking care of the smallest trifles, he marveled at the attention to small detail that women perform so well, and felt only a huge surge of love in his heart.

The afternoon drew to a close. Catherine and María retired to their rooms to rest before dressing for the evening.

De la Cruz, after inspecting every aspect of the preparations and expressing himself well-pleased with everything, went to shower and prepare himself for the celebration.

When he had completed his toilet, he stood for a few moments, looking at his reflection in the mirror, visualizing María on his arm, her fair beauty, the slender daintiness of her young woman's body offset by his dark, powerful presence. For a second he thought he saw her standing there beside him—some trick of the light, perhaps—but when he looked again, she had gone.

He shook his head and stepped away from the mirror.

It was time to give the final instructions. The mariachi band was due to meet him in the courtyard before the guests arrived. He wanted to be ready to meet them in good time, to discuss the evening's program. He had already planned the musical selection with Santiago, but what was important—and no one knew this better than de la Cruz—was the timing. Impact depended not only on content, on the piece of music chosen to heighten a dramatic moment, but on the exquisite timing of its introduction. This would require the full concentration of all the members of the band. He had written his instructions down clearly as a program for Santiago to follow, and he would make sure that there were no misunderstandings.

On hearing her father leave his dressing-room, María gave a sigh of relief. She had showered, and was dressed only in her petticoat. The bag for her departure was under the bed. Now she retrieved it, packed the last few items and closed the clasp.

Her heart was beating fast, not only from excitement, but from the knowledge that she was taking a final step out of childhood; a step that, whatever the future held, could never be reversed.

She looked around her room, and for the first time she realized the enormity of what she was about to do. She was leaving not only her home and her family, but a protected world, a place of safety that she had taken for granted. It came as a shock to her to acknowledge that, perhaps, precisely because it had always been there, she had been unaware of how safe her childhood world had been.

In that moment she saw her parents as two lonely individuals. She knew that by leaving in this manner she would cause them pain. Her father would manage his distress through his anger. How would her mother deal with her grief?

At the full recognition of her mother's bullied and broken spirit, María burst into tears. The last rays of the sun, shining through them, formed brilliant prisms which filled the room with tiny rainbows.

María went to the window which looked onto the courtyard, to see if Santiago had arrived with the members of the band. She almost hoped he hadn't; hoped, in some corner of her heart, that the whole day would fall through; that the party wouldn't happen, that the guests wouldn't arrive; that Javier and his family would change their minds; that she would go to sleep and wake up tomorrow, and look out at a new day, look out over the courtyard and the field of blue lavender, and smell the early morning mix of moist earth and juniper and herbs, and watch the white doves fly their tilting circles and spirals in the dawn sky.

María dried her eyes. She heard the hall clock chime, and realized it was getting late. Through the window she spotted Santiago's car, parked under the giant cottonwood. Her father would be occupied for at least half an hour with the band. It was almost the time for Salvador to meet her. She locked the door to her room, hoping that no one would discover this fact too soon, and hid the key in a drawer. Then she took down from its hanger the wedding dress that had been made for her, and completed only this week.

She had hated the fittings, thinking at the time that this was the garment that she would wear on the day of her marriage to Javier. Now it had become transformed in her eyes into a symbol of transition. In this dress she would leave behind all that she knew, and step into a future that contained only one certainty, and that was her love for Salvador.

Carefully she stepped into the soft ivory silk and began to button the little, covered buttons that reached from below her waist, up the low-cut back. The sweetheart neckline was trimmed with ruched lace to match the wedding veil, and below this the tight-fitting bodice was embroidered with tiny seed pearls.

Before going to rest, Catherine had come to María's room to braid her hair and pin it up into an elegant chignon for the evening celebration. Her father had impressed upon her again and again the importance of honor and dignity at all times.

"A woman has one important treasure, and she must guard it at all times!" he said on the occasion of her thirteenth birthday. "And that is her honor! A woman without honor has nothing! Do not forget this, María."

Now, with these words echoing through her mind, María stood in front of the mirror and removed all the pins and combs that held her long, heavy hair off her face, letting it fall like a river of fire, right down to her waist.

She gave a little sigh as she did so.

Her hair, as it always did when it was left to hang unrestrained by braid, comb or ribbon, began to emit blue sparks, as if some electric current lived in those tresses. That accomplished, she reached for the veil that she had worked on for all these months. She lifted all the heavy length of it and placed it over this shining mass and secured it with the small tiara of miniature white roses that Roberto had been specially tending for the occasion. She and her mother had spent some happy moments the night before, twisting the roses onto the tiara so that they would know how best to decorate it on the day of the wedding.

She stepped back from the mirror to survey the result, and found herself gazing at an image that she did not recognize. She stood in silence, staring at her reflection in the mirror.

She saw, not María de la Cruz, flesh and blood daughter of Don Lorenzo and Doña Catherine of the Hacienda de Las Palomas, dressed in her wedding dress, but a vision which resembled some elemental spirit, clothed all in white and hung about with rainbows and stars.

She moved closer and looked deeply into the cornflower-blue eyes, searching for any traces of uncertainty or wavering. She found none.

There was the sound of a pebble striking the window, the sign that Salvador was waiting close by. She moved swiftly across the room, making doubly sure the door was locked.

"Goodbye, Mamá. Goodbye, Papá," she whispered and kissed her finger-tips, blowing a loving blessing to her parents as she departed.

María floated across the room and out the window like a vision in a dream, or a slow-motion image from a film, the long veil floating behind her. She continued through the gathering dusk to the place where Salvador stood waiting for her, leaving a trail of light behind her.

If anyone had seen her passing, they would have crossed themselves, believing that this was a heavenly figure sent to test their faith in miracles.

As it was, only the white ceramic fantails that kept watch over her bed-room witnessed her departure, but they gave no sign of it, and remained discreetly still and silent in their customary positions on the wall.

The Best Laid Plans

De la Cruz heaved a sigh of relief. Everything was ready. The band had arrived. He met them in the courtyard, and was more than a little irritated to discover that only seven of the eight members were present.

"I engaged eight men," he said abruptly. "I see only seven."

"Yes, sir. My son Salvador is unfortunately unable to be here. He had a prior engagement. But I assure you, sir, you will not be able to tell from our playing. And we will sing our hearts out for the guests."

How could de la Cruz tell him that he had chosen this band with the express purpose of having Salvador witness María's promise to another man?

"I shall adjust the payment accordingly," he said churlishly. "Follow me."

He showed them where they would play, and went through the program one last time with Santiago.

"And you know the opening song?"

"Yes, sir."

He left them to settle themselves, and went to check that the waiters had arrived. He found the ten young people, who were to pass around eats and drinks, in the kitchen being inspected by Mercedes.

He checked the dance floor and the canopy. Roberto had finished fixing the long strands of scarlet roses around the canopy fixtures, and the strong fragrance of these blooms filled the dance floor. De la Cruz nodded his approval.

Diego and his son José had spent the afternoon setting the bonfires at intervals up the long driveway, and two some distance from the band. They would be lit just before the guests were due to arrive. In addition to this, they had lined the pathways, the courtyard and the whole length of the long porch with farolitos, to add a warm glow to the proceedings.

The food was ready, the champagne chilled. It was all going perfectly. The secret, thought de la Cruz, is all in the planning.

Neither Catherine nor María had put in an appearance yet, and he was about to go and call them when he saw the first car pull into the courtyard. De la Cruz went out to meet the guests, cursing Catherine under his breath for not being present.

While de la Cruz was busy greeting the first guests, Catherine, who had finished adding the last touches to her toilette, went to call María. When there was no response to her knock, she assumed that María had gone to be with her father. At this point Mercedes intercepted her, saying that the kitchen required another bottle of wine for the dessert sauce, and so Catherine went with her to the cellar to select a wine. She left Mercedes, and was confronted in the hallway by her furious husband, who wanted to know where on earth she had been.

"No, don't bother to tell me! Come and greet the guests. Everyone is arriving. Where is María?"

"I thought she was with you," Catherine replied. "She has probably gone to look at the dance floor. She helped Roberto all afternoon with the preparation of the roses."

She was about to go and call María when the Mayor and his thin, pinch-faced wife arrived and had to be welcomed. De la Cruz was muttering under his breath.

"Hush, Lorenzo. She will be here any moment, I am sure. Relax. You are meant to be enjoying this evening too. You have worked so hard for it."

At this moment the entire Otero family arrived. De la Cruz, casting a desperate glance at his wife, greeted them all.

"Ah! Javier! I think you'll find María out at the dance floor."

The rest of the Otero family made their way through the large reception room and out onto the long porch. They appeared to be rather overwhelmed by the elaborate preparations.

A steady stream of guests began to file up the pathway, all talking animatedly, admiring the farolitos which glowed orange in the fading light. Catherine and her husband were obliged to delay calling María until everyone had been received and directed to the porch.

At this point Javier, who had been unable to locate María, returned to de la Cruz.

"I can't seem to find María anywhere, sir," he said respectfully. "It would appear that no one has seen her yet."

Trying not to let his frustration be visible, de la Cruz nodded and said he would fetch her presently.

"Why don't you go and see that your parents have everything they need?"

A fresh wave of arrivals delayed him in his urgent task, but he managed to go through all the motions of a relaxed host. He greeted everyone effusively while steering them firmly in the direction of the porch.

"Please, make yourself at home. Champagne? Or would you prefer something else? Good. Good. Please. There are hot snacks coming round. Good. Excellent! I'll be right back. Yes. Thank you!"

De la Cruz made his escape and went in search of María. He was fuming. The pulse in his neck was throbbing above the silk collar, and he was starting to perspire. He mopped his face.

"Damn the child!" he muttered.

He went to María's room and, without knocking, attempted to open the door. Finding it locked did nothing to relieve his frustration.

Had the child fallen asleep?

He hurried back through the sitting-room, making his way through the guests, muttering "greetings" and "good to see you", and on to the porch and around to María's room.

He entered through the French doors. Discovering the room empty, he frowned. He was further angered to find no key in the locked door.

"What the devil—!" He strode back along the porch to check Catherine's room, thinking that perhaps María had needed something from her mother. Finding that room empty as well, he went to the kitchen and questioned Mercedes. No, she hadn't seen María, but then she had been so busy, she wouldn't have noticed if María had walked right past her.

De la Cruz asked Roberto what time he and María had finished the roses.

"That would be about four o'clock, sir. We had not quite finished, but María said she had to go and change."

Diego and José both shook their heads. Neither had seen María since about midday. De la Cruz went back to the house to find Catherine. In the dark, the small lanterns looked very romantic, but his mind was not on romance at this moment. It was full of rage at María for putting them in this embarrassing situation. And now, where on earth was Catherine?

Eventually he found her with a strained look on her face, listening to the Mayor's wife, who was recounting, in her thin, nasal voice and with the boredom of one who has never found life to be particularly interesting, a painfully protracted and minutely detailed account of her last visit to the gynecologist.

"Excuse us, Eusebia; Catherine is wanted in the kitchen for a moment."

Leaving her to find someone else to bore with stories of frailty and its supposed link to intelligence, de la Cruz almost dragged Catherine into his study. His lips were white with controlled rage.

"Where is she, Catherine?" he exploded. "I have organized an entire evening: food, wine, music, waiters, lights, flowers, everything! You had one thing to see to, and that was that María should be here to greet the guests. And she is nowhere to be found."

"You don't have to shout at me, Lorenzo. Even the guests can hear you."

He took a deep breath, as if trying to remain patient with someone of impaired intelligence.

"When did you last see her?"

"I went to her room and braided her hair at about five o'clock," she said. "She was almost ready when I left her. She only had to put on her dress."

"Well, no one has seen her since then."

De la Cruz consulted his watch. It was now half past eight. Everything was going wrong. They had planned to start with the ceremony, the gifts and blessings, and then serve the supper. He, of course, would make a speech and propose a toast. Now it was getting late. The food would be spoiling. The Mayor would be drunk soon if they didn't feed him. De la Cruz cursed. What was to be done?

It was Catherine who came up with the suggestion that they ask the band to start playing, and encourage everyone to dance.

"Well, see to it," he snapped. "I am going to get the men and see if she is anywhere on the property. Maybe something has happened to her."

Lorenzo never did have that first dance with his lovely María, as he had planned so carefully. He did not have that moment with her that he had dreamed of for so long. He did not hear those impassioned words that he had chosen to be sung as he held her in his arms and danced with her on this sultry evening beneath the full moon, and with the heady fragrance of roses wafting on the breeze.

And surely it was just as well so: for it was not a song for a father to offer his daughter.

It was a folk dance, a waltz sung by a young tenor who had been born and raised in Zacatecas, but who had been sent to stay with a cousin in Mexico City, there to study music and have his voice trained for opera. He had not lived up to his parents' lofty expectations, however, and had regretfully released his dreams of a brilliant operatic career. He had, nevertheless, a sweet voice that did very well with the less vocally taxing mariachi songs.

And so, to the accompaniment of guitars and sobbing violins, he sang—

"Hay unos ojos que si me miran—

"There are some eyes which if they look at me
Make my soul tremble with love
There are some eyes so exquisite
Prettier eyes I have never seen

"Ay! who could look at himself in them?
Ay! who could kiss them more
Enjoying always their sparkle
And never forgetting them?

"And everyone says I don't love you
That I don't adore you with a frenzy
And I tell them that they lie, they lie
That I would even give my life for you …"

He sang with such an excess of emotion, with such tremulous passion that, when the song was done, everyone, thinking that this surely was the way María would make her entrance, called out:

"Where is she? Where is the lovely María? Don't be shy. Come out, María with the—exquisite eyes! Come and dance with your future husband!"

And they pushed the blushing and self-conscious Javier unceremoniously onto the dance floor, where he stood wishing that María would indeed hurry and join him, so that they could end this discomfiting performance.

When María did not appear, the band launched into its next song.

"Amorcito Corazon—
Little love of my heart
I yearn for the kiss
Which is the sign of our love …"

Javier stood alone on the floor, his cheeks scarlet with embarrassment. The guests, who had begun to sing along with the young tenor, started a slow clapping.

Catherine, who had been greeting some late arrivals, on hearing the noise, hurried down to the garden to see what was happening. Some of the guests were stamping in time to the music. The subsequent crescendo had almost reached its peak when she arrived.

Seeing her, the Mayor, with many glasses of champagne under his belt, seized her, and ignoring the violent protestations of his wife, pulled her onto the dance floor. Once there he began to execute a tango of excessive flamboyance, paying no attention whatsoever to the rhythm or the tempo of the music. Catherine was spun this way and that, dragged, now shoeless, across the dance-floor, clutched to his breast and bent backwards over his arm so that her head almost struck the floor, until her customary, impeccable appearance was completely undone. The silver comb fell from her hair, causing those carefully groomed tresses to escape and fly about her head as if taken by a storm.

The guests went wild with delight, cheering them along with shouts of "¡bravo!" and "¡viva!", clapping louder than ever, stamping their feet on the wooden dance-floor to lend encouragement to the dancing pair.

It was at this point that de la Cruz arrived on the scene. When no one heard his shouts for "quiet!" he stepped onto the dance floor and seized his wife from the Mayor's grip.

That good gentleman did not appear to notice that he had lost his partner, and continued to tango back and forth, his arm out in front of him, straight as a ramrod, and his head thrown to one side in a dramatic caricature of arrogance. He was dancing to some compelling inner music, apparent only to him, and unable to see his direction, he tangoed himself right off the dance floor, and was last seen up on the hill, silhouetted against the flames of the bonfires.

De la Cruz signaled to the band to stop playing. With as much control as he could muster he announced, through white lips, that unfortunately María was indisposed, and would not be able to attend the party. He offered her apologies, saying that the ceremony would have to be postponed to another day. In the meantime, he invited all the guests to move up to the house, where supper awaited them. He promised to join them soon.

It was turning into a bloody circus!

De la Cruz cursed, took Catherine's arm in a grip that made her wince and literally dragged her up to the house and into his study. Before he even began speaking, Catherine could feel his rage pour over her like a wave. His face was purple. She had never seen him so angry.

"Look at yourself! You are a disgrace!" He was having difficulty speaking. "You look like a slut! A whore! Look at your hair!"

De la Cruz poured himself a whisky and downed it in one gulp.

"Have you any idea what you looked like out there? What a spectacle you made of yourself with that drunken old fool? And where is your comb?"

Catherine sat down and pulled her shawl about her, as if to protect herself. She was no stranger to the abuse that would follow, but after all these years, far from having become inured to his rages, her ability to withstand its violence had grown weaker. She felt sick.

"What has happened, Lorenzo?" she asked. "Have you found María?"

"All you had to do was to dress yourself, and help María with her hair. Is it so much to ask that you both manage to show up, on time, for this occasion?"

De la Cruz paced back and forth, striking his right fist into the other hand as he spoke.

"Your daughter," he choked with rage, "your daughter, who has been given everything on earth that she could possibly want, who has never wanted for a thing, who has been loved, and cherished, has on this, the night of her betrothal, in front of everyone we know, all the important people of this community—has run away!"

He was shaking with fury. He poured another drink and threw it back.

"She has made me—a laughing-stock. How am I going to explain this away? Tell me you know nothing about this! Tell me you had no part in this."

He stood glaring down at her, his face distorted with rage.

Catherine felt the familiar tears rush to her eyes. Her face was chalk-white, her lips bloodless. She felt she might faint. She struggled to retain some composure, but she could feel her chin and her mouth begin to tremble. Her whole body was shaking uncontrollably. When she tried to speak, she could hardly get her lips to form the words.

"How do you know this?" She made an attempt to sit straight. "Who told you this? Tell me exactly what has happened, Lorenzo," she managed.

"I will fire that good-for-nothing José! First thing tomorrow! After all that I have given him; done for him. The opportunities! The good education! And this is how he repays me."

De la Cruz poured himself another whisky. He walked over to the

French doors and looked out. The bonfires were still burning brightly. He returned and took a seat.

"I went to speak to Diego and José again. I wanted to suggest that we search all the grounds, in case she had met with an accident. The stupid boy, before he thought what he was doing, said he was sure she was all right—Salvador would look after her. Fool! I got it out of him.

"She and Salvador, that penniless son-of-a-bandleader, have run away together. José helped them organize this. They left shortly after five. They have been gone for almost five hours. I couldn't get anything more out of José. He doesn't know where they were going. I don't think he knows any of the details."

Catherine looked at him in disbelief. Her little María, Had she really done this? In spite of everything, she hoped it was true.

De la Cruz downed the whisky.

"Pull yourself together, Catherine. This is no time to go all weak and pathetic. Go and see that the guests are taken care of. I am going to phone every police station, and tell them to be on the look-out. And go and tidy yourself first. And get your hair up."

Catherine was about to leave the room when he remembered to ask what María was wearing.

"Well, she was to wear the new pink dress that was made for the occasion. She was about to put it on when I left her." Before she could stop herself, she added—"We can go and check in her room if you like."

Together they hurried to María's room.

With a curse de la Cruz remembered that the door was locked. Without explaining, he dragged Catherine up the passage. He attempted to look normal as they passed through the room packed with guests, lining up to help themselves to food.

"Yes, Mercedes, Catherine will be with you in a minute," he said in answer to her urgent whisper.

Finally, on entering the room, the first thing they noticed was the pink dress on its hanger, where it had been when Catherine was last in the room.

"So what is the wretched child wearing?" de la Cruz fumed.

Catherine searched the wardrobe, trying to remember what dresses María liked. She had so many that it was hard to tell if one was missing. She could feel her husband's impatience. She went through the garments again, trying to remember; wanting not to remember.

"Oh!"

"Well? What is it, Catherine?"

"Well, I can't remember, from all these dresses, what she might be wearing, but her overnight bag has gone."

She looked around the room.

"And her small basket of toiletries."

She paused, wanting not to give him the rest of the information.

If only she dared disobey him. Perhaps she could pretend that she had not noticed. She wanted so for María to be happy. She wanted her daughter, this one daughter, to know love: to marry, not because it was a suitable alliance; not because she would be wealthy; not because her father had selected a good-natured but extremely boring man, who would be easily manipulated and give in to her wishes. No. She wanted her daughter to know all the heights and depths that love and passion would bring. She wanted María to live the life she knew was possible.

But the years of habitual bullying had done their work. She had never been able to withstand his anger. Fear of this huge rage, and what she became when he loosed it on her, had always dominated any desires that she might have of her own. It was as if her will became obedient only to his commands; it had no independent life of its own.

And so, even as her heart longed to take that unfamiliar step, she heard the voice, of her fear and her obedience, utter the words:

"Oh, and I think she has taken her wedding dress, and the veil."

There. It was done. She had bowed to him, against everything in her heart, once again. This was her final betrayal of her beautiful, talented, passionate daughter.

De la Cruz would find her anyway, and bring her back home. He always got his way. In that sense it made no difference to María's fate.

But Catherine knew that there are other lives that we live, beneath the appearance of reality. She knew that a small door of opportunity had opened for her this night. It did not offer much; and it offered everything. And she had failed to step through it. Now she heard it slam shut.

Catherine cursed the person she had become; and cursed her cowardly fear, and her lack of courage.

The Lowrider

"María! Over here!"

María heard Salvador's whisper, coming from the cover of the thick hedge of lavender bushes which surrounded the gardens. She made her way towards the sound of his voice, keeping herself bent low so that her head should not be visible above the tall blooms.

After their initial ardent embrace, they stepped back and stood staring at the transformed beings they had become. María, regarding her lover's dark, handsome face and flashing white smile, felt her heart begin to beat, so fast she could scarcely breathe. His disguise for the evening was his mariachi costume—a brilliant solution to his need to be unremarkable, for no one would pay any undue attention to one of the band members.

Salvador stood rooted to the spot, staring at the vision he saw before him. He could not believe his eyes, and reached out to touch her, to make sure his senses were not playing tricks on him. He touched her cheek, her lips, and very softly he reached up to touch the flying tresses of her wild hair. He too was experiencing a pounding in his chest, so thunderously loud that he feared it might be heard up at the house, and would attract someone's attention.

"María!" was all he could say, in a voice thick and husky with emotion. "María!"

María was the first to recover some measure of composure, for she had, in spite of her delicate appearance, great presence of mind and an intensely practical nature.

"We must leave, Salvador, before they notice I am missing."

She pulled at his sleeve, so firmly that Salvador regained some of his senses; enough to point to the direction they must take to reach the car.

"I parked it some distance down the road, in case someone should notice it and become suspicious." Salvador took her arm. "We can walk along the arroyo, so that no one will see us. The car is parked very close to where it opens out onto the road."

"There it is," said Salvador when finally they climbed up onto the road. But there was no need for him to direct María's gaze, for the spectacle that awaited her had already attracted a small crowd.

At first María thought she might be hallucinating, a state brought on by too much exertion, or perhaps the evening light playing tricks on her.

What María saw stopped her in her tracks. There, parked at the roadside, in all its neon splendor and surrounded by a motley group of small children with huge eyes and grinning smiles, was a low, sleek, lime-green convertible lowrider, its chrome trim gleaming in the soft light. It was surely the lowest lowrider in all of New Mexico.

As they approached the vehicle, the small group, thinking that perhaps they were a bride and groom come all the way from Mexico, began to cheer.

"¡Viva la felicidad!—Long live happiness! ¡Feliz boda Mexicana! Happy Mexican wedding!" they cried, and waved their arms, singing and shouting and generally making such a huge din that a donkey, that was tethered in a nearby field, threw back its head, and added its staccato bray to the general hullabaloo.

Salvador, appalled at the noise that threatened to jeopardize his whole plan, attempted to hush them, afraid that someone would come to investigate the disturbance and that they would be discovered.

María seemed to be unaware of the noise, so entranced was she by what she saw. She walked around the car, staring at the artwork that adorned both the hood and the trunk, and the long, low length of both sides.

"Salvador!" she said eventually. "Where in the world did you get this car? And how on earth can we go away in this?"

She looked at him in wonder. "How will we ever be able to disappear in such a car? Surely everyone we pass will remark on it."

This last remark was superfluous: for it was a car that would be impossible not to notice. Not only was it a vintage lowrider of a particularly electric shade of lime-green, but it was spray-painted with a rapturous image of Our Lord Jesus, wearing a lilac robe, a garland of crimson roses and a magenta cloak.

His arms reached out over the hood, with rays of white light streaming out from both his hands, while in the center of his chest there burned a crimson heart bound with thorns, from which there sprang the flames of eternal love.

Spread across the width of the trunk, the Virgin of Guadalupe with her halo of fire, superbly executed in neon colors—yellow, violet, indigo and a rich blood-red—was surrounded by a profusion of scarlet roses.

On both sides of the car and down the whole length of it, garlands of these same painted roses twined around the wide chrome strip until, towards the rear of the vehicle, they transformed into a mass of leaping flames covering the rear tailfins in fire. Small images of The Flaming Heart adorned the centers of the chrome-rimmed hubcaps. The car's interior was upholstered in scarlet velvet. Just below the chrome rear-view mirror, on the driver's side of the car, inscribed in scarlet with violet shading, was the legend: 'Vivas Sueños'—Long Live Dreams.

It was certainly not an inconspicuous motor vehicle. It was like one of those dreams that are of such vivid intensity that ten, twenty years later they remain fixed in the mind. It was a work of art.

Salvador put María's small case in the trunk, and they both climbed into the car. The small group was cheering even louder. Some of the children had picked wild flowers from the roadside, and these they threw over the couple, showering them as if with confetti and shouting—"¡Viva!—¡Viva!"— and a variety of good-luck blessings for a happy life. In spite of their anxiety and their eagerness to be gone, the young couple could not help but enjoy the romance of the moment, and as if to complete the picture for them, Salvador leaned across to María and gave her a long and passionate kiss.

It is said that only one kind of kiss has the power to offer a miracle, and that is the kiss between two lovers whose hearts have remained true to one another through all the ages, since time began. Only a heart that has known such enduring passion will be of sufficient strength to bear the fate that such a kiss will bring.

Just such was the kiss that Salvador and María shared on that dusty strip of road, to the sounds of the children cheering and the discordant song of the burro.

Word has it that, after they left, it was discovered that the small boy with the withered leg had been made whole, and was jumping up and down in such a frenzy of joy that eventually he had to be restrained, lest he faint from exhaustion. This extraordinary occurrence, although they could have no inkling of it at this time, would play a part in the destiny that awaited Salvador and María in the future.

Salvador fired the engine. It responded with a throaty roar, and slowly the car pulled away. Slow is the only speed for a true lowrider, on account of its minimal clearance from the road. When María asked if they could not go, perhaps, a little faster, Salvador explained this to her.

"The whole idea of a lowrider is that you travel slowly, because you are supposed to draw attention to yourself, and the car. It is said that if a lowrider doesn't scrape the paving, it's not truly a lowrider—it's just another set of wheels with rims. This is a true lowrider. It is a major status symbol. Not even a limo is as romantic, or as prestigious, as a car of this caliber."

Salvador caressed the small, scarlet, leather-bound steering-wheel the way one might caress a lover's hand.

"When I asked Carlos if I could borrow his car, he neglected to tell me he had traded it in last year for this one. It was too late to try and find something else. We will make better speed on the highway, perhaps twenty-five miles per hour, but on these roads we must be satisfied with the speed we have now. I promised Carlos I would take good care of his—'amante'."

And so they traveled through the dusk, the sunset sky adding its glory to their passage. María thought she must surely be dreaming, for never had she seen so many flowers blooming at the roadside as she saw that evening: pink apache plumes, the many shades of cosmos, verbena and wild blue flax, and everywhere the fragrance of lilacs.

All along the way people in the small hamlets waved as they passed, calling out blessings. Some must have telephoned friends in other small villages, for everywhere they went the streets were lined with families who had left their houses to witness their passage and cheer them on.

As they glided along through the enfolding dusk, the slow speed and the light evening wind lifted María's veil so that her long, loose hair streamed out behind her, casting the familiar blue sparks into the evening air. As dusk slowly descended over the land, a radiant light could be seen surrounding the figure of Jesus, while the fire that sprang from his heart burned like a torch.

As the car passed them, the onlookers could see the image of Guadalupe, burning like neon, her hands clasped in prayer and benediction. There were cries of—"¡Viva! ¡Viva Guadalupe! ¡Viva Nuestra Señora!—¡Viva!"

And so they progressed. They left in their wake a brilliant trail of sparks and diamonds, which fluttered off María's hair and white veil, and a scattering of scarlet petals cast from the abundant garlands of painted roses.

The last glimpse the onlookers had of them came from the car's tailfins, from which tongues of flame leapt out into the indigo night like fiery salamanders.

Such was the passage of Salvador and María, on their way to conduct their personal and intimate ceremony; to exchange vows in the presence of Alejandro Jaramillo, Salvador's godfather, and to receive from him a blessing for their future.

Alejandro

Alejandro Jaramillo lived alone. It was not that he was in any way unsuited to the honorable state of matrimony, or that he lacked women eager to join their lives with his, for he was a tall, good-looking man with a face like a saint and a voice so gentle, it was said he could talk the birds out of the trees. No, it was not for lack of willing young ladies that he had never married; it was because he had never found the time for it. During his tenth year, while he attended the local school, Alejandro Jaramillo received what he later came to recognize as a divine call, a vocation, to serve 'The Heavenly Host'; a command to which he gave instant obedience and which, with the exception of a few unavoidable interferences, he had served exclusively since that time.

This calling came to him during a wood-work class at school. He entered the work room on that auspicious day with the rest of the boys, sharing jokes with his best friend, Santiago Fuentes. The wood-work teacher was a santero, well-known in the area for his unconventional interpretation of the saints—an interpretation that had been viewed with much criticism. It was thought that the influence of a visit to an exhibition and lecture on Picasso's work had so polluted his work, that the people of the community questioned his suitability as a teacher of young and impressionable minds. On the other hand, it was reluctantly admitted that while his interpretation left much to be desired, his craftsmanship was of an order rarely encountered, and it was on the strength of this that he was engaged.

He was, however, warned that if the school began turning out a procession of saints resembling tortured bulls and horses, he would be dismissed. It was pointed out to him that a screaming man with crooked eyes was not a santo.

The project he set that day had few specifications. Each boy was given a piece of cottonwood and asked to make a carving of whatever subject he pleased. When the carving was completed, it could be painted, as was traditional, if they chose to carve a santo; but they were also given the freedom to make secular work. They would receive their mark for the handiwork at the end of the semester. The project was allotted this length of time so as not to tax the small and unskilled hands unduly.

It was towards the end of this two-hour class, while the boys were putting their names onto the various pieces of wood that they had been carving—wood that now bore witness to some rough scarring not of natural origin—that it was discovered that Alejandro was missing.

Eventually he was found by the teacher in a corner of the playground, under the shade of a cottonwood, on his knees, deep in prayer. In front of him, resting against the rough trunk of the tree, was a most perfectly carved angel.

What the teacher who found him did not, could not know was that Alejandro had been visited by a member of 'The Heavenly Host'.

This had occurred towards the end of the two-hour period. It was while he sat contemplating his carving, an angel already completed, that it transformed into a being of light, transmitting rays of energy that induced in the boy feelings of great love.

Terrified that anyone might see the vision, he slipped out of the class with the angel tucked under his shirt, the light burning like fire against his chest, in the region of his heart.

He chose a corner of the playground where he was least likely to be seen, to ascertain if what he thought had happened had indeed taken place. He lifted the angelic presence—presence, not form, for it had no weight or apparent substance beyond that of light—out of its hiding and placed it beside the tree. There it hovered a little way above the ground, a shining, transparent entity, radiating into him such intense feelings of elevated and sublime love that they threatened to overwhelm him.

Without any thought on his part, and far beyond any conscious exercise of will, Alejandro found himself on his knees. It was at this moment that he heard a voice speak to him, saying that he, Alejandro Jaramillo, had been chosen and commanded by God to carve every angel of 'The Heavenly Host' that kept watch in the heavens. On asking how many that may be, could he be told the exact number of 'The Heavenly Host', the reply had been: "as many as stars."

"I will do it," was his immediate response, whereupon the light slowly faded and the angel resumed its wooden appearance once more. It was at this point that his teacher discovered him.

"Alejandro," he said softly, moved to find such a young boy praying of his own volition. "Alejandro, class is over; it is time to go home."

Then, noticing the perfect little carving, he asked the boy where he had found it.

"It is my work from the class, sir. This is what I made today."

"Impossible!" thought the teacher, but he kept this to himself. "May I?" he asked, indicating that he wanted to examine the carving.

Alejandro handed it to him. It was an astonishing piece of work. No master craftsman could have wrought more sensitively the folds of the garment, the small details of face and hands, the elegant wings. He was about to ask the boy to tell him the truth of how he had come by the angel, but something in the angel's face made him hesitate.

"You really carved this?" he asked inquiringly.

"Yes, sir."

Alejandro did not tell him the whole story, for he was not sure he would be believed, but he did confide in Santiago as the two boys walked home along the narrow lane, taking the short cut across the dusty arroyo to the square where their families lived in adjacent houses.

"That will take you your whole life!" Santiago said, astonished at his friend's sense of commitment to what sounded like an impossible task.

"Yes," Alejandro replied. "I know. It will be my life's work."

"How do you know this?" Santiago asked him. "You are only ten. How do you know you won't want to do something else next week, next month or maybe in a few years' time when you are older? We are just boys, Alejandro. We don't know enough yet to be sure of such things."

"But I do know, Santiago. This one thing, I do know!"

Santiago looked at his friend admiringly. He too had enjoyed the wood-work class, and he thought that maybe he would like to be a santero one day. A santero—or a musician—or maybe both. But to make such a promise, to such a strange request, when you were only ten years old: that took courage. Suppose you couldn't keep it up. Suppose you ran out of ideas for new angels. Suppose, suppose—he cast about for an example of what might constitute an irresistible temptation: suppose you were invited to be a conductor of an orchestra and you had to say no, because you had promised to spend your life carving angels? How might you feel then? No, he would not be able to make such a promise.

But as the weeks and the months, and finally the years passed, he realized that his friend had truly received a call from God, or from, as Alejandro stated, an emissary for 'The Heavenly Host', and that he intended to honor it.

His decision to commit his life to carving angels did not go uncontested. First his teachers, and then his parents challenged what they considered to be an unnatural occupation. As the months passed, they became increasingly worried as his seeming obsession with angels showed no signs of abating. He was taken to see a priest, who questioned him about his decision; but Alejandro, wisely for one so young, did not mention the visitation. He just told the priest that he liked angels. The priest, who could not find any fault with the boy's story, told him to say fifty Hail Marys and sent him home.

Observing their young son's growing collection of cottonwood and cedar, and any other timber that might be suitable for carving, his desperate and distraught parents consulted their doctor, who referred them to a psychiatrist.

The psychiatrist did numerous tests with ink and paper, every color and shade of ink from indigo to magenta, trying to see if he could gain some access into the boy's unconscious processes.

Alejandro enjoyed these tests, for he saw a surprising array of angels in the ink blots, and told the psychiatrist that he was pleased, at last, to find someone who could see what he was talking about.

The psychiatrist retreated, baffled, and Alejandro went home.

In his report the psychiatrist noted that the boy was either color-blind or a genius. He stated that both these conditions were difficult to diagnose with any degree of accuracy. Time might correct the first, but the diagnosis of genius, if it was correct, might prove more difficult to cure. He advised the parents not to put any pressure on Alejandro, but rather allow time to do its work.

As there did not seem to be any problem with Alejandro's sense of color, his parents reluctantly accepted the psychiatrist's other diagnosis, and eventually gave up what was turning into an unequal struggle. They gave their permission for their son to convert his small bed-room into a work space.

To accommodate the large work-table that he had made, he cut the legs off his bed, using this wood later to make four angels, and set it on the ground under the bench. It was here, surrounded by wood-chips, the strong fragrance of cedar and the subtle emanations of several hundred angels, that Alejandro slept the sleep of one whose heart is at peace, and who is content with the world.

For the rest, he kept only necessities, giving all his old toys to the children of the village and packing his clothes and school books into one small corner. He set up a series of parallel strings close to the ceiling, from which he suspended the angels as he finished them. Gradually his room became so filled with the heavenly presence which the angels carried, that people claimed they could see the love streaming out of the window.

The years went by, and Santiago went to college to study music. Alejandro remained in the village. He bought an old, run-down barn which he renovated, turning it into a work studio. It had a gallery that faced onto the road, where people might come and view his work. At the back, in what used to be stables, he built a small but comfortable living section.

Once all this was accomplished, he set about organizing himself for the great work. He managed to find a map of all the major stars in the heavens. This he enlarged, until it stretched right across one wall of the studio. He designed and built a piece of equipment with which he could examine and count all the smaller or more distant stars that he could see in the heavens above him. These he marked off onto the corresponding area on his star chart. It became a familiar sight, something that the villagers looked out for on those dark, moonless nights: the sight of Alejandro, standing on the hill behind the village, wrapped in the night wind and gazing up at the heavens, his eye pressed against the small grid, counting every last star in those trembling constellations.

"Did you find a new one last night, Alejandro?" they would inquire the next day. "How many have you got now?"

He would just smile at their teasing and wave them away. He knew that they were proud of him.

When Santiago returned from college, he became a music teacher and married his childhood sweetheart.

Alejandro became famous, and there was no gallery for miles around which did not carry his work. The region was as well-known for his angels as it was for its red chili. His work attracted many buyers, and generally brought much prosperity to the small community. There was not a single house in the region that did not have an 'Alejandro Angel' watching over it. And if the man was a little touched, as some said he was, well then, everyone knew just who had touched him. No one was going to argue about that.

When Santiago's wife died giving birth to a son, Salvador, it was Alejandro who, in addition to being godfather, became like a second parent to the boy, and it was partly through his influence that Salvador had been drawn to composing sacred music.

And it was he, Alejandro Jaramillo, when he attended Salvador's concert and heard his godson sing the duet with the young María de la Cruz, it was he who recognized that here was a marriage made in heaven, and that no man on earth would ever be able to come between these two young people, or change the destiny that awaited them.

Alejandro was a man who knew true love when he saw it: but he also knew the price that must be paid by those who are touched by the Almighty.

———————

But the future had not happened yet. As always, he thought to himself, we are spared from knowing what lies ahead of us.

Now, as he stood outside his studio, awaiting the arrival of Salvador and María, wondering what could have happened to delay them, his heart was full of joy for them; only joy, and blessings of love for the beautiful young couple and their future life together. He knew all about the difficult circumstances that surrounded their love for each other, but these things did not trouble him. Difficulties—were part of a world that had little meaning for him. Difficulties—should never be allowed to interfere with the course of true love.

As he stood waiting, the night cast its purple veil over the land. He watched the slow moon rise over the mesa. Somewhere a coyote howled. Tonight was not a night for stars, he thought. Tonight was a night for love.

Shadows

Ever since the disastrous engagement party a cloud had hung over the Hacienda de Las Palomas. Even on the finest of days people passing in their motor cars on the highway would look to their right and see a strange phenomenon that looked like a dark veil, suspended over a section of the land. It never moved, no matter how strong the wind might be, but cast a dolorous shadow over the house and the surrounding fields. The locals called it 'a cloud of suffering', for word had traveled of the attempted elopement of María de la Cruz with her young sweetheart, and of her father's heartless interception.

De la Cruz did not notice the cloud. He was in too much of a rage to see it. He was still smarting under the sense of embarrassment he felt at being made to look such a fool in front of so many people: particularly those of high social standing.

Catherine, while deeply upset for María's sake, was so familiar with the oppressive nature of her life that this was, for her, just another of her husband's brutal manoeuvers to control life at the Hacienda. She had already buried from her conscious mind any admission of complicity; any part that she had played in it.

The story of the event, and the miraculous healing of young Pablito, was told and retold by the locals, gaining many embellishments in the process until, through the passionate telling, María and Salvador had become elevated into a category approaching sainthood.

The brutal behavior of María's father, who had sent the police searching for her in all directions, was also well discussed, and whenever he made trips to town, all through the small hamlets people would point to his car as he passed, and hurry their children away for fear he carried some kind of curse.

It was known that María and her lover had eventually been found on the Interstate, driving southward towards the Mexican border. Their progress had been impeded by the nature of the vehicle in which they were traveling, and by the crowds they attracted whenever they made a stop for gas or to buy some refreshments.

They might still have made it to the border had it not been for the miracle that had occurred to the small boy, Pablito, and the attention it had attracted.

When de la Cruz roared out of his driveway onto the road late that night, leaving his wife and the guests to make what they would of what had become more a fiasco than the well-orchestrated evening he had intended, he was held up by a strange procession of people carrying torches, candles, lanterns and a banner on which was emblazoned the image of the Virgin of Guadalupe.

He was hurrying to take photographs of his daughter to the police station when the gathering obstructed his path. It did nothing to improve his temper. He blasted his horn and shouted at them to move aside, but so loud was their ecstatic chanting that, when no one paid any attention, he climbed out of his car and seized the leader of the march, telling him in no uncertain terms that he wished to pass.

The leader either did not hear or did not understand, for he nodded and thrust a branched candle-holder into de la Cruz' hand and continued with his chanting. When eventually de la Cruz managed to stop the discordant song, he learned about the miracle that had occurred when the 'Mexican Wedding' couple had kissed. Hurriedly he produced a photograph of María for identification. She was instantly recognized, and her likeness was seized by the people, who fixed it to the banner while offering thanks and praise and a profusion of blessings.

"Si, si, señor. That is the face of the angel. See how our little Pablito is healed!"

And little Pablito was pushed forward and told to roll up his trouser-leg. A torch was produced to throw light on the miracle.

De la Cruz looked at the grubby little boy with distaste. He could not see anything miraculous about his appearance, but he was persuaded to bend down and examine the leg from which, they claimed, rays of light still shone, remnants of the healing that had occurred. No, he did not want to touch it. Yes, he was convinced. Now could they please tell him in which direction the 'angels' had gone?

As one, they all pointed to the sky.

"She went that way, señor. She and the young man; they both rose up to Heaven. Our Lord Jesus led them, and we saw Guadalupe follow them. See! She left us these red petals."

And they produced a basket filled with sweet-scented, red rose petals.

"We thought they were a wedding couple, but now we know they were angels come to heal our little Pablito here. Now we are going to walk all night and tomorrow until we reach the sanctuario to offer her our prayers, and give thanks to the Blessed Virgin for the milagro that we have received."

Familiar with the flexible imagination of the locals, de la Cruz asked what kind of car 'the angels' were driving when they went to Heaven. When he heard their garbled description of the car, he decided not to waste more time with such superstitious peasants.

It was when he arrived at the police station, and learned that a wedding couple in a lime-green lowrider had been seen five hours earlier traveling south along the Interstate, that he realized that they had been telling the truth. He shook his head in disbelief. What on earth was Salvador thinking to be driving such a vehicle? It would be easy to trace. He wondered what their plan might be; whether they would leave the highway and take the back roads, or try to get across the border into Mexico. They might think that he would not be able to do anything once they were safe in that country. They would be wrong.

He suggested that the police spread out into all the small villages, and ask around if anyone had seen the couple. He would take the Interstate and go south. His suspicion was that this would be their plan. He would phone in from time to time to check on the progress.

De la Cruz drove as if the devil was on his heels. Cars moved to left and to right, even as the waters of the Red Sea had parted for Moses. He appreciated this courtesy, and pressed his foot down even harder. What he had not noticed was that in each town he had aroused several bored traffic officers who, seeing the speeding car flash by, had turned and given chase. It was for this reason that the other motorists had moved aside. By the time he reached Socorro, he had more than thirty cars, all with blue lights flashing, trailing behind him like the tail of a comet.

At Socorro the chase ended. As de la Cruz entered the city limits, he encountered a posse of cars with flashing blue lights spread across the road, waiting for him.

The next few hours were a nightmare for de la Cruz. The officers were not interested in listening to his story, and when he grew abusive, he was handcuffed. He was booked for dangerous driving, for driving over the speed limit, for ignoring traffic lights, for abusive language, for attempting to obstruct an officer in the execution of his duty, for attempting to resist arrest and finally, after an officer thought he could smell alcohol on his breath and he subsequently failed a breathalyzer test, for driving under the influence. He was thrown into the back of one of the cars, taken to the nearest police station and put behind bars. It was only then that he was allowed to make a phone call.

By the time he was released, he had lost a total of four hours. It was only after signing an admission of guilt, in triplicate; after having persuaded a slow and extremely thorough official to contact his local police station and arrange for them to vouch for him, and the driver's license, which he had not brought with him; and after numerous phone calls to arrange the payment of a monstrous fine, because he did not have any money or identification on his person, that he was permitted to leave his cell. However, he was obliged to drink several cups of black coffee, and consume numerous hamburgers, before he was considered sober enough to continue on his journey.

By the time all of this was done, de la Cruz was barely holding onto his rage, but he managed to look suitably contrite for the traffic officers, who were observing him closely. If he had known that he had overtaken Salvador and María while they filled up with gas some thirty miles back, he might not have managed this deception.

When he pulled out onto the Interstate, to his great frustration, he was followed by a stream of flashing blue lights, and was obliged to keep steadfastly within the speed limit. It was only when he saw them turn off at San Antonio that he put his foot on the gas, and drove southward as fast as he dared. He had no doubt that they would have phoned ahead, for officers to keep their eyes open for him.

It was as he was approaching the lights of a small town that de la Cruz saw before him some kind of vision. He shook his head and rubbed his eyes, but the brilliance remained before him. He thought it might be a traveling rock star with his band, but as he got closer he dismissed the thought.

What de la Cruz saw, what lit up the road in front of him, was a Technicolor image of the Virgin of Gauadalupe, painted with luminous paint on the trunk of a lime-green lowrider, a long, white veil that sparkled with diamonds—or stars—and the wild, red hair of María de la Cruz, flying like fire in the night.

De la Cruz overtook the slow vehicle and with skill, despite the violence that thundered in his chest, he forced them off the road and onto the soft shoulder, where eventually they came to a standstill.

Salvador, taken completely by surprise and with matters of love uppermost in his mind, was no match for María's enraged father. One punch from that powerful man sent him flying backwards into the night. Without a word, de la Cruz grabbed María and literally threw her into his car. He made a U-turn and drove off up the Interstate, leaving Salvador lying dazed at the side of the road.

Not a word was spoken on the long drive back to the rancho. It was past daybreak when they pulled into the courtyard. A white-faced and shocked María was dragged into the house and taken to her room. De la Cruz locked the door and retained the key. He went round to the porch and secured the shutters over her window. These too he locked. Then he went to his study, poured himself and drank a glassful of whisky. It was here that Catherine found him.

"Don't say one word!" was all he said. One look at his face was enough for her, and she left him.

All day the house was silent. The servants knew what had happened, and that María was back at home. Everyone kept their heads down and did their work in without speaking to each other, clearing away the debris and tattered remnants of the fateful celebration.

It was during that morning that the cloud appeared over the Hacienda: and all the birds stopped singing.

Pepita's Tail

It was evening when de la Cruz finally unlocked the door to his daughter's room. He entered without knocking. Finding her lying across the bed, still in the bridal dress and veil and looking like a crushed water-lily, he snatched the veil off her head, and with force tore the wedding band from her finger, leaving her delicate hand painfully bruised. He said nothing to María about the party or the elopement.

"Get into some proper clothes," was all he said, and left the room.

It was Catherine who, going in to her daughter some time later, found her sitting on the floor with a pair of scissors, surrounded by a mass of what looked like colored ribbons, busy cutting a long, narrow strip off a piece of material. To her horror Catherine saw that María had almost finished cutting up all her dresses.

"Oh, María."

She sat down on the floor next to her daughter, and took her in her arms.

"Mi querida."

María continued to cut the long strips of material. She said nothing, but a tear welled up in the corner of her eye. Relieved, her mother took her more fully into her arms and began to rock her, singing the lullaby that she and her mother before her had sung to comfort their babies when they were small.

María dropped the scissors and began to weep uncontrollably.

What manner of love was this that her husband felt for his daughter, that it could be so brutal? Intuitively Catherine knew that she didn't want to have this answered.

María's sobs were growing quieter. Catherine continued to hold her, stroking her hair and humming softly. When at last the weeping was done, Catherine released her. María sat up, blew her nose on a scrap of magenta chenille and took a deep breath. Then she looked at her mother.

It was a look that you will find on many women's faces in an unguarded moment. It is a look that fixes itself to a woman's face, sometimes early in life, sometimes later. It is a look which may come to include bitterness or may reveal a growing numbness. Catherine knew the look. She had seen it a thousand times in the mirror.

"Oh, my sweetheart," she said as she wiped tears from her own eyes. But what could she say? What hope or reassurance could she offer?

"Tomorrow we will take the car and go into Santa Fe, have lunch and buy some new clothes."

"Papá will never allow it. He is so angry."

"Papá will be away for a few days." She smiled at her daughter. "He is leaving first thing tomorrow morning. Then we will go and have a good time together. We'll clear this up. Your father does not need to know about it. I am going to ask Mercedes to bring you a snack, and some hot milk. Tomorrow you will feel better, and we can talk about what is to be done."

She gave her daughter a fierce hug and left the room, closing the door softly behind her.

Over dinner that night Catherine was silent. De la Cruz was so obsessed with himself and his own thoughts that he seemed not to notice this. When Mercedes had cleared away the dishes, Catherine rose and left the dining-room. She did not join her husband in the sitting-room, as was her custom, but went straight to her room and closed the door.

For the first time in her life she allowed herself to feel all the rage that lay beneath the resentment and bitterness that the lonely years of her marriage to him had brought her.

In a flash of violent rage she picked up a cut-glass perfume bottle and hurled it at the mirror. Staring back at her she saw the shattered image of her face.

With a scream that ripped the curtains apart and burst open the windows, she tore the silver comb from her thick hair and flung it out into the darkness. It was followed by flashes of light and shards of broken glass from the shattered mirror that flew out through the window and into the night.

Catherine threw herself onto the bed, screaming into the pillow and beating the bedclothes with her fists until she had no strength left.

That night she had a dream from which she woke sobbing so loudly that old Mercedes, in her small room across the courtyard, was wakened. She put on a gown and came across to Catherine's room to see what might be the matter. Still full of her dream, Catherine clung to her like a little girl, and between the sobs told it to Mercedes. It came out in disjointed bursts.

"I am looking everywhere for my little dog, Pepita. She was my closest friend. I got her as a puppy when I turned six. I don't know how she got lost."

As she clung to Mercedes' arm, she did indeed look like a frightened little girl.

"I am running down the road. I look everywhere. I can't find her. I keep calling her name as loud as I can, but she doesn't come. Where is she? Where is my Pepita? The road is so long."

Catherine stopped sobbing and looked at Mercedes. There was a look of shocked horror on her face as she remembered the dream's ending.

"One of my father's workmen has found something. It is Pepita's tail—her little white tail. I take it, and I think that maybe I can keep it in the drawer with my underwear, but I am not sure if it is proper. It looks quite clean. I take the tail and walk to my room, but as I walk I discover that the tail has started to bleed. There is a trail of blood behind me, and it is flowing out of the tail, like water out of a tap. I have all this blood on my hands. It is dark blood, almost black. Somehow I know that it is very old blood. Oh, Mercedes! It was horrible!"

Mercedes stayed with her until she was quiet, and then tucked her up into her bed the way you would a child.

"Sleep now, Catherine. It was just a bad dream. You will feel better in the morning."

But she did not feel better, for she woke to the sound of her husband shouting in the kitchen, and then a door slamming and a car pulling out of the courtyard.

At breakfast she learned from Mercedes that Roberto had found her silver comb on the roof of the stables, something he had chosen not to disclose to de la Cruz.

But worse than that, he had discovered that all of de la Cruz' prize roses had been mysteriously cut to pieces during the night, and that they lay on the ground, fragments of leaf and stick and thorn, with all their crimson petals liquefied into a pool of red fluid, as dark as blood.

The Days That Followed

Nothing was ever the same at the Hacienda de Las Palomas after the disastrous engagement party debacle. In the weeks and months that followed it each of the three de la Cruz family members sought and found their own particular means of escape from the overwhelming burden of suffering and mental anguish that the recent events had unleashed.

It was shocking to discover the bankruptcy that lay beneath the semblance of contentment; that the mask they presented to the world was just that, a mask. The outward appearance of success and harmony that the family had always projected in society, that they themselves had accepted as more or less typical of family life, now that it had been stripped away, revealed something unclean and sinister; an unexamined shadow, no less oppressive than the one that hung above them in the sky.

For Catherine there had always been the hope that María might manage to achieve the life that she, Catherine, had never lived; that through her she might gain a sense of fulfillment, of meaning; some consolation for all the opportunities that had been denied her. She had taken some comfort in the thought that even if her life and her freedom had been sacrificed, at least some of her gifts, and certainly her passion, might find expression in the world, through her youngest and extremely gifted daughter, María.

But when she saw her crushed and mortified daughter being dragged ignominiously into the house by a furious de la Cruz; when she recognized the same pattern of violence that she had endured being visited on her daughter, and realized that she was powerless to prevent it, all hope for the fulfillment of these dreams died in Catherine.

When she was with María she tried her best to comfort her, but there was a far deeper wound in her own soul, the pain of which now became unbearable. She wondered how she would endure the sense of terrifying hopelessness that had seized her, and the violence of her rage.

When not spending time with María, trying to comfort her through her terrible loss, her grief and the rage and powerlessness that she was feeling, Catherine would shut herself in her room and lie on the bed, unsleeping, staring at the overhead fan, trying to blot out the panic that was welling up inside her like a tidal wave.

At last a merciful door seemed to close on those acute feelings, leaving her senses deadened. In this benumbed state she was able to move about the house automatically, attending to the various house matters and doing whatever she could for María. In this dispirited state, and with her face as white as the little descansos crosses that marked the hills and roadsides, she managed to pull both her daughter and herself through the initial shock of the traumatic event.

And then deliverance came for her in an extraordinary form.

Nobody ever knew what had brought about the sudden and inexplicable change in Catherine de la Cruz, but a few months after María's return from her attempted elopement a transformation occurred in her mother.

Although nothing notable appeared to have happened in Catherine's external circumstances to explain it, it was noticed that she seemed to have discovered a new and invincible serenity. Her family, the staff and close friends who came to offer their consolation found this unaccountable. They thought that after the recent traumatic events—her husband's devastating embarrassment at María's failure to appear at her engagement party and the humiliating loss of face that he had suffered in the eyes of the community—Catherine would have had more to bear than usual: and yet this did not seem to be evident from her new and almost radiant presence.

Nor did María, who was close to her mother, have any notion of what had brought about this change. Ever since the dreadful night of her return, the night her father had dragged her away from her lover, the bond between María and Catherine, always strong, had become almost conspiratorial. But although she spent time with her mother and was grateful for her warmth and gentle support, María could feel that Catherine was slowly slipping away even from her. There were days when it seemed to María that her mother lived in a different world, a world from which she felt excluded.

Unknown to everyone, several days after the disturbing dream about Pepita's tail something happened, an occurrence that was to be a turning-point in Catherine's life, and it related directly to the dream—and to Pepita in particular.

Catherine had wakened to the sound of her husband's customary anger. He was still furious about the as yet unsolved mystery of the devastated roses, but Catherine sensed that he was using this as a focus for his anger at his daughter.

De la Cruz' humiliation was a deep wound to his pride. His feeling of impotence—the fact that he could not buy or manipulate his way out of the situation, was a foreign experience, and it terrified him. Anger was the only emotional response he knew, and the roses had offered him an outlet for his mix of feelings.

On that first morning when it was discovered, he examined the damage, noting with horror the dark pool of what looked like blood in which the ravaged plants lay in pieces. He made enquiries of all the staff as to whether they had seen or heard anything, but to no avail. Whatever, or whoever had wrought such destruction remained a mystery. This lack of information had done little to appease his temper and, as always, unable to contain his anger, he indulged in his customary abuse, shouting at everyone he saw and generally upsetting the entire household. Although this was not an unfamiliar occurrence, it was nevertheless profoundly disturbing, leaving everyone feeling strained and nervous and creating an uncomfortable tension in the whole house. No one who stood before a furious de la Cruz, or who found themselves anywhere close to his field of energy, could help but feel the waves of his rage penetrate their bodies, right to the core. His outpourings of anger were experienced by all as an invasion, an attack by some intractable and often irrational hostility, a primed and primal aggression that dwelt uneasily within his powerful body. It was a rage which seemed to be constantly alert, like a caged panther, watching only for that small gap when it could leap out and snarl at all who crossed his path. He seemed to be incapable of containing, or taking any responsibility for these intractable emotions.

On this morning Catherine was relieved that she was not yet dressed, and as such was avoiding direct contact with this latest tirade. She took a shower, and it was while she was toweling herself dry that she suddenly remembered her dream of Pepita. She sat down on the small bathroom stool, wrapped in steam and the fleecy softness of the large towel, retracing the steps of the dream. With the few days that had passed since she had dreamed it, some of the horror had faded, and the feeling with which she was left was one, predominantly, of curiosity. What could it mean that she should have the tail of her childhood pet returned to her? Why a tail?

While she completed her toilette in the bathroom, she mused on what the dream might be telling her. She returned to her bed-room, and while still pondering the enigma of the tail and its possible message, she selected a dress from her wardrobe, and the shoes she would wear. It was going to be a hot day.

Catherine sat at her dressing-table, brushing her long hair. She allowed the morning breeze, still carrying remnants of night, to cool her. She arranged her hair in the familiar coil and fixed it into place with the silver comb, which Roberto had cleaned before he returned it to her. Standing, she allowed the towel to drop and moved slowly across the room to the chest of drawers. She opened the drawer to take fresh underwear and a silk petticoat for the day, and was about to dismiss the dream altogether when her hand touched something that was lying on top of the neat piles of intimate clothing. Catherine stood quite still. Oddly she was not surprised. It was as if some part of her had known what she would find.

With a thrill of nervous excitement, and a delicious sense of illicit anticipation, she opened the drawer further and peered inside. There, resting on the softly folded lace and satin undergarments was Pepita's tail. She was relieved that there was no trace of blood to be seen.

When Catherine finally went to take her breakfast, she left the tail wrapped in a soft linen handkerchief and hidden in a small brocade bag, in the back of her closet. It gave her great comfort to know that it would be waiting for her when she returned.

When she entered the breakfast-room, she seemed not to notice the thunderous expression on her husband's face. She offered a smile, but it was clear she was distracted.

"Good morning, Lorenzo. How did you sleep?" She turned to Mercedes, and said that she would just have toast today, as she was a bit late.

De la Cruz looked up and scowled. "I suppose you don't know anything about the roses—you or María?"

Catherine poured herself some coffee and reached for the butter.

"No dear. We have been through this already."

Her husband, noticing that she was not giving him her full attention, began to raise his voice.

"Someone hacked all my roses to pieces. If I lay my hands on him—or her—I'll see to it that they are punished."

Catherine looked at him directly. She was completely without fear.

"There is no need to shout, Lorenzo. I can hear you perfectly well." She buttered a piece of toast. "You know, Lorenzo, you really are such a bully. It is most unattractive. And no, I have no idea what happened to your roses."

Catherine ate her toast and drank her coffee.

Lorenzo de la Cruz stared at his wife. He could not believe that Catherine would ever say such things. She would not dare. No woman of his would speak that way.

"What did you say, Catherine?" He felt he must have imagined it. Catherine had never spoken to anyone like that in her whole life.

But Catherine wasn't listening to him. Her mind had wandered off elsewhere. Something was calling to her. She turned her head, as if listening for a sound, a voice, some kind of invitation, something that beckoned to her. She looked uncertain for a moment, like a person at a crossroads, wondering which path to take. And then the indecision passed.

She rose with great composure, and laying her folded table-napkin neatly back on the table, she prepared to leave the room.

De la Cruz stood up and faced her directly.

"What did you say, Catherine?"

Catherine saw that he was about to launch into one of his tirades and held up a hand.

"I'm sorry, Lorenzo, that I can't stay to listen," she said over her shoulder as she departed. "I have to go. I promised Roberto I would show him where to put the new herbs. I see I am late."

And with this she left her astounded husband standing at the head of the table, with his mouth open as if about to speak and—speechless.

De la Cruz began to feel less and less in charge of his life and, with Catherine and María's close friendship and his daughter's refusal to speak to him, increasingly like an outsider in his own home.

He would sit in his study until late at night, or till the early hours of the morning, smoking as many as three cigars and drinking whisky until he was very drunk. He told nobody that there was a new reason for this late-night vigil. His boyhood dream had returned with all its feelings of fear and impotence. Now he was afraid of going to bed, to sleep, where he knew the dream waited for him. Again there was the long passage with the many doors; again his mother would come running and sobbing down the length of it; and he would be there, standing in each of the doorways, helpless. Only now, on some nights it was not his mother who ran past, but María: María in a wedding dress and veil, her long hair flying out behind her like a wild storm and the front of her dress covered with blood.

He took to making frequent trips, sometimes of long duration, down to Mexico, often staying away for weeks at a time. Some of these trips were necessitated by business matters, but more often they were a means of escape.

In Mexico City, with old friends who had no knowledge of his life in his home town, he did not feel the sense of shame that he suffered at home. Here with people of his own kind, he could still play the 'hombre de pro', the worthy man, and hold his head high. Here he could enjoy wild nights with friends, see the occasional bullfight, even enjoy a night out with a beautiful woman. Here he felt that people appreciated him, and ever the entertainer and story-teller, he blossomed under their laughter. He felt himself expand, break out of the strictures that small-town respectability imposed.

He felt the way he imagined a butterfly must feel when it has finally dragged its cramped wings out into the sunlight. Mexico City did not have the same small-town obsessions with other people's lives, and he enjoyed the freedom and the anonymity that the place afforded him.

But there were always the nights: and the dream.

Every time he returned home, he experienced a sense of loss, of claustrophobia; a growing resentment at the confines of his domestic life. He felt like a man who had put on someone else's clothes, clothes that were too tight, too small. He felt too large for the town, the community, even for his family, which had meant so much to him. He felt that he had outgrown his old life, that he had come to the end of a dream; and yet he remained tied to it.

This realization both dismayed and baffled him. He had not identified his own contribution to this lack of life and aliveness, or that it was he himself who had closed so many doors.

Alone in his study he could feel, beneath his anger, a growing fear: an almost overwhelming sense of disconnectedness.

He would never have admitted, even to himself, and even if he had recognized it, that beneath all his blustering rages and his attempts to dominate them, so much of who he considered himself to be rested in

Catherine and María's approval and admiration: that there was an empty place in him that was forever hungry for this.

He was a man who lived in two worlds, and although the one knew nothing of the other, the success of his life and loves in Mexico, when he made those trips to get away, nevertheless rested upon the stability and comfort of the home he shared with Catherine: a place to which he could always return. He didn't realize it, but it was the place that defined him; and for all his restlessness to leave such domesticity, there was always a moment when he needed to return.

It was as if some cord had never been cut.

At the Hacienda, Catherine and María had taken to spending many afternoons at the piano, singing, even composing music together, but their songs only served to make him feel more alienated, and listening to their intimate chatter, hearing the occasional laugh, made him feel painfully excluded. He knew, by their coolness towards him, that he was being punished. But it was the change in Catherine that disturbed him the most.

What nobody knew was that Pepita had returned to Catherine. At first, only the tail; but as the days passed and Catherine spent more and more time talking to her friend, remembering her childhood, more and more of the little dog began to manifest, until she managed to assemble all her parts—even her bark.

For Catherine it brought back the happy days, when she and Pepita would set off together, fearlessly roaming the hills around her family home, Pepita leading and Catherine, a beautiful little girl with a mass of red-gold hair just like her daughter's, following the little, erect tail that flashed at her through the sweet-grass and the sage bushes.

Now these days had returned to her. Catherine would set out on long walks early in the morning, returning bright-eyed and with sun kisses on her cheeks, in time for morning tea.

De la Cruz could not understand her behavior. Catherine never accompanied him on hunting trips, and he thought that she did not enjoy outdoor life very much, but here she was, neglecting her duties and running around the countryside like a child.

On several occasions he suggested that he accompany her, for he was eager to see where she went, but it was clear he was not welcome.

"Oh, Lorenzo, you wouldn't like it. You would be so bored."

And so he would watch her departure, puzzled at the slow metamorphosis that occurred as she walked away, disturbed to see his wife's customary, dignified deportment dissolve right before his eyes. Within seconds she became a running-and-skipping little girl, apparently engrossed in some delightful and animated conversation.

Catherine, in following the little dog, discovered a world beyond the dark cloud. All her new joy rested in the delight she felt at being reunited with her childhood friend. Pepita had always had an invincible spirit. It had always been remarked that it seemed to be impossible to upset or confuse the indomitable sense of self that reposed in that small animal. If she had been human, it would have been impossible to insult her, so contained was her inner serenity.

This new presence in her life seemed to give Catherine the strength to initiate some changes in her surroundings. The changes were small enough, to be sure, but the act of taking charge of some of the aspects of her world illustrated a new independence, which upset her husband greatly.

First she had all the electric lights removed from her bed-room and bathroom. She said from now on she wanted to spend her evenings in candle-light. She gave instructions for the large cushion that she had placed at the foot of her bed to remain there. She gave no explanation for this, and so the warm dent in the middle of it that Mercedes discovered every morning remained a mystery.

Every evening before she went to her room, she would go to the kitchen and fetch a small plate of food—in case she got hungry during the night, she said—something that she had never done in all their years of marriage.

Her husband could think of nothing that would explain her strange behavior. On a few occasions, while she was out walking, he surreptitiously searched her room for some clue, but found nothing. He wondered if she might be meeting with Salvador, and for weeks he watched her, followed her on her walks, throwing away all dignity and darting around like some third-rate sleuth, hiding behind junipers and ducking into arroyos to remain unseen.

On these occasions he was angered to see that as soon as she was away from the house she would find a seat, and very deliberately remove the silver comb and let her long hair fall about her shoulders. Then, leaving the comb on the rock or log where she had been sitting, she would run off with the wind blowing her hair behind her like a stream of silver and gold. She looked, he thought, like some wild creature. Catherine! His wife! He saw no sign of Salvador, or anyone else, but he was mystified to see her throwing sticks around and laughing like a mad woman. However, when she returned, her hair would be neatly gathered up once more with the silver comb in place: and she would walk into the house looking as if she had just been sitting in the garden for a few quiet minutes, watching the doves.

De la Cruz became a haunted man. He looked for ways to escape his feeling of powerlessness, searching for any reason, any excuse he could think of, to absent himself from his oppressive environment.

And there were always the nights: and the horror of the dream.`

The most notable change in María was that she refused to speak one word to her father, or to meet his gaze. She was quiet and well-behaved, doing nothing that could invite the slightest criticism from him, but there was a new defiance expressed through this silence; a separation that she established through it; an estrangement which he found unbearable.

He tried to coax her out of it through every means he could imagine. He offered her gifts, clothes, jewelry, a trip to Mexico, a trip to Europe, to France to visit some of her mother's relatives, anything she wished. There was a show that had just opened in New York that everyone was raving about. They could all go and see that, and spend a few days shopping.

All his attempts were fruitless. She appeared not to hear him. He thought that as time passed and she recovered from the shock, they might regain some of the closeness that they had once enjoyed. In his complacent arrogance he could have no idea of how irreparably he had destroyed that relationship; and so he continued to think of ways to win her back to him.

But as time progressed and he was unable to come close to María, a new and unfamiliar fear began to grow in his heart. It sounded within him, like one of the insistent drums that could be heard coming from one or other of the Indian pueblos during the time of their festivals: a pagan sound, to his ears, that seemed to go on and on and on, without any change in rhythm or volume—a sound so old, so implacable that nothing in his world could come near it. From time to time he would experience this as an unendurable pain that would lie in his heart for days at a time; a pain that took many glasses of whisky to make bearable.

There was no such turmoil in María's heart, however. After the initial shock at her father's violent rage, she felt her love for Salvador surge in her heart with a renewed strength. She would not be defeated.

While her father was occupied with his world, she considered ways to get word to Salvador. With José no longer working at the Hacienda, she had no means of having letters delivered undetected. She was sure that Salvador would come for her, but when? She had no knowledge of the charge her father had laid with the police, or that he had demanded that Salvador be informed that he would be arrested if he was discovered within ten miles of the Hacienda.

It was while she sat on the porch, looking at the ceramic pigeons on the garden wall, that she remembered the story her father used to tell to guests who asked about the name—Rancho de Las Palomas. She remembered being allowed once, as a special treat, to come into the dining-room to hear it. She could still remember the laughter and her father's deep, rich voice.

"Well, legend would have it," de la Cruz began, "that in 1781, the time of the smallpox epidemic, when Juan Bautista de Anza was Governor, an eccentric small-time sheep farmer, with more desperation than good sense, moved his family away from contact with anyone who might carry the disease. He came out here, which as you know was quite a considerable distance in those days, built a makeshift house and settled his long-suffering wife and three children into it. In order to stay in touch, should there be an emergency, he brought his homing pigeons with him, having arranged with a neighbor to check his pigeon-coop each evening."

De la Cruz rose and poured more wine for his guests.

"They were soon followed by his small flock of sheep, driven by two youngsters, who wanted to earn a few dollars. The sheep were watched during the day by his three small sons, and herded into a pen at night.

"Over the weeks and months, in spite of these precautions, the number of sheep began to dwindle. Some fell into arroyos, others were killed by coyotes. The farmer would run out at night when he heard the coyotes yipping close by, and scream and shout at them, firing random shots into the darkness. He would run to the pen where the terrified sheep were baaing and bleating, running from side to side, only to break out of the flimsy structure and disappear into the night. Here the coyotes would grab one, tear it to pieces and run off with blood dripping from the chunks of still warm flesh. He was always too late. If it hadn't been such a desperate time it would have been absurdly funny.

"His wife pleaded with him to let them return home. They could not continue this way. It was only a matter of time before they starved to death or died at the hands of the Comanche. But the farmer was a stubborn man. He refused to leave, and he refused to send a pigeon with a note to ask for help.

"'Those wretched birds are breeding at such a rate we will soon have no corn left. You are taking food out of your children's mouths with your stubbornness.' She raised her arms to heaven. 'Why the Holy Mother should have sent me such a fool of a man, I will never know.'

"And then it happened." De la Cruz paused dramatically.

"The youngest boy fell ill with a high fever. Within a day he was delirious. His distraught wife told her husband to send a bird or she would leave him and walk home with her sons, carrying the sick boy on her back.

"'I would rather die of smallpox than spend another day with you and your birds!'

"The farmer accepted what felt like an ignominious defeat, but his wife, watching the bird rise into the air, felt only relief. At last the ordeal was over. At last they could go home. Back to familiar things; back to friends and comfort and certainty; back to civilization.

"But the unexpected is never far away."

De la Cruz gave a chuckle.

"As the farmer and his wife stood with their eyes raised to the sky, following the pigeon's flight, to their consternation, they saw it circle once and fly straight back into the coop."

To the guests' inquiring looks he replied, "It would appear that from the pigeon's point of view, after all this time—this was home."

The guests all laughed.

"And what happened to the family?"

"Ah! Legend does not record what happened to the farmer and his family. That aspect of the story carries no romance, and has been forgotten. The birds, however, were still there when the land was bought some years later and the original Hacienda was built. Their numbers had swelled enormously, which is surprising with all the buzzards we have. In honor of the birds the Hacienda was named after them, and has kept the name to this day."

"And the birds you have now? Are they the descendants?"

"No," de la Cruz replied with a smile. "Those I had brought here when María was born. But the original ones—well, it would appear that at some time in the intervening one hundred and whatever-odd years they must have remembered their address and gone home. When we bought the place, there were just those fantails on the wall."

The story had given María the idea. She was delighted at its simplicity. She asked Roberto to buy her some pottery clay, and to set up a work-table in one of the old feed rooms behind the stables.

Every morning, María left the house after breakfast and set to work. By lunchtime on the first day she had finished making three small doves. She covered them with white slip and fashioned a little groove close to the left leg of each bird, where a note could be safely fixed, after the manner of a carrier pigeon. She used one of her tears to smooth down the soft curves of the breast, just over the heart. Then she placed them to one side to dry.

The next day and the next, and every day thereafter, María spent her mornings making white pottery doves. As soon as she had a batch of nine doves, Roberto took them to be fired. On their return María inspected them to make sure they were perfect. Satisfied, she inserted blue glass beads for eyes and lined them up on the shelf above the work-table.

Each day she wrote a note to Salvador, telling him how she missed him, promising undying love, and that she would wait for him, forever. This she folded carefully to include a small curl of her hair. Each day, in the early afternoons while her mother was resting, she climbed the hill behind the house, taking with her just one bird, with his precious missive tucked safely into place.

After pressing a kiss onto its white breast, she launched it into the air, telling it to fly to Salvador with her love.

And so, every day, anyone who happened to be looking in that direction saw a white dove rise up out of the dark cloud and wing its way across the vastness of the blue New Mexican sky, flying straight as an arrow in a southerly direction.

It became a game for the children who lived nearby, in the early afternoon, to wait and see who would be the first to spot the white dove. They would stand in a row, their faces turned up to that vast dome of sky, their eyes straining to be the first to see the little bird fly by.

Every day the cry would ring out from one small child or another—"There it is!"—and they would all dance up and down in the pink dust like an untidy row of jumping beans, laughing and pointing to the small, white speck as it flew over them.

Salvador Comes for María

Exactly one thousand and ninety-five days had gone by since María and Salvador had attempted to elope. María knew this, because she had been keeping a careful count of the white doves that she released each day.

She knew that they had reached him, and that Salvador had received her messages of love, for she could feel his love for her, burning in her heart.

She had never lost faith that he would come for her and take her away just as soon as she turned twenty-one. On that day her father would have no legal power to prevent her from leaving home. As the final weeks passed and the day of her twenty-first birthday approached, she began to make preparations for her departure.

Nobody noticed any change in her behavior, partly because she took great care not to advertise her plans by even the slightest change in her routine, and partly because everyone was preoccupied with their own affairs.

Catherine retreated further and further into a world that kept her safe from any of her husband's rages. María tried to join her, attempted to enter that world, but it seemed to her that just as she was about to make some contact, touch her in some way, her mother, right before her eyes, would walk through an invisible door—invisible, but no less impenetrable than if it had been made of steel.

Eventually María accepted that her mother had found a way of being happy that, of necessity, had to exclude all attachment to her family. She marveled at the way she seemed able to go through the motions of being a wife, a mother and occasionally even a hostess, without actually being emotionally present.

De la Cruz, recently returned from one of his numerous trips to Mexico City, was busy preparing for the hunting season. He spent long days in his gun-room with his whisky and his cigars examining, re-cleaning and oiling all his guns, testing the smoothness of their action, looking critically down the sights, checking his supply of cartridges and shot and honing his hunting knife until it gleamed with sharpness. This occupation brought him much pleasure. He loved the feel of the rifle against his shoulder, the weight of it; the knowledge of the power it held, a power that, matched with his skill, could bring down an elk with one shot from a distance few men could better.

With Catherine becoming increasingly distracted, much of the running of the house fell upon Mercedes' capable shoulders. This made it necessary for Encarnación, Roberto's wife, to come and help in the house. To everyone's relief, not least Encarnación herself, she had finally stopped having babies, and with the youngest now being cared for by the grandmother, she was free to take on responsibilities around the house. She and Mercedes made the lists of what provisions needed to be bought, and once a week Roberto drove his wife to town to purchase them.

It was in this fashion that life continued, uneventfully, one day following another, at the Hacienda de Las Palomas. One might almost say that the occupants, all but one, had fallen into some kind of lethargy, only a day short of the kind of sleep that princesses are wont to follow in fairy-tales.

It was punctuated sporadically by de la Cruz' tyrannical outbursts when he was at home, but even he seemed to have been lulled into some sense of complacency with regard to his family, and he filled most of his time, when at home, peacefully enough, inspecting his estate, talking to Diego and Roberto about certain maintenance matters or reading in his study.

María's twenty-first birthday was to be a quiet family affair. She did not mind at all that it would be so, for she had plans of her own, and it would all be much simpler this way. This time nothing would go wrong—she would see to that: and in her last note to Salvador she had suggested that he come to fetch her in a regular car.

María was expecting Salvador to contact her the evening before her birthday. She suggested that this would be a suitable time for them to make their departure. They would have the whole night before it was noticed that she was missing. This would give them plenty of time to reach the Mexican border and disappear.

Although she received no word from him, she was perfectly certain that he had received her missives and that he would arrive on time. So it was with a beating heart, on that last evening, once her father had retired to take his evening whisky alone in his study, that she said goodnight to her mother and kissed her tenderly on the cheek. It is possible that Catherine felt a difference in her daughter, for she drew her close, kissed her long and tenderly and hugged her tightly.

"You know how much I love you, my sweet María," she said with a suggestion of moisture in her eyes. "And I do bless you. Sleep well, my sweetheart. Tomorrow is a special day for you."

María looked closely at Catherine. At times she still had the child-like belief that her mother knew what she was thinking. Could she possibly know what she had planned? She looked again and felt reassured, for the familiar, distant look had returned to Catherine's face.

She left the room and went to say goodnight to Mercedes in the kitchen. She had spent time with the other members of staff during the day, but Mercedes was like a mother to her. She was the only one who had the strength to stand fast during her father's tantrums, and it was she who offered María a place in her large, uncomplicated heart, to recover from the violence that he had done to her love and her dreams. María felt a deep pang at the thought that she would not see Mercedes again.

She drank the warm milk and ate the cookies that Mercedes always kept aside for her. They exchanged a few words about the coming birthday, and María thanked her for the cake that stood on a shelf in the pantry. Then she hugged Mercedes goodnight, and was halfway through the door when she turned and ran back into her arms and held on to her tightly.

"Why, María! What's the matter?"

"Oh, I do love you so, Mercedes."

"Why!—child!" Mercedes wrapped both her arms around María and held her close. "And I love you, and I always will; even when you turn twenty-one and are all grown up."

She made her voice sound light.

María made her way to her room in what used to be known as the children's wing. It was an extension of the original house, which de la Cruz had ordered to be built when María was born. It had once comprised six small bed-rooms, but later, with her sisters' departure, five small rooms had been converted into a play-room, and later a music room for María.

She removed the packed suitcase from its place of hiding, under blankets in the linen cupboard. Everything was ready. There was not much to take: a few clothes, some blue jeans and sweatshirts and warm jerseys. She had packed her coats, several pairs of boots and the beautiful shawl that her mother had given her after Salvador's concert, a gift to cheer her up after the loss of the singing lessons. She did not take any of the jewelry that her father had bought for her, but she planned to wear the silver and gold locket that had belonged to her great-great-grandmother, which her mother had fastened around her neck on the night of the concert.

Her father gave her his birthday gift early, so that she could wear it on her birthday, he said.

She received it in silence, and only opened it later in her room. Now it lay on her dressing-table, still resting on its pink tissue wrapping: a silver hair-comb which he had brought back from his latest trip to Mexico. It was similar to the one he had given his wife over four decades earlier, but it was more delicately wrought.

From almost as early as she could remember her hair had been braided in compliance with her father's wishes. On the few occasions that the braids had come loose and she had entered the house with her hair flying around her head, a wild, tangled mass of red-gold ringlets, her father, usually so gentle where she was concerned, would snap at her, telling her to go to her mother and get her disgraceful untidiness made straight. Over and over she had heard him say that only women of loose morals wore their hair unrestrained; that morals, dignity and honor, these were a woman's only assets. If she lost these, no one would want her. A woman with loose hair was being provocative. She was signaling that she was available. No woman of his would shame herself in this way.

She looked at the silver comb with incredulity. She could see that it was a work of art, fashioned with great skill by a master silversmith, and intended to enhance a woman's beauty. Coming from her father, it was but a symbol of ownership and domination. María gave a small shudder.

Ever since her sixteenth birthday she had felt uncomfortable about her father's professed love for her, but not until the night of her attempted elopement with Salvador had she seen the unnatural possessiveness of his affection: and it shocked her. It made her feel unclean to be around him.

Now, as she considered her mother's life—her lack of freedom, bound as she was to her father's will, and the ultimate cruelty, his refusal to allow her to use her one talent, her beautifully trained singing voice—she saw a man so different from the father she had loved as a little girl, that it appalled her.

Now she understood all the years of her mother's depression; the unhappiness he had caused her by his blind self-centeredness. She realized that her father did not see his wife at all: did not see anyone, except they served his needs in some way. Catherine was an object, a possession. He had tried to turn her into a puppet, a beautiful doll that would wear the clothes he chose, speak when she was spoken to, agree with him in everything, never argue or have an opinion of her own.

But now, just when he thought he had succeeded, she had finally found a door out of her prison. María shook her head. He was a blind, stupid, arrogant fool. And now he wanted to offer her the same tyranny, in the form of this gift.

She looked out through her window. One by one the lights were put out as the various inhabitants turned in for the night. Only the light in her father's study still burned, throwing a glow into the courtyard. She wondered if he was still awake. She knew about his heavy drinking and his habit of falling asleep in his chair.

María turned out her light. She did not light the candle, which she was to set in the window as an indication to Salvador that everyone was asleep. She wanted to be quite sure that her father had gone to bed. It would not be safe until he left the study. Everything in the house was quiet. Everything outside was quiet, but still the light burned in the study window.

María waited. She knew he would be very drunk by now, for she had on occasion witnessed his unsteady progress as he made his way to bed. These past years his drinking had become heavier: yet with his remarkable constitution he was able to rise each morning, if not exactly clear-eyed, at least full of energy for the day.

The light in the study window went out. María waited another half-hour before lighting the candle. Now that the moment had arrived, she felt her heart skip a beat. Would Salvador really come?

She did not have to wait long. Within five minutes she heard a faint tap at the glass-paned doors. Within seconds they were in one another's arms, and Salvador was kissing her passionately.

"Oh! María! Oh, María!" was all he could say, in between the kisses that she returned with equal passion.

He lifted her effortlessly and carried her over to the bed, kissing her face, her eyes and her mouth. Accompanied by María's soft protestations that they should leave at once, he started to unbutton her blouse. The last cautious protest left María as she felt Salvador's warm body touch hers: one last moment when she was aware of herself, when she felt the wonder, the miracle of what was happening to her, and then she and Salvador were one, and all thoughts flew away.

De la Cruz had not gone to bed. He was spending a last few late-night, pleasurable moments in his gun-room. It was while he was inspecting, with satisfaction, the razor edge of his hunting knife that he heard the sound. He listened as attentively as the whisky would allow, in order that he might discern where it came from. Perhaps someone was attempting a burglary.

But as he listened he recognized, as well he should, the unmistakable rhythm of two people in the throes of passionate love-making. For one wild and desperate instant he hoped he was mistaken, but even as the thought occurred he knew that this was not so.

He knew, with an instinctive certainty as only a passionate and insanely jealous father can know, that the sounds he heard, the accelerating rocking and banging, the moans and the cries of pleasure, were coming from María's room.

De la Cruz was a big man with more than a bottle of whisky coursing through his bloodstream, but he moved through the house at the speed of an Olympic runner whose life depends on victory. He flung open the door to the music room and raced across the length of it, sending chairs and small tables flying as he passed.

A music box, that had been a farewell gift to María from the church choir, fell to the ground, was activated and began to pluck out—'Lead us, Heavenly Father, lead us'—in crisp, staccato tones. De la Cruz entered María's room in a rush, the hunting knife still grasped in his hand.

The two lovers sprang apart.

"Go, Salvador!" María screamed, even as she reached for her silk gown which hung close to the bedside.

Such was the compelling urgency in María's voice that Salvador found himself running naked into the night, leaping over lavender and sweet basil as he raced in the direction of his car. Only when he reached it did he come to his senses.

He threw on a shirt and some jeans from the suitcase of clothes he had packed for their journey, and made his way back to the Hacienda. There he found that de la Cruz had locked and barred the exterior doors to María's room, and he could gain no entry. He hammered against the windows, but such was the noise inside the room that neither of the occupants heard him.

Through small gaps in the shutters he saw de la Cruz, his face purple with fury, shouting at María, gesticulating furiously with the hunting knife. She, in an effort to protect herself, held the red silk robe in front of her nakedness. Perhaps the flash of scarlet had awoken some instinctive response in de la Cruz, or perhaps it was the sight of María's gleaming hair, that hung loose about her shoulders and over her naked breasts, that inflamed him further. He charged forward, wrested the floating, red silk from her grasp with the blade and tossed it to one side, striking her a blow across the face with his left hand as he did so.

"Whore!"

María staggered backwards, but de la Cruz was at her again. Seizing hold of a long lock of loose hair, he attempted to cut it off, but she was too quick for him. She pulled herself sharply away, but there was nowhere she could run to avoid him. He reached out and grabbed her, threw her back on the bed and stared down at her nakedness, his right arm raised, the knife still in his hand.

It was at this point that Salvador, who had been throwing himself against the French doors in an effort to come to María's aid, burst through the door. He catapulted himself into the room amid splinters of wood and glass and leaped at de la Cruz, seized the knife and hurled it across the room. Then, like a madman, he attacked the older man and struck him a blow, well-known by anyone who had had the misfortune to tangle with Salvador in a fight; a blow which sent de la Cruz, blinded with pain and the blood that sprang from his eye, reeling backwards, momentarily senseless. Salvador followed it up with another well-aimed cut to the jaw that saw the big man stumbling across the room, where he collapsed into a chair.

No one moved. There was the rasping sound of de la Cruz breathing as he struggled to recover. His chest heaved with the effort of it. Salvador never took his eyes off him. When at last the older man could speak, it was in tones that sent a chill down María's spine. She reached for some bedclothes and wrapped them around her nakedness.

"How dare you!" De la Cruz attempted to rise, but fell back into the chair. "How dare you enter my house!"

De la Cruz felt a sharp pain in his chest that momentarily took his breath away. His face was purple.

"How dare you come creeping into my daughter's room!"—He struggled to breathe. "Under my roof," he gasped, "In the middle of the night!" He pulled himself up in the chair. "Who in God's name do you think you are?"

"I am her husband! That's who I am!"

De la Cruz, with the blood running down his cheek, his heavy shoulders hunched upward and his head lowered like an enraged bull about to charge, leaned forward in the chair.

"Get out of my house!" Each word sounded like a pistol shot. "Get out of my house, this instant! Leave my house, and my daughter, and never set foot anywhere near her again! I will see you dead before I let you touch her. Return—and you will regret it. I will see to it that she receives the punishment intended for you."

He took a handkerchief from his pocket and wiped away some of the blood. "Is that perfectly clear?" He touched the cut on his lip, and then scrunched up the handkerchief and thrust it back into his pocket. "Do you understand that this is not an empty threat?"

His cheek, next to his right eye, had begun to twitch. His lips were very white. Catching a glance from María's shocked, white face, he continued.

"Look at her, Salvador. She knows. She will tell you that I do not utter threats that are not in my power to execute."

De la Cruz rose from the chair and stood unsteadily. With a hand that shook he smoothed his disheveled hair.

"Do not think for one second that I don't mean it. I am a powerful man. I can arrange things. I have many contacts. Do not underestimate me,

Salvador, or you will regret it. I guarantee you this. There is no choice here, Salvador. Either way you lose her. Go!"

Salvador stood still. He looked at María. He read on her face that what de la Cruz had promised, was not just an attempt to intimidate him; it was not an empty threat. But he also read a new spirit of defiance.

"Salvador is my husband, father. And I am twenty-one. You have no right to stand in our way."

"You are not yet twenty-one," he thundered, "and I am your father! And you are not leaving this house. I will call the police and lay a charge of breaking and entering."

"And I will say I saw you threaten your daughter, with a hunting knife," Salvador said with rage in his voice.

"And who do you think they will believe?"

With this de la Cruz left the room. He returned within a minute, carrying a pistol.

"If you don't leave now," he said, "I will shoot you."

"You must go, Salvador."

Salvador looked at her in disbelief. "Come, María. Come with me."

"If she takes one step out of this house, you will both live to regret it!"

"Go, Salvador," she said. "He will do as he says."

Salvador stood staring at her. It could not end like this.

"María," he began, but she cut him short.

"Salvador!—if you love me!—go!"

He hesitated.

"Go!"

Salvador turned and left through the broken door. María watched him make his way across the garden, growing less and less distinct, until the darkness swallowed him.

"And you go too, father," María said with her back to him. "You are nothing but a coward and a brute."

De la Cruz stared at his daughter. He crossed the room and retrieved his hunting knife. Returning to María, he gripped her arms and pulled her around to face him.

"What did you say?"

With the point of the knife beneath her chin, he raised her face to meet his angry stare.

"Don't think that you can give me orders in my own house," he said through white lips, "you little slut!"

He tore away the bedclothes that she had wrapped around her nakedness and flung her down on the bed: stood staring down at her, breathing heavily. María didn't move.

From the music room could be heard the slow notes of the music box, which had almost completely unwound and was playing the last slow, mechanical lines of 'Lead Us Heavenly Father Lead Us'. It had the effect of bringing de la Cruz back to his senses. With an oath he turned and left the room, leaving her lying there, naked, bruised and beaten, as surely as if he had raped her.

Blood

De la Cruz stormed out of María's room in a passion of rage. He made no effort to contain his emotions, but beat his fist on furniture and slammed doors as he strode through the house to his study. He entered it and locked the door behind him. Then, moving over to the liquor cabinet, he seized a bottle of whisky and began to drink straight from it, pacing up and down the length of the room between gulps.

The more he drank, the more enraged he became, until, swearing loudly, he crossed to the gun-room where the light still burned and opened the gun cabinet. He seized his hunting rifle, the bag of shot and hunting necessities, snatched his thick coat off its peg near the door and stormed out of the house and across the dirt yard to his pick-up, where he threw the gear into the back and, without a backward glance, roared out of the courtyard and down the drive.

It was a long drive to the Valle Grande, but it did nothing to diminish his fury; if anything, he grew more and more enraged as the miles passed.

Ignoring all the signs requiring him to decrease his speed, he roared through pueblos and the small villages, a high-pitched, metallic whine, cutting through the stillness of the night.

Soon he was climbing the steep mountain pass and entering the tree-line and thick snow. He would reach the caldera before dawn. Cursing and swearing, he forced the pick-up up the rough road, the engine protesting, the wheels slipping on the patches of ice, causing the whole vehicle to slide dangerously close to the outer edge where the snow-banks fell away sharply down the forested slopes.

It was about a half-hour before dawn when he arrived at the valley. As he rounded the last bend, he saw it stretched out in front of him: that vast, white space, the snow glistening in the half-light; a silent world where nothing moved.

His anger had changed. Now it was like ice. Once more he felt himself to be in control. As he climbed out of the car, it was as if a cold hand lay over his heart.

He put on the thick sheepskin jacket with the warm hood; put on the leather gloves. He loaded the rifle and fixed the shot belt around his waist.

He left the car and moved into the cover of the trees; moved on several hundred yards, and stopped to listen and survey the valley.

He saw a small pack of coyotes some distance ahead. They crossed in front of him, about two hundred yards away, and melted into the forest. He proceeded, staying in the cover of the trees, circling round the edges of the valley, his eyes scanning the white plain for a tell-tale sign of movement. He moved on a little further, right to the outer edge of the forest, where he might see more clearly.

And then, there they were.

An antler had moved, and that focused his eye upon the slight irregularity in the whiteness. He had seen the stags.

The overnight snow had given the elk a light dusting, enough to act as a camouflage. Now he picked out the cows some distance away on the other side of the stream. It was still early dawn, and the herd remained alert. No elk ever grazes at night. It is the time for predators.

They heard him. That slight movement that had caught his eye was an elk turning its head in his direction, although he thought he had made no sound. He stood still. But the herd had sensed a presence, and they rose and milled about, sniffing the wind.

Damn the brutes, he thought. Next thing they would take off and he would have made the trip for nothing.

He moved further into the forest and ploughed his way through the thick snow, trying to keep quiet and not break any branches. His heart was like ice. Gone was the bombastic host, the teller of stories, the lover of fine wine and beautiful women.

He was filled with a cold desire: to kill.

He hoped to circle round, and so be in position when they crossed in front of him; but they had turned and were heading north. He paused to consider which way he would go.

A pre-dawn breeze blew the light snow that was starting to fall against his face. If it snowed any harder, he would not be able to see a thing. He climbed up a small, wooded hill to give himself some elevation.

It was while he paused to get his breath on the steep incline that he saw, standing on a rocky outcropping, a magnificent bull stag with eight points to his rack.

He was standing proud, searching the wind, etched like a statue against the white sky with the light snow-flurries, soft as mist, swirling about him. Now the great head swung around to face in his direction.

De la Cruz knew he wouldn't get another chance as good as this one. Slowly he raised the rifle. Don't rush it now, he told himself. He took careful aim. Not the head: it is too far. The heart. Aim for the heart. He aimed for the heart, and fired.

The sound of the shot echoed across the valley. For an endless moment he thought he must have missed his mark, for the stag did not move. It stood there, still looking in his direction, the snow swirling around it. Then it took a faltering step backwards.

It seemed as if the brain could not comprehend this death: had no way of preparing itself or that warm system of blood, nerves and adrenalin—all those centuries-old mechanisms for fight and flight—for this unknowable adversary. There had been no warning to activate that system for self-preservation. The attack had been invisible.

The head, with those magnificent horns, raised itself, showing the full curve of the throat. Its muzzle pointed up to the sky. It looked like the bronze sculpture that de la Cruz had standing on the corner of his huge desk. It stood as motionless.

And then it fell.

María Leaves Home

Lorenzo de la Cruz was dreaming.

He was standing in a bullring, dressed as a matador, facing the gate through which the bull would enter the ring. In his hands he held the scarlet matador's cape. Across the ring, some distance away from where he stood, the picadors sat motionless on their bony, broken-down horses. There was something wrong with the dream; something missing. All was silent. And apart from the scarlet cape he held, there was no color. Everything was monochromatic.

Looking up, he saw that the entire stand, all the way around—the front seats, the boxes and the gallery seats—were empty. No one had come to see the fight. The gate had not opened. There was no sign of the bull.

A sudden movement in the stand, to the left of where he stood, caught his eye. Someone, a woman in a large, black hat, entered one of the boxes and took a seat. He could not make out her face under the shadow of the wide brim of the hat, other than its chalky whiteness and large, dark eyes.

He turned and bowed to her: then, with both hands grasping the heavy cape, he executed a slow veronica, pivoting on the balls of his feet, the scarlet silk spreading out from him as the imaginary bull charged. The woman stood and threw a blood-red rose, which landed at his feet and broke apart, casting red petals over his shadow that stretched out long and thin in front of him.

Then, turning her back on him, she removed the black hat, drew out the silver comb that held the mass of her black hair and allowed it to fall down her back. Slowly she turned her grinning face to him, and he recognized La Muerte, the death figure.

As if this had been some kind of a sign, there was the sound of a heavy bolt being released and the screech of the gate opening. The sound was shockingly loud. The horses turned their slow, skeletal heads towards the noise.

And then the gate swung open, and out of the shadows of the long, dark passageway stepped a little girl. María.

She was wearing the white dress with the appliqué design that he had brought for her from Mexico when she was eight. Her red-gold hair floated about her face like a halo. The colors on the dress were bright, startling against the drabness of the rest of the scene. So too, the scarlet stain on the front of it.

She came to a standstill twenty paces away from him and put her hands up to the top of her head with the two index fingers pointing forwards to imitate the horns of a bull.

"Look, Papá! I am a bull. Are you going to kill me?"

De la Cruz woke with a start, the sweat pouring from him. "God—what a dream!" he muttered.

He rose and went over to the wash-stand, poured some water into the large bowl and splashed handfuls of it over his face. He stood there for a moment, leaning on his arms over the basin, aware of the faint trace of lavender in the scented water that dripped down his neck. He forced his mind away from the dream, back to the room, back to the day ahead. He reached for a towel and patted the water from his face.

Standing there, he looked at himself in the mirror. What he saw reassured him. He looked the way he always did: strong, handsome: self-assured. He wet his face again, and dried it. He felt better. The nightmare that had woken him, although horrifying, meant nothing to him. He was not a man given to introspection. A dream was just a dream. Nothing more. He put on a light silk dressing-gown, and after patting some cologne onto his face and combing his thick, dark hair, he made his way through the quiet house to his study.

As he passed the kitchen door, he heard the muted sounds of Mercedes and Encarnación preparing the breakfast meal. He gave a rather grim smile of satisfaction. No talking was permitted in the kitchen this early in the morning. De la Cruz did not like the sound of chattering women.

In the study he poured himself a whisky, which he took over to his armchair. He set the glass down and seated himself, leaning back into the cushions, staring out over the garden. He had dismissed the dream. Everything was quiet and peaceful. On this auspicious day de la Cruz did not want to feel troubled in any way. He did not want to feel anything. He took a few sips of whisky and made a mental note to remember to pick up another case when next he was in town.

Through the panes of the French door he caught sight of the doves that had been let out of the aviary for their morning flight. The sight of the white birds awoke in de la Cruz a memory, and some unwelcome associations that made him feel uncomfortable. He averted his eyes, turning instead to reach over to the humidor which was close to his armchair. With much consideration he selected a cigar and smelled it, inhaling the rich fragrance. He removed the seal, clipped the end very precisely, and taking up his heavy gold lighter, he lit it carefully. He took long, slow draws of pungent smoke; savoring the flavor, watching the smoke curl upwards and taking frequent sips of whisky.

He wondered what he should wear on this important day: something dark, casual, but not too casual; perhaps the new, navy-blue linen jacket that Roberto had collected from the tailor. And black slacks. Yes—and a crisp, open-necked shirt. His mind went over the preparations he had made for the day.

Roberto was to drive María to the small retreat which de la Cruz had decided was a suitable future home for her; a place that would care for her and break this new, rebellious and intractable side of her that had become so unseemly; teach her the behavior suitable for a well-bred young woman.

Catherine had not succeeded in doing this. Now it was in his hands.

He had ordered the car for eleven o'clock, which would allow ample time for farewells and still get them to the retreat in time for lunch. He, de la Cruz, would leave the house before María. He would not say goodbye. He would leave that tearful scene to the women.

All the arrangements had been made several weeks ago, not long after Salvador's unwelcome intrusion into his house; the incident that had prompted this drastic decision. Once his rage had subsided, de la Cruz had set about making enquiries. His fury had been replaced by a cold, clinical detachment that the members of the house found more terrifying than his rages.

María was to be sent to the small retreat, known simply as The Adobe, that was situated on the other side of town, about a two-hour drive from the Hacienda. The retreat was run by nuns, and a young man called Sebastián Chávez, under the guidance of Father Octavio. De la Cruz vaguely remembered having met Sebastián, but he couldn't recall where that might have been. It was certainly of no importance. The inclusion of Father Octavio on the board of trustees had given the place credibility in de la Cruz' eyes.

He had driven out to inspect the facilities, to make sure they were suitable for his daughter; that she would be well cared for and suitably tutored in religious matters. Satisfied with both the accommodation and the staff, he duly finalized the financial agreement for María's permanent residence at The Adobe.

He had not consulted Catherine on this matter, nor had he informed her of the retreat's name or location. The staff had been told nothing. Roberto, who was to drive María to her destination, was sworn to secrecy with a threat of ruin for his family and his future. If it had not been for his love of Catherine, he would have left immediately.

A sudden, sharp bang on the glass pane of the French doors had de la Cruz springing to his feet. The glass slipped from his hand, tumbled and fell to smash into shards on the polished tile floor, leaving a mess of whisky and broken glass at his feet. Looking over to the French doors, he saw that one of the doves must have mistakenly thought the reflection of sky in the window-pane to be a new flight path, and had flown into the glass, leaving a smear of blood on it in doing so.

"God damn it! Can't a man have any peace?"

He went over to the corner and rang the bell. After a few minutes there was a soft tap at the door, and on his command Mercedes entered the study.

"Some bloody bird has broken its neck outside the door, and there is a mess of glass on the floor. Have Roberto come and clean it up."

He did not look at her, but stepping carefully over the broken glass, he bent down to stomp out his half-smoked cigar in the brass ashtray. She in turn said nothing, but left, closing the door quietly behind her.

A fine beginning to the day, he thought to himself. Better get on with it, then.

He left the study and went to his dressing-room: but his sense of calm detachment had been upset. Bloody bird, he thought.

In the end he wore his ordinary, every-day clothes. He dressed quickly. He went along the passage and tapped on Catherine's door to see if she was awake. Hearing her voice, he entered the room.

Catherine, her face pale, was sitting in bed, propped up by a pile of cushions. There were dark smudges beneath her large, blue eyes, eyes that stared at him almost, he thought—defensively. No, that was not it. He was shocked to recognize that it was—anger that she directed at him. Uncomfortably aware that he could not meet her eyes, he lowered his glance. He ignored the ridiculous cushion at the foot of the bed.

"I will be away for a few days." He spoke to the room in general. "I have ordered the car for eleven. Roberto will drive her. Mercedes has everything ready. Is there anything you need?"

Catherine said nothing. She was aware of him, and all that was happening, as if she was watching a play. She chose not to speak to this particular actor.

"Well, all right, then. I'll see you at the weekend."

He bent to kiss her cheek, his one hand just touching a lock of hair. She did not turn away, neither did she reciprocate the gesture, or even appear to register it.

De la Cruz left the room and made his way to the kitchen.

"I won't be having breakfast today," he informed Mercedes. "See that María eats before she leaves, and make sure everything is packed into the car."

He left the kitchen, and not long after she heard the sound of his car pull out into the drive and leave the house.

———

Catherine's bell rang in the kitchen, and Mercedes hastened to the bed-room at the far end of the passage.

"Good morning, Señora Catherine."

Mercedes moved across the room and opened the window a little, letting in the already warm morning air. It was going to be a hot day.

"I won't be taking breakfast today, Mercedes. Please ask María to come and see me. That is all, Mercedes."

Mercedes left, closing the door quietly. Catherine remained sitting in the bed, gazing across the room at nothing in particular.

Mercedes hurried to María's room and found her, chalk-faced, hanging over the basin, retching.

"Oh, my poor child—this is a terrible day! There—let me make you some mint tea with chamomile. It will help to settle those nerves. And I will bring you my drops. There, there, my poor baby."

She reached for the face-cloth, wet it and sprinkled a few drops of lavender water onto it. Then, taking María into her arms like a child, she held the cloth to her forehead.

"There, now. Old Mercedes is here."

She rocked María gently in her arms, from time to time turning the cloth that she might find the coolness for her.

María rested her head on the softness which was Mercedes' ample bosom and gave herself over to the comfort of that strong embrace. She closed her eyes. She had known this place all her life. More than anywhere this was home, this was where she felt safe, this was where love lived so strongly for her. It made no difference that Mercedes was a simple peasant woman. She was the wisest and most compassionate soul María had ever known. Not even her grandmother could surpass Mercedes in María's heart.

"There now, I'll bring you some tea and breakfast here in your room. Your father has gone out, and your mother is not well. She asked for you, but first I will come and take tea with you."

She shuffled back to the kitchen, her moccasins making a soft whisper on the polished tile floor.

"I don't understand these people! Not for the life of me! I don't think I ever will, even if I work here for the rest of my life. Your daughter is leaving, perhaps forever, and you can't say a proper goodbye? Could you do that, Encarnación?"

The younger woman shook her head.

"Are they both mad? Do they think that they will ever have this time over again?" She shook her head.

María was dressed when Mercedes returned with the breakfast. She had tied back her hair with a black ribbon and was packing her toiletries. Her face was deathly pale. Mercedes set the tray down and took a seat. They sipped the tea in silence.

Examining María's face, Mercedes saw the change in it. There was a new look in her eyes—an expression, a quality that women recognize instantly. María had become a woman. Mercedes saw too that María's spirit was not broken. Her father had the power to do much, but he would not be able to bend that fierce spirit to his will. The old woman's face held an expression of grim satisfaction.

Thank God for that! she thought. But then, she was always a free spirit, my little María.

It was just after ten o'clock when María entered her mother's room. Catherine was dressed and sitting on the side of the bed. She looked up when her daughter entered.

"María," she said, and patted the bed for her to come and sit beside her.

"How I love you, Mamá."

She knew that this was the last time she would see her mother. What could she say that would be of solace to her?

"I love you, Mamá, and I think I know how hard it has been for you. And I must thank you for all the many times you protected me from Papá's anger. I felt your love for me then, even when he overruled you. I have always felt your love."

Catherine's eyes filled with tears. This was no longer a play. María was leaving, and she had no words. What possible comfort could she offer?

"Spirit will always out, María. Sometimes we have to wait a long time. But the time comes. The time always comes." She wasn't sure she believed it.

"And it will come for you too, Mamá. It will come soon."

María leaned down to look into her mother's eyes, as if searching for something.

"You will sing again, Mamá. You will find a way to unlock that door."

Catherine said nothing.

María reached into her pocket and pulled out the silver comb her father had given her. It was still in its wrapping.

"I will never wear this."

She laid the comb on the dressing-table, opened the drawer and took out a pair of scissors. María smiled at her mother. Sitting on the stool in front of the mirror, she undid the black ribbon that held her hair off her face.

Slowly and deliberately she proceeded to crop her hair close to her scalp. It fell, handful by handful, into a shining heap on the floor.

When she was done, she regarded the mass of locks with satisfaction. Her father had attempted to cut her hair on the night of Salvador's visit. Very well, the hair was cut: but by her hand. He would never hold power over her in this way again. She felt an immense sense of relief in knowing this.

María looked at the unfamiliar reflection in the mirror. The white face, framed by the roughly shorn hair, stared back at her. She gathered up the thick mass of her hair and twisted it into a rope. Then she pressed the comb through it. Taking the heavy brass doorstop, she hammered the silver teeth until they were inextricably fastened together around it. She held it up and examined her handiwork approvingly.

"I shall leave this as a farewell gift to Papá," she said.

Catherine had her hand over her mouth. Her eyes were huge.

"That is for both of us, Mamá," she said, and she bent down and kissed her mother.

They heard the chimes of the front doorbell, signaling the arrival of Roberto. "I must go now, Mamá."

María kissed her mother again, and turned to leave the room.

"I will write to you soon. Goodbye, Mamá."

Catherine held up a hand. María paused.

"Don't lose your song, María. It is the one thing nobody can take away from you." Catherine's face was suddenly flushed, and her voice was surprisingly strong.

"I know, Mamá." María wiped away the tears.

"¡Dios le guarde! God be with you, my darling."

"I love you, Mamá."

Before going to the car, María slipped back into her room for a scarf to cover her head. Then she made her way quietly to her father's study. No one was ever permitted to enter this room without his permission, but such things were now of no consequence.

She opened the door and crossed the room to the trophy wall, where several magnificent elk stag heads hung, mounted on wooden plaques with small, silver inlays bearing his name, Lorenzo de la Cruz, and the date on which they had been shot. By pulling up a chair she managed to reach an empty plaque waiting, no doubt, to receive some new conquest.

"Well, here it is, Papá," María said aloud as she fixed the silver comb into place, leaving the long, red-gold tresses hanging free.

She replaced the chair and stood back to contemplate what she had done. She thought how fitting it was that her contribution hung close to the great elk stags. She left the room, closing the door quietly behind her.

Roberto loaded all the suitcases and boxes into the car. There was not a lot of luggage. At the retreat María's needs would be simple. She had, however, taken her wedding dress and veil, although she was not quite sure why.

Outside the front door the little band of Hacienda staff stood in a line, waiting to say goodbye to María. One by one they embraced her.

Diego wrapped his arms around her, and held her as if he would keep the world away by the sheer force of his love. Ciprianita, and José, who had come to the Hacienda especially to say farewell, with tears running down their cheeks, hugged her; and then Encarnación, who said she would pray for María every night, that she might soon return home.

Mercedes, now that the moment had arrived, was almost overwhelmed by the realization that she was about to lose María forever. She could not believe that what had filled her heart with joy for twenty-one years was leaving—forever. She knew with absolute certainty that María would not return to the Hacienda. She held her, one last time, in her arms. She did not weep. María felt the strong, steady heartbeat and was comforted.

"I will always be close, María."

"Oh, Mercedes..."

Roberto held the door open, and María got into the front seat. The door closed. He settled himself behind the wheel and shut his door. The engine started. María looked up at the faces of the people she had known her whole life. She kissed her hand and pressed it against the window-pane. She tried to smile, but the corners of her mouth slipped downward. All she could do was kiss her hand to them once more as the car moved away.

Then she was gone.

From where they stood in the driveway the small party watched the car roll away in a cloud of dust.

A sudden wind, rising out of nowhere, caught them by surprise. They heard a rushing sound, and looking upwards, to their astonishment they saw that the white doves had once again left the aviary and were flying over the garden.

They flew in urgent spirals, low over the flower-beds, with such speed that all the petals of the flowers were torn from the stems and rose in a cloud of fragrant color, swept along in the wake of the doves that now were flying down the driveway to follow the disappearing motor vehicle.

As if refusing to be left behind, the white ceramic fantails that had stood on the wall overlooking the herb garden for almost forty-five years, placed there by Don Merejildo, no less, now raised their wings, made one or two wing-stretching, flapping motions, as if to shake off the immobility of the decades, and then they too rose in unison to join the others and the cloud of flying petals.

The onlookers were about to speak when they saw one last, solitary bird, with a red stain on its breast, lift off from the front porch. It flew slowly at first, but then, growing stronger as it gained altitude, it turned and flew swiftly after the others.

Mercedes stared after it and whispered a silent prayer. She crossed herself.

"Holy Mother of God!" she whispered under her breath.

Tenderness

The Hacienda de Las Palomas became a house of shadows and whispers. The staff performed their duties in silence, and kept their heads down when de la Cruz entered the room where they were working. It became a house filled with shame.

Mercedes, appalled by de la Cruz' banishment of María, wondered that God did not strike him down, right then and there. No natural father would treat a daughter in this manner. She prayed to the Holy Mother to intervene and soften his heart; to bring her little María safe home again, even though she knew in her heart that this would not happen.

Every day she went into María's room. She opened the windows to let the sun and fresh air carry in the fragrance of the lavender. She swept and dusted and set fresh flowers on the dressing-table, and smoothed the bed-clothes that were always straight.

Roberto cleaned out the dove aviary, and when the weeks turned into months and they began to realize that María would not be coming back, without consulting de la Cruz he dismantled it and stored it away in the back of the barn.

With María gone and with Lorenzo's strict command to Roberto that her mother should not visit her, Catherine lost all interest in external events. It was for her as if the real world had flown away with the doves, leaving her strangely detached but comfortable in a world from which her husband was excluded.

Lorenzo tried to bring things back to some kind of normality by inviting guests out to the Hacienda, by suggesting that they attend the theatre or spend an evening at some favorite restaurant. None of his suggestions met with any response, other than an odd little laugh.

"What quaint ideas you do have, Lorenzo."

De la Cruz was beside himself. He found the silence of the house oppressive. Without fully understanding what was happening to him, he found himself listening for María's voice; even the singing, from which he had felt excluded, would have been preferable to this feeling of absence. His drinking became heavier, and those who knew him saw that he had lost his fire. The raging bull had retreated into the comfort and oblivion of alcohol.

He became surprisingly tender towards Catherine, and oddly it was the one attention she permitted. At night-time, after she had retired, he would go to her room and sit beside her on the bed, humming softly, almost under his breath, a song that had been popular when they were courting. Catherine wondered at this new gentleness. Perhaps, even after all these years, after all that they had endured together perhaps, in the end, she didn't know him at all.

"Come in, Lorenzo."

Her husband entered. He crossed the room, and bending over her, he removed the silver comb and put it on the dressing-table. He picked up the silver-backed brush and the ribbon which lay beside it. He took a step around the big pillow on the floor, to sit beside her on the bed.

With a sigh of pleasure he ran his fingers through the long tresses, again and again, more for the sensual gratification it afforded him than to loosen any knots. When her long hair hung loosely down her back, he began the long, rhythmic strokes with the hair-brush, one hand drawing the brush through the heavy mass, the other lifting it in readiness for the next stroke.

Catherine closed her eyes and surrendered herself to the enjoyment of it. Under the spell of the slow brush-strokes and the hand that, from time to time, lifted the heavy mass of hair to reach the brush under it, she was carried back to the days when her Mamá had sat and brushed her hair, just so. For the moment she was back in the safety of her childhood.

She wondered at these hands: that they always seemed to know so intuitively how to do things. It struck her as a strange anomaly that his hands could be so sensitive in their execution of a wide variety of duties while his will, with seemingly no sense of the violence it wrought in people's lives, demanded submissive obedience.

Now, as he braided the long hair, he told her about the day's events— small matters relating to the rancho and the stock; the price he was hoping to get for the young steers; matters that were of no particular interest to her: but the sound of his voice was strangely comforting. It was almost as if this tenderness was only possible for them now that so much else had been lost.

"Thank you, Lorenzo," she said as she settled under the covers.

He adjusted the windows and drew the curtains back a little, revealing the still desert night. Catherine liked to be able to see the stars from her bed; it helped her to feel less alone, knowing that somewhere beneath those very same stars María lay sleeping.

"Take care of her, mother," she whispered to herself. "Take good care of her."

Lorenzo bent down to settle the bedclothes around her, the way one tucks a child in for the night, making sure the pillows were the way she liked them. He kissed her on the forehead. "Sleep well, my dear."

De la Cruz retired to his study, to the comfort of a last cigar and a generous whisky. In the past it had been his custom, at these times, to sit in his comfortable chair and reflect upon the day. Now he found that such reflection brought with it unwanted images, and he had taken to pacing outside when the weather was fine. He found the immensity of the night somehow comforting, as if it brought some sense of perspective into the turbulence inside him.

Of late a third and a fourth whisky, and often a fifth full glass of the strong, neat alcohol helped him to dull the thoughts that persisted in surfacing, thoughts and feelings that he refused to allow any entry.

But they were there; always there, just beneath the surface of his thinking, waiting to be heard. He could dull them, but he could not eradicate them. They lived in him like malicious, independent beings, whispering to him, even on the edge of sleep. He knew they would never leave him: that they would haunt him forever.

And then there was always the pain in his heart.

The Songbird

Catherine sat up in bed, leaning against the pillows, the five letters clasped to her breast. Five letters: one for each month that María had been away. She knew Lorenzo would be furious if he found out about them, but then Lorenzo did not need to find out. During the day, she kept them locked away in her closet. It was only at this time of evening, while her husband sat with his after-dinner port, savoring the heavy wine and mulling over the events of the day and his plans for the following one, that she took them from their hiding-place, settled herself in her bed and began to read. Tonight was no different.

Catherine opened the first letter.

"My most beloved María..."

Sometimes this was enough. Just those four words had the power to summon to her the presence of her child. Then Catherine would close her eyes, and María would be there with her. Sometimes it would be María the young woman who came and sat quietly on the bed, but more often it would be the child who would run into her room, her eyes bright with excitement about something she had just discovered. And sometimes the two of them would lie lazily in the hammock, watching the swooping flight of the doves, sipping lemonade that Mercedes brought them.

Tomorrow was Catherine's birthday. It would be her first birthday without María. Each of her children had their special place in Catherine's heart, and with each of her first five daughters' departures she had felt as if she had been robbed of some part of who she was: more so because Lorenzo had fought with each one of their husbands, and visits were now stressful and often stormy affairs, and consequently infrequent. But the loss of María was the hardest to bear, not only because she missed her company, nor solely because of the shocking circumstances surrounding her departure, but because she was the last of her children to leave. Her idea of who she was and what defined her changed utterly. She felt empty.

Catherine looked at the clock. He would be through soon to say goodnight. How strange it was, she thought, that this one small ritual survived when all other communication between them had died.

Catherine crossed the room and locked the letters safely back in the closet. She was in bed when her husband entered the room.

De la Cruz sat on the bed and began to loosen his wife's hair, telling her about his day and asking after hers. Catherine thought he was unusually tender. She closed her eyes and gave herself over to the soothing ritual. She still had not found it in herself to refuse these attentions, and she wondered at the complexity and the contradictory nature of her feelings for her husband.

The hair was brushed and braided. Catherine lay back and pulled the bedclothes around her, relaxed and sleepy. Lorenzo kissed his wife and turned to leave the room. At the door he stopped.

"Sleep well, Catherine. I have a surprise for you, tomorrow."

Catherine, somewhere between waking and dreaming, mumbled a response.

"Oh. Is María coming home?"

De la Cruz was shocked. How could she possibly think such a thing?

"No, Catherine! Of course not!" His voice was sharp. The soothing calm of the evening ritual had vanished.

"When will she be home, Lorenzo?"

De la Cruz stared at his wife. It was not like Catherine to be so focused; so direct.

"Oh, come now, Catherine! We have been through all this before." Lorenzo drew in a deep breath. With a show of patience, and speaking slowly, as if to one of diminished intelligence, he said—"She will return when she has come to her senses."

"And what does that mean?" She was wide awake now.

"Oh—for God's sake, Catherine!" De la Cruz was struggling to keep his temper. "It means," he said, speaking with exaggerated clarity, "that she will apologize for her disgraceful behavior; she will promise to marry Javier Otero—if he will still have her, after her shameful conduct; and she will settle down, and be a good and obedient daughter and wife."

It was Catherine's turn to stare.

"But she will never do that, Lorenzo!"

"Then she will never return to this house."

"I see."

"Goodnight, Catherine," he said. It was a dismissal. He attempted to keep the anger from his voice. He did not succeed. It was always there, Catherine thought. It would always be there.

"Goodnight, Lorenzo."

The following morning de la Cruz rose early. He dressed quickly in rough denims, and without shaving, went out to meet Roberto and Diego in the old feed room behind the stables. He had come to check that the goods that had arrived by special delivery the night before were in good order.

The goods, a large and extremely heavy crate and a small box with air holes drilled into the side of it, marked: 'Live bird. Handle with extreme care', had been placed in the feed room so that his gift would remain a surprise for Catherine on her birthday.

The surprise was a South American songbird and a large cage of filigree ironwork that had been made to de la Cruz' specifications in Mexico. Both had been freighted up by train and had been delivered, by special request, to the rancho. De la Cruz had done much research, and had spoken to a number of dealers in exotic birds before he was satisfied that he was making the right choice.

The bird, a five-thousand-dollar, brilliantly-colored songbird from Colombia, came with a guarantee that it was young, male, healthy, and that it would sing.

Roberto and Diego were to carry the cage over to the house and suspend it from a rafter in a corner of the front salon, from which place the bird would, no doubt, fill the silent house with song. De la Cruz was well-pleased with his gift.

The crate proved to be far too heavy for two men to carry all the way across the courtyard.

"Perhaps we can load it into the pick-up, and then back that up to the entrance. That way we will only have to carry it a short distance into the front room." It was Diego's suggestion.

"Good idea."

Diego went to fetch the pick-up while Roberto and de la Cruz started to open the crate. They were interrupted by Diego's return.

"The pick-up is not in the garage. Did you perhaps arrange for it to be serviced?"

De la Cruz looked at him blankly. "It has just been serviced. It should be in the garage. I drove it yesterday, up to the back pasture. I put it in the garage myself, at about five o'clock."

"Well! It's gone!"

"Impossible."

The three men left the feed room and went to the last of the garages, where the missing vehicle was usually housed. The garage was most patently empty.

"I had better phone the police immediately, and report this. Get the cage out of the crate. It will be lighter to carry. Oh, and you had better give that damn bird some food and water. I don't want it dying on me."

With which compassionate remark he left them to make his call.

It was over an hour before he managed to contact the superintendent, after having a long and fruitless conversation with a sleepy member of the overnight staff who had spent most of the night playing poker in the back room with friends. De la Cruz reported the theft to the superintendent, who said he would be at the Hacienda shortly. In the meantime he would put out a call for police to be on the look-out for the vehicle. He wrote down the description and the plates' number, and rang off.

De la Cruz went to his room. He showered, shaved and dressed quickly, and was ready to receive the superintendent when he arrived. He ushered him into the front room, and was about to ring the bell for Mercedes to bring them some coffee when there was an urgent tap on the door and Mercedes entered the room, requesting that she might speak with him.

"Don Lorenzo! Please, sir. I need to tell you something."

"Not now, Mercedes. Can't you see I am busy?"

"But it is important, sir."

"Nothing, I am sure, that cannot wait. And bring some coffee through to my study."

But Mercedes would not be silenced.

"I must speak, sir. I don't think it should wait."

De la Cruz' face was thunderous. The superintendent was watching with interest.

What was it with women?

"Go and make the coffee!"

Mercedes left the room. She returned fifteen minutes later with a tray of coffee and cookies. De la Cruz was speaking to the superintendent.

"May I speak now, please, sir?"

De la Cruz gave a gesture of irritation, and was about to say something when a white-faced Roberto appeared in the doorway, signaling that he must speak to de la Cruz.

"Good God, man! What is it now? Can't it wait?"

Roberto twisted his cap in his hands and shook his head. He seemed to be having difficulty finding his voice. Seeing this, a determined Mercedes stood in front of de la Cruz and met his eyes.

"I have been trying to tell you about Doña Catherine. She's not—"

De la Cruz interrupted with a curse. "For God's sake, can't you women manage your lives for one second? Can't you see we have been robbed?" He made an extravagant gesture with his hands.

Mercedes would not be silenced.

"Doña Catherine is not in her room," she said firmly, "and I can't find her anywhere."

She paused.

"And she has taken the big cushion from the end of her bed."

De la Cruz was about to make some exasperated remark when Roberto finally found his voice.

"It's about the songbird, sir."

De la Cruz' face was purple.

"What about the bloody bird?"

Roberto could not look de la Cruz in the eye.

"I don't know how it happened. We were putting some food into the box, as you suggested."

He looked like a man facing a firing-squad.

"It seems that the one side of the bird-box had become damaged, during transportation. It was loose. One minute the bird was there, in the box, and the next minute..."

Roberto's voice was shaking. He cleared his throat. De la Cruz' face was unreadable.

"The next minute—he was out."

Roberto cleared his throat.

"Anyway, he's flown away—sir. Right out the door. He's gone!"

PART IV
HERESY

The Retreat

Snow had fallen heavily during the night.

It lay over the fields and the roof-tops, the orchard and the bare branches of the cottonwoods, obscuring the many paths and clearings between the buildings, creating a sense of space and emptiness.

It became a ritual for María, each morning and evening to sit at her window and watch the doves which, released from the protection of the aviary, unfurled their wings and spirits and soared out into the vast expanse of sky. It took her back to the happy times spent with her mother when she was a little girl.

She loved the way the birds rose up in a ragged cloud of flapping wings; how they moved into formation, with the last few stragglers joining the slow spirals. They would fly out over the surrounding fields, rising to clear the rows of cottonwoods, and then return, swooping down low over the herb and vegetable garden, flying towards the building where María and the nuns had their rooms. There they would rise up, a cloud of white wings, breaking the whiteness of the light with their wing-beats so that the momentary flickering reminded María of those early black and white cowboy films she had watched as a child.

They would vanish from sight as they made another graceful turn above the chapel, and then repeat the pattern with many subtle variations as new doves moved to the front to replace the tired leaders.

María would sit entranced by the shifts of light and image that the birds offered as they flew either into or across the light; by how that slow, parabolic glide with the light full on their wings would curve round until they became small, dark specks, which would quite suddenly vanish from sight. She would wait breathlessly for the completion of the turn, the moment when their banking flight into that new arc would reveal them, white and startling with the light full on their wings once more.

She recalled an evening at the Hacienda when a group of flamenco dancers, invited by her father, had come to entertain his guests. She remembered vividly the fierce intensity of one particular dance. A male dancer, dressed all in black with his face painted crimson to represent a fighting bull, and a female dancer in a scarlet dress, had emulated the blood-rage and passion of the bullfight. The woman had used her full skirt with its vermillion and crimson flounces, and a fan made of scarlet feathers, to incite 'the bull'. She could still recall the erotic energy of the dancers; their proud arrogance, a characteristic that distinguishes the art of flamenco—that fingerprint of Spanish culture. She loved the relentless intensity of the music; the raw, passionate voice of the singer and his guttural Moorish voice with the taste of blood in it, and the explosive clapping and stamping, punctuated by the sharp, staccato clack and rattle of the castanets, a sound that made María think of death. She marveled at the delicate turns of the wrist, the slow unfurling of the fan that imitated the matador's cape, creating in those graceful veronicas an illusion of presence, only to reveal the emptiness of that illusion.

The flight of the doves was for María a graceful and silent echo of this sleight of hand. Then, as now, she was held spellbound by the poetry of the movement.

And the memory of another time, when she was older, came back to her: how she had shuddered when her father spoke of the Duende. He had learned about this dark and ancient energy from someone at a bullfight in Mexico City: how it comes when death is possible. Perhaps that dark wind had touched her, even then, and now the doves were a reminder, an invitation—to what? Her death?

But still she thrilled at the rush of air as they rose steeply over the low buildings. And it was not only the beauty of it. Something in the repetition of appearance and disappearance, the awareness that the patterns of flight were timeless even though the life-span of each bird was transient, moved her deeply. In their shifting disappearance and reappearance she felt that they expressed the idea of death and resurrection, and as they passed over her and she heard the sudden, rushing sound of the wind thrown out by their collective flight, she fancied that they were angels come to watch over her.

And—that the Duende was not far away.

Maria had been at The Adobe for a little over five months. Each day began with the release of the doves, and the sound of the chanting of the nuns. Shortly after this she would be visited by Sister Piadosa, who would bring her a jug of water for washing. She would dress and make her way to the small communal area where she would eat breakfast with the nuns who worked in the school and the clinic.

It was not long after her arrival, indeed barely a week, when her attacks of nausea, thought to be brought on by the upsetting circumstances, were recognized by Sister Piadosa as the early signs of pregnancy. She recalled that Señor de la Cruz had offered no reasons for his abandonment of his child. Now, she thought, things were clear. He did not want the shame of an illegitimate child to fall on his illustrious life: foolish man. Did he think it would just go away? Not an original story, she thought grimly, and unfortunately not an unusual one, but some families had more compassion for their daughters thus afflicted. She was nevertheless surprised, for she had not thought María to be a foolish or promiscuous young woman, and she wondered what might lie behind the story; what had not been told.

The knowledge of her pregnancy, when it was made clear to her by Sister Piadosa, came as a surprise to María, but not a shock as the good sister might have expected. Indeed, she appeared to be overwhelmed with joy.

Looking at her, Piadosa had the sense that a fire had sprung up within her; for her face, her eyes, her whole presence had become suddenly radiant.

"You surprise me, María. But then, surely you knew you were pregnant. I assumed that this was why your father brought you here."

"My father knows nothing of this. I was not aware of it before today. But no, I am not upset. I think that this must surely be the most wonderful thing that has ever happened to me."

She smiled at the baffled nun.

"It is a long story."

The two women spent the morning together, Sister Piadosa to hear the story of María and Salvador's love for each other, a love that had been forbidden and obstructed at every turn by her father since she was a young girl, and María to unburden herself of the pain she felt at her father's treatment of her and the man she loved.

"But why can Salvador not come and fetch you from here? You are of age. You can have your informal marriage blessed by Father Octavio, and you can go away with Salvador and have your child in peace. What is to prevent this?"

"You don't know my father, sister, or how angry he is: or how jealous. No one is ever allowed to question his decisions, not even my mother."

Sister Piadosa's lips tightened.

"And be very sure, even though he has not called or been to see me, or you, he would know the instant I left this place. He has threatened to kill Salvador, and me, if he ever tries to see me again. He is a man of enormous power and influence. And he will do it. I believe he will do it."

The nun stared at María in a silence of disbelief. Surely María was exaggerating her father's anger. Surely he could be brought to his senses by some reasonable and gentle intervention. And yet, Sister Piadosa thought as she remembered how she had felt when de la Cruz had come to make the arrangements, perhaps not: for she recalled how she had felt herself then to be in the presence of something very dark—she hesitated to use the word 'evil'. How is it possible in today's civilized world for anyone to get away with such abuse? It was something entirely outside her experience.

She had often wondered what evil might look like; if it existed. María's description of her mother's life and what she had become as a result of it was almost impossible to believe, but the story of María's departure from her home and the sight of her brutally shorn hair convinced her. A young woman did not adopt such drastic measures unless in extremis, or if she was unbalanced: and María was most certainly not unbalanced. A fighting spirit, that was what she had; fighting for the right to determine her life.

"Oh, Lord," she thought, "you do test the ones you love."

Everything in her kind, compassionate heart went out to María, who had done no harm other than to rebel at her father's unjust and brutal treatment. Her initial 'sin' was that she had fallen in love, and her second 'sin' was that she had not wavered in her loyalty to the man she loved or to herself. What possible blame could there be in that?

Sister Piadosa was relieved to learn that María and Salvador, while not, strictly speaking, married in the eyes of the Church, had a marriage that was recognized as legal and binding in the eyes of the world, and that the child would be legitimate and would take his father's name, Fuentes.

She wondered if she should speak to either Father Octavio or Sebastián about the matter, but found herself hesitating. Intuitively she felt that the fewer the people who knew about María's condition, the better.

In the end she said nothing to either of them. While she admired and respected both men, and knew that she was supposed to inform the priest of such matters; that to take things into her own hands would be considered disobedient if it was ever discovered, this, she felt, was something for women to decide. So be it. María was not going to be the only one to show a little independence.

She confided in Sister Ana, and together with María they decided to put it out that María was considering becoming a lay nun. This would provide the rationale for her wearing a loose-fitting habit which would disguise her condition.

"Sister, see if you can find a habit that will fit María. Oh, and a veil as well," she added,

"and bring them to her room."

Sister Ana, thrilled to be included in this plan to help María, ran along to fetch the garments.

María, as she sat now, dreamily looking over the white landscape, was aware that it would soon be Christmas, and that this would be the first year she did not celebrate it at home. It was painful to consider how the world would go on, seemingly without missing a beat, and she would not be there. What are we then, she wondered: a footprint in the sand? One rain—and it is gone.

Her mind went back to the Hacienda. All the preparations and decorations would be underway for the Christmas Eve dinner. María loved the kitchen at this time of year. She loved the warmth and the industrious goodwill, and all the spicy fragrances that Mercedes used in her dishes. The delicious aroma would spread from that room right through the house and mingle with the pungent scent thrown out by the burning cedar-wood fire.

Roberto would bring armfuls of fragrant cedar cuttings into the house and, with Catherine's guidance, would fix them to the beams and lintels. Later it would be María's task to fix little stars and angels into this greenery. There would be large and brilliant arrangements of poinsettias in every room, and the dried lavender that had been hanging in the kitchen since late summer would be used to fill the lavender bags for the guest rooms.

Every year her five sisters, with their husbands and their families, came to the Hacienda the day before Christmas. They would be settled into their respective rooms by Catherine, the adults in the various spare bed-rooms and the children on collapsible beds and mattresses in what used to be the play-room.

While Mercedes and Encarnación slaved to have everything finished in time for the evening meal, the family would rest before setting off to attend an early Christmas Mass. In their absence Roberto and José would bring in and decorate the Christmas tree, a wondrous surprise for the children when they returned.

There would be the splendid dinner, interrupted by the news that Encarnación had gone into labor. She went into labor so regularly on Christmas Eve—seven of her eight children having been born on that illustrious night—that de la Cruz finally arranged for the car to be left in the driveway, so as not to waste a second in getting her to the hospital.

María smiled at the memory: how after all her father's meticulous planning for the evening to proceed smoothly, year after year would find the family running around to help Roberto load his wife into the car and hand the previous year's 'Christmas gift' into the tender keeping of Mercedes. Then they would all gather round Encarnación and wave goodbye, wishing her blessings for an easy delivery. The meal would be cold when they finally returned to it, but no one, with the exception of Don Lorenzo, minded in the slightest.

After everyone had eaten and drunk their fill and de la Cruz had made his obligatory Christmas speech, it was time to open the presents. This would pass in a flurry of torn paper and screams of delight, and then the little ones would be put to bed, the sisters would catch up on all the news and the men would sit and drink with their father-in-law and discuss business deals.

Of late Catherine would be exhausted by this time, and would excuse herself and go to bed.

"Poor Mamá," María thought. "You made everything so beautiful, and you were so unhappy."

María brought her mind back to the present. Beneath her hands, which rested on her now gently swelling belly, she felt the small movement of the new life that was growing in her. Very softly she began to sing the lullaby she had heard Encarnación sing so many times to her new-born infants.

With her hands stroking the secret within her, María sat looking out at the strange blueness of the early-morning shadows in the snow, singing the timeless song from the old country to her unborn child.

A Love Affair

Father Octavio knew he was in love.

It was a strange admission for a priest, he had to admit, and it was not an admission he was about to take to his superiors, nor to anyone else for that matter—for behind this passion there lay a secret that he had kept to himself for well over a year. It was a secret, the forbidden nature of which both thrilled and dismayed him.

He was as deeply in love as a man can be.

He was amazed, now that he had become aware of the depth of it, that it had taken him so long to acknowledge the presence in his life of this powerful and complex set of emotions: and yet perhaps he had not wanted to admit to them, for it was not the love of God that was uppermost in his heart, even if perhaps it should have been—'forgive me, Father', he thought—but a love that had been unsought, unexpected, and was now the most bewildering mix of joy and pain that he had ever known.

How could it be, he mused, that in the eleven years he had known her, he had failed to recognize how deeply he loved Magdalena?

Looking back now he thought he must surely have been blind not to see it. But it was only on that unforgettable evening, the night she had first called him by his name, Octavio, the night she had told him she was dying, that it had come to him how wondrously, and yes, how passionately he loved her.

He remembered vividly how he had bent down and kissed her, and all the thunderous emotions that had followed that spontaneous act. It was the only time he had ever kissed a woman on the lips, kissed a woman at all other than perfunctorily, and he could still feel the sweetness of her mouth on his. And she had died, just as this wholly new and breath-taking world had opened up to him.

"How I love you, Octavio." It lived in him like a flame.

In the time that had gone by since her death, there was not a day that passed that he did not think of her. He would wake up like any young, love-struck youth, with her name on his lips, and he would fold her into his last prayer at night. How many times in his mind had he not replayed that moment when he had kissed her? A hundred? A thousand? He could not say, but he was sure that whatever the number, it would count as a sin of the greatest magnitude in the eyes of the Church.

Who could he confide in? Who could he possibly tell about this feeling that possessed him? Should he confess it?—and if so to whom? Certainly not the Bishop. He was about to retire, and his mind was most certainly on other things. And he did not feel he could speak of this to Sister Piadosa, although he had written a letter of wishes not unconnected with this matter, which he would ask her to keep safe and open after his death. And certainly he could not go to Sebastián, a young man who had recently suffered much loss, and say he was in love with his mother, and the fact that she had died made no difference to the power of his love for her; that he felt all but consumed by it.

With all of this going on inside him, Father Octavio drove slowly along the familiar road to The Adobe. The journey was taking longer than usual because of the thick snow on the road and the occasional drifts that needed careful negotiating. Once he had left the highway, he stopped to put on the snow chains, a difficult task with such thick snow on the ground. On straightening up from this exertion he felt a sharp pain in his chest, and he leaned against the car, breathing carefully into the pain until he felt the constriction ease. Only then could he proceed on his journey.

This would be his last visit to The Adobe before Christmas. He would conduct an early Christmas Mass followed by confession. There were two babies to baptize and there was a marriage to perform. The latter would take place in the late afternoon, and would be a short ceremony so that the couple, who had been living together for the past eight years, could take their smaller children home to bed.

"And who are you to judge them, Octavio my fine friend?" he thought. "Given the opportunity, I wonder what you would do."

He frowned. He was trying to remember what had first drawn him to the priesthood, and he found he could not remember very clearly. He knew he had always cared very deeply about people and their suffering, but now he wondered why he had not chosen some other path to be of service. He wondered now why it was considered necessary to forgo the simple pleasures of family life, the love of a woman and the fulfillment of his sexual desires in order to do God's work. Did God really require such a sacrifice, and if so, why?

Octavio knew all the conventional and traditional answers to his question, just as surely as he knew that he was not supposed even to be asking it in the first place: but to his great consternation he found himself questioning their merit.

So what did you do with a thought that just seemed to think itself? Ignore it? Feel guilty and metaphorically, or even literally, beat yourself? Ask forgiveness for a thought that seems to rise of its own volition, as naturally and as autonomously as breathing? What was there to forgive? And what about feelings? Were they sinful? A sign of weakness?

Or was it not perhaps that here was a man, wondrously and gloriously alive with love and not separate from the love of God and all of His creation?

Octavio in all his years had never known anything like this. "This," he thought, "is the test and the measure of all my convictions." He felt as if the solid ground was being pulled out and away from beneath his feet.

He knew that he had come to—no, he had already crossed over some ultimate divide, a chasm of incredible depth which, although it had been crossed in an instant so brief as to be immeasurable, was also vast beyond comprehension, and there was no possibility of return.

He saw that his life, in spite of many hardships and not a little disappointment, had been essentially simple, uncomplicated, in a sense prescribed. He had lived a good life doing good work. Nothing had challenged him unduly, and his approach to life, his chosen path of obedience, his simple view of life and his earthy philosophy had served him well until now. He had lived a life beyond reproach: and it was not enough.

The simplicity of goodness was gone forever. A new voice had entered that place of comfortable—or was it complacent?—acceptance, and had thrown all his unexamined certitude to the wind.

The memory of a Sunday school lesson he had conducted in the village came back to him. He could see the small room and the pool of eager faces looking up at him. They had been reading about the city of Jerusalem and its wide entrances—north, south, east and west—and how the great gates would be closed at night to keep the city safe.

"But," he said, "there was a small entrance that remained open so that travelers, or people returning to the city late in the evening, could gain entrance. It was called 'The Needle'. Why such a name?"

The children could not guess.

"It was because it was so narrow, like the eye of a needle. And where do we learn this? Who spoke of this?"

There was much whispering, but no one could come up with any information. Father Octavio fingered through the pages of his worn Bible until he came to a place in the book of Matthew. He looked up, gave the children a smile and read Christ's words in the short verse.

"It is easier for a camel to go through the eye of a needle, than for a rich man to enter the kingdom of God."

The children heard the brief text, but what did it mean?

Father Octavio said that anyone who had ever seen a rich man's camel would see at once that, with its load, it would never be able to pass through 'The Needle'. A poor man would be able to lead his unladen camel through quite easily.

This had come back to him now with an additional significance. He saw that the nature of the load was irrelevant: wealth, stolen goods or good deeds; it was still a load, and it would still not pass through the narrow way. The accumulation of wealth or the unexamined preoccupation with good deeds, were the idols that could not pass through the narrow entrance into that holy place.

A panic seized Octavio, and he felt suddenly overwhelmed by the heavy burden of his unexamined goodness.

Why now, in his sixtieth year—he who had served his God and his people well, who was much loved and trusted by all who knew him—why now should he be presented with this knowledge that threatened the very foundations of his faith, that questioned all his principles: this knowledge that he had neglected, until recently, one essential act—the act of disobedience?

Father Octavio had read extensively from the Spanish writers and poets: St John of the Cross, Lorca and Machado. He recalled reading that no one who dares to fall deeply and passionately in love can avoid the Duende's touch and the terrifying self-examination that it evokes. Indeed, until now, although he had examined his heart and his conscience very deeply and had spent many hours in prayer over decisions which had no simple or clear-cut solution, he had never felt the call to such profound soul-searching before, let alone this challenging summons to let go of all that was familiar and be empty again. But then, he had never fallen in love before, certainly not in this way, with a woman. This longing to know her as deeply as was possible; to know her love, her heart and her mind and her body intimately—he had never faced this temptation before. But there was no avoiding the issue now, even though no one would ever know this inner conflict, ever know what divine madness raged in his heart.

He could not avoid the devastating truth that something that had been true for him for his whole life—a truth out of which he had lived and on which he had based so many of his decisions, a truth in which he had believed utterly—was simply no longer valid for him.

He felt as if someone had taken a huge mallet and struck at the very cornerstone of his beliefs, and he feared that unless he could find some new way of visioning his faith, the whole edifice might tumble down. He saw that he would never truly know God—know himself—until he had taken, without apology or remorse, that forbidden step and allowed himself to feel, right to the depths of his being and with unfettered heart, all of his love and his extremely human longing for Magdalena.

Father Octavio interrupted his thoughts to negotiate the narrow descent where the road crossed an arroyo that snaked between two steep hills. It was always a problematic stretch of road, eroded by the water which would rush across it during storms and shadowed by the close proximity of the hills. Today it was filled with snow-drifts that had piled up against the banks overnight. Cautiously he navigated the route past them, and then resumed his self-examination.

Had he deserted his faith? Had he, at this late hour, been tempted by the world and fallen in love, failing not only God and the Church, but himself? Surely that was far too simplistic? And though many would so judge it, this was not for other men to judge. This matter was between him and God. He, Octavio, would bend the knee to no man, not even to the Pope, about his right to know this love. He would accept whatever consequences might follow. How often had he quoted: "If you will but take the first step, God will show you the way: but you must take that step alone; He cannot take that first step for you."

Of course He cannot, Octavio thought, struck by the realization that the step into oneself is, and necessarily must be, an act of disobedience. In the deepest possible sense it was an act of autonomy, a commitment to that inner voice: for where else would God speak but directly into an unfettered heart?

He knew then with a clarity that filled him with awe that this apparent act of disobedience was a response to a far older law; that in taking this step he was obeying a calling, deeper than anything he could articulate; one that he dared not, on pain of betraying all that he held sacred, ignore. And who, in the end, is being disobeyed—God or man?

'And I will show you the way, and I will bring you home at last.'

Father Octavio rounded a bend and moved out of the shadow of the hills. In front of him bright sun slanting through the growing mass of thunderheads fell on the blanket of snow, blinding him. He slowed the vehicle and finally brought it to a halt, waiting until his eyes grew accustomed to the brightness.

He knew himself to be at the beginning. He knew he had taken a step into a terrifying place; that he stood face to face with his ultimate aloneness—even as God is alone, he thought. If I cannot bear this, I will never be able to bear His truth: and I feel it approaching. He was filled with awe that all of this should have come to him through his love for Magdalena; filled with awe, and a deep and very terrible joy.

"Oh, Magdalena," he whispered, "we know not what we do or who we are—but life will surely tell us!"

He drove on, engulfed by these feelings, and finally reached the familiar turn at the bottom of the line of cottonwoods that led up to The Adobe. Looking up he saw in front of him, high on the hill, the small, white cross that Sebastián had set there in memory of his mother. That at least was still there. It was barely visible for the snow that lay thickly around the stony base. Although much had changed at The Adobe over the years, the approach was the same as it had always been. Straight ahead was the small cottage that had been Magdalena's home. In spite of everything he still could not believe that she was gone; that if he just looked hard enough, he would not see her waving to him from the doorway.

Must it always be that we only know the true nature of our love, the profound depths of it, after the beloved has left us?

The Vision

An icy wind was blowing in from the south, bringing with it notice that a storm was brewing and the likelihood of fresh snowfalls before Christmas. María was about to leave the chapel where she had been decorating the altar, and had just wrapped her cape around her in preparation for the dash back to her room when Father Octavio pulled up and parked his car close to the chapel entrance.

"Greetings, María!" he called out to her through the wind.

"Hello, father!—Greetings to you too."

She walked over to the car, holding the cape tightly around her. The wind blew the veil up and away from her face so that Octavio, looking at her, thought how very beautiful she had grown of late—almost not of this world.

"She looks like one who has come through some testing ordeal," he thought, "but there has been a price."

He wondered what lay behind this decision to become a nun. It was not in keeping with the María de la Cruz he knew, or thought he knew. And yet there was of course that quality that had been evident since her early childhood, and which might point to this choice; that extraordinary spirituality and purity which could be tangibly felt by all who heard her sing. When she sang, he thought, it was as if the angels possessed her. Perhaps, at last, they had.

"But still it is a wonder. I would have thought that she and Salvador would have wanted something different. Come to think of it, I haven't seen that young man about lately. I must speak to Santiago this week at choir practice."

All this time María had been standing, waiting for Father Octavio to open his door.

"Deep thoughts, father," she remarked and laughed. Then, seeing all the boxes and baskets he had to unload, she offered to help.

Father Octavio brought his mind back to the matter in hand. "Oh, just some foolish wool-gathering. Yes, thank you, María. All of this must go to the sacristy. But,"—he indicated the various items on the back seat—"but the large box in the front contains gifts from the congregation in town, and it must go to Sister Piadosa to hand out to the children on Christmas day."

He climbed out of the car, opened the rear door and removed the small, black suitcase in which he carried the liturgical objects and vessels: the container which held the Host, the altar cloths and incense, the oils for burning and for blessing and a well-worn Bible. A white linen surplice and a change of clothing, all freshly washed and ironed for him by Elena, lay folded next to it. He gathered it all up and turned to pass it to María, but she was already reaching for a box of new hymnals intended for the Sunday school.

Father Octavio was halfway into the chapel, carrying the suitcase and the bundle of clothing, when he heard María give a cry. He turned round, dropping the suitcase, in time to see her fall. The suitcase burst open, scattering its contents over the paved chapel entrance. He left it where it fell and ran towards her.

"Oh, my dear!—María!—Wait!—Let me help you." But when he reached her he saw that she had fainted.

Father Octavio turned around and called for help.

"Sister Piadosa! Sister Ana! Someone! Over here! Quickly!"

He turned back to María. She was deathly pale. Gusts of wind blew her cape and veil this way and that so that the fabric made the fluttering sound of a sail caught in a capricious wind. He bent down, thinking to loosen her collar, and it was then that the wind, blowing the fabric of her habit close to her body, revealed the unmistakable nature of her condition. The child was pregnant!

Distractedly he noticed that the consecrated wafers which he had brought for the Eucharist Service had broken free of their small container, and were being lifted high into the air and blown into a whirling eddy like so many white flower petals. So too the white linen surplice which, filled with the stormy up-draughts of winter air, was flying white and bright over the chapel roof. It was too bad. He would deal with that later. Where was everyone?

"Sister Piadosa!" he called again, and was relieved to hear the sound of running footsteps.

"Oh, María. Child. Here, father, help me carry her inside out of the wind."

Together they carried her into the small chapel and laid her on the bright, woven Navajo rug that ran the length of the narrow aisle.

"Wait with her, father, while I fetch some help."

She returned shortly with a blanket which she lay over María, and tucked in the sides. "Sister Ana has gone to fetch two of the men and a stretcher. They will be here any second now."

She searched his face, and he nodded.

"Yes. I noticed."

"We can talk about it later."

At this point Sister Ana arrived with the two men. Very gently the two sisters lifted María onto the stretcher.

"We'll take her to the infirmary," Sister Piadosa said, and the little party hurried across the windy yard.

It was only when María was safely tucked up in the infirmary bed, and although still deathly pale, had regained consciousness and had taken a little of Sister Piadosa's special tea, that the latter accompanied Father Octavio to her office and closed the door.

The small office was crammed with boxes of goods waiting to be delivered. Sister Piadosa made space on two of the chairs so that she and Father Octavio could be seated.

"So—sister, María is pregnant, and presumably you have known about this for some time. Perhaps you would like to tell me about it."

"First let me apologize to you, father. I should have told you of course, as soon as I learned of it, but I didn't want to compromise your position in any way."

"You mean you didn't want anyone to interfere with the plans you so obviously have made for María." Although the words sounded harsh, there was a twinkle in the priest's eye. "Come, sister, you don't have to apologize to me; indeed, I salute your new independent spirit. This must be something you have picked up in the country. I don't remember such boldness. But perhaps you had better tell me the whole story. I assure you I shall not feel compromised in any way."

So Sister Piadosa related all that María had told her, and the plans that she and María had agreed on for the babe after the birth.

"There is no knowing what her father might do if he ever heard about the child. That is why I have told no one—except Sister Ana, and torture wouldn't drag the secret out of her. She loves María dearly. This way the child will be brought up almost next door. María will know that he is close by. The woman's child is due at about the same time as María's. She and her husband have agreed to have it known that she gave birth to twins. No one else need know about this."

Father Octavio sat digesting the information. His intuition that something very strange had been taking place at the Hacienda de Las Palomas had been proven to be correct. His concern over Catherine's strange behavior, María's sudden absence from singing lessons and the rather hurried arranged marriage, all pointed to something extremely unhealthy in the family. He brought his thoughts back to the conversation.

"You say that they were married and blessed by Alejandro. I am not sure that, from the Church's point of view, the marriage is viable. They are correct in saying that it once would have been, but that was at a time when access to priests was difficult. I don't know if the old rule still applies today, or if it does, under what extreme circumstances it might be considered binding. But Alejandro is a sworn deputy justice of the peace, and so the marriage is certainly legal."

"It is all almost unbelievable: that a young couple who are both of age and willing to take responsibility for their lives, who ask for nothing, are unable to marry, live in peace and raise their child." Sister Piadosa shook her head.

"Do you think that María might have exaggerated a little?" But even as he asked it, Father Octavio knew that she did not.

Looking back now at all the incongruities that had surrounded the de la Cruz family, he could understand so much better what lay behind the scenes, and the tyranny that María must have suffered at the hands of her father. And Catherine too! No wonder the woman was always ill.

He was seized by a feeling of utter outrage at what cowardly bullying had been hidden behind the appearance of sociable conviviality. A rare anger filled Father Octavio, and with it a clear resolve to do everything he could to foil de la Cruz' plan. He knew exactly what he would do. Of course he would discuss it with María, but he did not anticipate any resistance from her. Yes! He was decided.

"I am going to find out where Salvador has gone, and arrange for him to come here," he told the amazed sister. "I will need your cooperation to make sure that no one ever knows about this. And then we will conduct the marriage in the chapel and bless them both, and the child that is on its way. I will set about it as soon as I return to town."

"You amaze me, father: and I thought I knew you. I think I rather like this touch of defiance; but are you sure this won't land you in trouble with the Bishop?"

"What the Bishop doesn't know won't worry him!" Father Octavio said wickedly. "And even if he did find out, I do not have much left that I am not more than willing to lose. Such is the freedom that comes with age."

"Father Octavio!" But it was her turn to smile.

She rose from her chair. "Well, I suppose we must be getting on. There is still so much to do."

"Before you go, sister, there is just one other thing. I am pleased we have this opportunity to talk. I have a request. There is something I want you to do for me; a promise I would like you to make me, should you see fit to do so."

He turned to face her and she saw that whatever the request was, it was serious.

"Of course, father."

"I have a letter that I want you to keep safe. It is a letter of wishes."

Father Octavio searched in his breast pocket and handed her a long, white envelope addressed to her, indicating it should be opened on the death of Father Octavio Ascencio Córdova.

"Briefly it states that when I die I want my funeral service to be held here, in the chapel; and I want to be buried in the old graveyard here. I have written this most clearly, and have put aside an amount of money to cover any expenses. The letter also states that I leave whatever little personal money I have to Sebastián, for the running of The Adobe."

Sister Piadosa took the envelope and looked questioningly at him.

"I am just putting my house in order. We never know when our hour may come." He gave her a reassuring smile.

"You may encounter opposition from the Bishop: that is why I have written the letter, and I have had a lawyer examine it to make sure there are no loopholes. The Bishop, no doubt, will say all the usual things about how irregular it is; that I owe it to my congregation; that it is too far from town, and so on. But I do not think when a man is dead that he owes anyone anything, and I would be surprised if people objected to a delightful trip into the country to say farewell to their priest. Will you do this for me, sister?"

"There is an empty place in the graveyard next to Magdalena's grave," Sister Piadosa remarked by way of indicating that she would undertake to see that it was done.

Octavio searched her face, but it was as matter-of-fact as always. He thanked her and left to go in search of his lost wafers; to rescue those that perhaps the wind had not carried too far and to retrieve his surplice from the chapel roof.

After he left her Sister Piadosa closed the door, sat down in her chair and burst into a fit of unaccountable weeping. When the storm had passed, she rose and dried her eyes.

"Don't be a sentimental old fool," she muttered. "What is there to weep about anyway, and with so much work still to be done?"

Still, she did not hurry away, but went over to the window and stood for a while looking out at the white landscape.

She saw Father Octavio making his way across the yard towards the chapel, leaning into the wind. On approaching that building she saw him look up at the roof and then, to her great surprise, watched him fall to his knees with his hands raised.

She looked at the chapel and up at the snow-covered roof, but saw nothing untoward in its appearance. What on earth is he doing? He must have tripped.

But Father Octavio had not tripped.

He had fallen to his knees in adoration of what he now beheld on the chapel roof. For it would appear that the consecrated wafers had risen, and through some mystical agency had transubstantiated into the body of Christ, which now stood like a vision of light, wearing Father Octavio's white linen surplice, its arms reaching out as if in blessing of the small valley and all who dwelt in it: and standing beside him was the radiant form of Magdalena.

New Year's Eve Mass

With difficulty for the pain in his chest and the feeling of breath-lessness which had been getting steadily worse over the past weeks, Father Octavio brought the New Year's Eve Midnight Mass to a close.

All through the service he had felt Magdalena's presence close beside him.

He was hard-pressed to pay attention to the words of inspiration and gratitude which he had prepared for his short sermon when everything in him felt drawn to her; when every part of him longed to walk away from all the words, to be alone and surrender to this feeling of union with her.

Finally the service was over. Father Octavio stood in the doorway of the small church and leaned against the door-jamb for the waves of pain flooding through him. Still, he shook hands and exchanged good wishes and blessings for a peaceful new year with one and all.

One by one they thanked him for the uplifting service and expressed their wishes for his continued health and happiness. In the fullness of all the laughter and New Year spirit, much of which had been imbibed in liquid form before the service, many having come from parties held earlier in the evening, they did not notice that their priest was not quite himself. If they had, they would have seen that he was extremely pale and bore a strangely haunted look about his eyes.

As Father Octavio watched the last of the families depart the church and move off across the snow-covered plaza, he was seized by another attack of extreme pain in the area of his heart. He managed to make his way back into the church, close the door and take a seat in one of the pews, his hands clutching his chest. He felt dizzy and a little nauseous. He could no longer feel Magdalena's presence. He was alone.

He had not sat in his own church for many years, and he found it strange to be sitting there with the empty seats all around him, looking towards the altar. He raised his eyes to meet those of the Christ on the cross directly in front of him, in whose painted, wooden gaze he seemed to read a question.

"Yes!" he heard himself reply out loud. "It is enough. It is my time."

He looked around, half afraid that someone might be there, might have heard him, but the dim shadows were empty and silent.

What on earth was he saying? What did he mean? What was enough?

But even as he asked the question, he knew the answer. He knew with a certainty, a sudden and absolute clarity that his days as a priest were over.

He had no idea how this would be received, what repercussions such an announcement would incur, but it made no difference. He knew that nothing could change this profound insight, this recognition of self-betrayal, for it was no less: the certain knowledge that he could no longer wear the persona of a priest, an identity which he had carried so willingly for so many years. Because of this he had denied that sacred, other gift, given by God, no less, with no instruction so to deny it; the full and holy expression of his love for a woman. Had not God Himself said that 'it is not good for man to be alone'? Well, he would not compromise his vows; neither would he suffer the guilt brought about by the belief that his feelings of love for Magdalena were anything less than blessed.

For too long he had been living a life that he had not stopped to question; living by the truth and interpretation of it, and the decisions made around it—by others. Why had he never questioned it before? It was time that he, Octavio Ascencio Córdova, disobeyed the Church's ruling and listened to his heart. Now that he had permitted this realization to come to his conscious mind, he could no longer follow this path with integrity. He could no longer serve as a priest. Just when this thought had first come to him, however dimly, he could not say, but there it was: his lifetime vocation was done, complete.

Even as he thought this, miraculously the pain in his chest lightened and then left him completely. He sat in disbelief, breathing gently, listening to his heartbeat, waiting to be sure the pain did not return. When it did not and he realized that his strength had returned, he rose and walked down the aisle towards the altar and stood there, looking up into the face of Christ. He stood there a long time. Then he made the sign of the cross.

"Dear, sweet Lord, I feel your touch on me," he whispered.

He crossed himself once more, put out the lights and left the church.

Octavio walked the short distance back to his house through the glistening snow and the gentle brilliance of the full moon. All around him the vast night lay silent and mysterious. The last of the New Year revelers stood in small groups around the square, huddled for the cold, exchanging a last few words before finally retiring to bed. Later, when they were to report what they had seen, it would be suggested that they were intoxicated, but they swore it was not so, and certainly no alcohol had passed the lips of the young ones among them.

Octavio entered his house, lit a candle and fetched a pen and two sheets of paper from his desk. He sat down at the scrubbed-wood kitchen table where he had eaten his simple meals alone for over thirty years, and considered his life.

It was a long time to be alone; too long.

He felt tired but elated. The experience in the church burned in him like a flame. He sat on the hard, upright chair, thinking about the evening, about his life in the town; thinking about what he already knew he would do. He took up the pen and began to write. When he had finished, he folded the letters and addressed them to Sister Piadosa. Now he was ready.

"Sweet Jesus, be with me through this. It is not you or your teachings that I surrender, but rather the weight of all my clothing. I would come to you naked, as a man."

He stood up and went across the room to the small dresser where he kept, for his personal use, the silver goblet and a bottle of wine. He brought them back to the table. He poured a little wine into the goblet, blessed it and set it on the table, covering it with a white cloth. Then he knelt down on the hard floor to pray. He prayed for a long time. Through the window that opened onto the plaza, the moon cast her light over him and over the halo of white hair on the head bowed in prayer. When at last he rose, his face was clear as if a weight had been lifted from him. The deep lines of tiredness had vanished, and had anyone been present to witness it, they would have seen the radiant face of a young man.

Octavio uncovered the goblet of wine and drank deeply from it. He set it down, replaced the white cloth and closed his eyes while he prayed.

Finally, he lifted the chain and the heavy cross that he had worn since the day of his ordination, from around his neck and laid them down beside the goblet. He removed his white linen surplice, folded it, and placed it beside the cross. His shoes and socks he placed under the table. The heavy, black cassock that he wore for warmth, his thick vest, black pants and under-garments—all were folded and placed on the table. Octavio stood naked, his arms reaching outwards as if in invitation, as if to receive—what? The moonlight shining through the window fell on him, sculpting the strong, muscular body with her milky light.

He moved across the room, threw open the door and stood in the full, cold brilliance of the winter light. Snow was falling. Light, feathery flakes floated towards him. He stepped outside into the small rectory garden and stood with the light full on him, lifting his arms to receive the blessing. No manna ever fell more softly tender, or more silently.

It was what happened next—a sight witnessed by the few people remaining in the plaza—that became the main topic of hushed conversations in the village in the weeks that followed.

Seemingly out of nowhere, out of the moonlight or the falling snow, a vision of light appeared and floated slowly across the square.

Outside the rectory gate the astonished onlookers saw, standing in the moonlight, the figure of what appeared to be a young man, but one who resembled their beloved priest—naked, clothed only in light.

The other being, similarly clad, resembled an angel, but was perhaps a tall and very beautiful woman. The onlookers could not be sure about this.

It was at this auspicious moment that a resident in one of the houses overlooking the square decided to play some celebratory late-night music. It streamed out into the night like a ribbon of fire and wound itself around the two figures. To the glorious strains of Musetta's Waltz Song by Puccini the man and woman embraced in the center of the plaza. Then, very slowly, very tenderly, they began to dance.

The small group in the plaza stood transfixed. Many felt tears come to their eyes. It was a dance that seemed to be part of the softly falling snow, the silent stars and the moonlight glistening upon the white carpet that covered the ground over which they moved. As they crossed the square they left no footprints, but seemed to float, having scarcely more substance than those beams that caressed them.

The onlookers fell to their knees, many openly weeping at such beauty. Surely it must be a sign: of what they could not say, but they knew that something had changed in them—that such beauty changes us forever.

The following morning, when Father Octavio did not appear for Matins, old Elena came looking for him. She found him lying naked on his bed, a smile of such intense happiness upon his face that she bent down and kissed him full on the lips.

"That is for Magdalena," she said in a conspiratorial whisper, and wiped away a tear.

She found the old, worn bed-cover on the chair, and with great tenderness pulled it up over him. Then, with difficulty for her age, she knelt beside him and said a prayer for one of the gentlest men she had ever known. When she was done, she rose slowly and stood looking down at the face of the man she had served without condition or reservation for all those quiet and fulfilling years. She crossed herself and left the room.

And so it was not once, but twice that Father Octavio was kissed full on the lips, and on both occasions by a woman who loved him most dearly.

Father Octavio's Funeral

"Bendito sea el Dios y Padre de nuestro Señor Jesucristo, Padre de las misericordias y Dios de toda consolación, que nos consuela en todas nuestras tribulaciones, para que nosotros podamos consolar también a los que sufren, dándoles el mismo consuelo que Dios nos ha dado a nosotros."

The familiar words of the service, uttered at the entrance to the chapel, poured out of the loud-speakers towards the crowd who stood gathered in the courtyard, all come to pay homage to their beloved priest and friend, Father Octavio Ascensio Córdova.

Father Octavio's body, which had been prepared for burial the day before, had been brought to the chapel by two senior members of his church for the velorio, the wake, for which they stayed and sat vigil with Sister Piadosa.

It was a little after midnight when they heard men's voices chanting the alabados somewhere across the fields, and their hearts warmed to know that Father Octavio's vigil was being thus honored. It was only later in the morning that they made the surprising discovery that the grave, next to Magdalena's, had been dug in preparation for the burial. In spite of questioning everyone at The Adobe, Sister Piadosa could not discover who had performed this duty.

Sister Ana knew.

"Surely you know, sister? It is the Hermanos!"

Sister Piadosa smiled at her.

All afternoon cars and other vehicles made their slow way down the winding dirt road to the small valley, to where the life and death of Father Octavio would be honored and blessed in a late-afternoon funeral service. This would be followed by his burial in the small camposanto close to the chapel.

Among the vehicles, negotiating the twists and turns with extreme difficulty for the unevenness of the road and the thick snow, was a long procession of lowriders driven by some of the town's wildest young bloods. Through their passion for their outrageously splendid vehicles, variously sprayed with the images of their adoration, ranging from Elvis to a portrayal of Christ carrying the cross, they had found a creative way to express themselves and ultimately their love of God. It was a group who had always felt their priest's deep affection for them and his acceptance of their idiosyncratic, elegant and very original style of worship.

Sebastián and Sister Piadosa anticipated a large gathering, and bearing in mind the limited seating in the chapel, and that most people would be standing outside in the snow and the chilly evening air, they decided to set large bonfires at intervals around the yard to offer light and warmth.

That morning Sister Piadosa, in accordance with Father Octavio's letter of wishes, had set farolitos, the small votive candles in brown paper bags traditionally used at Christmas, to mark the path of Magdalena's labyrinth, which wound its way through the herb garden. After that she went to place the large pots of dried lavender to mark the place where the priest would stand for the Blessing of the Grave. Here she observed an unusual sight. The yuccas which Magdalena had planted around the graveyard had, overnight, sent up tall stems full of buds on the point of bursting into bloom. Sister Piadosa stared in amazement.

She called to Sebastián, who was up on the chapel roof.

"Sebastián! Come and look at this."

Sebastián descended the ladder and came to stand next to her. "Isn't that rather unusual?"

"More than unusual: it is unheard-of."

Neither of them had ever made mention of what they both knew to be true: that Father Octavio and Magdalena had loved one another as deeply and as passionately as only true lovers may. That Magdalena should command these blooms from beyond the grave was both mysterious and, paradoxically, entirely believable.

"It is extraordinary," Sebastián said. "But then, my mother always did have a way with plants. You wait. The blooms will open tonight, I am sure of it."

"Bendigo el cuerpo de Octavio Ascensio Córdova con el agua bendita que recuerda su bautismo..."

At the entrance to the small chapel, Father Santana, Father Octavio's most intimate friend, sprinkled the body with holy water, and made the traditional blessing.

He had discussed at length the extremely unorthodox funeral with Sister Piadosa and Sebastián, and knowing that the full body of the Church Council would attend the service, he had also consulted his superiors. After some deliberation and not a little consternation, they had come to the conclusion that, while eccentric in the extreme, the proposed service did not actually challenge any doctrinal law that they could think of. As Father Octavio had anticipated, they were shocked that he should request that the service be held in a little chapel that no one had ever heard of, but again, as far as they could surmise, no principle or law of the Church had been contravened.

The procession, led by Father Santana and followed by the open coffin carried by Alejandro, Raho, Santiago, Sebastián and Rafaél, and a young man from Father Octavio's church, made its way into the chapel.

Father Octavio lay resting on a bed of lavender, holding his well-worn rosary in his hands. He was dressed in a pair of casual denims and a check shirt, with an expression of the most utter and sublime joy on his face. His feet were bare.

The mourners who gazed on it saw a face which, far from wearing the customary pallor of death, bore the shining radiance of one in ecstasy.

It was noted with shock by the attending clergy that Father Octavio was not wearing his priest's robes, and on challenging this and demanding to know who was responsible for the oversight, they were shown the note which Elena had found on the table on the morning she found him lying naked on the bed. It stated quite clearly that he wished to be buried in his everyday clothes. They were told that he had even left them folded with the note.

"So he knew he was dying! Why did he not call for someone to hear his confession?"

Sister Piadosa looked at them, but ventured no explanation. They would see the service sheet soon enough.

The coffin was placed in front of the altar. The Bishop, the priest from the cathedral, all the priests from the surrounding parishes and a substantial gathering of influential members of the Church Council for whom places had been reserved in the front rows of the chapel, followed and took their seats.

The choir, Sister Piadosa and the nuns, and Encarnación Martínez from the Rancho de Las Palomas moved to the front and stood on one side of the altar. Encarnación, by Father Octavio's request, would sing a solo.

Soon the chapel was full. Those outside gathered at the doorway, or stood around the large bonfires for warmth. The service proceeded, not with the customary psalm, but with verses chosen by Father Octavio from The Song of Songs. Some years earlier Santiago had set excerpts from The Song of Songs to music, a work that had moved Father Octavio very deeply at the time. Now one of these excerpts was what he had chosen to be sung for him by the choir of The Adobe nuns.

"I am come into my garden..."

The clarity of the nuns' voices against the silent, white landscape somehow accentuated the erotic nuances of the poem.

"I have put off my coat;
How shall I put it on?"

Many of the members of the clergy found it an extraordinary choice.

What could it mean? It was hardly appropriate. And to come to your own funeral with no shoes was unnecessarily provocative.

"I have washed my feet;
How shall I defile them?"

But there were others inside and outside the chapel who were moved by the beauty of this naked expression of love.

From the small campanile, the bell-tower that Sister Piadosa had requested to be built above the room where the nuns meditated, María sat listening to the service. She could not attend it for obvious reasons, but she had asked if she could watch and listen from the tower, which would afford her a view of the proceedings.

Unobserved, she watched the arrivals. Her heart ached when she saw the familiar form of Encarnación enter the chapel. She searched for Mercedes and Diego, Roberto and José, but in the crowd of people, all muffled up for the cold, she could not see them.

She saw her father striding across the snowy yard, his head lowered, his shoulders hunched. From her perspective, standing up in the small tower, he looked oddly small; small and suddenly old.

Now, as she watched him cross the yard, she felt herself filled with an unexpected compassion for his utter loneliness. He was a man who had known and experienced many things, but he had not known love.

He was not accompanied by her mother, and she found this surprising, for Father Octavio had been such a favorite of Catherine's, and she would have wanted to pay her last respects to him. María concluded that her mother must be having one of her bad days. It would have to be a good reason to prevent her from attending Father Octavio's funeral.

She was brought back from her musings by the voice of Encarnación, singing what, María read from the Order of Service, was Father Octavio's Confessión, a prayer written by St Augustine. She was amazed. A confession being sung publicly!

The wondrous voice filled her with memories of her childhood. Once again she felt those strong arms around her in an embrace that was instantly familiar; an embrace that would protect her from all harm, all evil, from the Devil himself. She could hear in Encarnación's rich voice the infinite patience and endurance of those who live close to the earth, and who know that suffering is also beautiful; whose lives are made bearable by the absolute certainty of the invincibility of love. She closed her eyes and listened.

"Too late have I loved you, O Beauty..."

Through the words she could hear Father Octavio's voice; his gentle sadness.

"You touched me and I burned for your peace..."

María opened her eyes and gazed out over the familiar fields and the bare cottonwoods with their snow-covered arms reaching up to Heaven; at the mountains and the gentle contours of the foothills. All was tinged with the rosy light of the sunset's afterglow. The strange, blue light that haunts the shadows in snow had deepened into a shade of indigo, as if night were already breathing itself into that whiteness. In the courtyard more than two hundred small candles, lit by the people listening to the service, cast their small brilliance over the trampled snow.

Gregorio, who worked at The Adobe and whose task it was to keep the bonfires burning, threw bunches of dry lavender and armloads of piñón logs onto each blaze, and now bursts of sparks rose like streams of stars into the darkening sky. Even from where she stood María could smell the pungent scent of the smoke which drifted up to her. This fragrance and the soft silence of the snow, the pink sky and the leaping flames of the fires, and over all of it the voice of Encarnación singing a testament to love and redemption: she thought she had never witnessed such beauty.

"Take, O Lord, and receive all my liberty, my memory, my understanding, and all my will, all that I have and possess. You have given all of these to me; to you I restore them. All are yours; dispose of them all according to your will. Give me your love and your grace; having but these I am rich enough and ask for nothing more."

María's attention was caught by the sound of chanting.

"Santo, Santo, Santo es el Señor,
Dios del universo.
Llenos están el cielo y la tierra de tu gloria.

Hosanna en el cielo. Bendito el que viene
en nombre del Señor.
Hosanna en el cielo."

What was it? María couldn't be sure if the words she heard came from
the hillside or from the chapel. She heard the Lord's Prayer rising up into the
evening like a great wave.

"Padre nuestro, que estás en el cielo…"

She could not see anyone, but she could hear them. The voices which
came from the direction of the graveyard were not separate from those of
the mourners. María found herself uttering the words of the final prayer
even as she searched the darkness for sight of them.

"En tus manos, Padre de bondad, encomendamos a nuestro
hermano…"

Was it her imagination, or was there a band of men gathering around
the graveyard?

"Anunciamos tu muerte,
proclamamos tu resurrección,
¡Ven, Señor Jesus!"

"Dying you destroyed our death,
Rising you restored our life.
Lord Jesus, come in glory."

The priest left the chapel, followed by the pall-bearers carrying the
coffin. The women remained in the chapel while all the men of the congregation began to make their way to the small graveyard. María wondered what
the priest would make of a band of men standing around the open grave.
Surely there would be some surprise; some questions. Soon they would
meet.

She bent down to gather up her shawl that had slipped from her shoulders. When she looked again, the graveyard was empty.

The procession rounded the corner of the chapel and stepped into the brilliant light of the camposanto. The priest came to an abrupt halt, as did everyone following him. Sister Piadosa, who had followed at a discreet distance and now stood above the camposanto, away from the pall-bearers, was the first to identify the source of the light that streamed out into the darkness. The yuccas! Magdalena's yuccas had bloomed.

At first the pall-bearers were unaware of what had occurred, but as they drew closer they saw what could only be described as a miraculous occurrence.

"Milagro!"

Father Santana raised his hand for quiet. A hush descended on the gathering. With extraordinary composure and presence of mind he asked the gathering to be still.

"Let us not be disturbed by this glorious manifestation of beauty. Let us rather offer a silent prayer of thanks that this should be granted to a man so loved by all of us."

The grave was blessed and the coffin lowered into it. The prayers for burial were spoken, and the people made their responses. Finally the service was concluded with the Lord's Prayer.

Father Santana invited Sebastián to read the last word before the people cast their handfuls of dirt or petals or flowers onto the coffin and said their personal farewells to Father Octavio.

"And death shall have no dominion..."

Sebastián had chosen the Dylan Thomas poem deliberately. He wished he had spoken more fully to Octavio about the gratitude he felt towards the man who had been like a father to him, for all the years of his gentle wisdom. He wished he had acknowledged how deeply he respected the love that Octavio and Magdalena felt for each other.

He knew why Octavio had 'put off his coat'.

"Though lovers be lost, love shall not;
And death shall have no dominion."

Father Jean-Luc Sel

The welcoming party, made up of Elena, Gregorita, who was to replace her, two young women, Josefa and Gloria, who would help her keep the church and the rectory clean; Lina who tended the church and rectory gardens and was responsible for flower arrangements; the Women's Church Activities Committee, the Women's Social Services and Counseling Church Group and a group of children not yet old enough to be attending school—stood huddled together just inside the church entrance to shelter from a mean wind that was blowing in from the south.

They were awaiting the arrival of the man who was to be their new priest: Father Jean-Luc Sel.

Just outside the door, but also attempting to find a little shelter, the inevitable and almost obligatory pack of thin and perpetually hungry mongrels, which witnessed most of the town's comings and goings, stood with their heads lowered, their backs roached for the cold, their tails tucked tightly between their shivering legs.

The priest had been expected earlier, but reports of fresh snowfalls in Santa Fe probably accounted for the delay. The children, out of cold or boredom, or both, began running races up and down the aisle and hiding under the pews, so that the small church rang with the sound of their laughter.

While the women waited, talk obviously turned to speculation about what kind of man they might expect, and those few who had managed to learn anything about his background shared what little information they had gleaned about the new priest with the rest of the group.

A man of great intellectual ability was what had been reported to one member.

Although this was supposed to be a recommendation, the town's people were not unduly impressed, and would have preferred to have heard that he was a man of simplicity with a generous heart. Father Octavio had been one such, and it was perhaps only human that his replacement would be measured against his standards.

"It would be unfair of us to compare him to Father Octavio. We must remember that he might find our ways a little different. We must do everything we can to make him feel welcome."

What they did not know, and what no one had been told, was that Father Jean-Luc Sel had left France rather hurriedly, for reasons which had not been disclosed to the public or to the relevant dignitaries in New Mexico. Indeed, he was being sent away, against his wishes, because of a certain matter that was causing not a little embarrassment in the ecumenical ranks of the Church in his home country. Those in authority thought that the best way out of the compromising situation that his actions had precipitated, and which had taken much skillful negotiation to keep confidential, was to send him away so that all the excitement could die down, amends could be made to the wronged party and the unfortunate incident could be forgotten. It was fortuitous that a position should have become vacant so far from home, and he had been dispatched forthwith.

He left his comfortable parish, resentful that he should be forced to suffer the ignorant opinion of fools and tight-lipped after receiving his orders and a cursory blessing, which carried little warmth and even less conviction, for his future success in his new appointment; a blessing uttered by a relieved bishop, a man who was several years younger than Jean-Luc; a man he considered to be intellectually his inferior.

And so it was that he left France, the country of his birth, in order to come and take up the position which had become vacant following the death of Father Octavio.

Members of the clergy in New Mexico were told that he was a man of high intelligence with many published academic papers to his credit; commentaries on the history and precise meaning of certain doctrines, observances and rituals. Apparently these papers dwelt at length upon the importance of maintaining such rituals in their original form, insisting that any movement away from this, any new interpretation or cross-pollination from other, false religious expressions or practices was not to be countenanced.

It was when arguing the value and merit of the confessional that the full extent of his rigidity became apparent.

"Only," he said, "in the true and contrite and regular practice of a profound confession can members of the Church, at their death, be assured of forgiveness, redemption and a place in Heaven. Outside these parameters there can be no absolution. All others, not members of the true Church and not observing this practice, will not be saved."

It was his opinion, stated as fact, that the serious observance of these rituals had been allowed to slip in recent years, and it was a matter he sought to rectify.

Father Jean-Luc was not by nature a man who wanted to bring the Gospel to those uncouth, unwashed and uncultured nations that lived anywhere outside of Western Europe. Others might choose to do this, but he was of the opinion that savages were not intellectually capable of conceptualizing an abstract God, or any god, unless it was made of sticks and feathers. Indeed, he deemed even those neighbors close to France to be, by his standards, lacking in refinement.

He preferred to involve himself in things French, France being a country which, to his mind, had achieved in its art, music, literature and philosophy, in its very culture, everything that could be held to be elegant and uplifting for the spirit.

This exile to a place which he considered to be at the very edge of the lowest expression of civilization came as a heavy penance. He would, however, make the best of it—wasn't that what our Lord had always taught? Through the car window he observed the emptiness of the country, the strange geological conformations of the land—all very foreign to his eye. He paid scant attention to the few small towns they passed, and contemplated the trailer homes and small, ramshackle houses with distaste. He hoped that the town of his destination would be substantially larger than anything he had seen en route.

It was at this stage of his reflections that the car made the sharp turn into the narrow road which led to Las Madres and the small plaza. It negotiated the erosion caused by the arroyo which flooded across the road during the rainy season, and finally came to a halt inside the square.

"We've arrived, father." The driver pointed to the small structure that was identifiable primarily from the small cross on the roof.

Father Jean-Luc stared out of the window of the car in dismay. There must be some mistake, he thought. Surely this could not be where he was to spend his days; in a village which, as far as he could tell, was built of mud. This could not be called a town.

But there was no mistake. There was the line of women waving to him. Oh, God! Must it always be women?

He raised his hand in formal acknowledgement of their presence.

The welcoming committee saw a thin man of no determinate age, with a stoop that suggested a mild deformity of the spine and a sallow face that looked as if it had been put together out of scraps left over from other, more generous visages. Everything about him, from his thin, bony nose with its pinched nostrils to the thin-lipped mouth with the deep grooves on either side of it, suggesting an attitude of habitual disapproval, and the rather too close set of his eyes, looked mean. Even the cloth of his black cassock, although of a superior quality, had been cut to extremely narrow specifications, offering evidence of an angular frame, gaunt to the point of emaciation.

As he alighted from the taxi which had brought him from the station in Santa Fe, Elena stepped forward to greet him.

"Welcome, father. I am Elena." She offered her hand which, rather reluctantly, he shook.

"And this is the Women's Church Committee, come to say hello and wish you a very long and happy stay in our town and in New Mexico, and to say that if there is anything you need, you only have to call on them."

He nodded to the women.

"And this is the Women's Social Services and Counseling Group, who work in close association with the Church."

There was another curt nod.

"And allow me to introduce you to Gregorita and the three who will assist her: Gloria, Joséfa and Lina. Gregorita will replace me in looking after the church and the rectory. Please consult her about any needs you may have. She will help you to get settled."

"Father."

Gregorita gave a shy nod and held out her hand, but seeing the priest's face, gave a small bob instead, something between a genuflection and a curtsy, and stepped back.

"And now let me show you to your house. The women have prepared a hot lunch for you. It is inside. You must be very tired."

Following the rather ancient Elena, Father Jean-Luc walked the short distance to the small gate that opened into the rectory garden. He entered the house and stood for a while, taking in the low ceiling and the small, shuttered windows. His gaze passed over the scrubbed-wood table, the two crooked chairs, the dresser with its odd collection of cups and plates and the rough adobe walls. He was appalled by the simplicity of the house which he was supposed to inhabit. Everything about it, and this god-forsaken country to which he had been sent, looked rude and savage to his eyes, accustomed as they were to the elegant refinement of French culture. His eyes fell on the two large, covered pots of food, and he wondered what manner of abomination had been prepared for him. Elena noted his disapproval.

"I will have no need of Gregorita's attentions. I would prefer to have a man work in the church and assist with certain requirements in the rectory. If you could set up some interviews for the position, I would be grateful."

It was at this point that Elena noticed Father Jean-Luc's hands.

Ever since she had been a little girl she had been fascinated by people's hands. She had discovered that, while sometimes even eyes could dissemble, adopting a look of wide-eyed ingenuousness, feigning an artlessness which could be misleading, hands could never lie to her. It was almost as if she could hear them speaking. She could read a person by the shape of their hands and the way they held them: the spread of the fingers, the smallest gesture, the flick of a finger; and, while in no way a clairvoyant or a fortune-teller, she could tell so much of a person's character from them as to make it possible to predict much of what fate held in store for that person in the future. It was a gift which made it impossible for people to lie to Elena. Everyone in the village knew this.

Father Octavio's hands had been large and strong with blunt, square fingertips. They were farmer's hands, burnt dark from the sun, and although they were not shy of hard work, they carried a tremendous quality of peace and serenity. They were hands that were visible, open and inviting; hands that could bring to the bereft not only his compassion, but all the force and energy of his spiritual strength. Those hands would soothe a fever with a touch, comfort the contrite and close the eyes of the newly dead. It had been noted by parents who brought their infants for baptism that even the most fractious infant would grow quiet in that strong, gentle hold.

By contrast Santiago, the music teacher, had hands that were elegant, with long, sensitive fingers: fingers that could pluck from a guitar chords so sensuous that all the women would fall in love with him. He could caress the keys of a piano with such softness that people would feel the music breathing into them.

And then, of course, there were Alejandro's hands. Now there was a pair of hands for you! There was a pair of hands that could coax angels out of solid wood.

Looking at the priest's hands now, Elena thought that she had never seen hands like these before. Professionally—for the study of hands had become for her a discipline—she was fascinated, but she was nevertheless shocked at what she saw.

The priest's hands were long, thin and narrow like the rest of him, and white; very white, and somehow evil. She was surprised by the thought. They looked like hands that had lived in the dark, that had remained hidden from life; hands that had never felt love or sun or earth, had never played in the water of a stream. She doubted they had ever touched an animal. They had not worked; neither had they ever held, caressed or been caressed. They were not the kind of hands that touched—anything or anyone.

How strange, she thought. Hands that do not touch. She was sure they would be cold. But it was the whiteness of them that so appalled her. They had the look of something that has been buried, or has lain long in deep, dark water. They looked like those blind, white things that one finds beneath a heavy stone when it is lifted for the first time. Their whiteness was sepulchral and strangely unclean.

Now, as Elena observed them, they began a strange movement as if they were washing themselves. Over and over the hands turned and washed, and washed and turned. It was a hideously compulsive activity resembling a sexual act, a strange copulation where it appeared that the entangled creatures struggled to separate even as they writhed and clung together in their ritual. She would not want such hands ever to touch her, Elena thought, and the very idea of taking communion, of receiving the Host from those thin, white fingers filled her with disgust. What was it they were saying to her?

She bent closer in an effort to hear them speak, but for the first time in a life of listening to all manner of speech from the palms and fingers of young and old, she could hear no voice. They had no speech. The hands were mute. What could have happened to them that they should be so appallingly silent?

But no, there was something there, something hidden, sly. She moved closer. It was not a voice, but something else she sensed rather than heard. She bent closer still. Yes, there it was.

Behind the muteness and the white impotence of their fixated contortions she heard a child weeping.

Elena caught Father Jean-Luc staring at her, and she blushed with embarrassment. Mumbling something, she stepped away, averting her eyes. What a shocking thing to have done. Even if he had no idea of what it meant, all the women would know. How could she have been so indiscreet?

"Well, yes, then, father, I'll arrange the interviews," she managed to stutter out. "And now we'll let you get settled in. I will call a little later. Would four o'clock be suitable?"

She was anxious to leave.

"Four o'clock. I'll be waiting."

Although nobody said anything as the small group split up and each went back to her separate occupation, there was one over-riding sentiment that each carried: one of dismay.

It was not an auspicious start to an important relationship that might, quite possibly, last for decades. None of the women dared to allow what was moving in their hearts to become a thought, but if they had, it would have been that they disliked the new priest and had a quite irrational but very profound sense of mistrust of the man. It was a feeling that nothing in the following days did anything to dispel.

Father Jean-Luc Sel's narrow preaching did not find favor with the people who attended his church. The people continued to come to Mass as they always had, to take communion and pray, but they did not pay attention to his long and tediously condemnatory sermons. Nor did many of them seek his services in the confessional, a matter on which he commented frequently with strong disapproval and concern for their spiritual fitness.

"There are many among you who have sinned and who have not come to me for forgiveness. It is in my power to bring you safe unto our Heavenly Father, but not without your abject confession. Get on your knees and beg for it, and I will intercede for you."

Who on earth did he think he was?

They continued to shun the small, curtained chamber and fidget during the long, censorious sermons. Noticing this, he surmised that they did not have the intellectual capacity to understand what he was preaching. There had been others similarly afflicted.

His mind went back to his home country, and a certain over-reaching young priest who thought he could advance himself through his own intellectual capabilities, without consulting Father Jean-Luc.

Yes, well. Those short-sighted fools of bishops had believed the young man's account of what had happened, and now he was sitting pretty in a fine city parish, marked for promotion while he, Jean-Luc, who knew as much or more about matters of spiritual excellence than the Pope himself, had been sent to this backward little village and left to deal with these dullards.

The town continued to suffer his letter-of-the-law approach in silence, but he had no friends among them. He had no friends at all.

Oh! That God should have set him down among a stubborn and simple-minded people!

But he resolved to be equal to the test that God had set him. In vain he tried to wean the people off the Virgin of Guadalupe, who, he reminded them was a resurrection of the old, pre-Columbian earth goddess Tonantzin, a black idol worshipped by the Mexican Indians. Her blackness spoke of her evil origins; black as night or death, and far too earthy for his refined senses. For him she carried the taint and memory of idolatry in her black heart.

In addition to, and along with her he decried all the idols that stood behind the altars in churches all around the state. The people listened and said nothing. They tolerated everything he said with unconcerned indifference. It would pass, the way all things pass.

This opinionated little French priest would not last long. Nuestra Señora, La Morena, the Dark Virgin, La Lupita would see to it. Of that they were sure. Certainly he was not going to take their beloved Guadalupe away from them: who then would hear their pleas for intercession? Could he but know how many of them had her likeness tattooed upon their bodies that she might never be far from them!

This wretched French puritan was not going to come here with his repressive Anglo ideas and disturb their worship of a much-loved, gentle and serene Moon Mother who had watched over them for more than three hundred years; whose roots reached down into the dark earth—earth stained with the blood of so much suffering; full of compassion and tenderness and fierce protection for those struggling with the pain and sorrows of life. She had protected them at home, in their travels, in battle, in gambling dens, in the bullring, in taxis, cars and houses of ill repute. She did not judge their human frailty. Why then should he? Against her the priest was impotent; his words were as dust. Nothing he said could threaten the personal relationship they had with her, nor separate them from the comfort of her unfailing kindness.

The Birth of Sofia

The pains began before dawn on Easter Sunday. Sister Ana, looking in on María on her way to the chapel, found her sitting on the chair, white-faced and groaning, bent over the cramps. With a word to María that she would be right back, she ran to call Sister Piadosa.

As was her custom every Easter, Sister Piadosa had spent the night in prayer and vigil in preparation for the celebration of the resurrection of Christ. In the past Father Octavio, in spite of his many commitments, always managed to find a way to hold a Mass in the chapel for the small community. This year, with the new priest in office, anyone who wanted to attend the Easter Sunday Mass would have to make the trip into town.

With a hasty prayer Sister Piadosa snuffed the Easter candle and all the altar lights, and then she and Sister Ana hurried to María's room.

One look at María, and Sister Ana was dispatched to fetch the immediate necessities: hot water, a basin, towels and all the various bottles of herbal remedies. These were kept in a box for when the sisters were called out for a delivery on one of the farms nearby.

"There now, child," said Sister Piadosa as she helped María onto the bed. "We'll soon be welcoming this new little soul into the world."

She set about organizing the room, moving the table closer to the bed and opening the window as wide as it would go.

Everyone had predicted a hot summer, but Sister Piadosa could not remember an Easter as bone-dry and airless as this one. Although it was only the beginning of April, barely spring, the early morning air hung in the valley like a blanket, undisturbed by the barest breath of wind.

Sister Ana returned with the water and towels, and once she had arranged everything on the bedside table, she left the room again to go and brew a blend of herbs: mallow, chamomile and ground juniper to help María through the delivery.

While Sister Ana was gone Sister Piadosa bathed María's hot face and made her as comfortable as she could, and when the next pain came she showed her how to breathe her way through it until it had passed.

By midday Sister Piadosa knew that the delivery would be a long and difficult one. María was fine-boned and slender, with narrow hips. Not good child-bearing hips, Sister Piadosa thought to herself. And the baby is big.

In addition there was the delicate state of María's health to be taken into account, for it seemed that in the past months, as her belly grew ever more swollen and distended with the new life growing inside her, she herself became insubstantial, almost translucent in her frailty.

Sister Piadosa prayed to the Holy Mother and to Saint Bartholemew that María would come safely through this ordeal, and that her own knowledge and experience would be sufficient to deliver this baby, for they did not want any outsider to know of this child.

A trustworthy woman from the village had been found to foster the babe. She had given birth to her own child barely two days ago, and she and her husband were willing to take the infant and present it as a twin. They did not ask where the child came from. If the nuns, who did so much for them, asked this of them, it was sufficient. They were happy to give the child a home.

The day grew hotter and hotter. Sister Piadosa sat with María, sponging her arms and face and fanning her to comfort and cool her. She encouraged her to take frequent sips of the brewed herbs to relax her and help dull the pain. But each time the contractions came, the slender body was seized as if by invisible hands, and suffered the urgency of their demands.

María surrendered herself to the inexorable pains, but as each contraction passed she lay back on the pillows, exhausted, with eyes closed, her body limp beneath its swollen belly. Through it all she never uttered a cry.

"It is quite all right if you cry out, my dear," the sister said. "Women in labor do, all the time. It helps to let the pain out."

But although María registered the words she made no sound other than the groans that were forced from her by the contractions.

The afternoon wore on. From time to time Sister Ana came into the room with fresh water and cooling drinks. María, however, could only take small sips before sinking back onto the pillows. And then the next contraction would come and take hold of the frail, little body, each time drawing from it a little more of its strength.

Evening was drawing near, and the shadows were lengthening. The setting of the sun brought with it the relief of evening coolness, but the waters had still not broken and there was still no relief for María from the heaving pains and the heat of this dry labor.

Finally Sister Piadosa made a decision. She went to the door and called for Sister Ana.

"Sister, bring me the enema tray and some warm, soapy water. Oh, and bring an extra lamp with you when you return. We will need some light here. Then I want you to come and help me."

The little sister ran off to do her bidding.

"María, we are going to give you an enema to help things along a bit. I want you to try and relax. We will soon have this baby making its appearance."

Although she spoke the words with assurance, the sister was far from feeling confident. The labor was going on too long, and María was growing weaker. If only the waters would break, they might achieve something. Sister Ana returned with the enema tray, and together she and Sister Piadosa went about their task.

María groaned, and her body strained spasmodically under this added invasion, but eventually it was done.

"It will soon be over, María," Sister Ana whispered as she sponged her feverish brow, "and then I will wash you with sweet lavender and chamomile water and give you a fresh gown that has clean air and sunshine in it, and you will feel better."

She did not say, she did not dare say that she knew that, when the child was born and removed from the room—removed before María could catch even a glimpse of it; before she could touch or hold it—that far from feeling better, María was going to have to endure a pain far worse than the physical ordeal she presently endured.

Although the matter had been discussed early on in the pregnancy, no one had mentioned of late the arrangements for the child. María had been so delicate during the pregnancy that it was considered better to deal with one thing at a time.

But María, by this stage, was too exhausted, too worn out by the pain to even open her eyes. She had found that place where, unable to respond any further to the physical demands of the labor, she could rise out of her body, float above the pain, above the bed, detached from the drama that was being enacted below her. Her eyes closed as she drifted into this quiet place, away from the room and the sisters, away from life's urgent demands.

The two sisters, seeing this, knew that they must work fast, or they would lose both the babe and mother.

"Oh, Holy Mother of God, help me. Have I made a mistake in not calling for a doctor? Have I been arrogant? No time now to ask this, but please help me."

Her prayer was interrupted by a sudden groan from María, accompanied by a contraction and a rush as finally the waters broke.

"Thanks be to God," muttered Sister Piadosa. "Now we can get on with it."

It was as if the breaking of the waters was a signal for which María had been waiting. She opened her eyes, threw her head back and drew in a deep breath; a breath so deep that the light from the lamps streamed in with it.

The two sisters thought she was going to scream, that the pain, finally, had become unbearable.

But they were wrong. It was not for the pain that she drew in this breath, breathed in the lamp-light, the night wind and the indigo-colored evening sky. No, María was not about to scream.

María de la Cruz, in the middle of her labor, with the child of her womb beginning that long, slow, curving journey into life—began to sing!

It was a wild song that remembered an ancestry older than history. It was a song without words; an ancient song that came from the cave, from the rocks, from the dark earth. It flowed from her like a river; like a storm-wind rushing through a forest; like the silence of mountain snow.

The sisters were shocked. They listened in awe to this voice with its unearthly cadences and its primitive resonance; this song that was like an echo of the ages of time. They could not reconcile this voice with the frail young woman lying on the bed, and it put the fear of God into them.

What strange and awesome power has entered her, thought Sister Piadosa, and she crossed herself. It was like some primitive supplication, as if she sought through it to invoke some pagan deity! To her ears, accustomed as they were to the soft chanting of prayer and praise, this raw utterance, although utterly beautiful, sounded almost barbaric. She thought to hush María, but the labor was going so well that she refrained from doing so, but bent to the task of guiding the small head through the cervix, preparing for the infant's delivery into the world.

The song ended. There was silence.

It was into this silence that the sound of an infant's wail entered the small room. María's daughter had been brought safely into the world.

"You have a beautiful little daughter, María," sister Piadosa said, and there were tears of compassion in her eyes.

María reached out her arms to receive the babe; then let them fall.

The child was taken away by Sister Ana. María did not catch even a glimpse of her face.

Outside, night fell. Moths fluttered against the glass lamp, beating their fragile wings against the invisible shield in their struggle to reach the light. It seemed to Sister Piadosa that their attraction to the light was as irresistible as their failure was inevitable.

"Oh, God," she groaned, "sometimes I think you set us up in order that we may fail. And fail we do, again and again. All we do, like these poor moths, is bruise our souls against your greater will. And yet, like the moths we return to you again and again."

She paused a while to reflect.

"And if we did manage to reach you, would you consume us?"

She turned to María.

"I think you know, María, don't you, that we cannot keep the child here. We cannot allow the truth about the birth of this child to become known."

María had her hands over her face. Her body shook with the sobs that welled up out of her, while the tears poured down her cheeks.

Sister Piadosa knelt down to be close to her. She put her hand on María's arm and spoke through her own tears.

"I cannot begin to know your pain, María, and I feel helpless in the face of it: not to see your child. But it would be harder if you were to hold her." She stroked María's arm. "I give you my word that I will make certain that she is loved and cared for. We have found a foster-mother for her. She is a good woman. She will be very close, in a family—as a member of the family—where no one will ask questions."

María looked at her with eyes wide from exhaustion and the after-pain of the birthing. Of course she knew this. But now the overwhelming pain of her ultimate loss made itself known to her. She turned to face the wall.

Sister Piadosa could feel her aloneness. This was not how it should be. She had seen the look of wonder on so many mothers' faces: wonder at the miracle of this new being that had come from them. She had seen them looking at the new little face, all the features, committing it to memory; and all the time filled with the joy of this extraordinary experience, which although it happened millions upon millions of times throughout history, was always new. She should not be alone.

"I will stay with you tonight María. If there is anything you want, I will be here."

What sister Piadosa did not say was that with such a birth song, although they might keep their secret for a time, all of nature already knew and proclaimed the birth. It was only a question of time before such a child stepped into her destiny. Then the inevitable questions would be asked.

Although María would never be her mother in the traditional sense of the word, although she would not be with her as she grew up, she had already given her what few mothers have ever been able to give to their children: she had given the child her song.

On the window-sill the moths fluttered their bruised wings in their futile attempts to reach the light, only to hit against the invisible glass barrier.

She never did hold her. She did not ever see her face. All she knew, all she would ever know of her daughter was her cry. And she heard this one cry over and over in the days to come, while her arms ached with the weight of their emptiness and her heavy breasts throbbed with the pain of their engorged fullness.

She wept tears of pain and longing for that part of her that had been taken away too soon, too soon even for the body to comprehend its loss. The pain of labor, the pain of birth was nothing to the pain she now felt.

She held that cry in her memory, etched into a part of her brain where it would forever resonate with her love for her unseen child. She fixed it there that she might never forget it, never mistake that cry, that particular sound. She lay and listened for it, listened with all of her heart, for this was the only sense she had of her: that cry. And she wanted by this listening, by the quality of it, by this rapt attention, to send her daughter all her love; as if this listening might reach her, hold her: so that in some mysterious way, through this intense concentration, the child might know her mother.

The Baptism

It was the second Sunday in May, and as such it was the one day in the month when Father Jean-Luc made his reluctant trip down to the small adobe chapel. He would conduct Mass, hear confession and deal with any matters requiring his attention that had arisen during the previous four weeks. This Sunday he was to baptize the twins born to one of the local farmers' wives, and he had come prepared.

He did not enjoy these visits, partly because it took him away from his work, for he was writing a paper on Idolatry—The Trend Towards Paganism in Rural Communities, but more particularly because it meant he would have to spend time with that wretchedly perverse little nun, Sister Piadosa, who ran the place.

This was what happened when you gave women too much authority: they lost all sense of propriety. He had recognized it the second he laid eyes on her. Where was the meek obeisance, the downcast eyes, where the hands clasped and preferably hidden, the submission to his greater knowledge and authority? She was, it appeared, a stranger to these virtues. Instead she had met him with a direct gaze and had put out a hand to shake his, a gesture which he had ignored. He had found her behavior most unseemly, and oddly challenging. Well, it might take a little time, but he would set the record straight. Once principles were allowed to deteriorate even a little, there was no telling to what depths of decadence and depravity they might slide. Moral corruption began with just such matters.

These were some of the thoughts that occupied Father Jean-Luc's mind as he drove along the narrow, twisting road to The Adobe, the dust blowing into his nostrils and irritating the thin, sensitive membranes of that exquisitely delicate organ.

Even as Father Jean-Luc made his way to The Adobe, Sister Piadosa was busily preparing the chapel for Mass and the subsequent baptismal ceremony. The traditional forty days, the time allowed for the mother to recover her strength and be able to attend the baptism, had passed: not that the strong peasant body of Refugio Montaño had required any such pampering, for indeed, the rhythm of her work had scarcely skipped a beat with the arrival of her lusty son.

For María it was different. She had been frail during the pregnancy and the long, hard labor had sapped so much of her strength that Sister Piadosa, looking at the pallor of her face, worried about her and hoped that the summer heat would not deplete her energies further.

She realized that it was not only the physical labor that had caused her condition. She knew, although María never mentioned it, that she was suffering deeply, grieving the loss of her child; and it was a loss that she felt to be as final as death.

María would not be able to attend the baptism, but to make up for this she would decide on the chapel flowers. She chose lilacs for their fragrance, wild blue flax, fern verbena and cosmos if any were blooming yet, and of course lavender.

"—and as many fragrant herbs as you can spare, sister. I want Sofia always to associate her song and the feeling of being loved with the fragrances of this place."

Sofia's birth song was María's gift to her child. It was not the song from the old country, although there were similarities. It was a song that came through her, as old as the elk and the shining valley with its stream and its wooded hills; as old as the land she loved. She had sung it; first as Sofia was being born—and later when she was stronger, standing at her window.

She would look out in the direction of the small farm-house which, she was told, was Sofia's home, and will that Sofia should hear it; should hear it, and through it know of her love, that it might forever be associated with all the fragrances and wild scents of that other valley.

On several occasions, people working nearby paused in their labors to listen to the song that rose like that of a songbird, shocking in its wild and virgin sweetness, to fly out over the land. María's song would float out over the desert, flowing like a river down the dry arroyos and then out and upward to the hills. People commented on how the trees inclined their heads to listen to the singing, as if some ancient spirit dwelt in her song, and it was noticed by all who heard it that even the birds ceased their industry and became still, and listened when she sang.

It was like the old song that María used to sing, the one she had learned from Encarnación, the one she had sung to the baby elk, Santo; but now an older power even than that had entered it. She had made it her own. And now she gave it to her child.

And there was one other who heard María's singing: Father Jean-Luc Sel.

It was on one of his monthly visits, a few days before María was due to give birth to her child that, as he was leaving the confessional, a similar song floated over the small chapel and straight into one of his ever-vigilant ears.

He turned to Sister Piadosa, demanding to know from whence such free and unorthodox singing could originate. She told him, with a face as clear and unclouded as the blue New Mexico sky, that there was a nun in the infirmary who was not well.

"Well enough to sing, sister," he remarked dryly. "Perhaps I should visit her. She should be encouraged to receive the Eucharist and make her confession."

"Very well, father. If you will just give me a minute to make sure she is prepared to receive you, I will take you there."

Sister Piadosa hurried away, trying to achieve the appearance of one who is efficient but calm, a condition she was far from feeling.

"Oh, dear God," she muttered as she went to find Sister Ana, "I know it is asking a lot, but if you could work some kind of miracle here, I promise to thank you more properly when Father Jean-Luc has gone."

She was aware of the ridiculous impropriety of including God in her

deception, but she was not convinced he would want to support the sanctimonious righteousness of the priest.

If Father Jean-Luc had taken an instant dislike to Sister Piadosa, he
might have been surprised to know how vehemently it was reciprocated.
With every fiber in her body Sister Piadosa mistrusted the new priest. She
was shocked by the depth of the antipathy she felt towards him, and had
taken the matter with her into her meditation time to try and see what evil
might be rising in her breast. She prayed to the Holy Mother to take away
her uncharitable feelings and added many a Hail Mary to her list of prayers,
all to no avail.

It was almost as if in his presence she could smell something shameful
and unwashed; something that had been kept from the light; something
unspeakable locked away in a dark, foul place, which had begun to fester and
feed on that darkness; something revoltingly unclean.

Her powerful feelings of revulsion caused her profound distress.
She had never in all her life experienced such settled aversion to anyone or
anything, and even though she disliked the priest intensely, her response dis-
quieted her and left her with many questions about the source and nature of
such things. In her own way she experienced something similar to Elena.

She sought out Sister Ana and briefly informed her of the priest's
intended visit. She, Sister Piadosa, would delay him as long as possible,
and would Sister Ana please think of something to do that would conceal
María's very obvious condition?

"Put her to bed and do something creative about her stomach. Oh, and
Sister Ana, tell her to stop singing," she said as she hurried back to join the
priest.

When finally Sister Piadosa was unable to defer Jean-Luc's visit to
María with any further distraction, the two of them made their way to the
infirmary. On entering the room, Sister Piadosa could barely hide her amuse-
ment.

The shutters were fastened, so that only chinks of light lit the dim
room. María lay flat on her back with a huge cradle, such as is used to relieve
the weight of bedclothes from a broken leg, placed over her chest and
stomach and covered with a sheet. Her eyes were shut. On the bedside table
was a little tray holding a glass of water and numerous bottles of medicine.
Sister Ana sat at the bedside, as if in constant vigil, holding a bowl of fragrant

water and a sponge. She rose when the priest entered, and made a little bob before leaving the room.

"Sister María, can you hear me, dear?" María didn't respond to the nun's soft inquiry.

You had better hope that God has a sense of humor, thought Sister Piadosa, or he is surely going to punish you for this. She tried not to notice how much she was enjoying the priest's confusion.

"This is the person I heard singing only a while back?" Father Jean-Luc asked with a frown.

"Yes, father. She has a fever, and sometimes she calls out in her delirium. Sometimes she sings."

The priest leant down and felt María's forehead.

"She feels perfectly cool to me, sister."

"Sister Ana has just this instant sponged her, father."

You will burn in hell, Sister Piadosa thought to herself.

"Well, it would appear that she is unable to make her confession today. You must call me if her condition worsens."

He made a blessing, and the two of them left the room. Sister Ana was waiting outside the door.

"Call me if you feel anxious, sister, or if the fever breaks," she added wickedly. The two nuns took great care not to let their eyes meet.

"Delirium or not, I do not approve of such singing. It has pagan overtones to it. She should be discouraged from it at all costs. When she recovers, I want to speak to Sister María. I am not happy about this."

"Yes, father."

––––––––––

In response to Sister Piadosa's inquiry María said she had decided on the name Sofia. She wrote the name on a card, and gave it to Sister Piadosa together with the exquisitely embroidered christening robe that she had made during her pregnancy. Looking at the fineness of the handiwork, and aware of how much love lay behind it, Sister Piadosa felt tears come to her eyes.

"It is the most beautiful christening gown I have ever seen, María." She examined the fine pin-tucks, the sprays of white flowers and the small silk bows and ribbons. "I will ask Refugio to wash it after the service and pack it away safely in tissue to keep for her when she is older. One day, perhaps when her own child is christened, she will look at the fineness of this work and know how much you loved her."

All of this was drifting through Sister Piadosa's head as she arranged the flowers on the altar and tied small bunches of lavender and herbs onto the end of each of the pews with white ribbons. The scent of lilacs and lavender filled the small chapel. She arranged the extra chairs at the back, hoping that they would be enough. Refugio would be bringing her family and friends as well as the godparents. Godparents! She realized she had forgotten to ask María if she had any wishes in this regard. She hurried to the infirmary.

"Would you be her godmother, sister? That way I will feel closer to her."

"I am honored to be chosen, María. I will always do my very best by her."

"And could we ask Gregorio to be the godfather? I have had many chats with him. He is a kind man. Would you ask him if he is willing?"

At that moment they heard the sound of a car's engine straining its way up the track. Father Jean-Luc's car always sounded as if it was about to expire.

"Don't worry, María. I'll see to it."

She hurried away to meet the priest.

_____

By the time everyone had squeezed into the pews, or found chairs or standing-space at the back, the small chapel was ready to burst at the seams.

To Father Jean-Luc's intense displeasure Manuel and Refugio Montaño sat in the front pew, right under his nose, each holding one of their twin babes concealed in a white christening shawl.

While experiencing an aversion towards the fairer sex at the best of times, he felt profoundly repelled by this large, big-breasted woman, who seemed to exude a kind of fecund earthiness that he found intensely distasteful.

And yet, try as he might to control them, his eyes kept returning to the one button that held closed the straining cotton blouse which housed Refugio's two bountiful, milk-turgid breasts. In spite of himself Father Jean-Luc was transfixed by their heaving amplitude. With each breath she took they rose, tugging against that one closure, reminding him of the sea swell held at bay by the harbor wall in that small fishing-village off the coast of Brittany. That was the place where occasionally his family found time to leave their dairy and pig farm and take a holiday, away from matters carnal and repro-ductive, that otherwise monopolized their thoughts and the bovine tenor of their lives.

While the last stragglers were finding seats, Jean-Luc's thoughts wandered back to the past.

Those days spent at the coast with the wild sea rolling in and the fresh tang of the ocean blowing up into his face, were the only happy memories he carried of his childhood. It was the one time his parents managed some measure of light-heartedness. For the rest, their life was hard and mean.

The profits they made from the small farm at the end of the day were meager, and it was a constant struggle for them to meet their financial obliga-tions, their son's education being one of them.

Jean-Luc's father found his spiritual peace in imbibing copious quanti-ties of red wine, a constant source of tension between the two parents which, with the slightest added provocation, would erupt into a fight. Frequently the small boy could hear their raised voices shouting violent threats from behind the closed bedroom door, and later, when his mother emerged, her face tear-stained, he would hide away and pretend he had not seen or heard anything.

His mother found her solace in religion, and it was she who took the young Jean-Luc to Mass every Sunday, something to which he looked forward passionately the whole week.

He loved to sit in the small church, looking up at the figure of Christ upon the cross with the five wounds so vividly displayed, with all the icons, the paintings of Jesus and Mary and all the saints hanging down the length of the side walls and the stained-glass windows with the light streaming through them. The windows reminded him of certain pictures in his Bible, showing stormy skies with the clouds parting and God speaking out of just such light. There was always 'And God spake...' inscribed beneath the illustration, followed by some divine decree.

He was enthralled by the richness of the rituals: the candles, the heady fragrance of the incense, the wafers, the wine, the shining silver goblets and small silver boxes which stood on the spotless linen and the large book resting on the lectern—all of it was a joy to him.

The priest's vestments fascinated him, and he longed to own a white surplice and a rosary. His parents said they could not afford such a luxury; that he would be given a rosary when he was a little older, but the young Jean-Luc could not wait for that time.

Instead, he set about whittling a small crucifix, a task which took many days and for which he displayed extreme patience, shaping the intricacies of the suffering figure with small, inexpert fingers, finally sanding it until it was as smooth as the skin on the palm of his hand. From his tin of small-boy treasures he selected the prescribed number of shells, which he had collected on one holiday at the coast, to represent the beads, and threaded them onto a piece of twine that had been used to tie the sacks of pig food. To this he affixed the small cross. Assembled, it became Jean-Luc's treasure; his most precious secret that he kept on his person constantly. Morning and evening, in the relative privacy of his makeshift bed-room off the kitchen, the small boy would sit cross-legged at the head of his bed, his eyes shut tight, his fingers moving over the shells, his whole being given over to passionate and fervent prayer.

The happy days of his childhood were not to last for very long, for it was in fact just before his eighth birthday that the first of two events occurred: two events that were to come together in Jean-Luc's mind in a way that left an indelible and devastating effect on the small, sensitive boy.

The first powerful event that occurred was Jean-Luc's inadvertent witnessing of a pair of copulating pigs. Of course he had seen the heifers practice-mounting one another before, but he had thought that it was some kind of game they played.

This was different.

He was attracted to the sty by what sounded like two pigs fighting, and on climbing up onto the sty fence and looking over it, he saw a huge male pig mounting a protesting female who had fallen onto her front knees with her snout rooting at the mud, struggling in an attempt to rise and run away from her ardent suitor. Her grunts and screams were what had attracted the boy's attention. The male, with his short, fat, muddy forelegs fastened around her flabby, pink middle, winked his sly, pink eye at Jean-Luc while his wide, pig-grinning mouth stretched open, grunting vociferously with his straining efforts to keep his balance in the thick mud and maintain the short, thrusting spasms of his service.

Jean-Luc experienced a combination of horrified fascination and disgust. He hung on the fence right until the end of the violent act. When he climbed down at last, he knew that he would not speak about what he had seen, although he had no notion why he should have made such a decision.

The second event happened when he awoke on the morning of his eighth birthday and found that he was holding, in both of his slender hands, his painfully erect penis. To his surprise he found that it was most pleasurable to stroke this new and strange phenomenon that seemed to have risen in the night, and which had taken on an exciting life of its own.

He lay beneath the sheet with his eyes closed, enjoying the mounting waves of pleasure that were coursing through his body, swelling through him like the powerful notes of the church organ and the voices of the choir, rising and falling, only to soar upward again and again. Tingling sensations reached right down to the tips of his toes while he felt wave upon wave of painful sweetness, which in his mind's eye was akin to those great swells that rolled in from the sea, dashing themselves against the rocky Brittany coast and throwing up tall plumes of white foam: only now they were surging through him, coming faster and faster, so that he felt his chest pounding with the intensity of it. It was at the moment of orgasm, just as an involuntary cry burst from his lips, that his mother entered his bed-room.

"What is this?" she cried as she tore back the bedclothes and saw the now spent member resting limply in his small-boy hands.

"Pig! My son is a pig! You are all the same! All men are pigs!"

She took both his hands and beat them down again and again onto the now completely subdued member. "Filthy pig!"

Holding her son by one ear she dragged him, red-faced, out into the back yard. In one corner stood the bucket of lye which was used for sluicing down the cow-shed and the stys. She gripped her son's two arms and plunged both his hands into the strong solution: and held them there. He made no sound all through this.

Only when she released him and he pulled his two hands out of the bucket—hands which were now red and burned as if they had been in a fire—did he utter little moans, for he realized that his rosary had fallen out of his pajama pocket and into the bucket of lye. Still he said nothing: only reached into the bucket until his arm was immersed right up to the shoulder, before he managed to retrieve his treasure.

The subsequent scrubbing with the yard-brush of those two red members, to which he was forced to submit, left his hands so excoriated as to never fully recover. The resultant painful blistering caused him to lose all the skin from his hands, leaving them scarred and necessitating for ever after that he refrain from exposing them to the sun.

The pain of this discipline, however, was completely eclipsed by his mother's removal and destruction of the rosary.

"How dare you defile the Lord with your filthy practices?"

The whipping that he received from his father that evening was nothing to the shame that filled him; a shame that did nothing, however, to control the wayward life of that awakened member, for in spite of the punishment he received it continued to demand attention several times a day and gave him no rest at night.

The young Jean-Luc lost his ruddy complexion and took on the pale, haunted look that he was to keep for the rest of his life.

On the following day the small boy crept into his parents' bed-room to look in the Bible that lay on the small table between their twin beds. He thought that perhaps it might offer him some words of comfort. Hadn't their priest said as much? The book fell open of its own accord, and Jean-Luc read, as best he could for his limited skill, the portion that was marked with a pencil line.

'Therefore God handed them over to impurity through the lusts of their hearts for the mutual degradation of their bodies. They exchanged the truth of God for a lie and revered and worshipped the creature rather than the creator who is blessed forever. Amen.'

Over the years, as his understanding of these words and the place he felt called to play in them grew, Jean-Luc's life became a torment, for he felt he was being torn apart by his will on the one hand and certain shameful lusts on the other.

On his sixteenth birthday he resolved to enter the priesthood and devote his life to removing the temptations and lusts of the flesh from all who were led astray by such carnal motivations.

It was initially a hard battle, with the will of that wicked organ ever the victor, for try as he may, it would seem that he had no control over it. A random thought, the sight of bare flesh, it didn't matter whether it was of man or woman, and he would feel that stirring and curse himself for his sinful weakness.

It was only through a long process of self-punishment, and excessive purging which he took to the most extreme lengths, that finally he managed to subdue his flesh. Through the total deadening and denial of anything relating to the body and its appetites; through nurturing a revulsion of things earthy, all things feminine or female; anything touching on any aspect of feeling or imagination; every aspect of soul and the senses, particularly the sense of the numinous, which had its roots in pagan worship and was therefore highly suspect, he managed to silence that part of his anatomy that had been such an offender during his youth.

Now he was highly frustrated to find that Satan had placed yet another temptation before him in the form of Refugio's heaving breasts. He forced his mind back to the text, but his eyes betrayed him again and again.

That in itself was bad enough, but when the swarthy babe that she was holding began to wail in the middle of his reading from the holy Gospel according to John and he saw her pull out an alarmingly swollen breast and plug it into the child's mouth, he felt he might be sick.

He tried to ignore the horribly physical act that was taking place in front of him, but found it impossible, for the child sucked like a demon, making noises that reminded Jean-Luc of a time when a heifer had got stuck in some mud and had to be pulled out by rope and tractor. The infant sucked throughout the entire delivery, pausing only to release frequent, explosive burps that punctuated the reading like rifle fire.

Perhaps it was on account of this, or because he still had to conduct the baptismal ceremony, that Father Jean-Luc skipped the sermon that he had worked on the night before, an omission that was most gratefully received. Whatever the reason, he raced through the responsorial psalms, delivered the liturgy of the Eucharist and prayer over the gifts appropriate to the period after Easter at speed and proceeded with the communion.

It was only when Refugio unplugged the child, and passed him to the godmother, before taking her place in the line of people waiting to take communion, that a blessed quiet returned. Nevertheless, when the time came for Jean-Luc to offer the Host to Refugio, his hand shook and he averted his eyes, which otherwise would have been forced to take in the full amplitude of those magnificent breasts with which she was endowed.

After the service everyone moved outside while Father Jean-Luc prepared for the baptism. There were many congratulations to the parents for being blessed with not one, but two babes. Several people asked to peep at the infants, but one and all, after doing so, drew back in confusion.

"They don't look like twins at all!"

"That's because they are un-identical twins."

"The fair one doesn't look like either of you."

Poor Refugio was starting to get flustered when Sister Piadosa intervened. She explained that the smaller child, the girl, favored a great-grandparent no longer living, God rest his soul—and God rest mine, she thought.

Father Jean-Luc signaled that he was ready, and everyone took their seats again. He asked the parents and godparents to step forward and present the children for baptism. The traditional questions were asked and answered, and Father Jean-Luc leant forward to sign the infants' foreheads with the sign of the cross. He too stared down at what little he could see of the two dissimilar babes, but made no comment. All proceeded uneventfully, and to Jean-Luc's relief both babies remained quiet.

There followed the various liturgies and responsorial psalms, and eventually they came to the prayer of exorcism and the anointing before baptism.

"Almighty and ever-living God,
You sent your only Son into the world
To cast out the power of Satan, spirit of evil..."

The words rolled off the priest's tongue as if he particularly relished all notions of sin, darkness and evil. He enunciated the name, Satan, through clenched teeth, his lips drawn back in grotesque emphasis.

Both children were duly anointed on the breast.

"It's not a good sign when they're quiet." It was a penetrating whisper. "It's better when they yell a bit. It lets the demons out."

Her husband shushed her.

There followed the blessing over the baptismal water, the questions and answers by the parents and godparents, who promised to reject Satan and sin and the glamour of evil and to uphold the faith, and finally the moment came to move to the font.

The larger child was presented first. He was fast asleep—and no wonder, thought Jean-Luc, replete, no doubt, after such a meal. He looked down at the fat, sleeping face and tried not to remember where those fat little lips had just been.

"Is it your will that Pedro Manuel should be baptized in the faith of the Church, which we have all professed with you?"

"It is."

Father Jean-Luc poured the water over the sleeping child's head three times and blessed him. He then returned him to the godmother.

Sister Piadosa stepped forward with the second child. Father Jean-Luc looked at her and raised an eyebrow, but said nothing. He took the child and pulled back the shawl that almost covered the entire head and face. He stopped. He stared down at the child in his arms. The face was familiar. He searched his memory. Was it a painting he had seen somewhere? He could not place it.

The small child with the alabaster skin, the pink cheeks and small, rosebud mouth, the large, cornflower-blue eyes and red-gold hair smiled up at him, waving two pink fists, overjoyed to be free of the shawl. He looked at Sister Piadosa as if expecting some explanation. He received none. He raised the card and read the name.

"Is it your will that Sofia should be baptized in the faith of the Church, which we have all professed with you?"

"It is."

Father Jean-Luc baptized Sofia in the name of the Father—and of the Son—and of the Holy Spirit.

It was at this moment that a trace of a song blew into the chapel. Although it was very soft, it was shocking in its clarity.

Many people made the sign of the cross, and some fell to their knees in prayer.

Father Jean-Luc Sel uttered a gasp of recognition. But it was not only the singing, beautiful though it was, that startled him so. It was the song itself: for he had heard that song before—or something very like it. He had heard it coming from the little nun, Sister María, who had been so unwell. He now suspected that something else lay behind her feverish indisposition.

Father Jean-Luc lifted his cold eyes and stared at Sister Piadosa.

"So!" He did not need to say more.

She stared back at him, seeking to interpret the look that she witnessed in his eye, a look which she had difficulty identifying. It puzzled her. Was it anger? No—but something else: not anger; not even displeasure. And then it came to her.

What she saw in the priest's eyes was—triumph!

Father Jean-Luc's Crusade

Father Jean-Luc, whose paper, Idolatry—The Trend Towards Paganism in Rural Communities had so monopolized his thoughts and filled him with such zeal that he barely took time to eat, had indeed found the taint of paganism, if not outright heresy, being practiced at the center which called itself The Adobe.

It was a discovery that brought all his self-righteous concern to the fore, and with it no small sense of satisfaction. He felt vindicated that his initial assessment of Sister Piadosa, that she was lacking in humility and showed a marked tendency towards disobedience, had been proved to be correct. The whole deception that lay behind the baptismal service pointed to a willful disregard for the authority of the Church, a matter that would be serious in any person of the Catholic faith; but in a member of the Sisterhood, in a position of authority, such behavior could not be tolerated.

He was, however, far from down-hearted. Indeed, he felt elated. He had wondered what possible reason God could have had in mind when He sent him to this small, backward part of the world. Now he had his answer. He, Father Jean-Luc Sel, would bring the wandering sheep back to the fold: no less.

It was with this in mind that, on the Sunday following the baptism, he made an extra trip down to the small valley, there to take Sister Piadosa to task and help her to see the error of her ways.

The discussion began quietly enough with Sister Piadosa informing Father Jean-Luc of the marriage between Salvador and María, and that Father Octavio had said it was certainly a legal marriage. Whether the old laws that once held what was called an 'Entriega de los Novios' as a valid contract recognized by the Church would still be considered so, was something he was going to investigate. It was his plan to marry Salvador and María in the chapel and give them his blessing. Then, of course, he died before he could do this.

"If it was valid, why all the secrecy?"

Sister Piadosa explained María's fear that her father might come and take the baby should he learn of its birth, for to date he had no knowledge that María had been expecting a child. He had not come once to visit her neither had he telephoned to ask after her welfare. She did not want him to know about the birth.

"And why not? It seems he would be better able to see to its well-being than she would, or some peasant woman who is barely literate, I am sure. A daughter should bow to her father's wishes."

"Even if the father is unjust?"

"She must have deserved it. The father knows best."

"We could argue that."

"Just as I know best in this matter, and I will not be dictated to by you!"

"Be that as it may, father, you cannot get around the fact that in legal terms María is married and is the mother of the child, and the child therefore is legitimate. Her father rejected her. It is natural that she should want to protect her child from a man who can treat his own daughter in such a fashion. He took everything away from her, threatened Salvador with her death should he ever show his face again and threw her out of the house."

"For disobedience."

"She was twenty-one years old. And don't tell me you justify death-threats!"

"She was probably exaggerating."

The argument raged on.

"Your behavior in all of this is a matter of the gravest concern. Instead of being so obstructive you should have a care for what may happen to you. I shall most certainly report all of this, and your reprehensible conduct, to the Bishop."

"Please do. You will find that I am on extremely good terms with him, having assisted him in his work for many years. It was he who recommended me for this position."

For the first time Father Jean-Luc felt he might be losing ground. He glared at Sister Piadosa.

"He might not be so happy when he learns how you have lied to me, leading me to believe that María was one of the sisters under your supervision."

"She is considering devoting her life to the Church in this way."

"Do not play clever games with me, sister. I heard you lie before the baptism, saying that the child Sofía resembled one of her great-grandparents. It seems to be a habit of yours."

"Well, it happens to be true. María showed me a picture of her grandmother—a certain María Jacqueline Latour. María and Sofía both take after her."

"Latour?"

"Oh, yes. María's great-grandfather was a Latour who came over from France—your country, I believe—in 1869."

Father Jean-Luc's pale face became suffused with anger. Never before had he encountered such sly insubordination, such arrogance, from a woman; a nun, no less. He was unaware that his hands had begun to twist in their involuntary and habitual washing movements.

"You will burn in Hell, sister. María is young. She can confess her sins and do her penance. There is still hope for her. But you—you are no better than all the rest of this superstitious community with their pagan 'folk' Catholicism. Do not think that I don't know what goes on around here. I don't know what Father Octavio was about when he let things go this far, but I intend to put a stop to all these pagan customs; all this talk of miracles and unnatural practices."

It was Sister Piadosa's turn to grow angry. Up until now he had directed his criticism towards her, but now he had gone too far.

"How dare you, father—you who have been here a few short months?

How dare you presume to know anything about the lives and the faith of the people of this country? What gives you the right to judge us?

"You know nothing of the centuries of hardship, of frontier life that my people have suffered; of watching their babies die for lack of doctors; of having to rely on their own healing skills, often insufficient; of keeping true to their faith when there were no priests to help and guide them. And the pagan customs, as you call them, are evidence of the people's deep spiritual connection to their faith.

"The Entriega is not a new invention. It has been around since the late eighteenth century. It was an accepted form of marriage, officiated with the utmost solemnity. It was what served the people when no priest was available."

Father Jean-Luc Sel was about to interrupt, but Sister Piadosa put up a hand.

"It was only when a priest finally arrived at their village, usually several months, even half a year later, having traveled through dangerous territory on the back of a mule, that he would bless the marriage. He had compassion for the difficulties people had to endure to keep their faith intact. He knew faith when he saw it. He knew the passion that lay behind the ceremonies, and he blessed all of it, as did Father Octavio.

"And may I warn you, Father Jean-Luc, whatever else you may or may not say: for your own sake, do not criticize Father Octavio in this community."

"Are you threatening me?"

"I am warning you. And as for the legitimacy of María's marriage, I know for a fact that these two people married in good faith, in a ceremony conducted by a much-respected member of the community, a deeply spiritual man, a santero who, it so happens, is also an appointed, honorary justice of the peace."

"That is scarcely a recommendation: a santero, as you call him." With hard, thin lips he put all the disparagement he could muster into the word, "santero."

"It is not acceptable for such people to take these matters into their own hands. They have not been ordained into the Church to do such work."

"So in the absence of a priest, father, what do you advocate they should do?"

"They should wait."

"Oh—really? And should they wait to die as well?" Sister Piadosa struggled to get a grip on her temper. "Come, father. You are in need of some serious reflection if you are to remain here. You will not be able to convince the people that they are wrong and you are right. Centuries lie behind our traditions. You will only make a fool of yourself."

Unnoticed by him, the priest's hands were twisting obscenely. Sister Piadosa struggled to keep her eyes off them.

"You want to bring your dogma to the people, but dogma does not sit well with mystery. Your dogma is empty words for them. Perhaps it does more harm than good. Where in dogma does compassion lie?"

"Are you saying I lack compassion?"

"I am saying that dogma and reason are for intellectuals. But mystery, those signs and symbols that touch the heart, that is far better suited to those who live close to the earth, to poverty and the painful struggle just to survive. If God speaks to such people through what seem to be miraculous events, who dares to come and—dare I say it?—turn their wine back into water?"

"Are you proposing to lecture me?"

"I have witnessed again and again how a simple faith can touch the heart and bring love and comfort where the most elevated thinking fails. Be very careful that what you are about does not destroy something so precious."

Father Jean-Luc could not believe that he was hearing correctly; that this little village nun was daring to lecture him! It was preposterous.

"How dare you speak to me in this manner? Insolent woman! Don't tell me my business! As a matter of fact, I have already begun proceedings after learning some most disquieting facts about someone who, I believe, comes here frequently; a young priest in training: Rafaél Montdragón. If he is an example of the caliber of priest you are training out here, I am not surprised that the people are worshipping idols like savages. I have informed his advisors that he is in no way fit to become ordained. He is in great need of spiritual guidance himself. Not only that: he is questioning his calling to the priesthood. He thinks he wants to be a santero. There is much confusion and evil in him."

Sister Piadosa laughed. "I never heard such nonsense. Who could possibly have made up such lies?"

"Not lies, sister. He told me himself."

"He told you this? And when did you have this conversation?"

"It is none of your business, but since you ask, he confessed it to me about a month ago. He spoke of his grandfather, the 'Penitente Santero', and his painting. I heard all about the atrocity. And he told me how he felt he might have turned his back on his true calling!"

"He came to the rectory?"

"No, sister. He came to the confessional. The weight of his sin was obviously too heavy for him."

"Are you telling me that you have betrayed the secrets of the confessional?" She was appalled. "Do not tell me that you have done this."

"It is for his spiritual well-being. His soul must not be allowed to stray. He was considered to be their most promising novitiate. He was to be given, as his first position, a parish of excellent standing. They were grateful to receive the information."

"And did you tell them how you came by such knowledge?"

"Certainly! I told them he had volunteered it."

"And I don't suppose you mentioned that it was during confession."

"It is irrelevant."

Sister Piadosa was shocked. She sat down. She looked in wonder at the calm face of the priest, who seemed completely unaware of the seriousness of what he had done. That it would eventually be discovered seemed not to be a concern. Did he not fear for the consequences of his action? His face looked untroubled.

"Have you any idea of what you have done?" she asked.

"Certainly! I hope to help save Rafaél's soul from Hell and damnation. And I have saved the seminary and those who were about to ordain Rafaél from the embarrassment of sending a completely unsuitable person into a parish of civilized people. I have applied for the position myself, so you may soon be rid of me here. But don't think I intend to give up on the work that I see is needed here. I will be in a far better position to be effective when I am accepted."

Father Jean-Luc looked down his thin nose at the speechless nun with a feeling of profound satisfaction. She had got more than she bargained for. And when he was accepted and had moved to the large and wealthy parish, he would make sure that he would have her removed from her duties.

All in all, he felt the talk had gone rather well. Difficult initially, but right had prevailed. With a nod he dismissed the nun in her own office, walked to his car and set off in a light-hearted mood to prepare for the evening Mass in Las Madres.

Alone in her office Sister Piadosa considered what she should do. She wished with all her heart that Father Octavio was still alive, that she could take the matter to him.

She resolved to write a letter to the Bishop, stating her profound concern and distress.

It was at this moment that Sister Ana burst into the room.

"Come! Quick, sister! It is María. Something is wrong."

The Departure of the White Doves

It was early morning. María lay awake, looking out through the window, waiting for day.

First light was just beginning to reveal the dark silhouettes of the hills. Always this meeting of light and dark, morning and evening: for how many millions of years? There was no hurrying it. It was not possible to know what lay in that obscurity, only that it was there and that we must be patient and wait for it to reveal itself.

Morning and evening. Now the dark would win, now the light, only to be defeated once more at nightfall. There was no overall victor in this twice-daily engagement, she thought. Indeed they could not exist without each other. Was it the same with life and death?

She remembered how she used to fret as a child when something exciting had been planned for the day, a party or perhaps an outing with Diego. She would wake early and dress, wanting so for the day to begin. She would run to the window again and again, wishing the light to come, impatient with its slowness when there was so much living she wanted to fit into the day. Now she savored every moment of it, lying with her head turned sideways on the pillow, watching the slow, infinitesimal shifts and changes with quiet joy.

Now the light was stronger, but not yet lit by the sun. It was the coolest time of day; grey dawn. There were people María mused, whose faces looked like this; unlit by warmth. How awful it must be to live feeling like that inside, having no passion.

She reflected on her short life. I have known much passion, she considered. It is my treasure, and if there is a price to pay, then I gladly pay it many times over for the love I hold within me. She knew that no one and nothing could take this from her.

Sister Piadosa had given her a book to read, The Labyrinth of Solitude, written by the Mexican writer Octavio Paz, and it was from these essays that she had drawn strength. The book had been her constant companion ever since. She thanked God that he made people who could share their thoughts in this way. She blessed the writer, whom she would never meet, but who had a place forever in her heart. He wrote that it was not happiness that we ask for, or even repose. The true longing, he said, is simply for an instant, just an instant of what he called—'that full life'—where opposites vanish—where there is no separation.

Through the window María could hear the birds begin their song. These past months she had slept very little, lying quietly in the darkness, waiting for day. The sound of the birds was always the first sign that day would arrive, and that she was not alone. She found their busy chirping and twittering comforting, and often would fall into a light sleep, reassured by their presence.

For weeks now she had been watching the small, round buds on the Russian olive which grew outside her small room, waiting for the day they would burst open. Each year she marveled at the earth's remarkable powers of renewal; that indomitable patterning in animal and plant life, that fortitude in the face of the severe extremes that nature in all its manifest displays presented.

The creatures look out towards the light, she thought; always out into the world, into that blue sky that reaches over the land like a vast dome; into the very eye of God. It is in that gaze that they experience themselves not separate from nature and the eternal. They do not waste energy and spirit as we do—continually turning our gaze inward—observing ourselves. I wonder why that is, for it is this that separates us from ourselves.

She paused in her thought as she listened again for that one cry, that sound that she had bound to her heart; the place where she held her child through the pain of separation.

If only we could face life with such simplicity, she thought. We say it in our prayers—'the Lord giveth and the Lord taketh away; blessed be the name of the Lord'—but do we bless him? I wonder if we can say truly that we do. It is hard to surrender our will and our desires to a will that can at times seem to be so cruel and capricious. We pay a high price for our reflection and memory. The animals are spared that, at least.

But still she found it inspiring, the way they faced hardship, adversity, death: head-on. There was a covenant, it would seem, between the animals and this force of nature, a promise that said: "I will give you the wilderness, the trees, the shrubs, the grasses; and I will give you water and offer places of shelter; and I will give you a nature, an instinct, that you may know your world. In return I will take from you what my nature needs. Not more. Not less."

Since the birth of her child María's health had become increasingly delicate. The long and bitter winter cold and the demands of her pregnancy and delivery seemed to have drained what little strength she had. Ever since her fall, the week after Sofia's baptism, she had been overtaken by sudden dizzy spells.

Sister Piadosa had called a doctor, who now came regularly to check on her, but he could find nothing physically the matter with her. She should rest, he said. But the rest seemed not to have helped. Now she could barely raise herself off the bed, and had to be helped across the room to the chair while the sisters changed her linen and made the room fresh. It seemed that as nature outside budded and blossomed, even so María began to fade away. She ate very little and lay, not sleeping, but listening, always listening. The nuns would ask her what she could hear, what she listened for so intently, but she only shook her head.

"Just the birds—and the wind in the trees."

She did not tell them that she was listening inside herself, listening to her child the only way she knew how.

But it was more than that, and far, far deeper. Sister Piadosa knew that much. She recognized that María had been touched by a passion of spirit that was drawing her to unite, not so much with her child for whom she longed so greatly, as with what she symbolized: a state of innocence; a state beyond good and evil. She was being drawn into a marriage, a union: and it would appear that there was not sufficient will in María's frail, little body to do anything but surrender itself to be drawn into the light.

Sister Piadosa saw a new spirit enter into María, and feared that it might consume her utterly. But there was something else, too, for as her physical condition deteriorated, even so did the luminosity that seemed to light her from within grow stronger. The nun, seeing the light stream like fire from her eyes, was amazed at the strength and intensity of it, coming as it did from one so delicate. María seemed to glow, as if a current of electric energy flowed through her.

Sister Piadosa took to spending all the time she could spare with María; taking her flowers, telling her what was happening on the lands, what the chili crop looked like this year, how bountiful the lavender was. She had not yet written the letter about Father Jean-Luc to the Bishop, having learned that he was away on a six-month sabbatical, and she did not want to discuss the matter with anyone else. Sebastián would be back soon, and she would speak to him.

The sun had risen, and now María could feel the first trace of warmth blowing in through her window. It would be a hot day. The scent from the lilacs that covered the porch area and from the blossom on the apple trees that was just starting to fall like soft, pink snow filled her nostrils with their sweetness. These and the clean, fresh scent of earth still moist from the early morning dew, and the ever-present, pungent scent of juniper and the mingled scent of herbs from the herb garden were, she thought, like a symphony. She breathed in their bounty. Her child would come to know all these intense fragrances.

Sofia, she thought, would soon be a year old. My daughter.

She spoke the name softly. "Sofia."

Sister Piadosa looked in on María after Matins and brought her something to eat, but María waved away the tray of food.

"I am not hungry, sister," she said, "but stay with me a little while."

The sister sat beside her on the small, upright chair.

"Have I sinned, sister? Father Jean-Luc insists that I have. Is it a sin to love so deeply? Is it a sin to want to live your life in your own way, whatever the cost may be? Is it a sin to love another with all of your heart and all of your flesh; to surrender so completely to that love that a child is born of that union? Can this be a sin?"

Sister Piadosa contemplated her reply.

"It is difficult for me to answer this. I have taken certain vows, so I must always seek to honor them; and then it must be remembered that I live in a particular world, where many of life's temptations and opportunities have been removed. The temptations we face are different from those of people living in the outside world.

"I have no experience of such love, so I am not qualified to speak of it. But I find it hard to believe that God would give us our fine bodies and the capacity for love in all its forms without wanting us to enjoy them. I sometimes wonder what life would be like, even here within these walls, if it were not so directed by patriarchal values that were set so many, many hundreds of years ago and maintained to this day by men who seem to be so mortally afraid of the body and the physical expression of love."

She was shocked at her own words, and paused to reflect for a few moments before continuing.

"But I do question. And I do wonder what it is that makes it so sinful to question. If this system is beyond reproach, so strong in its moral and ethical conviction, why should a question be so threatening, be considered sinful? And so I do struggle with this."

She paused.

"I do question why women are not awarded equal status with men; if there is any reason other than a patriarchal fear of the feminine. And so, my dear, in answer to your question I would say that you have challenged the accepted code of the Church. In its eyes, you are not married, and therefore according to the Church's interpretation of God's word, yes, you have sinned.

"However, if you choose to stand outside the Church, outside its protection, if you dare to stand completely alone, if you have the courage to stand before your God with no intercessor, if you are willing to take whatever the consequences of your decisions and actions may be—then only you can answer your question. You must search your own heart for the answer to it. This is what Our Lord did, and why he was crucified. To step outside the law as it is prescribed by those in power will never be accepted. It is far too threatening. If we choose to do this, we will most surely experience our own personal crucifixion."

María considered this for a while.

"How do I make my peace, sister? On the one hand I know that I have gone against all the values that I have been raised to love and honor. But against this, I seem to have been given a glimpse of a world that is not ruled by fear: a world that does not need those attributes, power and domination; does not need to have others define what God may be. I have seen that other world, sister.

"All this time that I have been lying here it is as if some grace has been granted me. How can I deny it? How can I turn my back on something that calls to me, even if it is a conviction that is hard to hold because there are other voices in my head saying—Sinner, Sinner? In spite of them I truly feel that to deny this voice that calls to me, out of me, to deny that—that would be a sin!"

Sister Piadosa bent forward and kissed the flushed face on the pillow.

"Whatever you decide, my dear, I am sure that God will recognize your sincerity, and I believe our Holy Mother will bless you for your courage."

What am I saying she thought? She shrugged. I will say my Hail Marys, she resolved, but I am not going to abandon this passionate soul—not now, not so near to the end.

"I do not believe that you have sinned, María," she said without a trace of doubt. "Our Holy Mother will bless you, and your child, even as her own."

"Will you read me the poem, sister?"

'The poem' was one of María's favorites: The Dark Night by St John of the Cross. Father Octavio had lent María his copy of the poetry shortly before he died. From the bedside table the nun took the book, which fell open of its own accord at the page. She read slowly and softly. It was when she came to the last two verses that María turned her burning eyes towards her.

"When the breeze blew ..."

María whispered the words almost under her breath. She waited for the line she loved.

"All things ceased …"

"All things ceased …" she whispered.

"… I went out from myself …"

María lay back and closed her eyes.

"Father Jean-Luc is going to want to hear my confession, but I have little to say to him. I fear he is going to be disappointed."

So here it was. The sister felt the shock of it.

It was always so sudden. Even though you expected it, even when it came to the very old, it never failed to startle one with its appearance. It did not wait to be invited. There was no polite knock on the door. Just suddenly it was there, bringing all its absoluteness with it: that finality that nothing can ever prepare us for, though we see it a thousand times.

"He will be here soon. It is his day to visit. Would you like me to stay with you till he comes?"

For answer María took her hand and held it tight.

María was lying with her eyes closed when the priest entered the room. She lay so still, and her face was so pale that he thought he might be too late. He took his seat next to the bed.

"You can leave us, sister," he said without meeting her eyes. Sister Piadosa left the room.

"Can you hear me, María?"

For answer she opened her eyes.

"Yes, father," she whispered.

"I am ready to hear your confession, María. May the Lord be in your heart and help you to confess your sins with true sorrow. What is it that you need to tell me, my dear?"

"Father, I want to thank God for my life. I want to say that I love my parents, and I am sorry they are disappointed in me. And I ask you for your blessing. That is all, father."

"But, my child, what about your confession? You must confess your sins before I can bless you."

"I have nothing to confess to you, father."

She lay with her eyes closed, her breathing shallow and irregular.

Father Jean-Luc considered what he should do. This was no time to enter into some lengthy debate about sin. He knew that Señor de la Cruz had sent his daughter here because of her willfulness. But this was something else. Perhaps she was wandering in her mind and had become confused.

"I think, my dear that perhaps you do not remember well. I must hear your confession before I can bless you."

She turned to look at him and shook her head.

"I do hear you, father, and I understand what you are saying. I have nothing to confess to you!"

Her voice, although low—barely a whisper—was clear. She did not appear to be confused. No. This was deliberate obstinacy. She was refusing the act of confession.

What did she mean when she said she had nothing to confess to him? Who was she, this slip of a girl, to challenge him, to challenge the Holy Catholic Church, the word of the Holy Father himself? She had been carefully taught. She knew the price of going against the ruling of the Church. She would be excommunicated.

"María," he said harshly. "If you do not confess your sins, there is nothing I can do for you. You will not receive the sacrament or my blessing. If you persist in this foolishness, I must tell you, God will turn away from you. You will not be received into Heaven. Your soul will be lost for all time. Are you aware of this?"

María opened her eyes, and the two regarded each other. The priest's face was flushed, angry; his lips were pursed and white. He tapped his thumb in an agitated fashion against the Bible he held.

María's face was calm. She took a deep breath. Still looking steadily at him, she raised her right hand a few inches off the bed and let it fall.

"So be it, father."

She closed her eyes and turned her face away from him.

Father Jean-Luc was furious. He struck the chair with the Bible.

"María! I offer you an opportunity to reconsider! You do not seem to understand what you are doing! I have a duty to you as a member of the Holy Catholic Church to hear your confession. Look at me, María!"

He leaned over the bed, bringing his furious face close to hers.

"Listen to me, María. You are doing a terrible thing. If you persist in this nonsense, you will indeed be severely punished."

There was no reply from the figure on the bed.

"You will burn in Hell!"

Father Jean-Luc hit the chair again. This chit of a girl had dismissed him. Well! She would pay the price for her heresy. He strode out of the room and down the colonnade towards the chapel.

Sister Piadosa, seeing the priest's angry departure, could guess what had transpired. She hurried into María's room.

María was struggling to breathe. The sister raised her and pushed more pillows behind her. María's face was drained of color.

"He would not give me the blessing. He says I am going to Hell."

"Then I will offer absolution, María, for any such sins as you may have committed."

María nodded.

"And then I will bless you."

"I have been very willful, sister, and I have felt anger towards my father. I have been devious, and lied to my parents."

A huge sob made its way up María's throat.

"And I have failed my child." This last was the faintest whisper.

Sister Piadosa took María's hand.

"You have failed no one, María, least of all your daughter; and when she is older I will tell her about you, and how you loved her."

She took María's hand, recalling as best she could the words of absolution:

"In quantum ego sum potest
Et tu indiges,
Ego te absolvo—

"Inasmuch as I am able, and inasmuch as you have need of it, I absolve you."

Sister Piadosa searched her heart for words of comfort to offer to María. Finally it was the words of another passionate soul that came to her. Long ago she had committed them to memory.

"Job said:
'Oh, would that my words were now written!
Would that they were inscribed in a record!
That with an iron chisel and with lead
They were cut in the rock forever!

"'But as for me, I know that my Vindicator lives,
And that He will at last stand forth upon the dust;
Whom I myself shall see: my own eyes, not another's
shall behold Him.
And from my flesh I shall see God;
My inmost being is consumed with longing.

"'This is the Word of the Lord.'"

María gave a deep sigh. "My own eyes, not another's," she whispered.
Sister Piadosa uttered a simple blessing and marked María's forehead
with the sign of the cross.

Outside the window the leaves of the Russian olive were motionless.
María lay facing the chapel, the garden, and the orchard with its carpet of
fallen blossoms. The herbs that grew between the meanderings of the labyrinth's footpath were in full bloom and filled the air with their sweet aroma,
and the rose bushes that had been planted many years ago, and now covered
the far adobe wall, were full of pink and yellow blooms: and all around the
courtyard hedges of lavender were filled with bees.

But she did not see these things. She did not see the small, well-tended
garden with its tidy paths and the cultivated beds of herbs and medicinal
plants.

What she saw was that great valley she loved; the beauty of that
mountain wilderness with its rim of tree-clad hills; that rolling valley that
had remained untouched for almost a million years. There, in front of her
eyes, lay the pristine whiteness, the valley veiled like a bride, reaching out
before her, all around her; that valley with the snow glistening in the sunlight,
reflecting the clear light back into the high, thin mountain air. She was back
in that place, that great expanse of open ground with its miles and miles

of snow and silence, uncorrupted by human footprint; back in that vast openness, looking out at the blue light that shaded the whiteness—a light that was more a haunting than a color—and on to where the snow-drifts had piled up and fallen away, where deep crevasses were shadowed with a deeper shade of blue, that quality of light so subtle it was as if something of the memory of sky lay captured in the cold ice.

She saw a child, a little girl, maybe eight years old, running as if in slow motion, running, almost flying over the snow, leaving no footprints. She wore a white cotton dress embroidered with scarlet rosebuds and with blue satin bows and ribbons that fluttered in the breeze. Her hair—long, thick tresses of red and gold—streamed out behind her as she ran. Alongside her ran the young elk stag with the same strange, floating gait. They ran as if suspended in time. They ran, but covered no distance. They were the time in which they ran, and the place, and the light. It was all one; beyond past or future: an instant and an eternity.

And then the image changed. It was as if the figures shape-shifted or transfigured into the form of a golden-haired child standing between the horns of the stag.

María's arms lifted off the bedclothes. Her eyes shone brightly.

"Sofia!" she called. "Sofia!"

But the snow began to fall: softly at first, and then, as the small flakes became larger, she could see less and less. María strained her eyes, struggling to keep the child in sight. And then the vision of child and stag began to fade.

"Sofia!"

But the snow closed in, and there was just this whiteness; this blue light in which white, feathery stars began to swirl about like birds, flying round and round; white birds, doves, white doves that flew up and into the light. She felt herself being lifted off the bed, out of the small room and up and into the clean air. And now she was weightless; flying with them into this light; into this brilliance; into the dazzling brilliance of this light that went on and on and on forever.

———

Outside there was a rushing sound. Sister Piadosa raised her eyes from María's face. Through the window she saw that the white doves had left their roosting-place and had risen in a cloud of beating wings. They flew upward in a ragged line, but once they had gained a certain altitude, they moved together and flew in formation as if one will dictated their direction.

Sister Piadosa watched them circle the garden, dipping low over the labyrinth with its fragrance of lavender and lifting to fly towards the small window that marked María's room. At what seemed like the last moment they banked and turned, flying back towards the hills and down again into the self-same pattern as if following a path carved out in the sky. And then they turned for the last time and flew outwards, over the orchard and the rows of cottonwoods, gaining height now, and on and out over the hills.

She watched as they circled the small valley, rising higher and higher with each spiral until she could see only the faint flash of white against the blue as the light just caught their wings. She strained to keep them in sight, but eventually she could not be sure if it was the doves she saw or the brilliance of the light.

And then she could see them no more.

Her eyes searched the clear, blue sky. But the sky was empty.

The white doves had flown out and away, through that blue veil that separates the worlds.

The Summoning

It was Father Jean-Luc Sel's unshakeable conviction that María was a heretic.

He would enter into no discussion on the matter; neither would he countenance any consultation about his judgment. Her heresy lay in her refusal to confess her sins, of which there were patently many, an act of volition which offended the union of Christian charity. As such he had withheld the sacrament of Last Rites. He had warned her—no! He, Father Jean-Luc Sel, had begged her to confess! He had put himself that far out for her! In her willful obstinacy she had turned away from him, and therefore from God. Now she was damned.

He would not conduct a Funeral Mass for her; neither would he permit her, a heretic, to be buried in the camposanto or in any consecrated ground. He issued strict orders to that effect. He had done his best, but she was a lost soul. Now he washed his hands of her.

Sister Piadosa, her lips white with anger, watched him drive off. She did not trust herself to say anything to him, but she had exercised all her will not to curse him. She turned and hurried back inside. She had much to organize.

She would have to arrange some kind of a funeral and burial ceremony for María. She sat down at her desk to collect her thoughts. First she would inform Señor de la Cruz and his wife, Catherine, of their daughter's death, after which she would contact Alejandro and see if he would be willing to conduct a service. Then she and Sister Ana would wash and prepare María's body.

She rang the bell for Sister Ana. The nun arrived, her eyes red from weeping.

"We have much to do, sister. I want you to arrange the vigil. As soon as I have made these phone calls I will come and join you, and together we can see to María. In the meantime, gather the oils and the box of Magdalena's herbs. Oh—and bring the wedding gown that María brought with her. We will put her in the wedding dress—and the veil—so that she will be a bride when she goes to meet her Lord.

"And ask Gregorio to pick flowers for the chapel and for the reception room, and something special for the coffin, and a posy of herbs for María to hold—a mix of the flowers she chose for Sofia's christening."

Sister Ana hurried away to carry out these tasks.

Before dialing de la Cruz' number she paused to reflect on how she would break the sad news. Even if he was a tyrant and a heartless father, surely to hear that María had died would be a terrible shock. Would he feel remorse, regret for a decision made in anger? Sister Piadosa was not looking forward to the conversation.

It was a woman who answered the call. Sister Piadosa gave her name and asked if she could speak to Señor de la Cruz.

"Good afternoon, sister. This is Mercedes speaking. I am afraid that Señor de la Cruz is away at present in Mexico. Can I perhaps be of help?"

"When do you expect him back?"

"He has gone for four months."

"Did he leave a contact number?"

"No. He is moving around, and he said it would be impossible to leave all the numbers. He said he would phone here from time to time to check that everything was all right, but he has not phoned us yet."

"And Señora de la Cruz—did she go with him?"

There was a long silence.

"Are you still there, Mercedes?"

"Yes, sister." Mercedes seemed to hesitate. "Señora Catherine did not go with him. I am afraid she is not here either."

"Do you, perhaps, have a contact number?"

"I am sorry, sister, I don't."

"Well, may I speak to you in their absence?"

"Certainly, sister."

"You don't know me, Mercedes, but María has told me so much about you. I have been taking care of her this past year."

"Oh, blessed Holy Mother! I prayed I would hear some word of her. We have been so distraught, not knowing where she was taken; not knowing how she was doing; not being able to visit or even speak with her. How is she, sister?"

Oh, blessed Holy Mother indeed! How do I tell her that María is dead?

"Mercedes, I am afraid I have some bad news."

She paused and then added, "Some very bad news."

"How bad, sister?" Mercedes asked, but already in her heart she knew the answer.

"I am afraid the worst, Mercedes. María died this morning."

The line went quiet. This is not something that should be told over a phone, Sister Piadosa thought. This woman was a mother to María, and far more. It was she who had loved and cared for her from the day she was born; far more of a true mother, by the sound of it, than the beautiful but fragile Catherine could ever be. When María had spoken of her she said that leaving Mercedes was the hardest of all things. How terrible it must be to receive a call from a stranger and be told that your child is dead.

"Are you there, Mercedes?"

For answer she heard a muffled sob.

"Yes." There was a long pause while Mercedes no doubt struggled to collect herself. "What brought about her death? She was so young."

Briefly Sister Piadosa told her of the illness, but made no mention of the child.

"I am arranging the funeral for Thursday late afternoon. Perhaps you could attend. Would you be able to find transport?"

"Diego is here, and he can take one of the cars. Where about are you? Is it very far from here?"

"About two hours by car." She gave Mercedes the directions.

"So close! All this time, just around the corner! We could so easily have visited her. It is wicked! That is what it is!" She did not elaborate. "We will all be there this evening to sit vigil."

As she replaced the receiver Sister Piadosa thought how strange were the workings of fate, that de la Cruz and Catherine should both be away and un-contactable at this time. María would have been relieved that her father was not to be there, and I can't say that I am not, she thought. She was curious to hear about Catherine's absence. From what she had gathered from María, her mother never went anywhere any more.

Putting the thought aside, she dialed Alejandro's number. There was no reply, so she dialed Santiago, for the two were known to be almost inseparable.

She spoke to a woman who, she learned, had been engaged to look after his house and feed his dog while he was away. It turned out that he and Alejandro had left three days before for New York to attend the opening of an exhibition called Artes Sagrados: The Sacred Art Tradition of the South-West, in which a number of 'Alejandro's Angels' were to be included. She did not expect them back before the middle of July, maybe a little later.

Who else could she turn to? For such a delicate situation Sister Piadosa could think of no one else in whom she could confide, or who would be willing to conduct a funeral where the regular priest had refused.

"We will have to do it ourselves," she told Sister Ana when she joined her in María's room.

"So be it."

She put the matter out of her mind, and turned all her attention to María.

Even in death, with her head shaved of its glory, María was beautiful.

"She looks like a Madonna," whispered Sister Ana.

"Yes."

The two sisters bathed the body with water prepared by Sister Ana, in which Magdalena's special, fragrant herbs had been steeping for the past hour with a mix of leaves and roots.

They sponged María's body, face and head. They dried her and anointed her with aromatic oils. They took long gauze bandages impregnated with a mixture of oil and the ground powders of anil del muerto, yerb de la sangre, lavender and yerba del caballo, and bound her body and limbs, leaving only her face free.

Sister Piadosa opened a small jar of some perfumed unguent and applied a little of the contents to María's face until the skin began to glow.

They dressed her fragrant body in the wedding dress that she had worn on the magical night when she and Salvador had driven off in the outrageous lowrider to exchange vows and rings in the presence of Alejandro and to promise themselves to each other until death.

On María's head they placed a white cotton nun's cap, to cover its bareness, before fixing the veil with its fine embroidery. As Sister Ana lifted it from the tissue, the dim room became filled with rainbows and flashes of light from the crystal tears that had fixed themselves to the fine lace the day María left her parents' house.

Now, in the white dress and with the veil falling around her, she lay on the narrow bed, a sleeping bride waiting to be awakened.

The two nuns stared at each other. Who, they wondered, or more specifically what was she, this strange little one who had come into their lives for a brief stay, and yet had made such an impact on all who lived at The Adobe?

Sister Consuela knocked softly and entered the room. She had come as arranged by Sister Ana, to sit the first vigil.

"Before you sit down, sister, would you run and ask Gregorio when he will have the coffin ready? And bring one of the large bags of dry lavender back with you."

Sister Consuela left the room.

"Mercedes and the rest of the staff from María's house," said Sister Piadosa, "are coming over this evening to sit vigil, and I suppose some of the locals may have heard of María's death. They may come, although they barely know her. Manuel and Refugio will come with the babes. I spoke to her on the phone. I think we will use the meditation room. It will be warm tonight, so we can leave the doors open. I have arranged for food and refreshments, but it is a small gathering, so we probably won't need much."

"Do you know how you are going to conduct the service tomorrow? You will have to leave out the Eucharist. Can you have a proper funeral without a priest?"

Sister Ana looked concerned. "What will happen to María if the service is incomplete?"

"I believe that when intention is sincere, and as much as can be done is done, God is not going to split hairs about a few wafers and a little wine."

"Sister Piadosa!"

"Yes, my dear. We will do all that we can. God will provide the rest." She moved about the room, covering the mirror and the three small pictures that María had brought with her. "I must go and see that the chapel is ready, and make some notes for the service. Wait here until Sister Consuela returns, and call me when the coffin is ready."

Gregorio had made the coffin from raw cedar that had only recently been cut. The strong pine fragrance filled the room. Sister Piadosa packed the base with long stems of dry lavender. Over this she spread a carpet of plump lavender heads. "So that you may rest well, María," she said.

She and Sister Ana lifted María's body into it, arranging the veil about her.

"She weighs nothing. She is like one of the feathers from her white doves."

White feathers are all that remain of them too, thought Sister Piadosa.

Sister Ana went to the door and nodded to Gregorio and the three men who were waiting to carry the coffin and its precious passenger to the meditation room.

They entered softly, and although they were big men accustomed to rough work, they tiptoed in as if afraid to wake the one who slept. Gregorio was visibly moved by the vision he saw lying in the coffin he had made. He leaned forward and whispered in María's ear.

"I carved a little dove just above your head to watch over you, María."

Sister Piadosa, catching his words, looked more closely at the coffin, and indeed, just above the crown of María's head she saw the small dove carved into the wood.

In the small meditation room the coffin was placed on two stools beneath the simple wooden cross that hung on the end wall. All the chairs had been rearranged and others had been brought from the dining-room. The room was filled with flowers.

Presently they heard a car turn off the road. Sister Piadosa stepped outside to meet the arrivals.

Diego parked the car, and the sad little party from the Hacienda de Las Palomas alighted. One by one they introduced themselves to Sister Piadosa. They had their emotions under control, although there was evidence that the women had been weeping. They followed Sister Piadosa to the small room and entered.

It was only when they saw María lying in the coffin that the full truth of her death came home to them. Mercedes knelt down beside the coffin, tears streaming down her face.

"Oh, María. Oh, my sweet little dove, my sweet one. Oh, María, how can this be?" She wiped her eyes with a large handkerchief. "I would have come to see you if I had known."

She broke down and sobbed. "I would have come. I would have come."

Diego, his heart full, stood looking down at María, at the Madonna-bride sleeping with plump heads of lavender between the folds of her veil. He thought he had never seen her so lovely. But beyond the sleeping figure, in his mind's eye, he saw the passionate face of the young child María as she watched her baby elk being set free. Such passion, he thought, demands a heavy price.

But somehow he could not feel too sad. It was always her destiny. One had only to look closely to see that.

Still he wondered at the great mystery that decides these things, and he said a prayer for the child she had been and for the young woman who lay so peacefully before him, whose life had been so short and so filled with beauty and suffering.

He was carrying a small package. Now he moved over to Sister Piadosa.

"I have something here for María, sister. It is something I was making for her and was going to give to her, but she left so suddenly."

He undid the wrapping, and Sister Piadosa saw the small carving he had made.

"The Zunis are better at this kind of thing, but when I saw how unhappy she was after..." He looked to see if the nun knew the whole story; she nodded that she understood. "Well, I thought I would make her a carving of Santo, the baby elk she helped to rear. Would it be permissible to give it to her now? Would such a thing be frowned on?"

He did not understand her rueful smile, but was pleased that she had no problem with the gift. He went over to the coffin and set it between María's breasts.

"So that he may always be close to your heart," he whispered. "May he be waiting to meet you, María."

Mercedes and Encarnación moved over to Sister Piadosa.

"Who is conducting the service tomorrow, sister?"

Here it was. What could she tell them? They of all people deserved the truth.

"Perhaps you would come to my office. There is something I would like to tell you, but not here; and I must ask you, for María's sake, to keep it strictly confidential."

They followed her past the herb garden and into her office, where she pulled up two chairs for them.

"Not even María's father knows what I am going to tell you, and I have given María my word to keep it from him if it is at all possible."

Wonderingly the two women nodded their assent.

Briefly Sister Piadosa told them the whole story. It was met by a stunned silence. They stared at her, unable to comprehend the fullness of the tragedy.

"And that is why the priest has refused to conduct the service. I have tried to contact Alejandro, who married them, but he is away."

"Will Salvador be here tomorrow?"

"I don't know how to contact him. Santiago left with Alejandro. I thought he might know Salvador's whereabouts, but nobody else does. María's father threatened him with death—and with María's death. Salvador believed de la Cruz might harm María, and he left. No one has seen him. I can't explain all this to any other priest, and I just hope Father Jean-Luc doesn't spread it about. So there is no one to conduct the service but me and the other sisters. We will do our best."

"Oh! But there is!"

It was Encarnación who spoke. Now she rose, and with a nod to Sister Piadosa and Mercedes she left the room.

"What does she mean?" Sister Piadosa looked enquiringly at Mercedes.

"Encarnación is a strange woman, sister. I think she will invoke the Hermanos—to come and conduct the wake and the Funeral Mass."

"But there are no Penitentes here any longer. They were all driven away from this area long ago."

"I think you will find that Encarnación knows otherwise."

They hurried outside, and saw Encarnación striding out towards a raised piece of ground just beyond the cottonwoods.

"What is she doing?"

"Encarnación's family comes from the old country. She is part Mayan, a powerful people. She knows the art of summoning."

Sister Piadosa put her hand over her mouth. She thanked God that Father Jean-Luc was not here. All his worst fears would be realized.

But it was she who had said to Sister Ana that God would provide. Perhaps this was His way. How could she be certain? She decided that she couldn't; but then, what could you ever be sure of? Stranger things had occurred, which later were considered to be the working of God's hand.

She was lifted out of her thoughts by the deep, throaty voice of Encarnación chanting.

It was a dark and guttural summons that grew and diminished in volume; something between a prayer and an invocation, that repeated over and over until the whole valley and the hills and beyond the hills and beyond, seemed to be filled with it. It poured out like a wild river, streaming, not from the lips but from the heart, and was flung out into the wind. It was a raw, untamed sound, and it held a terrible beauty.

The sound of it almost stopped Sister Piadosa's heart.

Who was she to condemn such power? Father Jean-Luc would have known it was the Devil: the very beauty of it was proof of that. He had the comfort of certainty on his side.

The silence, when the song stopped, was profound.

They waited.

Encarnación returned and stood with them.

And then they heard it: the distant sound of chanting.

The sound grew louder. And then they came, striding out of the foothills: a band of men, chanting alabados.

They wore long, black robes. Some of their number had hoods covering their heads. They made their way down the steep pathway that descended from where Magdalena's white cross etched itself against the late-afternoon sky.

The Hermanos had arrived.

PART V
SALVADOR

The Musicians

María de la Cruz had vanished off the face of the earth, or so it seemed to the distraught Salvador, whose frantic search for her had lasted for over two months.

He had done everything in his power to find her, but no one knew, or certainly no one was telling where she had gone. The only lead had come from José, who told him that she had left one day by car, driven by Roberto, and that the staff members of the Hacienda de Las Palomas were not given any information as to her whereabouts. On learning this, Salvador beseeched José to speak to Roberto, to plead with him to disclose where he had taken her. José had done so, but he met with no success.

"I have no idea why you should be asking me such questions, nor do I have any answer for you. And now, I am extremely busy."

"But father, I was there when you drove María away. I waved her goodbye. What has happened that you will not tell me?"

Roberto made no reply to this, but turned and walked away.

His father's behavior was so uncharacteristic that José guessed that de la Cruz must have some terrible hold over him. It made him fear for Salvador's safety. He asked some cautious questions around town, and everything he heard only served to reinforce his belief that de la Cruz was a ruthless man; not a man to provoke or defy.

"I think you had better keep well away from town, Salvador. I have heard people talking, and your name has come up more than once. De la Cruz is looking for you, and I would not take it lightly. Things have happened to others who have crossed him: unfortunate accidents. He is not a man to be trifled with."

And so it was, on a cold October day—with the snow falling heavily and causing the usual accidents and car pile-ups on the slippery roads—that Salvador returned to his small, rented casita and contemplated what his next move should be. He had exhausted all his ideas. He had left no stone unturned, but every line of inquiry had been fruitless. What else could he do? He racked his brains. What was it Alejandro used to say?

"Do nothing. How can the future find you if you are running around like a chicken without a head?"

That was all very well, but this was his life—and María's. This was their love for each other, and the future for which they had waited so patiently. They were married, for God's sake. She was his wife. They were not teenagers. This was no sudden infatuation. The angels themselves had blessed their union. The whole insane drama was like a nightmare.

"Curse you, Lorenzo de la Cruz!"

But because, and only because he could think of nothing else to do, he followed Alejandro's advice. He would find María eventually. He swore he would. No secret lasts long in a small community. Sooner or later someone would let slip a word and the truth would be out. Not all de la Cruz' power could protect him from the insatiable curiosity of small-town gossips and their ability to ferret out the truth.

"One day your death will come for you, de la Cruz. I wish I could say truthfully that I hope it is not too soon."

A fleeting vision of de la Cruz' skull grinning up at him from the grave with one long, yellow, bony arm reaching up out of it, beckoning to María to join him while the other bony fist grasped the hem of her dress, caused him to shudder. He closed his eyes and shook his head.

Christmas came and went—a lonely time for Salvador. He phoned his father on New Year and heard the sad news of Father Octavio's death. He asked Santiago to please light a candle for him in the church where so often he had played the accompaniment for the hymns.

He phoned again some little time after Easter, but still there was no news. He wondered if María was still in the country. If she was somewhere close, surely someone would have spoken up by now. Perhaps she had left the country. Perhaps she had been sent to someone in her mother's family in France. Perhaps it was all hopeless. Salvador did not phone his father again.

It was with a practicality that he was far from feeling that he returned to his work; to his pupils, a handful of eager, young would-be Elvis Presleys, all with outsized sideburns and the obligatory lock of hair falling into their eyes, who wanted to play guitar and become overnight rock stars; to the small band that he had put together, a group that made good money playing mariachi music for weddings and dances.

But he did not want to spend his life dressed up in a fancy hat, a ruffled shirt, tight pants and a waistcoat with silver buttons, singing about lost love, however topical that might be at the moment. He did not want to play other people's music. He wanted to compose and play his own: music that was both sensual and sacred, music that spoke of passion and ecstasy, of the pain and beauty which lay in the depths of his love for María.

He knew the music was there, waiting for him. He could feel it inside him, an ache that filled him, that pressed up against his heart. It felt as if a being lived in him, an entity longing to be released. But for all his efforts he seemed unable to reach down far enough into himself to lift the amorphous energy out of that deep place within him, where it burned like an ember, and give it a voice. Beneath the table which served as a desk there was a waste-paper basket filled with crumpled manuscript paper that testified to his struggle to make some kind of contact with that haunting spirit that possessed him.

The months went by. The seasons came and went. He paid them scant attention. It was only when he woke one morning to find the ground covered with snow that he realized almost a year had passed, and that he was no further with his life or his music.

"Oh yes, Alejandro! Do nothing! It looks as if I will spend my life doing nothing."

But fate, or divine providence, or whatever it may be that decides these matters, was more merciful than that: for even as Salvador sat ruminating on his future, filled with his longing and his love for María, a young man of twenty-eight years was making his slow but steady way home from Buenos Aires back to New Mexico: by cargo ship, by train and by hitched rides in transport trucks.

He paid his way by playing his particular and, to most of the listeners, strange brand of music. It was a sound that filled them with such longing and nostalgia that for most of the long journey home the young musician was accompanied by a series of men who, touched by his melancholy chords, felt compelled to sob out the sad and often intricate tales of their lonely and rootless lives.

Reuben Mendoza—for that was the young man's name—left home on a mission when he was eighteen, the mission being to study and indeed immerse himself in the whole culture of tango: its history, its people, its music and its dance.

To do this he had decided to travel to Buenos Aires, that great city which in the mid-nineteenth century had been such a melting-pot of immigrants, peasants and porteños—the marginalized, working-class natives of Buenos Aires—and others who had washed up on her shores. It was a group that shared a sense of homelessness, of nostalgia for their origins and a deep experience of up-rootedness and loss. This vigorous mix of peoples brought with them a rich diversity of dance rhythms and musical expression which forged a new and integrating ethos, out of which a passionate culture of music and dance and an entire philosophy was born.

This was tango. And it was tango that had resonated so deeply in Reuben Mendoza's young heart when he first heard it. It was tango to which he had surrendered himself utterly, as any hot-blooded and ardent young lover might surrender his body and soul to a beautiful woman who called him to her bed. He longed beyond all else to lose or find himself in her.

He especially wanted to meet the man who now, almost a hundred years later, was re-inventing tango, the great musician Ástor Piazzolla: if not to meet, at least once, to hear him play.

This was the dream he held onto during the long and lonely journey away from home. He was also determined to do whatever it took to become accepted as a pupil and be taught by a true artist; to play the bandoneon, that instrument that could evoke the soul of longing in all who heard its sweet and melancholic lament.

For Reuben Mendoza this was a calling, a vocation as powerful as any call to serve God. He had been seized by this fervent desire when he was a youngster, barely fifteen, when he first saw the tango danced to the scratchy sounds of an old Carlos Gardel 78rpm record at the local dance club. He had known no peace from its compelling rhythms since that time.

It was a hot September evening with a sky the color of ripe water-melon and only the very faintest trace of a breeze. Salvador sat on the small porch which faced onto Route 550, trying to decide what his next plan should be.

As he sat, looking straight ahead at nothing in particular, a large transport truck, belching diesel fumes from its two shiny exhaust stacks and carrying on its three-tier trailer eight brand-new just-out-of-the-box, sky-blue, two-tone Chevrolet Impala Hardtops, rolled slowly by on its way to deliver the same to a dealer in Albuquerque.

It was not its customary route, for at the last minute the driver had made a detour so that he might say hello to a cousin who had recently returned home after serving three less than comfortable years in a local establishment for something involving the disappearance of a company car.

Salvador barely noticed the truck's passing. His muse had deserted him—or so he felt. He was contemplating converting a nearby vacant shed into a work studio where he would return to the craft Alejandro had taught him so many years ago, for which he had an undoubted gift: that of making violins.

He was lifted out of his cogitations by a waft of some strange music that seemed to be issuing from the cab of the transport truck.

Yes! He was not imagining it. He stood up, straining to hear, above the grating noise of the gear-change as the truck slowed to negotiate a bend in the road, the unfamiliar sound that was floating out into the evening air. In spite of the grinding gears and the explosive sound of the brake engaging, he managed to hear a snatch of the most hauntingly sad music, which reawakened in him all his longing for his beloved María. It was a music which somehow managed to rise above the rumbling of the forty-eight outsized trailer wheels and the metallic clank and rattle of the vast body of the mechanical giant and the load which it carried; a music that floated out into the soft, indigo evening; a music that, like a soul finding at last its mate, made its way straight into Salvador's desolate and wounded heart.

Without a second thought he leapt up, rushed inside, snatched up his car keys, flew out the door, jumped into his battered Chevy Bel Air and sped off down the Interstate in pursuit of the transport truck, leaving a smoke-trail of burning oil and rubber in his wake.

In spite of the gathering dusk it was a simple task to follow the truck, not only on account of its vast size, but because of the visible streams of magenta music that flowed from its cab.

Salvador drove like a madman, possessed by a passion and an intense desire to meet the author of that bitter-sweet sound: for in the music he heard all of his love and longing for María; all the pain of their separation and his sadness and nostalgia for a dream that had seemed so real, and which now lay broken and lost.

But that was not all he heard.

In the music's deep undercurrents and the subtle and complex set of interweaving rhythms and counter-rhythms, that spoke of every artist's search for the expression of a poetic and transcendent perfection, he heard a call to his soul, and right there on Interstate 25, with the diesel fumes filling his nostrils and the music filling his trembling and ecstatic heart, he knew he had come home.

Tango Muerte

It seemed to Salvador that his body and that of the woman were one, not separate from the passion of the music. They were bound together in a dance so deep that the throb of their conjoined hearts was not separate from the rhythmic beat of the tango which held them so tightly in its embrace.

The room was dimly lit. Couples sat in the small, intimate booths which encircled the large dance floor, engrossed in whispered conversations, their heads almost touching, cigarette-smoke curling around them and drifting languidly up into the gloom. Salvador caught glimpses of flesh: a shoulder, the proud curve of a neck, the contour of a breast. Here and there a woman's leg, long and provocatively bare in its high-heeled dance shoe, caught the light. He could not see their faces, nor could he hear any sound issuing from their lips.

He and the woman were the only ones dancing.

The musicians, dressed all in black, sat in one corner of the room, bent over their instruments, intent only on the music. They allowed no pause between dances, but played on and on so that the very shadows were filled with the rhythmic undercurrents and the nostalgic chords of loss and longing.

In the center of the room there was a small pool of light, cast onto the dance floor by an overhead spotlight. Salvador was startled by its brightness. Somehow he knew that on no account must he be drawn into its brilliance, but as they danced, it became more and more difficult to avoid touching the white beam, for the light was drawing him inwards like a magnet, pulling him towards that illuminated place on the empty dance floor.

The music changed. All the musicians save one stopped playing, and the room grew strangely quiet.

Into this emptiness the bandoneon began to play a slow lament. The utter loneliness of the sound filled the room, and Salvador felt the woman in his arms begin to weep. He drew back from their embrace to look into her face. To his surprise he saw she wore a heavy, black veil through which he could see nothing of her features.

A staccato knocking on one of the windows startled him, and he turned towards the sound. The white face of de la Cruz stared back at him through the glass. He was holding a piece of paper that resembled a certificate, pressed against the window-pane. It bore a seal the color of blood. One thick, nicotine-stained finger jabbed at the paper as if insisting that Salvador should read it. He could see some writing, but he could not make out the words from across the room.

He turned back to his partner and noticed that the veil had shifted slightly, revealing the startling brilliance of her red hair, which seemed to have fallen free of its dressing. He moved to lift the veil, but she whispered urgently: "No, Salvador, don't—don't look—keep dancing—we can't stop, or he will come. We mustn't stop dancing!"

Her body pressed itself urgently into his.

The music increased in volume and tempo as the other musicians took up the soloist's theme. Salvador felt himself seized by its energy, so that he could no longer control his body. The beam of light grew wider and the music grew faster and more impassioned. The figure at the window rapped louder and louder. The finger jabbed more urgently.

"María? Is it you? I must know! I must look."

He lifted the veil, and simultaneously the two of them fell apart and into the beam of light. To his horror Salvador saw the blue eyes of María de la Cruz staring up at him out of a stark, white skull, her red-gold hair fanning out all about her like a fire.

Outside the window the grimacing face and jerking figure of de la Cruz danced back and forth to the frenzied rhythm of the tango, like some crazed marionette on strings. The window blew open, and the note fluttered into the room and fell at Salvador's feet.

On it there was just one word. 'Muerte'.

———

Salvador awoke with a start, his heart beating fast. During his sleep all his blankets had fallen to the floor. In spite of this he was sweating. Outside his window the full moon had just risen over the mountains. Snow had fallen. The night was cold.

He rose quietly so as not to waken Reuben in the next room, and made his way to the kitchen, where he mixed himself a hot drink. He did not switch on any lights, preferring the less intrusive quality of moonlight. He sat curled up on the large couch, his body wrapped in a thick serape, sipping the chocolate.

What were dreams that they felt so real?

His mind went back to María and the day he had left the hacienda where she lived. It was over two years now, and he still had not managed to discover her whereabouts, nor had he heard so much as a whisper of her name. Early on in his exile he had fretted and made daily phone calls to José and frequent calls to his father, but as the weeks and then months went by with no word of her, the calls became less and less frequent. Reflecting on this, he realized with a shock that he had last spoken to his father over a year before.

In his attempts to escape his pain and his feelings of hopelessness of ever finding María, he had blotted out of his mind everything connected with home. Because Salvador had decided, as a cautionary measure to change his name, his father could have no notion of his whereabouts, nor would he be able to locate him or obtain his telephone number. Now he felt remorse that he should have allowed so much time to pass. His father would be worried not to have heard. He resolved to write him a long letter and tell him that he was well and that he had met a musician called Ruben Mendoza. Ever cautious, he decided he would not put his address on the letter.

Since Salvador's meeting with Reuben in the Albuquerque car lot life had changed for both those young men. The very first time their eyes met they shared an instant of profound recognition of their mutual aloneness, which was in itself an identity of a kind and which set them apart from most of their contemporaries: Reuben on account of having been away from home for ten years, and Salvador because not only had he left his home town, but he could not return to it.

But this sense of disconnectedness was not new. Although neither of them had perceived it as such, it was a loneliness that had lain hidden inside each of them, and while the recent circumstances of their lives had served to make them painfully aware of their solitude, the circumstances themselves were not the cause of their sense of alienation. The roots of disaffection went far deeper.

Reuben had been born into an atmosphere of exile, his parents having left Germany in 1938, the year before he was born. Fearful of what was happening to Jews in Germany at that time, they changed their name from Mendel to Mendoza and managed, at a price, to have their documents altered, stating their religion as Roman Catholic. Through a contact, a man who worked for an underground movement and who was, they heard, subsequently arrested and sent to Auschwitz, they managed to secure a passage on a ship which took them to New York. From there they made their slow way by railroad to New Mexico, where they settled in Albuquerque and made a fairly satisfactory, if not comfortable living out of an import-export business.

Both Reuben's parents died of pneumonia within a week of each other, shortly after his eighteenth birthday. Their furtive life-style had kept them separate from the community in which they lived. This and the two-thousand-year-old legacy of the Diaspora, which his parents had made a point of impressing on the young boy, had been etched into Reuben's heart, making him forever a stranger—even, it sometimes seemed, to himself. In one way the death of his parents released him, but it also left him alone, without family or contacts and with no one to whom he could turn for advice. It was in the absence of any form of guidance that he decided to follow his dream and seek his fortune, which he hoped awaited him in Buenos Aires.

Salvador, although he had not consciously been aware of the loss, had grown up an only child without a mother. His father had been his closest friend, but he worked hard to support his son and had little time for recreation. Salvador, of necessity, became familiar with solitude. The only woman in his life was María, and their relationship had been a courtship filled with painful absences and longing. And now she was gone. The absence of his mother had been less painful in that he had no image of her. In a sense there was no one to miss. With María it was different. At the very first sight of her he knew he had met his beloved, his muse, his future wife; and something else that he would not be able to define, but something that completed him where he had not been aware of an absence.

Now it seemed that fate, at last, smiled on both Reuben and Salvador. It took them no time to decide on a musical partnership, and they enjoyed long conversations until late into the night about what form it would take and what they would call it.

They finally decided to run a music and dance studio which would embrace their many talents. They found an old, vacant warehouse that would suit their purposes and which would not strain their rather meager finances. It comprised a small apartment above a room which would easily convert into a large studio. In addition there were several small rooms behind this which they would use as offices. There was also a garage that Salvador said he would convert into a wood-work studio, for he had every intention of returning to the craft that Alejandro had taught him.

Salvador stood in the empty room, planning how he would organize the space. He remembered Alejandro's words to him on hearing him play the first violin that he had made.

"Poetry! Pure poetry, Salvador," was what he said then.

"When you work with wood you must caress it the way you would make love to a beautiful woman. That way she will bring all her gifts to you."

Salvador was surprised by his godfather's sudden display of earthiness. On mentioning it to his father, however, he was told of the many women who had fallen in love with Alejandro and who would have married him there and then, had he only found the time for it.

"But he is married to his angels, as you well know. This does not mean he has not known the love of a woman."

And so Salvador listened, and learned all that Alejandro could teach him. No father ever gave his son more gifts of sensitivity and interiority than those which Alejandro bequeathed to Salvador. No godfather was ever more loved by his godson.

A door opened down the passage, and Reuben entered the room.

"What's up?"

"Oh—a dream, I guess. Nothing. Just couldn't sleep."

"I'm going to make cocoa. Want some?"

"I have some."

Reuben returned with a steaming cup of cocoa.

"Do you want to talk about it? The dream, I mean."

Briefly Salvador recounted the dream.

"What was the music?"

"What do you mean?"

"I mean the music that you were dancing to. Could you recognize it?"

Salvador frowned. "It was more of a feeling than the actual notes. I don't think the music was anything familiar. Nothing I've heard before."

"Well, there you are! You could start by writing down the music; recreating the dance." He took a sip of cocoa, and curled his feet up into the chair. "You said you wanted to explore tango rhythms, and you already have so many notes and musical scores. Oh, yes! I have been aware of your late-night activities. Perhaps this is what you have been waiting for. It certainly has all the elements for a very dramatic work. Why not give it a try?"

Salvador gave a shrug.

"And while you are about it, make sure that you give the bandoneon a major voice in it. I want to be known as the musician who first played the brilliant works of Salvador Fuentes."

He thought for a moment. "If you get a move on, we can include it in the Albuquerque concert program. But you'll have to hurry."

"I will have to write it under my new name."

"Whatever. Write it under any name. But get to work while you have the energy with you. Until María shows up, let the tango offer you her muse. She is a lady worthy of much respect. She has known more sorrow and loss than you can imagine, and still she sings; still she dances."

Reuben shuffled back to bed. Salvador remained curled up in the warmth of the serape, his eyes closed.

Mestas, Mendoza and Company

The show, Tango Amor—Tango Muerte by Mestas, Mendoza and Company, was an overwhelming success in Albuquerque. It received standing ovations every night from audiences who wept openly at each performance.

Their copious tears might have been for the sadness of the story or for the beauty of the music, but the theatre manager, who watched the show each night, was similarly afflicted during each performance. He was astonished by his emotional response, for he was not by nature a man given to such outbursts.

He questioned Reuben one evening as to the possible cause of such excessive emotion. He learned that the two violins played during the performances had been made by the composer of the music. Through some agency that was a mystery even to the craftsman himself, his instruments, when played, aroused powerful emotions in all listeners. In the case of these two instruments, which Salvador had but recently completed, it was obvious that they held in every curve and plane of the glowing wood used for their creation, all of his longing and heartbreak and his many tears for the love he had lost, and for whom he had searched in vain.

"You don't say."

The theatre manager was deeply moved by this explanation. He made a point of mentioning it to one of the reporters, who intended writing a column about the show, and who was looking for a human interest angle.

Salvador was dismayed to read in the paper the following day an exaggerated account of this story, entitled 'The Weeping Stradivarius.' He feared that someone might guess his identity and inform de la Cruz. There was nothing he could do about it but request that no more personal details should be offered to the press.

The group was also interviewed by a music and theatre critic, who wrote a column almost unmatched in the history of that publication in its extravagant use of superlatives.

"Here, Salvador, listen to this!"

Reuben read from the music critic's page.

'...a new and most original composer, Angelo María Mestas, and a master of the bandoneon, Reuben Mendoza. These two young men, through their various empathic skills, have brought to life the very soul of tango.'

'A concert not to be missed.'

"That's us!"

The three principal dancers, who had worked so hard with Reuben to arrive at the dramatic combination of tango and mime to tell the tragic love story, received lavish praise, as did the creator of the masks, worn by two of the dancers, and of the puppet that had been carved and painted with such sensitive mastery to represent the child in the performance. Critics made particular mention of this most unusual feature, calling it 'a tender and moving passage—a new and innovative introduction of puppetry into the field of tango'. The choreographer was highly praised for his deeply moving sequences.

In writing the music for bandoneon, piano and two violins, as well as the story behind the music, Salvador had drawn heavily on his dream, but he was unwilling, even in a work of composition, to contemplate María as dead. Instead, he created the character of a prostitute for the woman in the story. However, to his regret, he was unable to control her ultimate fate. He wrote an extremely detailed account of the story-line for the dancers, musicians and puppeteer to work from and typed a copy of it for each member of the cast so that they could make their own notes in the margin.

Tango Amor—Tango Muerte

A young man of wealth and high social standing, Julio Romero, visits a bordello one evening and falls in love with a mysterious young woman who works there, known only as Corazón; mysterious because she wears a black veil over her face.

She is the daughter of a rich man who has rejected her and thrown her out onto the streets because she has disobeyed him and conducted an affair with a man of no social standing. It is to hide her identity and her shame that she wears the black veil.

Julio takes Corazón to a milonga where they dance together the whole night. He constantly tries to catch a glimpse of her face but she turns her head away and resists all his attempts. When dawn comes he cannot bear to leave her, and begs her to come away with him.

Although this is forbidden by the owner of the bordello, she goes with Julio and the two spend three months together, expressing their ardent love for each other through their ever more, passionate dancing. During this time she refuses all his requests that she remove the veil.

Three months pass, and Corazón learns that she is pregnant. Rather than telling Julio of this, she leaves him one night after he has gone to sleep. She returns to the bordello, where the owner lifts the veil and presses her with kisses, and cuts off one lock of her hair. He takes her to her old room where she sits down in front of the mirror, staring at her face through the veil, weeping when she sees what she has become.

In the morning, on finding her gone, Julio is distraught, and rushes out into the street, asking everyone if they have seen a woman wearing a black veil. No one can help him. He searches for many months. Finally he finds himself back in the rough neighborhood of the bordellos. He is not welcomed there by the residents, who mock his elegant attire. A bandoneon player, crippled in one leg, plays a rough tango full of shadows and seduction. Julio is about to leave when an Old Man dressed all in black, with the brim of his black Fedora turned down, obscuring his face, steps forward and says that if Julio will dance with him, he will take him to Corazón.

Julio agrees and the two of them dance together, a dance of great sensuousness that grows increasingly more passionate, more erotic and more explicitly sexual. The crowd in the street applauds wildly, and the bandoneon plays an ever more raunchy and seductive music.

Now the Old Man starts to caress Julio as if he were his lover, his body making suggestive movements that illustrate his desire. Julio is revolted, but submits because he is afraid that if he doesn't, he won't find Corazón.

Finally the dance ends, with the Old Man executing a brutal and deliberately off-balance desplazamiento. Julio is thrown to the ground, injuring his hip. The Old Man, who seems to have grown stronger during the dance, leads the limping Julio down a narrow street to a small, open door and up a steep staircase.

At the top, in a dingy room, Julio finds Corazón lying in bed. She is very frail. He bends down and lifts the veil. He is shocked to see a grinning skull with hollow eye-sockets resting on the pillows.

Now the Old Man steps forward, and with a flourish and a bow removes his black fedora, in turn revealing a grinning set of gold teeth in a skull with eyes as red as rubies. Julio is horrified to learn that he has been dancing with death. He moves away from the bed.

The Old Man reaches out his hand, inviting Corazón to dance with him. Gracefully she rises from the bed, and they dance a slow tango down the stairs and out into the street.

Julio hears a child laughing. He draws aside a curtain and sees a little girl sitting on a narrow bed. Her skin is pale like alabaster, her eyes are the color of gentians and red-gold hair frames her face like a halo.

Julio knows without a doubt that this is his daughter. He leaves the room, taking the child with him. In the street the bandoneon player sees them and starts to play a tender tango lullaby. In spite of his limp Julio begins to dance, holding his daughter in his arms.

In the shadows Corazón and the Old Man, with their white faces and crazy grins, mimic the dance; a macabre performance full of exaggerated jerks and turns, like two uncoordinated marionettes.

On opening night an abbreviated outline of the story appeared printed in a glossy program which included a list of names beginning with the composer of the music, Angelo María Mestas, and the choreographer and master of bandoneon, Reuben Mendoza, together with the names of the musicians and dancers and some information about the background of the group and its members.

With the popularity and success of the show and the many flattering reviews in several newspapers it was not surprising that word of a must-see performance of tango should have reached the attention of several music-lovers in Santa Fe.

No one had ever heard of Mestas, Mendoza and Company. It was a group that seemed to have sprung up overnight out of nowhere. For all that, a local concert manager was being inundated with calls, requesting that he engage the group to perform in Santa Fe. This worthy man managed to track them down through a newspaper, and spoke to Reuben about the likelihood of a two-week booking early in February. The fee was agreed and the booking made. The contract would be brought to them in Albuquerque for signature.

Salvador was nervous about playing so close to home, where there were people who might recognize him, in particular de la Cruz. At the same time he felt thrilled to be closer to where, he was sure—or rather he hoped María must be living in some kind of enforced confinement.

Perhaps José would have some news for him. Perhaps he would be able to arrange for her escape from wherever she was being held. Things were different now. He had become a man of means; a man with a future. The group was on its way, requests were pouring in for membership to their tango dance club and there were several orders for his extraordinary violins.

A recording company had sent them a letter, the contents of which dealt with the possibility of recording the music from Tango Amor—Tango Muerte, and he was full of ideas for his next composition. The future, which had looked so hopeless, was full of promise once more.

An Evening of Tango in Santa Fe

The small foyer of the concert hall was abuzz with excited anticipation.

Much of the conversation focused on the identity of the group and how it could have escaped notice until now. No one, it seemed, could throw any light on its origins. The names Reuben Mendoza and Angelo Mestas were completely unknown.

There was the usual activity, the greeting of friends not seen for some time and the perennial occupation of exchanging the latest news or gossip. In amongst all this there was much whispered surprise, expressed by those who knew him, at the presence at the concert hall of Don Lorenzo.

Everyone knew that after the disappearance of his wife, Don Lorenzo had refrained from appearing in public. Why he should choose to do so now, after the recent tragedy and all the startling revelations about his family that had been made so cruelly public, was a mystery. But he was there—not his usual, ebullient self, that was certain, and not flaunting his customary, scarlet-lined theatre coat, but dressed all in black.

His partner for the evening was a young, extremely beautiful and elegant woman who could not have been a day over twenty-five—the shame of it!—and him in his seventy-fourth year. This in itself was enough to set the tongues wagging, but under the circumstances it was quite shocking.

Another face in the excited crowd was that of Santiago Fuentes who, recalling the letter Salvador had sent him mentioning his meeting with a young musician, had recognized the name Reuben Mendoza from the advertised program. He hoped that Reuben might be able to tell him something of Salvador's whereabouts and how he might contact him. He wanted to inform him of María's death and suggest that he might consider returning home, should he wish it. It was to be hoped that de la Cruz would not continue his private vendetta now that his daughter was dead.

Santiago was accompanied by Alejandro, who had, it transpired to the amazement of everyone who knew him, a passion for tango music. He hoped that he might find inspiration for an angel, or even a series of angels, in this music which had been born out of such an extraordinary mix of peoples and passions. He had recently completed carving angels for all the stars around Taurus, Auriga and Orion, and was looking for fresh ideas.

Sebastián and Rafaél were interested to see just what Tango Amor—Tango Muerte was all about, and whether they might invite the group to give a performance at The Adobe, for it was with great excitement that they had decided to build a small theatre and make all forms of the arts a means of education and spiritual growth for the community which The Adobe served.

For the rest, the gathering was made up of regular concert-goers and a few out-of-town visitors who had come along to taste what culture Santa Fe had to offer them.

Santiago decided he would seek out Reuben Mendoza after the performance. After greeting several friends and colleagues he and Alejandro moved into the auditorium to take their seats with the rest of the audience. They had managed to acquire seats in the third row, which offered them an excellent view of the stage.

The lights dimmed, and the audience grew quiet. The owner of the concert hall appeared on stage in front of the curtain to welcome everyone and give a brief introduction to the evening. He said a few words about the two unknown musicians who had put together this most unusual program, which combined all the passion of tango with the erotic qualities of dance and the drama of a story-line.

He mentioned that the choreography was the work of Mendoza, while the music was composed by Mestas. He added that tonight's extraordinary music would be played on the piano, guitar, violin and the bandoneon, an instrument that might be unfamiliar to some concert-goers, but which was the instrument of tango. He informed the audience that the violins had been made by the composer.

On receiving this last piece of information a sibilant whispering fluttered through the audience like a small bird. What a talented man the composer must be!

Santiago and Alejandro stared at one another. There was only one person they knew in New Mexico who actually made violins, and that was Salvador. Who was this Angelo Mestas that they had never heard of him?

The lights dimmed for Act One. The curtain rose on an empty stage.

From the shadows come the haunting notes of the bandoneon, playing the Theme for Corazón. It is echoed softly by the violin, as if the two voices were speaking to one another. Simultaneously, behind a filmy gauze curtain, the ghostlike figures of a man and a woman begin to dance a slow, nostalgic tango. They hold each other's gaze, seemingly oblivious to everything save each other. They dance, thigh tight upon thigh, their lips almost touching, as if breathing one breath, maintaining the tension of their almost-meeting mouths until it becomes almost too painful to watch.

An audible sigh of appreciation rose out of the audience. Something in the music, particularly in the notes of the violin, spoke of such depths of sadness that several women began to wipe their eyes.

A full moon lights the dance, but slowly it begins to wane, growing smaller and smaller until the last thin crescent vanishes, and the dancers and the music with it. The stage becomes dark once more.

There was a profound silence in the auditorium, but not in Santiago's heart: for he had recognized in the composition, Theme for Corazón, echoes of the music that Salvador had composed for María de la Cruz when she had sung with him in his first public performance in Santa Fe.

How had the music come to be in this program of tango?

On the stage a street-lamp lights a narrow street in a mean part of town.

The bandoneon player with a crippled leg, a sad old man with frayed coat-tails, the smoke from a cigarette curling about his face, leans against the lamp-post, playing a rough tango full of shadows and the slashing sound of fast knives, street-fights and dark passions.

Behind him, in the shadows, the other musicians join him in what sounds like a musical labyrinth of tempo and counter-tempo, dark and violent.

Three men appear out of the shadows: macho images, all dressed in black with black Fedoras pulled down over their faces. Two men are engaged in a brutal dance, but are soon split up by the third. Flashing a knife, he throws the one partner down into the gutter and takes his place, his punishing steps a brilliant mirror to the violence of the music. The fallen man rises and dances alongside the other two like a shadow. In this fashion the three make their way down the street and enter a doorway over which there glows a single red globe. This is the entrance to the bordello, the whorehouse.

The stage becomes quiet.

From the far side of the stage a fourth man appears. He too wears black, but his suit is immaculately tailored and his cravat is white. This is Julio. In his lapel he wears a red rose. He seems to be unfamiliar with his surroundings, looking at street names for direction.

Now the violinist wearing a white mask with scarlet lips and a blue, painted tear below his left eye, steps out to meet him. He plays a slow, erotic milonga, inviting Julio to dance with him. Although the two do not partner each other in the traditional manner, they dance as if joined by some invisible thread, while the sultry notes of the violin speak of the promise of passion. Julio seems not to hear the faint echoes of sadness beneath the violin's sultry voice.

Several moans could be heard issuing from the audience.

Julio is drawn down the street by the violinist, who stops outside the same doorway and indicates to him that he should enter. The owner of the bordello, a sinister figure with his face completely shaded by the brim of his Fedora, also bids him enter. The violinist disappears back into the shadows and the music fades away.

Julio reappears with a beautiful woman, Corazón, dressed in scarlet. Her black, stocking-clad legs flash provocatively when the high dress-slits part in the dramatic dance steps. Her face is obscured by a black veil, and she refuses all his requests to let him lift it, but in her dancing she signals her readiness to grant him anything else he could wish of her.

As they dance his lips brush over the creamy whiteness of her throat, her shoulders and her breasts, while his hand moves slowly down the bare length of her back, over the inviting shadows of her buttocks, finally to slide suggestively inside the fabric of her dress, claiming her as his own.

Loud groans could be heard coming from the audience, and the ladies directed their fans towards the partners so affected in an attempt to alleviate the heat they must surely be feeling, but with little effect.

To what must surely be the most erotic and demanding tango ever written, Julio and Corazón express the love and the burning passion which has seized them in a dance so tight that all that the audience could see was a perfectly balanced, sinuous intertwining of limbs and bodies, as if indeed they were one flesh.

Slowly, as if reluctant to ever bring the dance to an end, they make their way down the street. The bandoneon leads the piano and guitar in the sensuous tango rhythm, but behind this voluptuous invitation, with all its delicious overtones of love and erotic union, the violin weaves in such an echo of sadness that Julio, looking backward over his shoulder, pauses for a moment, listening. From the shadows the owner of the bordello laughs quietly to himself as he watches them leave.

The curtain came down on the end of Act One to a thunderous burst of applause, some rather heavy breathing from the men and much dabbing of eyes with handkerchiefs by the women. The house lights came on for a twenty-minute interval. Amidst all the noisy chatter and excitement Santiago turned to Alejandro.

"Nobody else I know can play the violin like that."

"You think that is Salvador?"

"I am sure of it. It is not only the playing; it is the instrument itself. That is one of his making, and he has put his broken heart into it. Look what is happening to the audience! All his tears are in it. That is what they are hearing tonight. That is what is moving them so."

"You think he changed his name to Mestas? Let me look here in the program."

Alejandro searched the pages until he came to the full name.

"Ah! Angelo María Mestas."

"I don't know where he got the Mestas from, but the rest is fairly obvious. It must be his way of staying in hiding. The mask is ingenious."

"Do you think he knows about María?"

"Probably not."

"So he doesn't know that de la Cruz will in all probability have no further interest in pursuing him."

"Do I tell him tonight, Alejandro?"

A hand tapped Santiago on the arm. One of the young ushers whispered in his ear that he was wanted backstage. Would he follow him, please?

"Do I tell him?" He looked despairingly at Alejandro.

By way of reply Alejandro shrugged.

Santiago and Salvador greeted each other with emotion: Salvador with the joy of seeing his father; Santiago with a lump in his throat for what he was going to tell his son.

"I saw you out front! How wonderful that you are here, father!"

How can I do this, Santiago thought despairingly.

Salvador read the hesitation in his father's face.

"What is it?"

"Can we meet after the performance? Have coffee somewhere?"

"Tell me now, father. It is María, isn't it? Is she married?"

Santiago stared at his son.

"María is dead, Salvador," he blurted out. "She died last June."

So sudden. So blunt. Santiago looked helplessly at his son.

"María is dead?" he whispered.

"Yes."

A young usher put his head around the door.

"One minute, Señor Mestas."

One minute, thought Salvador. No. There were no minutes. There was just this appalling, empty now.

Before the curtain went up for Act Two a spotlight appeared at the side of the stage. Into this brightness Salvador appeared, holding the violin and bow in his left hand, the mask in the other. The audience was suddenly quiet.

Many of the regular concert-goers recognized him. Why was he here? Salvador Fuentes? What did he have to do with the performance? Was he the masked violinist? Why wasn't he mentioned in the program?

"Ladies and gentlemen, I have just this moment received some information. Before we continue with the performance, may I ask you all to rise?"

Astounded by this unusual request the audience rose to its feet.

"I wish to dedicate this performance, and the composition of this music, to my wife, María Teresa de la Cruz Fuentes, who died in June 1968."

There was a stunned silence.

"Thank you. Please take your seats."

Before the house lights dimmed a hushed whispering blew through the house like a wind, and the name María could be heard everywhere. This must surely be María de la Cruz! They had not known she had married!

Many heads craned to catch a glimpse of Don Lorenzo, who sat stony-faced, his eyes fixed on the curtain as if willing it to go up and relieve him of this embarrassment.

His young escort whispered something in his ear, but he dismissed her with an abrupt wave of the hand, and she fell back into her chair, her face red with confusion.

The concert continued. The audience was enthralled. Such music! They thought they might die of it. But it was the last scene that finally broke down what little control they had left to contain the passions that had been awakened in them.

The sight of the limping Julio removing the veil from Corazón, and discovering that she was dead, and the horrifying sight of her dancing with the sinister bordello-owner was too much for them to bear. Gasps and sobs began to rise from the auditorium.

But it was when Julio lifted the child into his arms and the bandoneon player with his crooked hat and frayed coat began to play a tango lullaby that there came from the front row of the audience the grotesque, strangled sounds of a man sobbing.

It was not just the sound of weeping, but deep, choking, inarticulate utterances of grief, as of one who is having the tears torn out of him. It grew into such a torrent of anguish that the ushers came running down the aisles to see if there was need for medical assistance.

All around the keening man, rows of people had risen from their seats and moved away, afraid that such profound grief might infect them.

From backstage the lighting technician, with great presence of mind, twisted the spotlight around and trained it onto the chair from which the sobbing, which showed no signs of abating, arose.

The white light illuminated the shuddering body and tear-drenched face of the man in black. It fell onto a face which, in the whiteness of the spotlight, was leached of all color and which, with the dark hollows of the deep-set eyes and the grimacing mouth with all its large, white teeth, resembled a skull wearing the obscene grimace of death.

It fell onto the broken face of Don Lorenzo Carlos de la Cruz.

PART VI
THE ZEALOT

The Inquiry

María's grave with its engraved headstone lay between the two large cottonwoods, almost obscured by a profusion of flowers.

It was the chosen place for those working in the fields to come and take their siesta during the heat of midday, and in the cool of evening before returning home to their families.

It was a place notable for the unusual sense of peace that filled those who came to sit there, and it was remarked on more than one occasion that María's song had been heard wafting on the summer breeze and echoing off the hills. During the fall Gregorio witnessed a band of elk browsing on the chamisa and clover which grew alongside the hedges of lavender.

Following María's funeral Father Jean-Luc arrived on his customary second Sunday of the month to conduct Mass for the small community.

Sister Piadosa found herself unable to meet the priest's eye. She kept her head down, answering him in monosyllables only when absolutely necessary.

He observed this with satisfaction, taking it to be a sign of submission and respect. But when he inquired where María had been buried, Sister Piadosa found that she was unable to speak at all. It felt as if a hand was held over her lips, so that even had she wanted to utter them, no words would have been able to emerge. It was only when he pressed her for the information that she finally managed to say that Gregorio knew where the grave was located, but that he was not at The Adobe at present, which was the best compromise between truth and evasion that she could manage.

Jean-Luc, instantly suspicious, took himself off to visit the graveyard to examine whether any earth had been turned recently. Finding it to be unchanged, he felt reassured.

On this particular Sunday there came a point in the interminably vituperative sermon when Sister Piadosa knew she could endure it no longer. His words felt like a poison to her. Looking at the congregants she saw the same look of confused revulsion mirrored on all their faces. His fervent and sanctimonious cant made the hairs rise on the back of her neck, and she felt the prickling of something in her thumbs. Everything in her wanted to run out of the chapel and away, into the sunshine and the air with its scents of earth and growing things; into a world where she could hear God speaking in her heart.

Father Jean-Luc's interpretation of the text fell into a category of such severe over-orthodoxy, such rigidity that it verged on religious mania. Sister Piadosa knew that many of the teachings about which he spoke were the words of Paul, from his letter to the Romans, but somehow Father Jean-Luc had added an emphasis that distorted the meaning and the intention of Paul's words, leaving the congregation feeling cheated, miserable and disempowered.

"The wrath of God is indeed being revealed from Heaven against every impiety and wickedness of those who suppress the truth by their wickedness."

Father Jean-Luc, spurred on no doubt by the recent experience with María, launched into his chosen subject: confession. He was quoting from his favorite and most studied book in the whole Bible, Paul's letter to the Romans. He had long ago forgotten, or suppressed the memory of when and where he had first read it.

"Therefore God handed them over to impurity through the lusts of their hearts..."

He stared at the cowered congregation.

"They are filled with every form of wickedness, evil, greed, and malice; full of envy, murder, rivalry, treachery and spite. They are gossips and scandalmongers and they hate God."

The rows of uncomprehending faces stared back at the priest. There was nothing that they could do with these words. A child had died; an old woman was sick; a father was struggling to meet his bills. The rains had not been kind to them; a valuable cow had died. What relevance did this sermon have for the harsh realities of their lives?

A number of people rose and left the chapel.

At last the priest drove away in his violently protesting vehicle.

Sister Piadosa went to her office, determined to take action. Sebastián had gone off for the day to collect new stock for the clinic, and would not be back until late in the evening.

She decided to phone the seminary and speak to Rafaél.

The secretary who answered her call informed her that he had left the seminary, having postponed his final decision on whether to take Holy Orders.

"Would you like to speak to Father Paz? He is Rafaél's advisor."

Sister Piadosa thought a moment, and then decided against it. She was alarmed to hear that Rafaél contemplated leaving the seminary, but felt she should speak to him first before she interfered in his affairs.

"Did he leave any contact number or address?"

She heard the sound of paper being turned. The secretary came back with the information that he could be contacted through a certain Sebastián Chávez, and she gave Sister Piadosa the number.

Sister Piadosa was back where she had started. She busied herself with some paper-work to pass the time until Sebastián returned. She would discuss it with him, but it looked as if the matter would have to wait until the Bishop returned at the end of December.

The months passed. Summer became fall, sending rivers of gold flowing down the ravines and along the water-courses that wound across the land. The sun, streaming through the yellow leaves of the two cottonwoods on either side of María's grave, cast their golden light over the fading flowers.

Sister Piadosa, on one of her frequent visits to offer a little prayer for María, thought that it was like standing in a cathedral, only far more beautiful!

Finally, in September, after the first fall of snow, Rafaél returned from his visit to his family in California.

Sebastián and Sister Piadosa listened, appalled, to his account of Father Jean-Luc's letter. But what to do about the priest's betrayal was quite another matter.

The attendance of Mass at The Adobe, once so popular, had fallen off so dramatically that now, apart from the sisters, there was barely a handful of locals coming to take communion. Jean-Luc saw this as proof of everything he feared to be true about the religious soundness of the people's spirituality.

He did not for one second stop to consider that there might be anything amiss with his exposition of spiritual matters, and it never entered his head for one instant to question his motives. Nor did he pay any attention to the hints given to him by Sister Piadosa, or listen to the complaints made by members of the congregation. He was not there to listen: he was there to teach and inform, as Paul had done in the early days of the Church. Indeed, he saw a parallel between his work among these religiously naïve people and Paul's work among the early Christians.

December came, but even this traditionally joyful period of celebration was marred by Father Jean-Luc's preoccupation with sin and confession. He made a point of emphasizing just how Jesus had died for our sins, and that anyone who did not come penitently to confess his wickedness and beg forgiveness with a truly contrite heart for his many sins of omission and commission had the blood of Christ on his hands.

"And there is not one among you who is not guilty of transgression!" he thundered. "There is not one of you whose hands are clean of the stain of sin!"

It was the last straw. The people had had enough. The congregation grew restless and exchanged meaningful glances, left and right; turned to look at those behind them. Brows were raised in inquiry and received surreptitious nods in response. Slowly, one by one, they rose and filed out of the church, leaving the priest standing alone in his pulpit.

Father Jean-Luc was not unduly surprised. He knew he had touched a nerve, and that these people were not used to examining their consciences. They had been indulged in a permissive laxity for far too long.

He stood for a while with these thoughts passing through his mind while, unnoticed by him, his hands began to twist and grasp at each other in their familiar, tedious and unclean act, each, so it would appear, attempting to hide behind the other.

"The man is mad," the Mayor was heard to say to his wife under his breath as they left the chapel. "Until this insane little French priest goes, I shall not set a foot inside that church, not for any reason, be it even my own death."

He considered a moment and then added, "Especially not my death. I refuse to be buried by this maniac!"

He paused to give a bow to a neighbor.

"¡Felicidad!—Pedro."

After exchanging greetings and blessings the families departed to return to their homes, there to set up their luminarias and farolitos and enjoy their preparations for Las Posadas. This was always a time of great excitement and awe for the children, as they waited to receive their costumes for the pageant of Los Peregrinos. This was a re-enactment of Mary and Joseph's search for a place to stay in Bethlehem. But their joy in preparing for La Navidad and Nocha Buena had been saddened for them, and many of the older ones remembered Father Octavio with affection.

Two days before Christmas Sister Piadosa, with great courage, called Father Jean-Luc on the phone and informed him that she and the sisters would be attending Mass elsewhere, because the locals had sent a communal note saying they would not be coming to the chapel on Christmas day.

"So we will not be in need of your services, father."

She tried to disguise the intense satisfaction she felt at imparting this information to the priest. He made no comment, but put the phone down abruptly.

For the first time in her life Sister Piadosa did not attend Christmas Mass.

Instead she went to her office and drafted a long letter to the Bishop, setting out the details as she knew them, stating what Father Jean-Luc had said to her about Rafaél and begging that the whole matter of María's alleged heresy be discussed by whatever group or council attended to such matters.

She emphasized that the priest's relationship with the people appeared to have deteriorated to a point where she doubted they would return to worship as long as he was in office.

It was a difficult letter to draft, for she wanted to be as clear as possible, and not make any statements that were exaggerated or mere hearsay. It took her the whole morning, but she felt she had served the infant Jesus well, although in a rather unusual manner. When the other sisters returned with the car, she would drive into the town and post it so that, in spite of all the holidays, the Bishop might receive it as soon as he returned.

———

The Bishop did indeed receive it on his return, just before New Year, and he phoned her immediately.

"I will pay you a visit over the weekend. When would be a good time for you?"

"The sooner the better—Saturday would be good. And we can offer you accommodation, so you could stay the night. As it happens, this Sunday is the day Father Jean-Luc comes to hold a service here. I can't promise a very large congregation, but you might like to stay and attend Mass with us."

Looking back on those many months following the Bishop's visit, Sister Piadosa was relieved to discover that she could feel some measure of compassion for Father Jean-Luc.

The beginning of the end for the French priest was the sermon he gave on the day the Bishop attended Mass in the small chapel. On learning that a disciplined and informed mind, capable of understanding the finer points of theology, would be present at his sermon, Father Jean-Luc poured all the contents of his tortured mind into its composition. He finished, with a flourish, a sermon of such violent scurrility and scorn that the Bishop felt faint.

Father Jean-Luc, on the contrary, felt victorious. Never had he delivered such a fine exegesis on the punishments awaiting those who denied their sins and neglected their duty to the confessional.

There followed, in the ensuing months, a long and wearisome process of inquiry, of meetings and letters and more meetings. A letter was sent to France to inquire more deeply into Father Jean-Luc's history and conduct to date.

It was received with dismay, for it now seemed that they had not rid themselves of the problem. Indeed, if anything, it had become worse. They did not want him back, but it seemed to be inevitable that he would have to come and face a disciplinary hearing in France, and it might be the end of his ecclesiastical career, for it would appear that this was the second time he had broken the Sacred Seal.

A series of meetings were held to discuss how the matter should be handled, but owing to the absence of some of the relevant persons the period of time was a protracted one. It was a very serious offense if it were proved to be true, which seemed likely, and was not a matter that could be hurried. He had been given the benefit of some very small doubt the first time. Now he would have to face the music.

Finally it was suggested that, before leaving New Mexico, he make some kind of amends to those parties he had harmed, should that be decided to be possible and appropriate. They would expect him back not later than the end of April.

There followed another set of meetings, hearings before councils, debates and flurries of letters, all to determine whether Salvador and María's marriage could be considered binding in the eyes of the Church. There was some doubt about the validity of the Catholic 'Folk Wedding Ritual', or whether it had been followed correctly.

The other relevant issue under discussion was 'the sincerity of intent'.

On this matter both Sister Piadosa and Alejandro Jaramillo were interviewed and questioned, separately and together. They said that there was absolutely no doubt whatsoever in their minds or their hearts that both Salvador and María were sincere in their belief that they had been married before God, in a ceremony that was recognized by the Church. The council deliberated for days. Finally Sister Piadosa received a call from the Bishop.

"I just phoned to tell you that you will be receiving a document later in the week, informing you of the Council's decision."

"And?"

"They have decided in Salvador and María's favor."

"Praise God!"

"As such, on that score she had no sin to confess. They are concerned, however, in spite of the confession you heard and the absolution you granted her, that she died without making a proper confession to her priest and without receiving the Last Rites. Under the circumstances they are willing to make an exception, as there seems to be some question, yet to be argued, of course, as to whether Father Jean-Luc was fit to hear it. I don't think there will be much debate on that score. However, they would like there to be some kind of ceremony, even though María is dead, blessing the marriage.

"María's body must be exhumed, of course, and reburied in the consecrated graveyard. It cannot be left to lie outside a sanctified burial-place now that all claims of heresy have been discounted. It has been suggested that Father Jean-Luc be present at this service as part of his amends.

"I will follow up with regard to Rafaél Montdragón's contemplated withdrawal from the seminary, but as far as you are concerned, sister, you can relax—and start arranging a service for María's re-burial.

"It has been suggested that Father Jean-Luc conduct the exhumation. There is a certain poetic justice to that, but I am considering investing Father Rafaél with the authority to conduct the rest of the ceremony, should he be willing to do so. I still think of him as Father, for he has been such an exemplary student: the very best. The Church will be sad to lose him if that is his decision."

"How do I thank you? I can't tell you how anxious I have been!"

"Another 'pollo asado' might do it."

"It is already done."

The Exhumation Service

The small procession, led by Father Jean-Luc, made its way past the camposanto and down to the solitary grave between the two cottonwoods. Sebastián, Father Rafaél and Salvador, followed by Sister Piadosa, walked ahead of Gregorio and the men with the spades.

There had been some strong words spoken about the sister's intended presence at the grave-site, but she had been adamant that she would be there, whatever tradition had to say about such things.

Some distance behind the rest de la Cruz walked alone.

Father Jean-Luc was profoundly uncomfortable. His request to be spared this ordeal had been met with a very firm—"no!" Now, unable to meet the eyes of Sister Piadosa and Father Rafaél, he walked ahead, anxious to get this humiliating experience behind him.

The grave was covered with bunches of bright, hand-made flowers, placed there over the months by unknown hands. At the onset of winter someone had brought a carved statue of Jesus and placed it close to the grave. Sister Piadosa discovered it there one morning when she went to clear the snow away and say a prayer for María. The figure was dressed in a white robe, his arms raised in blessing, the intense gaze of his cornflower-blue eyes fixed on some distant glory. A scarlet heart, emitting rays of golden light, was painted on his chest, a testament to an unswerving faith in salvation through His love.

To Father Jean-Luc's displeasure a small crowd had gathered under the cottonwoods. He requested that everyone stand back and remain quiet. The adults duly complied with his instruction, but nothing could contain the excess of excitement that filled the group of young children, and they wrestled and wriggled themselves away from the restraining hands of their parents, pushing their way to the front of the group, the better to see what was happening.

The two priests entered the small enclosure and stood at either side of the grave.

Looking to his left, Father Jean-Luc noticed that the statue's blue eyes were fixed upon him. He attempted to turn his back on the unblinking stare, but then found himself addressing a large cottonwood. Sister Piadosa, who observed the priest's discomfort and the reason for it, watched with interest. She saw him beckon Gregorio over to him and whisper some instruction into his ear, and was amused to see Gregorio step past the priest and surreptitiously give the figure a ninety-degree turn. Father Jean-Luc, who had feigned ignorance of the activity behind him, could not resist one glance over his shoulder. Satisfied that the disturbing gaze was now trained on the distant hills, he turned back to the matter in hand.

He was displeased to see Refugio in the front row, reaching down to restrain her lusty son from crawling towards the grave. As she bent forward the priest's eyes were drawn once more to her immense breasts, which were almost tumbling out of their tight bodice.

Suddenly there flashed through Jean-Luc's mind's eye the image of his furious mother pointing at him and shouting: "Pig! My son is a pig!" He pushed the memory down, but he could feel his whole body remembering the hideously painful event. He began to sweat. With difficulty he came back to the present.

With a face as white as death, and with shaking hands, he raised his prayer book, cleared his throat and began to read the opening prayer for exhumation. Few could hear him, however, and his thin voice shook as he uttered the final amen.

He gave a stiff nod, and the nuns stepped forward and cleared the grave of its decoration. Gregorio removed the figure of Jesus to a place behind the cottonwood. The men with the spades entered the enclosure, and the digging began.

"Milagros!"

The awed whisper spread through the band of onlookers. And indeed, with every turning of the spades a fresh fall of tiny, silver milagros slid down the growing mounds of soil.

The two piles of earth grew steadily as the men, sweating with the effort of their labor, moved deeper into the pit. Finally their spades struck the lid of María's coffin. They proceeded with care, until there was a space wide enough for them to slip the cords for lifting under each end. A hush fell as the coffin was swung up and out of the pit.

It was as it was being set down that one cord slipped. The coffin gave a lurch, and the brass clasp which secured the closure sprang open, loosening the lid.

The onlookers gave a gasp that sounded like the wind. They saw bright splinters of light slipping out through the narrow crack. Some of them made the sign of the cross; others raised their arms in praise.

Father Jean-Luc tried to ignore this response, but when about twenty fingers pointed to the coffin, he was obliged to bend down to examine it. Seeing the loose clasp, he made a fumbling effort to fasten it, but his hands were shaking so much that he was unable to do this.

This revolting ceremony was getting out of hand.

He ordered everyone to leave immediately, but he might as well have spoken to the wind. Wild horses would not have moved them. All stared at the shafts of brilliance that surrounded the coffin.

It was Father Rafaél who stepped forward and closed the clasp, fastening it securely. The crowd released its breath and waited for the priest to lead the way up to the chapel for the service.

But it appeared that Father Jean-Luc could only stand and mutter something under his breath. His face had broken out into a sweat, and Rafaél, observing his pallor, feared he might faint. With one arm supporting him, he loosened the priest's collar and directed Sister Piadosa to assist him back to the chapel and to have someone fetch a glass of water. Only when this was done did he join Alejandro, Santiago and Sebastián in carrying the coffin up the path and into the chapel. The crowd followed in silence.

De la Cruz, who was standing close to Father Jean-Luc, was furious that he had not been invited to be one of the pall-bearers, and cursed the priest under his breath for not explaining in detail the intended proceedings.

He was further put out, on entering the chapel, to find that no seat had been reserved for him. All his employees were sitting together in the second row behind Refugio, her husband and the two babes, Salvador and his family. Mercedes nodded to him when she saw him staring at them and moved up to make a place for him next to her and Encarnación, but he ignored the gesture and went to an empty seat some rows back.

The congregation stood until the coffin was settled across two low stools, beneath the cross which held the suffering figure of Christ. Father Rafaél disappeared into the vestry and re-appeared wearing a white surplice, customarily worn for weddings. He explained that today's ceremony was, among other things, a celebration, and that they should all feel joy for María on this, the day of her blessing. He called upon Alejandro Jaramillo to say a few words.

Alejandro spoke of the night María and Salvador came to him to be married. He spoke of the love these two people had for each other; a love that nothing, not even death, could destroy.

He told the congregation how he, in his capacity as honorary justice of the peace, had witnessed the vows made by Salvador and María, and that he had given them his blessing. He informed them that, at a meeting recently convened by the Bishop, unanimous approval had been given to this marriage, and that all allegations that their ceremony had not been viable, as had been stated by a certain party, had been revoked. At last María's burial outside the consecrated area, on the grounds that she was a heretic, was to be set right. Permission had been obtained for today's ceremony in which absolution, which had been refused at her death, would be granted, and a blessing would be conferred on her, before witnesses, sanctifying before God the vows that María de la Cruz and Salvador Fuentes had made to one another on the day of their marriage.

Alejandro returned to his seat and everyone, knowing who—'a certain party' was, turned to stare at Father Jean-Luc.

It appeared that the priest was not well, for he shook as if a fever was upon him. His hands, usually so compulsively engaged in their nervous activity, hung limply at his sides. He did not appear to notice the eyes turned on him, but stared up at the face on the cross, his chest heaving as if he were struggling to breathe. Later people recounting the events of the evening to others said that he looked like a man about to die.

Father Rafaél, having received some whispered communication from Salvador, announced that following the blessing a piece of music written for María would be played. Following this the marriage service would be read aloud and the two rings and the two rosaries would be blessed and received by both parties. He added that the coffin would be open for the duration of the ceremony.

Everyone in the congregation received this information in stunned silence.

De la Cruz was horrified. This whole farce was bad enough, but to open the coffin—of someone who had been buried for two years—his daughter!—was obscene!

He attempted to stand up and protest, but he was hampered by the cramped narrowness of the pews, and before he could object Father Rafaél had stepped forward and made the sign of the cross over the closed coffin, unfastened the clasp and raised the lid.

The onlookers gasped.

The tiny flames on the altar candles were drawn forward by the communal intake of breath.

Father Rafaél stepped back and raised his prayer book, about to read, but was halted by the expression on the faces of the congregation.

Later it was said that, with the lid raised, a stream of golden light had flooded out of the coffin and into the onlookers' eyes. When their eyesight recovered sufficiently, they saw that the light came from María's hair! María's brilliant, red and gold hair had escaped from beneath her veil and spilt out over the edge of the coffin—and was growing! It flowed down the aisle, they said, like a rippling stream of fire, emitting blue sparks all the way.

Everyone in the congregation leaned forward to peer over those in front of them in an attempt to see more clearly.

Salvador stepped up to the coffin. He saw María lying amid the fragrant lavender, as beautiful in death as she had ever been. No mark or stain was visible on her white burial clothes. There was even the faintest flush to her cheeks.

Standing beside her, as swarthy and full of red blood as she was pale, he gazed down on her with an expression of such ardent love and suffering that many, having witnessed it, commented later how like a santo he looked, and how tragic was his and María's story.

De la Cruz was outraged to see his daughter displayed in such a vulgar manner. It was worse than that revolting habit of carrying relics of saints about in little boxes and swinging incense all over the place.

He was shocked to see María—so unaltered by death. After all this time, surely one should expect—he was loathe to even think the thought—well, some change! Surely after two years some decomposition might be expected! What strange practices did those nuns know? Perhaps they had learned them from the Indians. And all those milagros. He shuddered with repulsion and passed his hand over his forehead as if to wipe away the revolting thoughts.

He was horrified to see his daughter's hair so alive, and rampant, he thought—and unbound! Displayed before all these people! It was all so shockingly common. He forced himself to ignore the curious glances that were being cast in his direction by the people seated close to him, and turned his attention to the blessing being offered by Father Rafaél.

"Jesus says:

'All that the Father gives me shall come to me;
No one who comes will I ever reject,
Because it is not to do my own will
That I have come down from Heaven,
But to do the will of Him who sent me.'"

Why did these priests always have to speak in riddles? De la Cruz had not the faintest idea what the young priest meant, or what Jesus had meant, for that matter. He lowered his head and examined a hangnail.

"'It is the will of Him who sent me
That I should lose nothing of what He has given me;
Rather, that I should raise it up on the last day.
Indeed, this is the will of my Father,
That everyone who looks upon the Son
And believes in Him
Shall have eternal life.
Him I will raise up on the last day.'"

Many in the congregation were dabbing their eyes, moved by the promise of these words.

De la Cruz was not one of them.

He was disturbed, however, to observe that Father Jean-Luc was suffering a fit of trembling so extreme that Sister Piadosa at last persuaded him to accept the seat that was made available to him. De la Cruz noticed that he groped his way to the pew like one who has lost his sight. The man should be removed. He was quite obviously ill, or unbalanced. Priests made him uncomfortable; but thin priests, he was sure, could not be trusted.

The service was to continue with the music composed for María.

Salvador stood and faced the congregation. He lifted the violin, settled it beneath his chin to strike the first note...

Later no one in the congregation could be sure that they had not imagined what followed. In any event, true or imagined, what they claimed they witnessed was the sight of the little girl, Sofia, in the front row, standing up on the pew, turning and reaching out to Mercedes, who sat behind her.

Mercedes rose with tears in her eyes and took the little girl into her arms.

And then Sofia began to sing—just the first few words of a song.

It was not the love duet that Salvador had intended. It was the song María used to sing to her unborn child; the song she had learned from Encarnación; the song from the old country.

Her little-girl voice was like a clear bell. Salvador, playing very softly, picked up the melody.

And now, as Sofia's voice faltered, Encarnación rose and took up the song. Her great voice welled up and filled the chapel to the rafters.

Listening to the song, Rafaél thought he had not heard anything so ecstatic in his life before. In that instant he would not have been surprised to see María rise up out of her coffin, for surely such beauty had the power to undo death itself.

Finally the song ended, and the last notes died away. There was silence in the chapel.

There were a few who had even begun to feel afraid.

De la Cruz was one of them.

For he had heard that song before: the song of the young child, Sofia.

He had heard it when Catherine sang lullabies to her babies. And he had heard it from María when, as a little girl, she used to sing with her mother.

Who was this child that she should sound so like them? What strange practices happened here, that a song should be lifted from the grave? De la Cruz didn't know, and he didn't want to know.

He felt a sudden, sharp pain in his heart that left him feeling dizzy.

The remainder of the service proceeded without further interruption. Only at the exchange of the rings the sight of María's pale hand receiving the ring was too much for old Mercedes, who finally broke down and sobbed.

At last Father Rafaél spoke the final blessing. It was time to carry María to the camposanto for the final prayer at the graveside and the burial. Father Rafaél moved to close and fasten the coffin when something in the whisperings coming from the congregation made him pause.

For years to come it would be discussed and argued just what had actually occurred in The Adobe chapel that evening. No one of intellectual mind, within or without the ranks of the priesthood, could offer any satisfactory explanation. It was left to those of enviable simplicity, who were able to live quite comfortably with the notion of miracles, to spread the word of what happened. By their reports they had seen the figure of María de la Cruz, surrounded by golden light, rise from the coffin and float like an angel right up to Heaven, with her hair streaming about her like a wind, leaving the coffin standing empty in front of the altar.

Certainly at this point everyone had closed their eyes—all except de la Cruz, who sat staring straight ahead, his usually florid face white. Never, in a life of power and dominance, had he ever allowed for one instant the slightest element of doubt to compromise his ability to control the world, and those around him. Now, in the face of these grotesque and surreal happenings, de la Cruz was deeply afraid. He looked around; behind him, as if seeking something familiar, some comfort, something concrete: the presence of someone he knew; the presence of, perhaps, miraculously—Catherine. But there was no one there for him.

The story became so embroidered with each teller's fantasy that outsiders who asked to be told what had occurred had difficulty making sense of the dramatically differing accounts. Some said that they had seen the transfigured body of María rise out of the coffin and ascend, as our Lord Jesus had ascended. Others said they saw a white dove, surrounded by an almost blinding brilliance of light, disappear into the sky. Still others, who had kept their eyes shut all the while, said that a hand had touched them, and they had felt a sense of peace such as they had never known enter their hearts.

All that could be agreed on was that when next they looked, the lid of the coffin had mysteriously closed and the strong brass clasp was firmly in position once more, apparently without any hand having touched it.

The word 'milagro' could be heard on everyone's lips, and in the days to come the wooden cross that Salvador made and erected on María's grave, close to the gravestone and the white-robed figure of Jesus, became adorned with hundreds of these small, silver blessings, offerings from the faithful, for whom the distinction between María and the Blessed Mother had somehow become blurred or had disappeared entirely.

It was thus that María de la Cruz, in the eyes of this small community, moved away from the wide, dusty plains, the ranchos with their grand haci- endas and the settlements of adobe villages that nestled in the river valleys; away from the earthy, pink foothills of the Sangre de Cristo mountain range and into the heavenly and timeless realm of the saints.

But it was not the only milagro that occurred that day, for when everyone in the small chapel finally managed to return to themselves they heard the sound of weeping. It came from the sobbing figure of the afflicted priest, Jean-Luc Sel; a sound so lonely that many in the congregation crossed themselves.

The priest had fallen to his knees beside María's coffin, sobbing like a child. His cupped hands reached out in front of him like those of one who seeks communion, it was said. Others said he looked like a beggar. Those close to him had seen his lips move, and although it was barely a whisper, it was said that they could hear his words—

"Bless me, Father, for I have sinned..."

It was what happened next that came to be known as the second miracle of the evening: for it was said that even as the priest looked up into the face of the one who hung above him on the cross, even so tears began to flow out of those blue eyes and down the painted cheeks, to fall into the pale hands of Father Jean-Luc Sel.

Whatever it was that happened, it was too much for de la Cruz, who had had as much spiritual hocus-pocus as he could stomach. With a cry he rose from his seat, scattering prayer-books and hymn-books onto the floor all around him. He did not wait for others to move aside, but pushed his way up the aisle, forcing his way between those who stood packed like sardines into the back of the chapel, and others who crowded the doorway, and strode out into the night.

Sebastián Speaks to de la Cruz

De la Cruz stood at the graveside, looking down at the freshly turned earth and the scattered flowers; a lonely figure of a man with the darkness and the silence closing in around him.

Rafaél and Sebastián watched him from the chapel doorway.

"I think one of us needs to go and speak to him," Rafaél said. "And I think it had best be you. I am a complete stranger to him."

Sebastián stared at the solitary figure.

"I really don't know what to say to him." He looked helplessly at his friend.

"What do you say to a man who has brought about so much suffering? I find it hard not to judge him, not to feel bitter. You didn't know María. You never heard her sing. It was not just that she had a lovely voice; an extraordinary voice. It was far more than that. I was at that concert when she and Salvador sang a love duet. There was just such purity in her voice, such purity of soul, that it touched the heart and drew everyone into another world. Her singing made me think of wind blowing over the wild sage, or of the trembling leaves of the mountain aspen. It made you recall a state of innocence; some distant time or place. Not only that: her singing made you feel the possibility that such grace might be found within yourself; that it was attainable. That is what moved all of us so deeply."

He paused.

"And he put a stop to her singing. He was jealous of anything that was not directly related to him and his relationship with her. And she challenged him. So he had her shut away. What is that, Rafaél? What kind of sickness is it, that a father should so destroy the life of his child? I don't even want to think what might lie behind such desperate measures. There is some horrible darkness in all of this, and it rests in that man. I do not understand it—this thing that feels like evil. What can I say to him when I hold such thoughts and feelings of aversion? What can I say?"

"Sometimes all we can do—all we need to do—is to listen. Whatever he has done, he must be suffering right now. The utter humiliation he must feel to have it known that his wife has run away, and now this. How will any of us come to terms with today's events? But if it is hard for us, think of him. To see your daughter in such a way! This must be unbearable for him. You tell me he has always managed to manipulate people and events to his own ends. Well, this is something about which he can do nothing. For such a man that is terrifying."

Sebastián made his way through the gathering dusk to the tiny cemetery. He walked up to de la Cruz and stood next to him. Neither man spoke.

A pale moon, just past the full, rose slowly over the dark hill to the right of them and cast its cold light on the fresh grave. Finally, without looking at Sebastián, de la Cruz spoke.

"She was my whole life. I did not know how empty I was until the day she was born."

De la Cruz took out a large handkerchief and blew his nose.

"And then she arrived; such a beautiful little being. She filled me with love; made me feel so alive, so…"—he searched for the word—"so complete. At her birth, when I picked her up and held her, I knew I would be willing to die for her. I knew that I would never be able to let her go. Not to him. Not to anyone."

He paused. Sebastián said nothing.

"And then she gave her love to Diego, and later to Salvador. I felt that my heart would break." He looked at Sebastián, as if searching for understanding. "I could not bear to let her go, you see."

Reading in the young man's face what appeared to be an invitation to speak, de la Cruz continued.

"I could not let her go, Sebastián—you can understand that, can't you? Not to some peasant. Not after she had known me! You must see that, surely. She was far too good for him. I could never allow that."

Sebastián was shocked. If ever there was evil, this must surely be the face of it. What he had thought might be the beginnings of remorse working in the man's heart, was nothing but a supreme arrogance. His daughter, by his own admission his whole life, had died, separated from her family, her lover and her child. He had banished her to this place because she had defied him—Sebastián considered a moment. No, he thought, that was not the truth. It was not her defiance that had brought about these desperate measures. No. It was because she had denied him! She had given her love to another man. He was jealous!

It was not that de la Cruz had never considered that she might have desires that differed from his, or that she had the right to exercise those choices. He understood that very well. He just could not suffer the reality of the separation that such differences would entail. He said he loved her, and Sebastián could believe that he genuinely thought this to be true. But it was not love. Such a man does not know love. This selfish obsession, this need to control was certainly not the measure of love.

Perhaps, in the end, for all his bragging and his power, for all his reputation as a shrewd businessman, a man of wealth, a hunter, a marksman; a man of sensual appetites; a lover of beautiful women, good food and of bullfighting—that pleasure he derived from watching a man pitting himself to the death against some enraged creature—perhaps in the end he was afraid. Perhaps, unacknowledged and probably unsuspected, it was fear that lay behind those black eyes. And it was not only the fear of facing death that hid in their blackness, but fear of life itself. He had been an observer in life, but he had never faced the bull. He had never taken that risk. Until today! Today, perhaps for the first time in his life, he had been alone in the ring, and the adversary who came thundering through the opened gate was death.

You cannot kill or destroy death; it is only life with which you may engage. Sebastián wondered if this man had ever truly lived his life. Had he experienced it only through others? Did he just buy and own the trappings of life? It appeared that his whole existence was concentrated in the external world: his fine house, his beautiful wife, his money, his powerful control of business matters, and finally his lovely daughter María. Sebastián wondered if he had ever really dared to seek the man behind the many masks and costumes; whether he had ever experienced any contact at all with the man who lived behind the complex and intricate web of worldly distractions.

He tried to summon some kind of compassion for the man; to find in his heart a measure of understanding for him, for whether de la Cruz knew it or not—and Sebastián suspected that he did not know it—he was a most tragic figure. He tried to detect some sense of contrition in the man's words; tried and failed. What he heard in de la Cruz was rage. It was combined with a ruthless arrogance and an almost pathetic sentimentality, but not remorse. He heard the pain and grief that things should have come to this, but he could find no evidence in the other man's words of any awareness that he might be largely responsible for his young daughter's early death.

"I would do anything to bring her back, Sebastián. If only I could have her back, I would take her back home to the Hacienda de Las Palomas and take care of her; see that no harm came to her. She could have anything she wanted."

Later Sebastián would regret the words that flew out of his mouth.

"You mean—she could have anything that you wanted her to have? Is that not what you mean?"

De la Cruz stared at him, his face suddenly hard, lips white with anger.

"You people are all the same," he said with contempt. "Peasants!"

He drew himself up to his usual, powerful stance, and without another word or a backward glance walked steadily away into the night.

The Storm

De la Cruz drove steadily along the ill-kept road, swerving from time to time to avoid the potholes. He was in no hurry. At the Hacienda the staff would have retired for the night. No one would be waiting up for him. The house would be empty.

He drove automatically over the familiar road, his mind occupied with the details of what he was planning to do. Above him thick clouds blotted out the stars and all traces of moonlight. In the distance he saw the first flashes of lightning, signaling the oncoming storm.

The first big drops were just starting to fall as he pulled into the courtyard. He did not put the car away, as was his usual custom, but left it close to the house, directly opposite the front door. He made a dash for the entrance just as the first squall passed overhead, dropping sheets of drenching rain onto the land.

After he had removed his wet jacket and shaken the drops of water from his thick hair, he made his way to his study, turned on the light and went to the liquor cabinet. He poured himself a generous, neat whisky, which he downed in a gulp. He poured another, and taking it and the bottle over to his chair, he set them down on the table next to the large ashtray.

He opened the humidor and selected the finest of all his cigars. He removed the red and gold seal and very precisely clipped the tip. Holding the cigar lightly between his thumb and finger-tips, he crossed the room and opened the two French doors that led out onto the long porch. He stood there looking out at the falling rain, thrilling to the electric tension that was being released. Filaments of electricity, like tributaries of a river, threaded their way across the vast night sky, and the land, with each flash of lightning, was etched in an eerie, electric clarity. Such was the magnitude, intensity and duration of each multiple lightning flash that it seemed to blot out distance, revealing the contours of the hills, each rock and stony outcropping, each tree-branch, each blade of grass in a stark, white light.

He lit the cigar, drawing on it to make sure it burned well, adding a little more flame to the one side and drawing some more. Over the years this had become a favorite ritual, and he honored an excellent cigar with impeccable attention to the correct way of appreciating it to the full.

The storm was blowing in from the north. De la Cruz counted the seconds between the flashes of lightning and the cracks of thunder. He counted about thirty seconds, and could calculate from this the approximate distance of the storm from the Hacienda.

He stood there, drawing on the cigar, feeling the rushes of wind that preceded each fresh thunder-roll and watching, with profound satisfaction, the magnificent electric display that was approaching. It was like witnessing the prelude to a grand opera, a tempestuous introduction to a drama of Wagnerian proportions, set on this vast desert stage, beneath a sky commanded by a pantheon of storm gods, each fighting for supremacy.

De la Cruz did not feel small in the face of this grandeur, nor did he feel frightened. He felt relieved. Nothing less than this could have matched the tumultuous emotion that was raging in his breast. For him this was the size of it. This was an expression worthy of his respect.

Leaving the French doors open, the better to hear the storm, and placing the cigar carefully on the ashtray, he went to the small closet in the corner of the room. He took out the soft, velvet smoking-jacket which Catherine had chosen for him many years before. She loved the rich, red tone, the scarlet sheen of it when it caught the light, and said that it suited his complexion.

De la Cruz took pleasure in it because it reminded him of a matador's cape and the blood of the bullfight. Of all his jackets it was his favorite. He put it on and replaced the heavy, wooden hanger in the closet. He closed and locked the door.

Crossing over to his chair, he pulled it around to face the doorway so that he could more comfortably watch the storm. Settling himself into its soft down cushions, he sat, alternately sipping his drink and drawing on his cigar, and watched the storm closing in.

There was less than an inch and a half of cigar stub left when a crack of thunder, so loud he thought it might split the house in two, sounded overhead. Now that the time had come, he noticed he felt strangely calm. He wondered at this.

He stubbed out the remaining cigar-end in the ashtray and threw back the last of his drink. He rose, and taking the bottle of whisky and the glass with him, he went over to the drink cabinet, poured another full glass and downed it in a few gulps, replacing both bottle and glass on the silver tray when he was done.

He walked slowly over to the mirror that hung over the fireplace, and stood looking at his reflection in the glass. He saw a cruel, handsome face, a face in which he could discern no weakness; the face of a man who neither asks for nor offers mercy. The black eyes stared back at him. There was no flinching in that stare. He reached up and straightened the collar of the smoking-jacket, smoothed the velvet lapels and fastened the middle button. He smoothed back his hair, giving a small, rueful smile as he stroked the white hair at the temples.

Then, with a nod, he dismissed that 'other' who was his sole witness.

De la Cruz entered the small gun-room. It was a wood-paneled room of obsessive tidiness. It was a man's room that smelt of leather and metal and gun-oil. It contained nothing extraneous to weaponry and the care and maintenance of fine weapons—with one exception. On the wall above the chest which held his store of ammunition was a portrait of María, painted just before her sixteenth birthday.

She was looking directly into the eyes of the viewer from a face as serene and lovely as that of a Madonna, but the eyes belied the gentle sweetness of the face, for in them—and the artist had captured the look to perfection—there could be seen evidence of a determined, fierce and unflinching integrity.

De la Cruz did not look at the portrait.

He took a key out of the heavy desk drawer and opened the glass-fronted cupboard that housed all his guns. For a moment he allowed his hand to move over them, caressing their cold steel as tenderly as any lover ever caressed his mistress' face.

But it was not a woman's face he saw, but the snow-flurries swirling around the magnificent head of the elk bull standing on the peak, with the proud eight-point rack etched against the sky. This was the image that haunted him: the great head swinging around to look directly at him; the shot that echoed around the peaks and resounded in his ears, so that he could hear it still—would never be free of it; the slow muzzle lifting towards the white skies and holding there for an eternity, so still, before the back legs buckled and it fell.

He remembered letting the gun fall to his side; how he had stood motionless, listening to the silence. Of all the aspects of falling snow, he thought as he stood alone in that mountain wilderness, quite the most notable one was the immensity of its silence. And it was in that silence, as the red blood pumped a slow stain onto the crumpled whiteness, that he knew, in a way he had not known anything ever before, that he had committed a transgression: not that he had shot an elk—any hunter may shoot a stag—but that he had shot it in anger. This would not be forgiven.

He reached up and removed from its holder the large revolver with the mother-of-pearl handle. The revolver had been a special gift of thanks, given to him by a wealthy Mexican businessman with whom he had conducted some rather nefarious business on one of his visits to Mexico City. The butt and the decorative filigree around the trigger mechanism were wrought in Spanish silver, the work of a master craftsman. The weapon was perfectly balanced.

De la Cruz opened a drawer of the chest where he kept a wide range of ammunition for the many weapons he owned. He selected one bullet, and loaded it into the revolver. He closed the cabinet and replaced the key in the desk drawer.

Outside the storm raged. It was directly overhead. The brilliant flashes of lightning lit the interior of the room, showing up the rich textures of the cushions and upholstery, the thick, woven rugs. He switched off the light and made his way to the French doors.

Between the brilliant flashes of blue and orange light the blackness of the night swallowed everything into its emptiness. He noticed how the image of each flash remained fixed in the retina, even after the light had gone.

There was a last flash of lightning that raced from west to east, from horizon to horizon in a jagged line across the sky. It snaked across the heavens, devouring the darkness as it passed.

He raised the revolver to his right temple; stood for a moment with that electric image etched into his brain, knowing that in one second the thunder would crack.

He waited all the timeless duration of that immense, eternal second.

The Face in the Mirror

The community of Las Madres was shocked to hear that Don Lorenzo had suffered a massive heart attack and was still unconscious.

For those who knew him it was almost unbelievable. He had always seemed larger than life, so powerful; utterly invincible. What an ill-fated family it had turned out to be! There were some who spoke about vengeance, but most, even though they disliked him, were more forgiving.

Sebastián heard the news when he made a trip into town for supplies. He was shocked. He had contemplated calling on de la Cruz that morning to make right his harsh remarks, made after María's service. Now he saw that in all probability he was the last person to speak to him before the heart attack; that his words, so self-righteously judgmental and spoken in anger, might have contributed to the attack, and it appalled him.

Close to some kind of panic, and without attending to any of his business in town, he returned to The Adobe.

Rafaél saw the pick-up from Sister Piadosa's office window and, surprised at Sebastián's early return, went out to meet him. When he saw the shock-white face he said nothing, but opened the car door. He took his friend's arm, and together they walked to Sebastián's casita.

"De la Cruz had a massive heart attack last night. He is still unconscious."

He did not have to explain to Rafaél. Remorse was written clearly in his drawn, white face.

"The housekeeper found him this morning in his armchair in the study. Oh, Rafaél, I wish I had gone round right away. This might not have happened."

Rafaél said nothing.

"The French doors were open and the chair he was sitting in was pulled round, presumably to look out at the storm."

Sebastián paused as if not wanting to add the rest.

"There was a pistol in his lap."

He looked at Rafaél, almost fearfully; almost as if he wanted reassurance.

Rafaél was listening.

"You don't suppose…" He broke off, waiting for some response. When he got none, he continued. "You don't suppose he was going to—going to, you know—actually—shoot himself?"

Sebastián searched his friend's face, hoping to find—what? Comfort?

Rafaél said nothing.

"Perhaps he had been cleaning it."

If it was a question, it received no answer.

"There was the stub of a cigar in the ashtray beside him, and an almost empty bottle of whisky on the dresser."

Sebastián looked distraught.

"The police found that the pistol was loaded." He rubbed his forehead as if trying to erase the thoughts that were flooding in. "With one bullet. Oh, Rafaél, what am I to do? I am no better than he is; no better than that unfortunate, over-zealous French priest."

Still Rafaél said nothing.

"The housekeeper says that the whisky bottle was full when she tidied the room the previous morning. He must have lost consciousness and just never woken again. He has been taken to the hospital in Albuquerque."

He paused.

"Oh, and another thing—she found a small, white dove with blood on its breast lying just outside the door, almost at his feet. Isn't that bizarre? It must have been wounded in the storm. She is nursing it in the kitchen."

Sebastián paced the floor.

"I feel so utterly wretched. All I had to do was listen. I had an opportunity to hear, beyond myself and my petty judgments. And I missed it. I heard only his arrogance, not my own. What have I done, Rafaél?"

"You spoke up for María."

Sebastián slumped into a chair.

"I did not even have to offer some profound counsel or wise advice. All I had to do was to open my heart. I failed him, and I failed myself. I know nothing about him; nothing about his past. Are children born with this evil in them? Or does some unbearable pain twist their innocence until it breaks?"

Even as he asked the question he remembered his own anger at life, fate, God. He remembered that day of shame when he turned eight.

Rafaél pulled up a chair and sat facing his friend.

"I think an angel in the most improbable disguise has given you a powerful lesson. Only recognize the face in the mirror."

Sebastián stared at him. "Are you saying—?"

"Yes."

"I don't think I can bear it."

"But you will bear it. And maybe you will even find a way to bless it." He touched his friend on the shoulder. "I won't offer to say a prayer with you. I know it isn't your style. But whatever it is you heretics do, now would be a good time to do it. Call me if you want me."

The Pink Hill

It came to him gradually, the way a raindrop on a window-pane will slide slowly down the glass. It creeps forward; it falls, it fuses with another drop, darts downward in small, capricious zigzag spurts, pauses, edges slowly to where another drop brims like a tear. It trembles. There is a tremulous moment of supreme delicacy, of exquisite balance. And then, quite suddenly, two or three drops merge to form a mass of some optimal size that slips swiftly to the bottom of the window-pane.

Even so did Sebastián's ponderings drift through his mind as he sat alone on the hill behind The Adobe. A little way above him and to his right Magdalena's cross, brave and white, stood surrounded by little piles of stones.

It was his favorite place for such ruminations. It was here, looking out over this harsh desert landscape, that he could most remember himself, could most feel the earth supporting him.

It was here that he could catch those mysterious whisperings that drifted like ghosts over the arid surface of the land; here where he could listen to the echoes of memory that lay embedded in the earth, as much a part of it as the strata of rock and clay. It was not only the bones of the dead that found their rest here, guarded by these hills and plains; it was memory itself. It was as if the silent land was a response to all that had taken place on it over the countless centuries; as if the hills and mountains, rivers and plains now embodied the energetic lives of all who had lived and died there; as if memory had become a palpable entity that lived there, separated from the physical world by the airiest of ethereal veils.

It was late afternoon, and the sun had lost most of its fierce heat. He noticed that the purple shadow cast by the rock had grown longer, and was now almost behind him. He had been sitting there for well over an hour. At some little distance below the rock he watched a cottontail's alert progress as it searched for and nibbled on green shoots and the tufts of sweet-grass that were just starting to sprout.

While watching the rabbit's activity he noted how completely it blended into its environment—so well, in fact, that from time to time he thought he had lost it, only to catch that slight movement again as it foraged further.

Sebastián recalled two lines from María's burial service that had touched him profoundly; two lines that had made his heart beat faster with the sense of recognition they evoked.

'All that the Father gives me shall come to me;
No one who comes will I ever reject …'

Absent-mindedly he constructed an edifice out of pebbles and fragments of weathered basalt. Stone by stone he built a small tower. The employment of his hands engaged and focused one part of his attention, allowing some other part of his mind the freedom to roam uncensored and unhindered.

What was the connection between de la Cruz and these words?

He tossed aside a stone too large for the small tower he was building, and then, as if on second thoughts, retrieved it and held it in his hand.

He stared at the rejected stone.

It came to him then: his fundamental solitude.

In this respect, were they not very similar? De la Cruz, for all his connections, his wealth and power, was the most solitary individual Sebastián had ever met. Had he too longed for some kind of absolution, perhaps without knowing it—without knowing how to ask for it?

Sebastián groaned.

Perhaps, he thought as he turned the pebble over and over in his hands, perhaps he too would not find forgiveness. Where could he go for it? Not to a priest. Not to the Church. He did not belong there. Where would he find pardon?

If only he had not hesitated. If only he had followed de la Cruz to his house that evening, might not something miraculous have occurred between them? He could not know what the other man's response might have been. What mattered was that he, Sebastián, apologize for his arrogance, his lack of compassion and his judgments. Just that might have been enough to make a difference. If not to de la Cruz, he realized with something close to panic, it would have made all the difference to him. He was the one who had judged.

He felt in his heart the full impact of what the hand of destiny had dealt him. His conversation with de la Cruz, and the man's subsequent severe illness, had only served to make it inescapable: that once life, or fate, had set you on that solitary road—the road full of mirrors—the doorway back to the comfort of belonging was forever closed to you.

That was it! It was not that he did not belong, but that he never would belong, anywhere.

The insight came with a rush of tears.

But it was more than that. It was the sudden realization that he could hold this—he could celebrate the paradox: that as much as he would never belong anywhere, he belonged everywhere. He was nothing, and he was all of it: he was the sinner, and the saint; the murderer and the victim. The painful search for that one place, that one identity, one belief, that one certainty—was over.

He realized, he would always be at the beginning.

He felt like a man set free.

He knew then that the traditional path to redemption was not his destiny. He would have to find—what—God, meaning, salvation—within himself? Was that hubris? Arrogance? Would he alone have to answer for and accept responsibility for the consequences of his actions, and all the questions that went with that? And did that mean that he could ask from others neither their acceptance nor their approval? It sounded appallingly lonely.

Sebastián shifted his position.

What had Rafaél said? That his atonement would be for a lifetime? That was terrifying. He remembered two lines from a poem, something about 'beauty was the beginning of terror'. Where had he read that? Of course. Rilke. Oh, but where was the beauty in all of this?

He recalled that the poem went on to say something about freeing ourselves from the beloved, for there is no place we can remain. Is that what Jesus meant when he said that 'the Son of man has nowhere to lay his head'?

That might be so. But against this, how he longed to be touched—to be taken. How he longed, above all things, to know and to be known. He longed for this even as he felt that a part of him would always be a stranger; that his desire to belong somewhere, to feel accepted, had been his attempt to avoid facing this ultimate solitude.

An explosion of dust, and the cottontail vanished into a heap of black basalt. The shadow of a hawk passed over the dark rocks.

He recalled Father Octavio's favorite quotation from a poem by St John of the Cross. It had been like a mantra to the priest, so often did he utter it: that 'he would not throw away his soul, for all the beauty there may be; only for something unknown, unimagined—that one may come on randomly'.

What was it that one came on randomly—so quietly that you could fail to recognize it? Whatever could it be for which one would be willing to 'throw away one's soul'?

A thought like a hummingbird hovered just out of reach, darting this way and that; a flash of brilliance—such speed, the eye cannot hold it—now here, now there.

But something about indifference—and love—just out of his mind's reach. Sebastián willed the thought to settle, if only for an instant. He closed his eyes as if to escape the world and its distraction.

And then the words came to him: that love, at its highest, was a state of divine and passionate indifference. It was as beautiful and as terrifying as that. Could he bear it?

He looked out over the land, stained red by the sunset.

Love was like this vast desert, he thought. It allowed space for the soul to be its own; to be spacious. It allowed all things: it was indifferent to the choices you made. But paradoxically—and this was the secret—by its nature it obliged you to be responsible for your life.

The shadow of the hawk passed over him. In that instant he knew that he had answered his own question. His heart leapt with the utter simplicity of it. It was not an insight. It was a revelation.

Sebastián stood up. He felt naked. Above him the sky was crimson. He kissed the stone in his hand and threw it with all his might, as far as he could, out into the gathering dusk.

Tears streamed down his cheeks. He raised his hands in the age-old manner of supplication and surrender. No words were necessary. The tower toppled and fell. The pebbles scattered in all directions.

'Only for something I don't know …'

He was filled with awe, with ecstasy—and the certainty that he had been touched—by whom—by what? He didn't know; only that it contained both joy and pain of such intensity that it took his breath away.

For an instant the fierce eye of the condor pierced his own, and he was back on that high ledge, seeing the crucified figure leap out into the void.

He knew now that he was loved. That he had always been loved. In that extraordinary paradox he knew, beyond any doubt, that even in his solitude he would never be alone.

And what was this love? The answer lay before him. It had always been there, but only now did he comprehend the depth and grandeur of the desert's essence; that it was the overwhelming magnitude of its utter indifference that drew him to it—the magnetic presence of that vast and dispassionate solitude. It lay clean, essential and uncorrupted. The soul of the land was indestructible. While it offered no mercy, it made no demands on his integrity. What greater love could there be? What greater terror? What greater compassion? He did not have to be or become, do or achieve anything. In this emptiness that resounded with the memory of ancient seas, he could throw away the masks and be who and what he was, and life would take him where he needed to go.

In a flash it came to him that it was life that was living him. He and this eternal 'other' that lived within him were not separate. It was all one: life, joy, grief, rage, passion and death; all of eternity; the entire song and silence of the universe, the divine laughter of the angels, everything—even disbelief, negation and denial.

It was as if a great sea of deliverance had rolled over him, leaving him washed up on some shining and foreign shore.

And then he heard it: woven into the very fabric of life, like a brilliant silk thread, or like the voice of the flute sounding above the fullness of the symphony, he heard the clear notes of his personal and uniquely individual song.

PART VII

THE BIGGEST SKY IN THE WORLD

The Telegram

"A telegram for you, Sebastián."

Sister Piadosa had just finished sorting the mail that Gregorio brought back from Las Madres.

"It's from Albuquerque."

Sebastián tore open the envelope and read the short message. He read it twice. Then he sat down.

Sister Piadosa, aware of the sudden silence in the room, looked up from the slips she was sorting, and noting the look of shock on Sebastián's face, asked if he had had bad news.

"It's from Georgia. She's in Albuquerque, and would like to see me. There is a phone number."

Sister Piadosa said nothing.

"She says she will understand if I don't want to see her."

Sister Piadosa sat with her hands resting on the table.

"For heaven's sake, sister, aren't you going to say anything?"

"Well, do you want to see her?"

"You go right to the point, don't you? I'm not sure—perhaps not."

"Oh well, then you can leave it, and when you don't contact her, she will realize that you have moved on with your life, and that will be that."

Sebastián stared at the innocent face, seemingly so free of guile, in disbelief.

"You really are far too wicked to be a nun, sister."

But her words had helped to bring resolve. "Of course I am going to see her. I'll phone you from Albuquerque tonight."

Sebastián snatched the telegram from the table, noted the contact number and hurried out of the room. Through the window Sister Piadosa saw him striding across the yard; saw the walk break into a run as he reached the path that led to his casita.

It was less than fifteen minutes later that she watched his car rumble away down the bumpy track, leaving a small dust-storm in its wake.

"God bless, Sebastián," she muttered. "Be wise if you want her. Pride has no part in this."

The drive to Albuquerque seemed endless. Road-works near Santa Fe had brought traffic to a standstill, and a broken-down truck that had skidded across the highway ten miles out of Albuquerque further slowed the heavy stream of vehicles. In addition to this, Sebastián, unfamiliar with the small hotel and its environs, became caught up in a series of one-way streets that led him back to the Interstate in a frustrating and time-consuming circle. Eventually he found the address of a small motel and pulled up outside number twenty-eight. Suddenly he felt both shy and terrified.

The door of the small bungalow opened, and Georgia stepped out into the sunshine and waved to him. Slowly he got out of the car.

"Hello, Georgia."

"Sebastián. I'm so glad you came."

What did you do, he thought—shake hands? He stood staring at the beautiful woman in front of him.

"I'm glad I came, too."

He put his arms around her and gave her a warm hug.

"There's a little park up the street. Let's take a walk."

Georgia took his arm, and the familiarity of it came as a shock to Sebastián. Did all the pain and ten years of separation just vanish with one touch?

They walked in silence through the late-afternoon sun. At the park they bought a soda, found a bench and sat looking out over the city.

"Where do we begin? There must be so much to tell. You begin, Sebastián. What have the past ten years brought to you?"

He sketched an outline of the events that had occurred; of how he was now sharing, with Sister Piadosa, the work of organizing and running the new and complex set of activities at The Adobe. He did not mention the matter of his inheritance. That could wait till later—if there was a later.

"And what about you? Are you a famous artist now? What brings you back here?"

It was a long story, and as it progressed Sebastián felt compassion for the series of disillusionments that Georgia had sustained.

"Monsieur le Noir was not only a great art teacher, he was a great collector as well: a collector of young, pretty, naïve and foolish girls who thought that they were going to be the next O'Keefe under his tutelage."

Georgia hesitated, and looked away.

"I was flattered by all the attention I received in Paris. Monsieur le Noir is well-known, and has a lot of influence in art circles. In this respect he was all that I had expected. He arranged an exhibition for me, and I worked hard to have enough canvases for that: I had only three months to prepare. It was a great success. I sold everything. That night we went out to celebrate."

Georgia hesitated.

"I ended up going home with him."

There it was. Sebastián felt sick.

"Shall I go on?"

There was such a note of pain in her voice that he nodded. If they were to end it, better to end it well.

"Yes, go on."

"A year or so later he was tired of me. A new Jamaican girl arrived. I had become something of an embarrassment to him. I was dropped from his life and from the school. I found an inexpensive place to live, and managed to pay the rent by selling my work. I wrote to tell my parents what had happened, and they said that I must find my way through. They sent me some money and told me to get on with it."

Sebastián frowned. He was surprised.

"Then things became more difficult. But fortunately I made a good friend. She worked as a model for an evening life-drawing class, and needed somewhere to stay. So she moved in with me and helped me with things during the day in lieu of paying rent. I don't think I would have survived Paris without her. I will be forever in her debt. Matilde. That's her name. So that was my time in Paris. Just over ten years. And now here I am. It took me a while to save up the air fare. I hope to make New Mexico my home."

She was leaving something out. Sebastián knew it. But then, so had he.

"What do your parents think of this idea?"

Georgia made no response to this. Instead she rose and took his arm again. "Let's go back to the motel. There is someone I want you to meet."

Slowly they made their way back to the small suite. Georgia called down the passage, "We're back, Matilde. Would you like to come and meet Sebastián?"

The door opened and a young woman entered. Holding her hand was a child, a boy of about eight years. He had golden-blonde hair and large, blue eyes; blue as cornflowers.

"Matilde, this is Sebastián. Sebastián, meet my very dear friend Matilde."

"'Ello, Sebastián."

"Matilde. Very happy to meet you."

Sebastián smiled and nodded, but his eyes were on the child. Georgia moved over to the boy, who removed his hand from Matilde, took Georgia's hand and walked with her across the room to where Sebastián was standing.

"And this is my son, Lucien."

The small boy took one step forward and nodded his head.

"Hello, Sebastián," he said gravely. "Bon soir. I speak English and French."

"Indeed you do," Sebastián said equally gravely. He held a hand out, inviting a handshake as befitted two men meeting each other for the first time. Lucien ignored the offered hand.

"Mama has told me all about you. You were at university together, non?"

Sebastián put his hand in his pocket and nodded.

The boy repeated the question. Surprised, Sebastián answered. "Yes, we were."

"And you live in a place out in the desert. I have never been in a desert."

"Yes, I live out in the desert—in a valley, actually, with desert all around. Maybe you will come and see it one day." He caught Georgia's eye and added, "Of course we will have to see what your mama's plans may be."

Georgia nodded to Matilde, who said that Lucien must come with her and have his supper. As they turned to go, Sebastián waved to the boy. Lucien did not return the wave. The two left the room.

There was an awkward silence as the door closed behind them. Georgia sat down on the small two-seater. Sebastián was the first to speak.

"I'm sorry about the handshake, if I embarrassed him. And I hope I wasn't out of line or upsetting any plans, inviting him to come and see the desert. He is a beautiful boy, Georgia. He looks like you."

He stopped, alerted by something in Georgia's face.

"Lucien is blind, Sebastián. He was born blind. I discovered it when he was three months old. The doctors can do nothing about it. He does incredibly well. He's very bright, and loves learning. Music is his first love. He is a very gifted song-writer. He wasn't being rude. He didn't see your hand."

Sebastián sat down and stared at Georgia. Finally he spoke.

"There is quite obviously a lot to talk about."

Georgia nodded. They were both quiet. Sebastián sat, frowning slightly into his hands. Finally he spoke again.

"I don't know the story, Georgia, but from the little you have said, you must have been through a very difficult and painful time."

Georgia looked back bravely, but he could see the chin begin to quiver.

"I don't know if you have commitments here, or whether you are going to California, to your parents. You didn't answer that question. But if you have no immediate plans, what would you feel about coming back to The Adobe with me? We have plenty of accommodation. It would offer you some breathing-space perhaps, and Lucien could see,"—he caught his words, and corrected himself—"Lucien could be introduced to the desert, and we could talk." He hesitated. "That is, if you want to, of course."

Georgia blew her nose.

"Oh, Sebastián. As it happens, it would be a Godsend." She looked hard at him. "I don't deserve it."

For reply he moved across to where she sat, took her in his arms and kissed her. The room was quiet. At last Georgia spoke.

"I have no plans other than finding work in the art field. I must earn a living. Of course I will be painting as well, but first I must set myself up with a studio, and for this I will need some regular income. But a breathing-space would be most welcome. The last ten years have been—" she took a breath— "difficult."

"We can talk about all of it tomorrow. It's late, but not too late to leave now. I could phone Sister Piadosa, and she would get a cottage ready for you. Or we could leave in the morning—whatever you say."

"Now! Right now! I haven't even unpacked yet. Lucien will probably fall asleep in the car. Oh, Sebastián!" She gave him a fierce hug. "I'll tell Matilde. We can be ready as soon as Lucien has finished his supper."

Watching her cross the room, Sebastián saw the Georgia he remembered. The years of separation vanished. He felt a lump in his throat, and was about to say something, but she was off through the door to tell Matilde the new plan.

The Biggest Sky in the World

"But I do see!"

Lucien was responding to Sofia's question. "I just see differently."

Sofia looked surprised.

"But tell me what you see, Sofia. Show me your valley."

They were standing hand in hand, facing out toward the pink hills. Sofia's gaze took in the whole sweep of land.

"I see big fields full of lavender—Sebastián's mother loved lavender—and further away, in the grazing-paddock, the two ponies are chasing Sebastián's cows. They are so fresh and naughty in the morning when they have just been let out. Have you ever ridden a pony, Lucien?"

The boy shook his head.

"I will teach you. It is such fun. Listen. I can make the sound of ponies galloping."

Sofia executed a complicated clap of her small hands, ending with both hands thumping her chest. The sound was remarkably realistic.

"Over there," she pointed, and then, realizing her mistake, she corrected herself. "Over to your left,"—she took his hand and pointed it in the general direction—"is the chapel, and below it is the camposanto where my mother is buried."

"Your mother is dead?"

"She died soon after I was born. But Sister Piadosa—she is my godmother—Sister Piadosa says she is not really dead, because she lives in me when I sing. I love to sing. Both my mother and my grandmother had beautiful singing voices." There was no sadness in the matter-of-factness of this statement.

"And you must meet my father, Salvador. He runs the music workshop here, and he writes music, and he makes violins. I love to go and sing with him. I just love him. He says I will be a great singer one day."

She was thoughtful.

"And you will meet Reuben. He plays the bandoneon."

"What is this? I do not know 'bandoneon'."

"It looks like a big concertina with lots of buttons, but it sounds so beautiful and sad."

Sofia looked around for what she had left out.

"Well, of course there are the two pink hills. The nearest one has a white cross on it. Sebastián put it there to remember his mother, Magdalena. And then the cottonwoods: they are starting to bud now, but you can still see their bony arms reaching up to the sky. And then there is just the blue sky. People say that New Mexico has the biggest sky in the world. It is so clean and clear, except when the airplanes fly across it. They leave long, white trails behind them. Sister Piadosa says, "There goes God, scribbling in the sky again.""

She laughed.

"Sister Piadosa says God doesn't mind if we say things like that. She says sometimes God feels lonely, because everyone is always whispering and praying and bowing their heads. She says she thinks he must enjoy a bit of cheekiness now and then."

Lucien gave a chuckle.

"And of course there are the white doves the other side of the herb garden. They are pigeons, really, but we call them doves. Come. Let's walk there. It's not far."

She took Lucien's arm and led the way to the aviary.

"My grandmother was given the white doves on the day my mother was born. I am told that they used to fly over the pram when she was a baby.

"But when my mother came here from the ranch where she grew up, she was very unhappy, and so when she left in the big car, driven by the foreman, all the birds left their aviary and followed her. They settled here, in a tree outside her window. So Sebastián built the aviary. When my mother died all the doves flew away, and they only came back two years later. "Sister Piadosa says that they flew all the way up to Heaven to be with her for a while, so that she wouldn't be lonely. And then one day they came back again, so we know she is happy. I love to watch them. Somehow I think that my mother flies with them."

"Tell me about them, Sofia. Tell me everything. Tell me what you feel like when you watch them." Lucien's face was alight with expectation.

Sofia considered his request. She had never thought about how she felt. She just let herself fly up and out with them.

"First you must hold one."

She unhooked the catch and reached into the aviary. Carefully she drew out the bird which was standing at the door, waiting to be released for the morning flight.

"Hold out your hands like a bowl, and when you feel the feathers, close them just slightly. Don't be startled if it struggles a little at first. It will settle down. They are used to being handled."

She put the dove into Lucien's eager hands.

"Just stand perfectly still."

Lucien stood, barely breathing. He could feel the fast flutter of the bird's heart against his fingers. He bent slightly over his hands, listening. He started when the bird shifted its feet, feeling the clawed toes grip the skin of his palms for greater purchase.

"It tickles."

"Can you feel its heart, Lucien?"

"Yes. It was beating very fast at first. Now it is getting quiet."

The bird turned its head this way and that. The boy felt the slight tremor of the movement, and asked what it was doing.

"It's looking around. I think it is wondering what's going on. Usually when they are taken out and held, it is to ring them or check that they are not injured. Sometimes one comes back hurt. One broke a wing once, and had to have a splint to make it better."

Lucien smiled his delight.

"When you feel ready, hold your hands up high and open them."

Lucien did as he was instructed.

"Oh!"

The utterance burst out of him. Feeling the release of the hands that held it, the dove broke free and, with a flapping rush of wings, lifted into the air.

"Where did it go?"

"That's just it, Lucien. They fly. Up and up. Up into space, where there is nothing but air and wind and light. They just move through space, far above the ground, with nothing holding them back. Sometimes when they turn they almost disappear, and you have to wait a few seconds, and then there they are again, soaring upwards. Sometimes when I watch them it makes me feel like crying. It is just so beautiful."

"You mean, like music?"

Sofia nodded. "Just like music."

"I will write a song for them—'The Song of the White Doves.'"

"And I will sing it."

Sofia took his arm and tucked it through hers. Together they turned to face the hills.

"And now, Lucien, tell me what you see."

She closed her eyes and stood breathless, wondering if she would be able to see his vision.

Lucien stood listening, his face turning slowly towards all the sounds of the valley.

"I see happiness," he said.

EPILOGUE

The Old Dog

Sebastián stood looking down at the roses he had placed on the four graves that lay in a row in the small camposanto.

It was part of his daily ritual to arrange fresh flowers around the headstones and to share his thoughts with these four much-loved souls: his mother Magdalena, Father Octavio, María Fuentes and Sister Piadosa.

Images from the past floated through his mind: days and moments; fragments of conversations; the particular intonation of much-loved voices; the sound of laughter. He recalled, with tenderness, distinctive gestures, so familiar that it felt to him as if he carried these now within him, almost as if they enjoyed some measure of immortality through his remembering them in this way. He gave thanks for all the love he had known, all the blessings he had received from these four people whose lives had been so inextricably woven together with his own.

The mid-morning breeze lifted the lock of grey hair that fell over his forehead. The day was hot, and his brow glistened with sweat.

Behind him the four dogs lay panting in the shade. They had been hunting cottontails at the far end of the field, where the rows of cottonwoods gave way to the steep hills. Although, as always, they had made no kill, they returned well-pleased with their efforts.

Sebastián uttered a blessing over each grave, and said a short prayer for the peace of the four who slept there so soundly. Then he turned to contemplate the day. It was early fall. All around him the leaves of the cottonwoods were turning and the early-morning sun streamed through the golden foliage, so that the trees appeared to be lit from within. He sighed contentedly. It was a fine day.

He made his way across the fields and began the slow climb to his seat on the hill. He paused from time to time to catch his breath, aware that there was a time when he could run this distance with ease. The old dog waited with him, panting, but the three young ones ran on ahead, turning from time to time to bark impatiently.

He found his rock, and he and the old dog sat contemplating the desert while the young ones searched among the basalt and juniper for cottontails and lizards.

It was well past noon when Sebastián made his way back to his casita. One could hardly call it that, he thought, for with the many additions that the years had made necessary it had become quite a substantial house. He would have it all to himself today, as the others had left early that morning for Santa Fe and would not be back before supper-time. He looked forward to having a quiet day alone.

For some time now he had felt an excitement growing inside him, and today, with the blessing of solitude, he planned to make a start on putting down on paper the words that had been clamoring to be heard inside him.

With a sandwich and a jug of iced tea he retired to his study. He sat for a long while sipping the drink, gazing through the window at the pink hills. On the wall beside him hung the painting that Georgia had given him before she left for Paris. The translucent quality of the canvas filled the room with its light. Next to it an old, faded, hand-woven poncho, in which she had wrapped the painting for protection, hung on a black wrought-iron rail on the wall.

Sebastián put down the empty glass and reached for a clean sheet of paper, which he fed into the old typewriter. He paused for a moment, and then typed a dedication.

For Lucien, Sofia and Octavia

He paused, staring out once more at the pink hills. The small, white cross stood bravely, clean and white beneath the vast dome of blue-painted sky. At the base of the hill the cottonwoods had just begun to drop the first of their leaves. For several hours Sebastián sat gazing out at the valley.

He was stirred from his reverie by a rushing sound above him. It was the white doves, released for their evening flight.

Sebastián breathed in deeply. He returned to the page and typed the first line.

'In the end it is all about beauty.'

Glossary

Acequia: an irrigation channel.

Adobe: sun-dried brick consisting of clay, sand, water and sometimes straw.

Alabados: an unaccompanied song in praise of God.

Amiga Negra: Black Lover.

Amigo: friend: lover.

Animado: spirited.

Arroyo: a usually dry gully created by torrential rains.

Banderilleros: the man who places the dart with streamers into the bull's neck.

Bandoneon: the instrument associated with tango: a type of squeeze-box concertina with buttons at both ends.

Bolo: a plaited leather thong with decorative metal or silver tips and an ornamental clasp that can slide up to form a kind of tie.

Bordello: a house of prostitution.

Buenos días: Good day.

Bulto: carved and painted statues of the saints: some carved so that the limbs can move.

Caldera: volcanic crater of great size.

Camposanto: country graveyard.

Carnero: sheep.

Chili ristras: long plaited strings of red chili pods.

Coleta: the pigtail worn by a matador.

Concho-belt: a leather belt threaded with silver medallions.

Condor: a large vulture: the largest flying birds in the western hemisphere. Black with a frill of white feathers at the base of the skull, it has a wingspan of up to ten feet.

Corazón: heart.

Curandera: healer.

Descanso: literally: the 'resting place' of a person who has died.

Descanso cross: a roadside cross where someone has died violently.

Desterrado: Exiled.

Duende: is something instinctive, animal and dark, yet with a touch of the divine: secret and shuddering. It is the struggle within the artist which creates true art. It never repeats itself. It is a form of genius; a mysterious force that everyone feels and that cannot be explained: the spirit of the earth. 'The duende won't appear if he can't see the possibility of death.' (Lorca)

El Desplazamiento: 'displacement of a partner's foot': one of the most powerful tango-leads.
El Estampido: The Boom/Detonation.

Farolitos: little lanterns: votive candles set in sand in small brown-paper bags.
Fuego: fire.

Golondrinas: swallows.
Guacamole: a mix of avocado, chili, tomato, onion, juice of a lime and seasoning.
Guacamole grande: a dish of corn chips, melted cheese, guacamole and sour cream.

Hacienda: a large estate: the house of the owner of such an estate.
Hermanos: members of the Penitente Brotherhood.
Hermoso: beautiful: handsome.
Hombre de pro: man of worth.
Horno: an outdoor clay oven for roasting chili and baking bread.

Juniper: a coniferous plant of the cypress family: may be up to 40 m tall in mountain areas: low and stunted in desert areas.

La Carretta del Muerte: the death cart, a small, wooden wagon with the figure of death sitting in it—a skeleton, sometimes with human hair and teeth and carrying bow and arrow or a hatchet.
Ladrido: bark(of a dog).
Lágrimas de Cristo: tears of Christ.
La Sagrada Corazón: the Sacred Heart.
Las Madres: The Mothers.
La Navidad: Christmas Eve
Las Posadas: The Inns. Beginning December 16 and ending December 24: a chorus of singers accompanies 'Joseph and Mary' seeking shelter in 'Bethlehem.'

Los peregrinos: Pilgrims.

Los Santos: the saints.

Lowrider: In New Mexico's Hispanic culture, a vintage model car, custom-made with the suspension lowered as far as it will go 'to make it ride like a Cadillac.' Most people agree that the classic lowrider was created as an affront to America's middle-brow factory cars as a statement of cultural pride and individuality.

Luminarias: Illumination: small lights.

Mariachi: a style of music developed as a folk tradition in Mexico.

Mayordomo: the title given to the ditch-manager for digging and clearing irrigation channels.

Matador: bullfighter: the one who kills the bull.

Mestizo: mixed breed.

Milagro: miracle.

Milagros: small silver or metal charms representing the miracle of healing in response to a prayer: the healed arm or child or animal etc.

Milonga: means 'party' or 'festival': a lively type of tango: a place where people go to dance milongas.

Morada: An adobe building, usually plain with a flat roof and a cross on top: a place where Los Hermanos, the Penitente, held their rituals.

Morillo: the large lump of muscle on the bull's neck which swells and rises when the bull is arroused.

Muchas gracias: thank you very much.

Muerte: death.

Noche Buena: Good Night or Christmas Eve.

Paloma: dove.

Parciantes: member shareholders who govern an acequia.

Penitente: a lay religious society.

Pepita: little pip.

Perro: dog.

Piadosa: compassion.

Parciante: member shareholders controlling ditch digging.

Penitente Brotherhood: Los Hermanos—a religious group, cast out of the church: have retreated into the hinterlands where they continue to develop a deep spiritual and mystical sense of community.

Picador: a mounted bullfighter with a lance—a pica.

Pick-up: a light motor vehicle with the front like a car and back like a truck.

Piñón: a type of pine tree.

Ponderosa: a type of pine tree.

Portenos: the marginalized working-class natives of Buenos Aires.

Querencia: Lit. homing instinct. In bull fighting it is the place in the ring which the bull feels to be the safest; to which he returns again and again to recover.

Querido: dear, darling.

Retablo: flat painted panels of wood, metal or animal skin—showing images of the saints.

Sangre de Cristo: Blood of Christ.

Santero: an artist who makes images of saints, painted, or carved and painted.

Santo: a saint.

Serape: a shawl or blanket worn as a cloak.

Sueño Mistico: Mystic Dream.

Suerte: a bullfighter's manoeuver.

Tango: is a sad thought expressed in music and dance: an impulse that challenges the dancers to explore their inner feeling through movement.

Toro: bull.

Veronica: a move in bullfighting where the bull is enticed to charge at the cape: called "Veronicas" after St Veronica who wiped Jesus' face with a cloth.

Vigas: wooden beams.

Yucca: a genus of plant native to Mexico and New Mexico.

Notes

Hispanic Surnames:

Most Hispanic people use two surnames called the first apellido and the second apellido. The first apellido is the surname of the father and the second apellido (coming after it) is the mother's maiden name (i.e. her father's surname). When a woman marries she may keep her name—a modern trend—or she may take her husband's surname as a second apellido. The woman in a marriage never changes her first apellido. Their children will take the father's surname (first apellido) followed by the mother's first apellido.

For example, Gabriel García Marquez is the son of Mr. García and Mrs. Marquez.

Readers' Guide

1. The pairing of death and beauty in the novel's title is echoed in many of its key passages. What is the relationship between death and beauty that emerges in the novel, and why do you think Fairhead suggests that they are so inextricably linked?

2. In the novel's prologue the reader is presented with a narrator who makes his own role as story-teller explicit and declares his specific intentions in telling this particular story. What are the implications of having such a narrator, and how do his intentions and priorities influence the way the story is told to us?

3. In Part I, "Las Madres," when Father Octavio Cordova blesses the Casa Magdalena, he comments on its "unusual juxtaposition" of imagery, and, throughout the novel, characters strive to reconcile or even celebrate opposite points of view in their own lives. Using the décor of the Casa Magdalena as a starting-point, what do you think is the significance of such a struggle? What are some of the crucial oppositions portrayed in the novel, and how is the struggle between them explored?

4. In Part II, after leaving home, the young Sebastián Chávez passes through a series of testing encounters—often with teachers of one kind or another, but also with aspects of his own nature. Is there a common thread between these encounters? How are we encouraged to understand what Sebastián is learning? Finally, what is the significance of the labyrinth as a key metaphor in this part of the novel?

5. In the chapter, "Lorenzo," of Part III the reader is given a glimpse of Lorenzo de la Cruz' childhood and the trauma that accompanied it. Is this account helpful in understanding de la Cruz' later actions and attitude towards his own family? Does it influence the reader's perspective on his later actions? Later on Sister Piadosa is hesitant to refer to him as evil: why?

6. In a particularly significant passage in Part II Father Octavio suggests to Sebastián that there is only one question worth asking about our own lives—are we in love? They are discussing Sebastián's future plans at the time, and it is clear from the context that "love" is used to describe a particular way of being in the world. Using the life and work of the santero Alejandro Jaramillo as a starting-point, how does the novel explore this definition of love?

7. Throughout Part III we encounter descriptions of Lorenzo, Catherine and María contemplating themselves in a mirror. What are the different ways in which this ritual functions for them, and what is the significance of Catherine's breaking of her mirror towards the end of this part of the novel?

8. Much of the novel's humour depends on descriptions of the same event or phenomenon from different, contradictory perspectives. One particularly striking example is a passage in Part III in which de la Cruz' search for his daughter María is hindered by a procession of ecstatic villagers. They claim to have witnessed a miracle, and are on a pilgrimage to the shrine of the Virgin of Guadelupe. De la Cruz' dismissiveness about such claims is made obvious, and all attempts at dialogue between him and the group fail. This failed dialogue is an important plot device—apart from being extremely funny—but it also fulfils another function. What does it suggest about the way in which unexamined beliefs determine what we are able to experience, and how does this determine the way characters relate to one another throughout the novel?

9. It is possible to read the description of the bullfight in Part III, "The Bull-fight," as an unusually sympathetic glimpse into the inner life of Lorenzo de la Cruz. Do you agree with this statement? How does the account of the bullfight resonate with the novel's larger project as stated in the prologue?

10. In Part IV, "A Love Affair," Father Octavio reimagines Christ's saying about the difficulty for a rich man to enter the Kingdom of Heaven in such a way that it leaves him overwhelmed by "the heavy burden of his

unexamined goodness." What does Octavio's insight about disobedience suggest about our ability to change and the cost of such transformation? At least one character in the novel is accused of heresy. Using Octavio's insights as a starting-point, how do you think the novel understands heresy, and how does this understanding differ from its more orthodox definition?

11. In Part VI, "The Inquiry," Sister Piadosa longs to escape from the oppressive atmosphere created by Jean-Luc Sel's sermons "into the sunshine and the air with its scents of earth and growing things." There are several instances throughout the novel in which the beauty and solitude of nature—particularly wilderness—becomes a metaphor for what is both unique and under threat in the self. Using María's experiences in the Valle Grande as a point of departure, how does the novel explore the significance of wilderness, and of humanity's place in it?

12. Throughout the novel artistic endeavour—Sebastián's poems, María's singing, Salvador's tango drama—is explored as a possible means of interpreting and transforming experience, and of course the novel itself, as told to us by the narrator, is also such a project. In particular the ability to identify and sing one's own song becomes a central theme. How and through which characters is this theme developed most fully? Are these themes resolved by the end of the novel?

13. It can be argued that the novel's main ideas are expressed most fully in the passage describing Sebastián's revelation on the pink hill at the end of Part VI. In the context of the events that lead up to this revelation, how can we understand his insight that "love, at its highest, is nothing but a divine and passionate indifference?"

14. In Part I, "The Kiss of the Patriarchy," in defending the inconclusive ending of her famous story, Magdalena says that "there are no endings. Only pauses." Using this remark as a starting-point, how are we to read the description of Sebastián and Georgia's meeting in Part VII? Why is it important that the novel should end as it does, with a dialogue between Sofia and Lucien? Are these names significant?

www.ingramcontent.com/pod-product-compliance
Lightning Source LLC
Chambersburg PA
CBHW031024030726
47497CB00004B/993